Feared &

Forgotten

*To the Dreamers
and the Realists*

Acknowledgments

Thank you to all of those who have helped either inspire this book or helped support me during the process of its creation.

Specifically, thank you to authors like Rick Riordan, Adam Silvera, and Madeline Miller for keeping my love for reading burning strong throughout my childhood and giving me something to live up to.

To AJ, for helping shape many of the character traits shared by Aska and Jay, for being my biggest supporter during the early years, and for being the first to take an interest in my writing.

To Brianna for Lily's positive and loving demeanor.

To my amazing cover designer Elementi.studio.

Thank you to all of my friends and family who have made this journey possible—to my family for always dealing with my excessive work, and to my friends for being my greatest source of creativity.

Table of Contents

<u>Prologue</u>

The young girl looked down at her shaking hands, trying her best not to make any noise. She could hear her mother's voice echoing through the small house, completely overshadowing her uncle's.

Shadows.

Over the past week, they seemed to crawl toward her; even now, she felt like the closet's darkness would consume her. The closet was hard to see in any case, and the flood of tears she experienced wasn't making it any easier, but she could vaguely make out a small wooden box in the corner. Her father abandoned both her and her mother four years ago; she was only three at the time but remembered he always had that box with him. It was the size of a briefcase and had a latch for a padlock, but the latch had been broken many years ago. She jumped as a glass shattered on the wall in the next room, prompting a fresh set of tears. Slowly, she turned back to the box and opened the lid. Inside was a collection of knives, spears, and guns, perfect weaponry for the perfect criminal. Another glass shattered on the wall, causing the girl to jump again. Suddenly, she held a small black knife in her hands.

A voice separated itself from the cacophony of sound downstairs; her uncle warning his sister to act rationally. The bruises on her face ached, but that voice coaxed forward a warm feeling in her chest. He couldn't always be there, but when he was, her uncle did his best to quell the raging storm that was her mother. For that, at least, she was grateful. Her mother hated her; she knew her mother hated her. She was a constant reminder that her mother's life was ruined; the reason why she was who she became.

Another glass shattered on the wall, and then something strange happened; everything went quiet, as though even the birds were afraid to speak. It was never quiet. The little girl held her breath and refused to move; still clutching her father's knife to her chest. Downstairs, she could vaguely make out someone crying.

Slowly, she stood wondering if the storm was finally over. No, that was impossible; it never subsided that fast. Dropping the knife on the closet floor, she inched across her bedroom and into the living room. Her mother rocked on the floor, back turned to the little girl.

"Mama?" Her voice cracked as her mother stopped rocking and sat completely still. The woman turned, revealing hands covered in blood and puffy red eyes. Her eyes. They were little more than dots looking straight ahead. Everything in the little girl's body froze solid as her mother's pupils slowly jerked down to her.

"YOU!!" The woman's voice was harsh and ragged. "This is YOUR fault! You ruined everything!" She lunged towards the small girl, slamming her to the ground. The girl's head buzzed, her eyes streamed tears and her breathing quickened as her mother hit her repeatedly. She felt something warm leak down her face but was unsure whether it was tears or blood. Her body felt dull, almost like she was sleeping; she knew this feeling well.

The beating continued for what seemed like hours but, it was likely only minutes. The girl could barely see through all the blood and was only slightly aware of the screams escaping from her mouth. She struggled against her abuser but lacked the mental awareness or physical strength to defend herself. Any minute, she would lose consciousness and likely never wake up. Her will to live was getting smaller with every moment. *What reason did she have to continue life? Would anyone even miss her if she died? What happened to her uncle?* Too many thoughts. Too much pain. *Maybe I should go to sleep.* She thought. *Yes, sleep sounds good . . . Sleep sounds comforting. . . Sounds soothing. . .*

"BAMM!" A single gunshot sounded and everything went cold. She lost consciousness and swam towards the deep, dark pool of sleep.

It was morning by the time the girl was awake. Her head was pounding, and she could barely breathe, but she was alive. Blood dripped down onto the little girl as her eyes slowly opened. She wanted to scream, but her throat was too dry. A numb body lay lifeless on top of her, causing her to scurry out of the way, determined to escape what was happening. She looked around the room, searching for the killer, but there was no one to be seen. Suddenly, she bumped into something behind her, cold and somehow comforting. Wanting to run and yet staying still, she turned, but there were only shadows. She was about to look away when something caught her eye; a pistol lying on the ground in the center of the wall's shadow. The girl examined it in her hand, and while checking the chamber, she noticed only one bullet missing.

There wasn't enough time to question anything; she had to find a way to dispose of her mother's body. Dragging it across the floor, they made their way to the garbage shoot.

The girl's head spun, and her body ached; she watched as her blood dripped on the floor with every step. Before the body even reached the garbage shoot, the little girl collapsed. She glanced over at the body; it was too heavy to move, and if she kept trying, she'd probably end up dead. *It can't stay here; I need to get rid of it!* She thought loudly to herself.

Suddenly, her body exploded in burning pain that increased by the second. It shot between her veins, indescribable pain, like a fever but 10000 degrees hotter. She spasmed on the ground, her blood pooling on the floor. The veins on her fragile arms turned a deep purple, and her skin's color drained. As her lungs began to collapse, her eyes shot wide open as she watched all the shadows in the room shift into a pure black circle under the woman's dead body. She was forced to watch in horror as they spun faster and faster, tearing into the floor and digging deeper and deeper until there was nothing but a terrifying black hole. Nobody. No floor. Nothing. Then everything disappeared except the pain which continued to spike until her vision darkened, leaving her seeing blinding red dots. It was the worst torment she had ever endured. In her mind, she knew she was dead or dying.

At first, all she saw was black, but then they appeared. It was unclear what exactly they were, but the sight of them filled her with more terror than ever before. She couldn't run or scream, so she stood there; hoping to remain unnoticed. Each one of the creatures was different from the rest; one had four long legs that bent in all the wrong directions. Another was taller than a truck, with a thin body and long arms. Still another slithered across the floor like a snake, its massive head swayed with each movement as the spikes along its back rattled.

Holding her breath so that the monsters would continue to ignore her, she remembered stories her uncle used to tell. The stories were all different in their own way, but they all revolved around a central primordial being that decided, among other things, who was a sinner and a saint. The sinners would be sent to a painful and terrifying afterlife while the saints would rest in peace. What had the little girl done to be considered a sinner? She was just an innocent child. Wasn't she? Her thoughts were shaken from her as one of the monsters approached. It had pitch-black skin and pearl-white eyes with no sign of a pupil. Its body was slouched with a hump on its back and four thin black legs that crawled in a way that made her body tremble. The temperature dropped with every step it took toward her—a faint buzzing sound emanating from its body. Soon, the creature was only a few meters away. The girl's feet seemed almost cemented to the cold gray ground, and despite the overwhelming urge to scream, her lips remained glued shut.

More stories that her uncle used to tell her swam through her thoughts, except this time, they were about his time as a dog sled racer. He would tell her of the younger, more arrogant men who didn't believe the horrors of winter nights in northern Quebec. In some severe cases, the men's skin would turn black and bitter from the disease called frostbite. The girl was sure this was the same experience.

Just as the creature was maybe two meters away, her vision turned a blurry shade of purple, and she felt herself begin to stir.

Just like that, she was back in the house. The bodies of her mother and uncle were gone; it was only her left. Sirens echoed in the distance, and her body tensed in fear. They couldn't be searching for her unless maybe the neighbors had overheard something. No, sirens at this time of night were common, but still, she crept upstairs, trying her best not to make any noise on the creaky steps. She only had one bag: a blue, black, and purple Galaxy backpack for school. She dumped its contents under the bed and began shoving clothes inside it. Before she left, she remembered the small wooden box in the closet and shoved it into the already cramped bag.

Finally, she snuck out the back door and fled to the woods towards the city, without knowing where she was headed or how long she survived. A flash of her young and handsome father presented itself in her mind: "Never return to the crime scene, Lunette. Never." He had done just that, and the girl nodded and swore she would follow his advice.

Part I:

Machigai

Chapter 1: Disappearance

The first disappearance was terrifying. All I could remember was waking up in the dead of night screaming. There was nothing strange there; we both often experienced episodes similar to nightmares but much more accurate and much more horrifying. An unspoken pact sat between us regarding these episodes: 1) The house was shared, meaning we were always welcome in each other's rooms. 2) Never. NEVER ask the other about their dreams.

The pact sounds childish to most people, to people with the bliss of regular nightmares, where you're horrified, but eventually, you wake up and realize it was nothing more than a dream. Ours never end; once you're awake, the pain is still there. That night was a particularly dull one, frightening, sure, but dull nonetheless. The monsters came close enough for me to feel their presence but never once touched me, leaving me with the warmth of knowing there would be no painful welts when I awakened. By the time that happened, my voice was hoarse, which again was nothing out of the normal. The cold chill slipping through the cracks in the wall convinced me to stay in the comfort of my blankets, so instead of utilizing the pact, I curled back under the covers and prayed for good sleep.

The following day, a bitter cold nipped at my flesh. It was Aska's responsibility to set the fire in the morning; the risk of keeping it lit at night was too high, but it gave us delightful heat during the day. He would light the fire while I made breakfast, and that was the way it had always been.

Last night, snow had leaked in through the wall, so the floor was freezing. I slipped a hoodie over my nightwear and put my winter boots on as I headed downstairs. As I guessed, the fire was still out from the night before. Panic began to rise from within me, causing the shadows to dance on the walls.

Get it under control, Onyx. No one wins with the shadows. I thought. Slowly, the walls stilled, and my breath steadied. After lighting the fire, I returned to Aska's room. My breathing turned shallow as the door creaked open, but it wasn't what I expected. Instead of Aska being frozen dead in his bed, he was just gone. His room was a disaster, per usual, but he was nowhere to be found. Caution was thrown to the wind as I started to search for him. He couldn't be stupid enough to leave alone at this time of day. The streets were full of posters marked with his face and a reward, along with thousands of people walking to work. They would have found him hours ago.

Thousands of scenes rushed through my head, pictures of my best friend hooked up to a machine at Toyls Academy. Teachers forcing him to activate his curse over and over again until he begged for death. I'd seen what his abilities could do to him, and it made my punishment look like a tea party.

The machigai curse is extremely rare but more common in colder places like Quebec and Moscow. It works like a disease, infecting all body parts and eventually killing the holder. The oldest known machigai lived to only twenty-five years old. Depending on the severity of the curse, that time could be halved. Aska's curse specifically allowed him to deal with punishment for sinners. Still, in doing so, he breaks a Major Ten commandment, creating a circle of pain as he receives the same punishments as his victims, the only difference being his natural system refusing to release endorphins or let him die. This leaves him dying without ever being granted the mercy of death, if that makes any sense. My curse, on the other hand, can control shadows, resulting in a variety of painful punishments. Dreams, or rather real hallucinations of demons living in the shadows, creatures so foul and cruel that they would make fully grown men wet the bed at night, creatures that burned flesh with their acid like touch, bubbling underneath my skin and creating pockets of poison. If you could imagine the pain of that multiplied by millions, you'd have a fraction of Aska's life. Therefore, the odds of him living after capture were very slim.

The next few days were filled with anxiety, pain, panic, and very little sleep. My wanted posters consisted of inaccurate drawings, mainly black shadows, due to my tendency to shield myself inside them. This granted me the pleasure of searching the streets in my regular clothes. I searched through alleyways, abandoned buildings, anywhere I could grasp the hope he might've gone, every time coming up dead empty. Sitting in bars or pubs staring at the TV became my new regular, waiting for the headline I knew was coming: MACHIGAI BOY FOUND AND KILLED!

After over a month, I started to give up. During the time I had spent searching, money and food had both run extremely low. I went days with an empty stomach due to not being able to "borrow" more money or food without drawing attention to the machigai, putting law enforcement on high alert, and indirectly putting Aska in more danger. By the time the first month had come to a close, my energy was burnt out. One night, as I was lying on his bed staring at the ceiling, I had a dream. Not the terrifying monster nightmares I usually have, but an actual dream.

I dreamt I was twelve again, five years after I had left home. I was freezing, frail, and starving to death in an alleyway, clutching my father's wooden box to my chest. My life was the picture of some cheesy English soap opera. In the last few years, survival had depended on dumpster diving and people's pity, but as I grew older, the people grew colder and far less generous. When it happened, I hadn't eaten in weeks, my clothes had been so worn they were practically shredded to bits, and the gas station was so close the hotdog's intoxicating scent engulfed the air around the alley.

Thoughtlessly, I followed my nose and found myself staring at all the different flavors of chips with my mouth watering and my stomach pleading for the barbeque-flavored ones. The security camera and the person sitting at the counter were barely out of sight. I started cramming as much food as possible into my backpack, and when that was filled, I watched my shadow turn a deeper shade of black than ever before. I started throwing even more food into it (a trick I had learned a year or so back), but I was already exhausted, so the hole could only hold maybe five bags of chips. My blood felt like it was draining to my feet and onto the floor. The hole clenched shut as ice radiated through my hands down to my frail legs, leaving me placing each step out of the store strategically to prevent myself from collapsing.

A hand tapped on my shoulder. "Excuse me." The ice in my blood somehow turned even colder. The man from the counter grabbed my arm tightly to ensure I didn't run away. "Bag, please?" Suddenly, every cell in my body was terrifyingly aware of how awful I must look with old torn clothes and the rotten stench that came with living on the streets, not the most trusting of appearances. Slowly, I handed my bag to the man, saving my strength for the inevitable. As the man took the bag and gave me another look, I tried to gain my bearings. Three other people were in the store: another man behind the counter and a woman with her young son. I couldn't even think about the hundreds of people outside the store heading home to live everyday lives with their families, their ordinary families.

The man threw chip bags and a water bottle back to the other man at the counter and finally found the box. My box. His hands slid over the soft mahogany, and panic forced me to make my move the second he reached to open the broken latch. The oh-so-familiar burning pain appeared, first behind my eyes, and then, like water breaking from a dam, it shot through my whole body, taking each inch by surprise. Already on the floor, I watched the shadows consume the two men and then the mother, leaving only myself and the little boy. Although no sound was audible, it was clear he was screaming; the look of terror painted across his face was enough to break a whole theater to tears.

Through fits of my own gasps and screams, I mouthed one single word to him: Run. As threatening as the words seemed, I hadn't killed him. It was never my intention to kill anyone, just maybe contain them, but the shadows had a mind of their own. A mind much more prepared to take lives. So, as my vision blurred and the world spun around me, I sat and watched him sprint away, hopefully far, far away. Then the monsters came.

The sound of sirens awoke me from the monsters. My entire body ached, and I desired nothing more than sleep, but I made it to my feet using a nearby shelf. Unimaginable pain shot throughout my body with that single movement, and somehow, I found myself vomiting.

The sirens were just outside the store. "Come out with your arms raised, try to activate your curse, and we'll shoot you dead," A voice said through a megaphone. My eyes darted from place to place, looking for an escape, but there were only two doors: one behind the counter that would lead me to the side of the building where the police most definitely had covered, and the glass doors right in front of me. There was no escape. I wanted to cry, to scream for help, but there was no mercy for machigai, no mercy for killers, even if they were children.

I approached the door quietly with my head down and arms raised. It opened automatically, letting me out. "That's close enough," A tall blond woman shouted through her megaphone. She nodded to one of the men who had his gun aimed at my head. The man pulled out a pair of handcuffs and headed in my direction, never letting his gun drop a millimeter. Finally, I broke, and tears streamed down my face. My fate was all but sealed when the man halted, clutching his chest as his eyes rolled back into his head, falling to his knees and then the rest of the way. Looking around, it was a strange sight with similar things happening to all the officers; some people merely fell, while others discovered bullet or stab wounds. Only one person was still standing. A bone-thin, tall Indian boy with blond highlights through his mess of raven hair. The boy was maybe 15 years old and was standing with his arms out and a pained expression of concentration on his face; he looked towards me with a pleading look.

"Run," he said. The same thing I had spoken to the little boy earlier, and then he collapsed to the ground groaning; obedience and fear swept over me as I sprinted down the streets. It took me only half of a block to realize what had happened: three innocent people were dead by my hand, and another was soon to come to the same fate. Not just a stranger though, a fellow machigai, the first one that had ever made contact with me. Guilt overwhelmed my fears; for once in my worthless life, I would do the right thing.

He was right where I had left him; we had at most five minutes till another round of cops would be on top of us. I tugged on the arm of his groaning, lifeless, doubled-over body. After being unsuccessful at pulling him to his feet, I knelt at his side, carefully placing my hand on his back.

"They'll have reinforcements here shortly; we either leave now or die in captivity. It's completely your choice." He managed to look me in the eyes. Briefly, every fragment of pain was visible through his steely gray gaze, so I tried to talk even softer.

"Please," I begged. He waited a moment, then gave me a slight nod. With his assistance and with me for balance, we made it a couple of blocks before neither of us could go on. Dragging him inside an abandoned house, we weren't even able to sit down before he started to vomit up a thick black fluid. Our savior was a small steel bucket in a back room. I awkwardly patted his back and tried to gain my bearings. We were in a small living room connected to a tiny kitchen. There was no electricity, and the building was extremely run down and probably infested with all kinds of rodents, but it was the best option to hide out for a while.

It took a while before the boy's vomiting slowed to a stop, and he curled up in a groaning ball on the ground. There was a sketchy staircase leading upstairs that I decided to explore. The upstairs consisted of two tiny bedrooms with rundown mattresses, crawling with who knows what, and a bathroom that I could barely fit in, but it was better than nothing. I headed back downstairs and sat next to the boy who had somehow managed to prop himself up on the wall with sweat beading on his forehead. I retrieved two water bottles and some chips from the black hole that I had taken to calling the void.

"Thanks," the boy said with a weak smile. The water turned an odd gray color as he drank it. He didn't seem to mind, but it made my stomach churn so much that I didn't even bother to drink mine.

"What's your name?" I asked him quietly.

"Soul Stealer." Something about how he said it, maybe it was how serious his face was, or the fact that such a small, bony boy would give themselves that name… made me laugh.

"What's your *real* name?" I said with a grin. Clearly, my smile offended him, but it was obvious he didn't have any other choice, so his expression softened.

"Aska. What about you?"

"Onyx." I responded.

"Your *real* name," he said, mocking my previous tone. I rolled my eyes with a playful smile.

"My name is Lunette, but I prefer to be called Onyx."

"Well, Luna, it's nice to meet you." He held out a hand and I shook it.

"Ditto." We sat there momentarily, listening to the sirens outside, before I stood up and brushed the dirt off my already filthy clothes. "If you're feeling a bit better, I found some beds upstairs. You can sleep, and I can ensure no one finds us." He gave me another weak smile as I offered my hand to help him up.

"Deal."

I helped him up the stairs, which proved more difficult than navigating the streets. It was still cold, but the walls protected us from the wind. Aska fell asleep almost instantly, not caring what diseases the beds held, and despite my vow to keep watch, I dozed off as well.

***

I woke from the dream, oddly calm. I half expected Aska to be right next to me again, but he was still gone. The dream convinced me to keep looking for almost another month. Most days, I found myself fiddling with the blue dye in the end of my hair. When we first met, Aska was 15, and

I was 12. Aska's highlights were blond, and I didn't have any. But after a few years, he switched his to blue, and taught me how to do the same to the tips of my own.

After almost two months altogether, I gave up on my search. It seemed pointless; he would've come home by now if he was still alive. I took over all of his chores, lighting the fire in the morning, heating the water for baths, and once a week, I covered myself in shadows and stole money from stores' cash registers (never nearby; it would be too easy to track). I also continued my chores, mainly cleaning, cooking, and shopping. It continued like this for another two months, although I never did stop sleeping in Aska's room.

Four months. That's how long he had been gone when there was a knock on the door in the middle of the night. I sat bolt upright, wondering if I had dreamed it, and just as I decided I had, another one came. Three simple knocks. It couldn't be him; we always knocked our unique way, two spaced apart and five fast. After another knock, my curiosity overcame my will to live, and I crept downstairs, careful not to make a sound. I was lucky it was night, where shadows were everywhere, fueling my abilities, instead of day where I would have been drained. Preparing myself for whatever, or more likely, whoever that was out there. I threw the door open, my father's knife placed steadily in my hand.

Chapter 2: BlueJay

"Aska," I whispered under my breath. He was there, but not the version I remembered. His beautiful toffee brown skin was covered in bruises, and he seemed to have shed an extra 20 kilograms, which he honestly couldn't afford to lose in the first place. Still, the most noticeable change was the fact that he was being practically carried by an African American boy about my age who was staring dumbfoundedly at the knife in my hand. In a single fluid motion, I was behind him, legs wrapped tightly around him, pinning his arms firmly down. One hand clung to the base of the boy's throat, the other caught Aska by the hood of his sweatshirt. My middle finger planted itself into the little indention on his neck, pressing in hard and up behind the windpipe, watching him struggle for breath. Finally, the boy began to collapse underneath me. I dropped down, letting his eyes flicker shut on the cold pavement. He wasn't dead, not by a long shot; I didn't have that much pity. Instead, I dragged him inside and focused on Aska.

I knelt beside his limp figure; he was still breathing, but the rise and fall of his chest was shallow and uneven. I propped him up against my own body and half carried half dragged him to the foldout couch that we constantly had pulled out just for this occasion. I draped a blanket over his still form, and my eyes fell on the other boy.

After a moment passed, nimble fingers laced the final knot, securing the boy to one of the kitchen chairs. Then it was all a waiting game. I didn't know what else to do, so I sat beside Aska on the bed. It never got easier, seeing him in his weakened state. A part of me believed that he had never looked worse, but logically, it was easy to see it was a lie forced forward by the suppressed panic. Nonetheless, he was beaten horribly and covered in excessive grime. I stroked his hair back and gently kissed his sweat-beaded forehead.

A combination of coughing and a strange gargling/choking noise came from behind me as the other boy woke up. I ran to the kitchen, grabbed a water bottle from the cabinet, and helped him drink almost half of it since his hands were bound. I took a few steps back, leaning on the corner of the couch, and watched as he gained his bearings until, finally, his eyes landed on me.

"Lunette?" I threw my knife, which had somehow made it back to my hands, at the spot just to his right, and he quickly corrected himself. "Onyx, my mistake! My name's BlueJay, call me Jay." Something was odd about how he spoke, drawing out the syllables slightly, making all his "a"s "aw"s. *He's American.* I realized.

"Okay, *BlueJay,* I have two questions. Answer truthfully or else, well..." I nodded toward the three remaining knives on my belt loop and then toward the one on the wall.

"Got it. I pledge to speak the truth, the whole truth, and nothing but the truth. I would pledge it to the bible, but sadly, my hands..." Another knife slipped from my fingers, this time scraping his cheek before landing on the wall next to the first.

"Strike one."

"No fair! I didn't lie!"

"Oh, did I forget to mention that vexing me is also against the game's rules? My mistake." I gave him my most dazzling smile. "So where was I? Oh ya!" My face went slack and then morphed back into a scowl as I leaned against the side of the couch's shell. "Question one: What did you do to Ask- Soul Stealer?"

"Long story short? He overused his ability and well- check under his shirt."

"What do you mean?" I raised an eyebrow at him.

"See for yourself." He shrugged.

Careful not to take my eyes off BlueJay, I moved around to the right side of the couch and removed the blanket from Aska's shivering body.

"I know, I know," I whispered. I sat my knife down on the coffee table. Cupping his face in my hand for only a moment, he seemed perfectly aware I was there. I moved my hand from his face down to his shirt and slowly moved it upwards, revealing a few centimeters deep cut on his side. It looked like a regular wound, except it was oozing black fluid. Suddenly, I wanted to cry, scream, vomit, and kill someone all at once.

"Pretty bad, huh?" It took me a second too long to realize that the voice came from behind me instead of in front, but by then, it was too late. A strong hand pushed me to the ground, my head slamming against the metal under the bed part of the couch. My head was as blurry as my vision, but I could see Jay standing above me, scowling. His foot was placed sturdily on my chest, preventing me from gaining enough oxygen to activate any part of my curse.

"Don't you know never to chain up a machigai? All the humor was gone from his voice, replaced by sheer anger. "I don't understand why Aska would put a human on his deathbed card and such a rude one at that!"

"Wha-" He pressed down harder on my chest.

"Now, let me make this very clear. I'm going to kill you and take Aska back to headquarters. If he ends up getting better, I'll tell him that overcome by his absence, you took your own life, and if he doesn't get better, we'll bury him among the rest like a hero instead of whatever horrible things someone like you would do!" For a brief moment, I truly believed that those would be the last things I had ever heard.

"Stay away from her, you dolt!" Aska's voice was surprisingly strong.

Jay stumbled backward, and for a moment, we were all silent. He was struggling to sit up, coughing so much I thought he would pass out again. My body knew what to do before my brain. Shockingly unopposed by Jay, I stood and got more water from the kitchen. When I returned, Jay knelt by Aska's bedside, the two whispering back and forth. I climbed onto the other side of the bed beside Aska and helped him drink a little water.

"Would someone care to explain what the hell is going on?" Jay asked irritably, still glaring at me.

"Don't look at me; I'm just as in the dark as you!" I shot back.

"Cut it out, you two," Aska groaned, leaning back into his pillow. "You don't need to know my motives, but you can't kill each other."

"The last hour or so begs the difference," Jay smirked, and Aska groaned harder.

"Jay, shouldn't you be leaving now, though?" Aska said hintingly.

"Technically, Burn's orders were to, and I quote, 'make sure he is properly taken care of'." Jay mocked. "I translate that as I can leave when you are dead and buried, or I can leave when you're alive, not this stupid in-between stuff."

"We don't have an extra bedroom."

"Since there's no way that you are making it up those stairs in your condition, we do," I interjected, with a shrug.

"Luna!"

"Sorry!" I raised my hands in surrender. "But it might've been fine for me to take care of all the chores when you ran off, but I can't feed two people completely on my own. I'd get caught within a day, and then we're both screwed!"

"Lun-" He stopped halfway through my name. His chestnut face turned white. "Bucket."

"What?" Jay asked. Aska shot straight up in bed, and I grabbed his shoulder, steadying him back.

"Next to the stairs!" I yelled. "Quick!" I saw a lightbulb go off behind his eyes as he turned to the stairs next to him, grabbed the bucket we kept there, and tossed it to me. It's the same one from all those years ago. I shoved it in Aska's lap as he turned green. The black liquid shot out of him like a fireman's hose. I kept my hand on his shoulder but made the best attempt to move as far away from it as possible. Even after all these years, it only seemed to grow more and more repulsive.

I looked up at Jay facing the wall with his hand over his mouth, and I was almost tempted to laugh.

"Hey!" I yelled at him over Aska's shoulder. "Go to the kitchen; the third cabinet to the right is filled with water; please bring a couple over for him." He retrieved five bottles of water, which was a little overkill, but I didn't complain.

"Here," I threw him a bottle. "You look like you're gonna pass out."

"Thanks," he muttered and sat beside me on the bed.

"You get why I attacked you, right? It wasn't anything personal." He nodded but didn't look me in the eye. "So why are you so angry?"

"Because you're one of them." He said it like it was the most obvious thing in the world.

"One of them?"

"Human, one of the people that decided that all machigai were bad, people like you make my life a living hell every day." The hostility in his voice hinted he wasn't even trying to hide his anger.

"That's why you hate me?"

"I hate everyone like you." He shrugged and looked the other way. "Don't take it personally."

"I think you might be confused."

"How do you figure?"

"Because she's not human," Aska coughed before lurching back forward over his bucket, which was getting pretty full. Killing two birds with one stone sounded like a good plan, so I opened a different portion of the void I called the outfield, where we threw anything that would give us away as machigai.

"Aska," I whispered, and he nodded and laid back, away from the bucket.

With a gag forming, I threw the whole bucket into the void. I counted the seconds before the bucket came shooting back out, sparkling clean, and placed it back in front of Aska who was leaning against the back of the couch with his eyes screwed shut.

I tapped on his shoulder lightly. He looked back at me for a moment, his eyes bloodshot and teary, and I motioned to the bucket on his lap, but he only shook his head, signaling he was done for now. I handed him a water bottle, but he didn't drink it; he just sat there. I bit my lip quietly; my anger towards him a moment ago had evaporated completely.

I sat next to him for a moment, then got up and headed back towards the kitchen. Wetting down a small rag with a different bottle, I squeezed out most of the liquid, dampening it and shaking it off a little more, stalling, to be truthful. A few tears leaked from the corners of my eyes, and I wiped them off.

"So," Jay started from my side, slightly less hostile than before. "You're a machigai"

"Of course. Why would you think otherwise?" I bit at him, rubbing my temples and leaning against the rickety countertops.

"Aska always said you were human, none of us ever really had any reason to assume he'd lie." Jay shrugged, and turned, leaning next to me. His anger seemed to have faded fairly quickly, but I was still cautious.

I turned to face him. "What?"

"He told me that he used to live with a human girl he met on the streets."

"He's a mystery. I'll give him that."

"I guess so," he shrugged, turning his gaze back to Aska in the living room. I wondered what the connection was between these two, how they met and whether they were friends or just allies of situation. From the sun's angle, it was 3-4 in the afternoon, which gave me the perfect excuse to get answers.

"Quick question?"

"Sure" He looked back towards me.

"How wanted are you?"

"With the ladies?" he said with a smirk and a wink. I needed him out of the house, so I laughed instead of slapping him.

"With the police, stupid."

"Not very, why?"

"It's way past lunch. I don't think any of us ate breakfast, and knowing Aska, he will prevent himself from eating anything for as long as possible; subsequently, we need to force him to."

Jay's eyes moved side to side slowly as if he couldn't believe the banality of what I just said. "So, you want me to go get food?"

"Precisely"

Chapter 3: An Explanation (sort of)

Jay followed me up the stairs. As I retrieved my wallet from my bedroom, I gave him a quick tour of the tiny second floor and sent him to get a large pizza.

Once he was gone, I returned to the kitchen and took a deep breath, steadying myself against the counter, grabbing the first aid kid, and heading back to Aska's bedside. Inspecting the contents on the table, I evaluated what needed to happen next: small bandages, athletic tape, medical gauze, rubbing alcohol, a thermometer, and antiseptic wipes. It'd been a while since I had used any of these things, much less on an injury this large, but there was nothing else to do.

"I'm so sorry, Aska," I whispered, putting on my gloves and pouring rubbing alcohol on a paper towel

"What?" He asked weakly just before I lifted his shirt to examine his wound more thoroughly. The black fluid and blood were binding to his ribs, making it almost impossible to tell the depth of the cut. It was a mess of black and red that almost made me gag. Realization vibrated through his body only seconds before the first towel made contact.

"Wait!" His hand grabbed my wrist, and a slight twinge of guilt pinged my chest. The alcohol touched the wound only gently at first, but my friend's entire body contracted in pain, and the grip on my wrist tightened dramatically. I tried to keep a brave face on for him as I continued cleaning the wound.

The towel consumed only a bit of the combination of blood and dried black fluid before needing replacement. Silently impressed with how well Bounty absorbed bodily fluid, I tossed it away and prepared another one. When I turned back to his body, still tensed in pain, my guilt grew. Looking down at the hand latched to my wrist, I guided it down, intertwining my fingers with his, and gave a gentle squeeze of encouragement.

The second paper towel was more challenging to use gently. My hands kept shaking, and the actual wound was becoming more visible, causing a lump of anxiety in my chest to bubble. It seemed never-ending, only getting deeper and deeper, but finally, it was as clean as possible. The cut was about four centimeters deep, but the skin around it seemed to spread away, revolting, just as I had done earlier. There was only one last thing to do, but it would undoubtedly be the hardest.

Moving towards the head of the couch, I held his hands between mine and whispered. "Aska, if you can hear me, you know what needs to happen. We can't let the cut get infected. Try not to resist too much; it'll make it worse." A small squeeze went through my hand, barely noticeable, but enough to tell me what I needed to know. Pushing back his blue and black hair, I gently kissed his forehead as a ghost of a smile whispered across his clammy face.

"It'll be over before you know it." Freeing my hand from his grip, I knelt beside him, pushing one arm underneath his shoulder blades to steady him.

"On three. One. . . two. . . three." His dead-weight body rolled into my arms as he screamed from the movement.

"Sorry, sorry, sorry," I muttered, propping him up against the couch's backrest so there were a few inches between his back and the sofa.

"I'm so sorry," I whispered to the still whimpering body in front of me. "Almost done." I took the space between the soft white gauze off of the table and started working my way around the wound. After about ten complete wraps, the wound was almost completely covered, and some of the tension had spilled from Aska's body. After about twenty wraps, everything below his chest was covered in clean white bandages, and his breathing settled.

I packed the kit and what was left of the bandages and delivered them back to the kitchen.

"Drink," I commanded once I returned to the bed, grabbing one of the water bottles that Jay had brought from the kitchen earlier. Aska's eyes were open, which I took as a good sign, though they were still slightly clouded. He seemed as if he was looking at nothing.

He let me help him drink almost two bottles before he stopped. I wondered if, when he was asleep, Jay ever actually gave him water; he probably didn't think of it knowing him.

Sitting next to Aska on the bed, things almost felt normal again; he rested his head on my shoulder and closed his eyes.

"I never thought at twenty years old I would still be here," he said quietly.

"I never thought of leaving; I assumed you were just as content." My voice made me want to escape to the shadows again, right back to the alley I came from.

"You know that's not what I meant." He shook his head, squeezing my hand just slightly.

"Then what did you mean?" I asked, not squeezing back.

"I mean, I never thought I would still have to have people taking care of me. All my life, I always thought there were only two options. Either I would die or be killed before I made it to adulthood, or I would grow and be able to control my curse, but here I am and--" a fit of coughing cut him off. I pressed one hand against his chest to prevent him from falling so far forward that he would fold his wound. My other hand raised in the air, summoning a shadow to throw the bucket over. I caught it in my raised hand and placed it gently on Aska's lap; he didn't throw up; instead, he coughed like he was losing a lung. Eventually, it stopped, and he laid back with watering eyes; his breathing deep as silent tears rolled down his cheeks.

"I never thought--" he said through gasps of breath, "That once I was an adult, I would still be burdening other people with the responsibility of taking care of me." I looked down at him without saying anything.

"That's not always a bad thing, you know," I said after a while. "Relying on others."

"Maybe not, in small doses, but it seems like I rely on you for everything; if not for Jay, you would be completely overwhelmed and probably get caught. If that happened, I don't know what I would do."

"You know I didn't mean any of that! I would always find my way back, even if Jay weren't here!"

"I know and that worries me," he said quietly. Again, all forms of conversation seemed strained. Aska leaned his head back on my shoulder and even took my hand. It was strange how natural this seemed to me, but I couldn't stay there forever; Jay would be back soon, and I had questions I needed answered.

"Aska?" I whispered.

"Hm?" He mumbled sleepily without opening his eyes.

"Why did you leave?" Apparently, my shoulder suddenly wasn't as comfortable because he sat up so straight, he towered over me until he slumped against the back of the couch. I saw the gears turning in his head, and they struck me with fear.

"I mean, I know it's not any of my business," I rushed. "We never agreed to stay here forever, but I was just wondering. You don't have to answer."

"No, it's fine. You deserve an explanation, I guess." He breathed slowly. For a moment, it seemed he was waiting for another coughing fit to save him. "I'm dying," he said at last. He must've seen the confusion in my face because he continued to explain. "Maybe not right now, but soon. I can feel it." He paused to let that sink in, maybe to him as much as me.

"I wasn't running away from you but towards something greater than us. The Machigai army. They've been fighting for our rights for years; if I could help them, once I'm gone, you can still live."

"I can survive on my own," I protested quietly.

"I don't mean just survive; I mean live. Have a life, a family, a job, be normal."

"Machigai can't have any of that."

"But we all could; if only we had a few more rights, we could be a part of society and live. We wouldn't be forced to use our curses to protect us." His eyes lit up when he spoke; he believed we could be more than just dead bodies marked for the kill. I wasn't too sure what I believed.

"Do you regret leaving?" I whispered.

"No. Sorry, I don't," he whispered back to me.

"Do you regret getting stabbed?" I jested, placing my hand on his stomach over his bandages.

He rolled his eyes. "No, I enjoyed it, the best experience of my life. Would do again if I ever had a knife," he said sarcastically.

"No need for that level of sarcasm." I laughed, nudging him.

"Don't ask stupid questions if you don't want stupid answers." He shrugged, finally relaxing a bit.

"Okay, how is this for a non-stupid question? Can I go with you?"

"Where to?" He looked over to me with his eyebrow raised, I traced my fingers over the blue lines of veins that swam over his forearm.

"To the Machigai Army. At least then I can do something to--"

"No," he said bluntly, tearing his arm and eyes away.

"But-"

"I said no! I didn't tell them you were a machigai cause if they knew you were, they would want you to join, especially with your abilities. They would take you on raids, you'd always be in danger."

"That's fine, I'm not scared!" I shot back.

"Ya? And what happens if you don't come back? Huh? What do I do then? What happens if they kill you? Or worse? You're just a kid."

"I'm seventeen years old, Aska."

"Listen, I said no, and that's the end of it!" He bit in a tone much harsher than the one I was used to.

"I'm back with pizza!" Jay burst through the door. He had a half-eaten slice in his hand and was chewing on a mouthful.

"Perfect timing, I'm starving," Aska said, clarifying that our discussion was over.

Chapter 4: Two Brothers and a Phone Call

"I gotta hand it to you, Onyx," Jay examined Aska's bandages while we dined on the pizza. "You did some nice handiwork on good ol' Soul Stealer here." He gently poked at Aska's belly button, causing him to flinch and wince, but Jay just looked up and smiled.

"Hey, Stealer," He prodded with his obnoxious grin. "How come you've been hiding this little devil from us? We could've been using her expertise at headquarters this whole time."

"We have Lily; we don't need to drag Luna into it."

"Who's Lily?" I asked, picking a pepperoni off the top of my own pizza slice.

"She's kinda like a dedicated nurse; her curse involves healing natural wounds at the expense of both her and her patient's energy, so it's pretty much useless to a bunch of machigai. Plus, it couldn't even make a dent in Stealers papercut here, not for lack of effort on her part." Jay explained.

"What does that mean?" Aska asked.

"She spent a week at the least trying to heal that thing, probably why you were asleep so long; it must've taken up a lot of energy on both of your parts, I guess." Jay took another bite of pizza.

"You said it only worked on natural wounds, right?" I asked.

"Ya, simple stuff like stab wounds and gunshots." He made a lot of elaborate gestures when he talked, miming out every word.

"The black fluid might've been the problem." I suggested. "It stems from his curse and is anything but natural."

"Possibly," He shrugged and took another bite of his pizza. "Still, I think you would be useful." He paused for a moment. "Do you know how to treat burns?"

"Vaguely. Why?"

"Just curious." I could see he was plotting something, but then again, when was he not? We all consumed our pizza in silence until it was all gone. Then we threw the box in the trash, and I headed back upstairs to clean Aska's room so it was at least livable for Jay.

It was a disaster. For the most part, I had done a good job of ignoring it for the last four months, since the rat's nest always reminded me of Aska, but now that he was back, I was gaining awareness of just how disgusting the place was. Clothes covered the ground, and old food was everywhere; I was half tempted to throw it all into the outfield. Instead, I tossed the food and the plates in the trash, but I spared the clothes (or most of them) placing them in the hamper instead and making a mental note to take them to the laundromat once I got the opportunity. Weirdly, it was relaxing; it was so quiet that everything felt like it was melting away: the worry, fear, and pain; for a second, I was allowed to be just an ordinary girl, cleaning her loved ones' room while they were sick. That wasn't the case though, instead of being stuck in bed with a cold, Aska was immobile downstairs with a dangerous wound, and instead of going back to school once it was over, he was going to run back to the place that caused it all. I tried to concentrate on the methodological cleaning but my head wouldn't shut up; nothing about this situation was expected, and nothing about us was normal. Machigai don't deserve normal. We sin to live, and we live to sin. We pretend we're innocent, but we are just filthy criminals.

"Looks good," Jay said from the doorway, then wrinkled his nose. "Smells… not as good." A laugh escaped from my mouth, probably the first one in years.

"I'll get some air freshener next time I'm at the store." It was his turn to laugh now.

"Seriously, I don't think Aska has cleaned this place since I was twelve." I sat down on the bed and he followed.

"When did you two meet?"

"When I was twelve," I repeated, thinking back to the small, frail boy he once was.

"Really, but I thought you were only 17?"

"Ya, so what?"

"Wow, for only five years, you guys make it look much longer." He leaned back with a sly smile.

"Well, when 70 percent of the population is trying to kill you, and 25 percent of the rest is turning you into the people who are trying to kill you, it's hard to be picky with whom you place your trust. We're all family in a certain way, so it makes sense."

"Seems fair enough, but even if someone is a machigai, how can you trust him so easily?" I thought for a second, trying to remember my thought process five years ago, why exactly I went back to him.

"Well, after they've saved your life a few times, it's easier not to worry about it." Jay nodded. "Why are you so concerned with trust? You've known me less than a day, and you seem pretty comfortable, especially granted I started the day trying to kill you."

He laughed and swung his head back. "I hate to say it, but you have a point. Somehow, the attempted murder might've helped, as ironic as it seems."

"I'm gonna just ignore that, only because I just got over the habit of sleeping with a knife, and I don't want to relapse."

"First off, sleeping with a knife is a good habit." He made a jabbing motion at the knives that still hung at my belt. "Second, I meant how you were willing to put yourself in danger of being found for Soul Stealer."

"I don't follow. How did I put myself in danger?"

"You didn't know who I was or anything about me; I could've had much stronger powers. Or, the less likely of the options, spent less time rambling before killing you."

"Kinda sounds like you regret it." I widened my eyes at him, picturing what might've happened if Aska had woken up only a second later.

"I-- huh?" He paused and stroked his chin thoughtfully before cracking a grin. "You might have a point there." He chuckled, nudging my shoulder.

"That's both concerning and deeply, deeply offensive." I rolled my eyes back at him, warmly excepting his returned smile.

"Well--" A quick, loud thud rang out downstairs. Instantly, I shot up, but Jay just sat there and took a deep breath. With his eyes closed and his head hung backward, he smiled and said. "Never gives up, does he?"

"Not as long as I've known him." I turned at the door to look back at him. "You coming?" He opened his eyes, shook his head with a sly smile, and laid back on the bed, rubbing his temples.

"I'll be down in a minute."

***

I helped Aska return to bed and fetched another water bottle from the kitchen. He fell asleep before I was back. It was already pitch-black outside, and the cold was seeping into the creaky house like water in a strainer. Shivering, I placed all the blankets I could find over Aska. It felt quite weird tucking a 20-year-old into bed, yet for what seemed like the thirtieth time, I realized nothing about this was normal.

Smiling, I gave him a peck on the cheek and made a cup of tea before heading back up the stairs.

"Jay? Jay?" A muffled voice echoed from Aska's room.

Slowly, I cracked open the door. "Jay? Is everything-?" My voice caught in my throat as I saw his body sprawled across the bed.

"Jay?!" I sprinted over to the bed and checked the pulse on his wrist. *Oh, thank god. He's just asleep.*

"Who's there?" The same muffled voice echoed. I saw a brilliant light bouncing off the ceiling and traced it to a small rectangular object on the other side of the bed: a cell phone. It was nothing fancy, just an average flip phone. Picking it up, I saw the word "Burn" flash across the tiny screen with a fire emoji next to it.

"Hello?" I said into the phone, clicking off the speaker phone for two reasons; firstly Jay was quiet for the first time since I met him, and it was peaceful, secondly I'd already seen him enraged once, and I didn't think he would respond well to me snooping through his things. So, instead, I held the phone up to my ear and listened.

"You aren't Jay," said the person on the other line quietly.

"And we have an Einstein in the building, or not quite." I shrugged, expecting the same lighthearted humor I found from Jay.

"Who is this?" It demanded back, not quite as amused by my fabulous joke.

"My name is Onyx; I'm a friend of Aska's." Someone on the other side released a deep breath.

"Oh, it's just you," the voice whispered gratefully.

"And who might you be?" A feeling of suffocation washed over me with the realization that I was deeply uninformed compared to the rest of the people involved in this fucked up situation. I didn't like feeling uneducated or unprepared. My uncle used to tell me that proper preparation could turn any scary situation controllable, unfortunately I didn't see a way I could have predicted this.

"I'm Burn. I knew Soul Stealer very well; I'm so sorry for your loss," he stated formally. I cracked a grin. Apparently, I was not the only one getting kept in the dark.

"Wait… wait, repeat that, please?"

"I'm Burn. I-"

"No, the last part." I interrupted.

"I'm sorry for your loss?" I laughed, wondering how much this boy knew about the events of the last 24 hours. "What?" I noticed that his voice had a little edge to it, like that of an army general.

"I'm very disappointed to tell you that Aska is still alive and kicking despite everything. He just went to sleep a little bit ago.

"Oh…" Burn's embarrassment radiated from the phone, but after a day always feeling a step behind, I enjoyed someone else having a turn. "What about BlueJay? Is he alright?"

I glanced over at the former stranger, snoring away in my best friend's bed. The corners of my mouth tweaked upwards. "He's fine, just tired, I think."

"Good, how much did he tell you?"

"Not nearly enough." I replied honestly, stepping out of the room. I crossed the hallway and clicked my own door shut behind me, sliding down against the wooden door with my knees held to my chest.

"Then, I'll offer you a deal. Tell me what you know, and I'll do the same." His voice was becoming steadier. I smiled, grateful for someone who wasn't trying to protect me from the machigai, because I was one of them, whether they liked it or not.

Chapter 5: Return

The next few months were okay-ish. I never ended up telling Jay about the phone call; always a little too afraid of ruining progress in our slowly burning new bond. It seemed that Burn also never divulged our secret, because Jay never asked me about it either. Aska slowly gained more movement, although it was still extremely difficult for him, and after about a week, I woke up to find Jay gone. I knew he couldn't have stayed, but it was still disappointing. Somehow, I had grown to enjoy the psycho's company. After he was gone, Aska became restless. He went from only trying to walk around when we were there helping him to me waking up in the middle of the night due to his falling. I constantly resisted the urge to yell at him; not only was he hurting himself, but it seemed like he was trying to make a clear point of how much he wanted to leave, and eventually, he did.

That day I woke up, and everything was quiet. I didn't even have to leave my bed before I started weeping into my pillow. I knew where he was; where he would go, and where he might not ever return from. So why did it still hurt so much?

Eventually, I found myself going over the events in my head. He first disappeared in January, returning just barely two weeks ago on the 29th of April, and now he was gone.

After a day in bed, I returned to work. Jay had used up the last of my spending money on his unhealthy obsession with pizza, so I had no choice but to steal again.

It was just barely a month when I awoke late at night to another knock at the door. I sprinted down the stairs and stopped just before the door. *Please be them.* I prayed. Sure enough, Jay with his dark skin, close cropped curls, and broad shoulders stood before me with his eyes locked on Aska, who was barely on his feet; arms wrapped tightly around Jay's neck. I opened the door with my arms crossed and my eyebrows raised. They continued bickering as if I wasn't even there.

"You have no say in where I take your corpse when you can't even stand!" Jay sounded so irritated, and I was surprised he didn't just stop supporting Aska right there.

"Did you seriously just say that? Of course I have a fucking say in it! How did you convince Burn to let you do this!"

"You think that guy knows anything about medical needs? All I had to tell him was that if Lily couldn't help you, maybe Onyx could."

"You only wanted to come to get off your scouting duties; this isn't a vacation home! Burn will be informed of this the second we get back, and there is no way he's ever putting you in charge again!"

"I thought I raised you better than to threaten the reason why you're still standing, Aska," I interjected. They both flushed as they saw me in the doorway, Jay flashing me a smile "About goddamn time. I thought you two would be bickering out here all night. Seriously, you sound like an old married couple. Come on already." I closed the door as Jay dumped Aska on the couch. Sometime, as they walked, I heard Aska mutter something along the lines of: "You raised me?!"

I had already stored a few water bottles below the bed for this occasion. I gave each of the boys their own, and Jay's seemed to disappear down his throat in seconds.

Sitting down next to Aska on the bed, my body relaxed. "So..." I said with a minor grin. "What happened this time?"

They told me everything. I couldn't figure out if they were too tired or too angry with each other to care anymore, but they spilled their knowledge out for me to examine without a second thought. Aska began telling me about a siege they had been planning for months.

"The police station recently took in two machigai children between the ages of five and twelve. Tresa saw the report on the news, but they were ready for us, probably trying to lure us out."

"They were waiting for us. Couldn't make it past the front gate." Jay muttered; there was darkness and hatred behind his voice.

"Anyways, gunfire was raining down, and that's all I remember." Aska continued. I couldn't tell if he realized it, but his hand had found its way to the side of his thigh, where I could tell there were minor amounts of blood seeping through his pant leg.

"And the kids?" I asked.

"Who knows? They could've been killed already and experimented on. Tortured. Or maybe they never existed in the first place. I haven't had much time to look into it. Our ranks were never that large, but now they're almost non-existent." Jay trembled; his voice quiet.

"How many are left?" Aska asked softly, his brow furrowing.

"Alive? Maybe about thirteen. It could've been worse, but still. . . there were so many casualties. Blaise got a bad beating from a guard, but he'll be fine. Blake, Alexis, and Yvette are all in severe condition. Chris… Chris didn't make it. Lily's been overrun with different patients, which is probably how I convinced Blaise to let me sneak Soul Stealer out. Figured the less stress for her, the better."

"You seemed to get out okay?" I nodded towards him. For someone who had survived such a seemingly intense battle, Jay didn't have anything to show for it. No scars or wounds, not even a scratch.

"It's easier for me. Small target." He shrugged, dismissing the idea with a wave of his hand.

"Small?" I almost would have laughed if not for the grim looks on both of their faces. Jay might not have been huge, but he was at least a half-foot taller than me and possibly twenty kilograms heavier than Aska.

"Ha. . . ha. . . ha. . ." He rolled his eyes sarcastically, then he was gone. My own eyes darted around wildly searching.

"Jay?!" Aska stayed unfazed, grabbed my hand, and pointed to the floor beside the bed. A small bird with blue and white feathers and hostile eyes glared at me. It was a strange sight, but my heart rate climbed back to normal.

"Huh? BlueJay indeed." I muttered. Aska tugged me back by my shoulders as the tiny bird flew up a few feet and landed on the bed. Once again, a slim African boy, Jay, lurched forward hard. For a moment, I thought he was laughing, then Aska threw out an arm to steady him as he began gagging and coughing, clutching his throat. Out of instinct, I retrieved Aska's bucket from the corner; by the time I returned, he had stopped coughing but was quietly shaking. I sat beside him and offered the bucket, slipping it into his hands. He spat a glob of soaked bright blue feathers into the bucket and sat it on the ground. I saw Aska shuffle his injured leg away as Jay leaned back onto his hands with a few tears slipping down his cheeks.

"Get it now?" He groaned.

"Ya, I guess. Why couldn't you just explain your curse? There was no point in activating it."

He gave a slight chuckle and shrug. "It's more cinematic this way I suppose; anything for the drama."

"Well, Mr. Theater, take a water bottle and go get some sleep. I put air freshener in the room."

"Sleep sounds good." He stood for a moment before teetering slightly backward. Both Aska and I steadied him as he placed his hand on the couch for support.

"I'll help you." I decided when he began to walk. I gave Aska a gentle squeeze on his calf. "Be back in a minute."

Chapter 6: A Chance or A Reason

They didn't stay long that trip. Aska was right, his injury really wasn't that bad- just a minor gun wound on his thigh. According to Jay, his curse activated on its own when he was shot, which was probably the reason why he lost consciousness so easily. There was something strange with the bullet though, someone else's blood was on it, but the blood was so light it could've been pink. If I had to guess, it was probably dipped in activated machigai blood. For the most part, a machigai's circulative system was identical to a human, but recent studies had shown that when a machigai's curse was activated; their blood changed composition. If this was the case, active machigai blood would be deemed an unnatural substance and could likely cause issues with Lily's curse. No wonder they were having so much trouble with the injuries.

The next day, Jay bounced down the stairs fully renewed from the previous night's affairs. When he saw Aska's leg, he gave me a look which I couldn't quite decipher before it disappeared only a second later.

That day became a trademark in my memories; something good to look back on when the shitty-ness of life's reality set it. Jay and I went to a nearby gas station and bought egg sandwiches for breakfast, a *real* breakfast. Occasionally, I would see him giving me the same look as before, but it was always brief; vanishing like a phantom before I had a chance to understand its meaning. Aska seemed to grudgingly be enjoying being away from the base, and even laughed at Jay occasionally when he did something stupid. Later that night, after we were all filled and rested, he fell asleep. I covered him in a blanket and gave him a small kiss on the forehead before retreating upstairs.

Jay's door was wide open and he was talking on the phone with a grim face. When he saw me enter the room, he told the person on the other end a quick bye and hung up.

"Everything okay?" I asked. He leaned back against his pillow and sighed.

"Burn isn't in the greatest mood today. We lost another machigai to their injuries last night, and there's still two in severe condition; Lily's powers aren't working, and she's exhausted out of her mind. Telling him that Aska recovered so fast because of you certainly didn't help."

"Could you call him up again?" I asked. Jay's eyebrow arched, disappearing into his forehead, scanning me up and down like he was surveying a child. To be completely honest, his composure, at times, was a little off-putting – it was the sudden changes that disarmed me the most. One moment he could be dancing around cracking jokes left and right, and the next his face was so serious it left you questioning if his stoney expression was a bit of some sort.

"Do you have a death wish?" He paused, but when I just smiled back with determination, he gave a gentle head shake of disbelief before continuing. "Ya, I guess but I doubt he'll be too happy about it." he relented, flipping the phone back open without removing his inquisitorial gaze.

"Just do it. And put him on speakerphone too." I sat down next to Jay on the bed as the phone rang.

"What!" An extremely irritated voice yelled from the other line. Suddenly my confidence declined and my understanding of Jay's need to get away cleared.

"Burn, play nice. Onyx wishes to speak with you, I think she has information." He handed me the phone and laid back on the bed with a gesture that could only have been translated to; *All you. Good luck.*

"Hello." *Hello? Who starts with that? Just try not to do anything too stupid Onyx.*

"Onyx," He acknowledged me with less edge to his tone. "Good to speak with you again."

"Again?" Jay muttered, lifting his head just slightly.

"I would like to pass a message on to Lily."

"Proceed."

"The bullets are covered in what I believe to be active machigai blood. The Machigai Enforcement Squad most likely knows you have a healer. Her powers won't work if any of the blood is left in the wounds, it's dried on the outside of the bullets, but by now I suppose it was cleaned off into the bloodstream. I'm not entirely positive, but my theory is that if you cleanse the infected area thoroughly enough, her powers might have more of an effect." For a moment he was silent. The air became dense around us as the sound of pencil on paper scraped through the tiny phone's speaker. Was he actually writing this down?

"Anything else?" He asked.

"No-No that's all." I waited for a reply but the phone screen went dark.

"I wouldn't worry about him, he's typically nicer but he's stressed right now," Jay said with his head still lolled backward. "Now let's talk about what he meant by *again*."

"Ohh wowww. . . look how dark it is." I started inching backwards to the door dramatically, stopping just barely in its frame. "You'd better go to sleep. I'll go check on Aska! Bye!"

"Wait!" He yelled as I reached the doorway.

"What's up?" I turned around to look at him staring me down with the same expression as earlier, this time I could read it perfectly. Desperation.

"You know, you could come back with me and Aska. We really need another healer and it would make it so that we don't have to travel here every time he needs help. You could have your own room, and no one would bug you. Us machigai should all be together; we are family after all."

"I-I'll" I stumbled for words. I've only had two homes my whole life, one was horrible and one was somewhat better, still not quite what I expected, but something inside of me didn't want to leave it. "I'll need to discuss it with Aska," I said eventually. The disappointment on his face was well hidden, but still noticeable. I didn't want to think of how bad things were at headquarters that he would be desperate enough to disobey Aska so openly.

"If you really think he will bend, I would talk fast cause I doubt this trip will be a long one."

"Good night, BlueJay," I said as I shut the door. I should've gone to bed right there but looking down the stairs, my legs seemed to glide away from my room and down the steps where Aska lay asleep on the foldout couch.

I climbed onto the base of the bed and sat on my knees, taking a second to just look at him. He always drooled when he slept. That seemed to be the only thing that hadn't changed in the past six months. His jawline was sharper, his bony frame had gained a small amount of muscle, and his chestnut skin had a more consistent color making him look less flushed. Flashes of our past made me wince. Robberies, and dinners. Meeting and leaving. The most recent of him yelling because I even considered going with Jay and him, but things were different. According to Jay, their ranks had slid down to thirteen people, only seven of whom were fighters. Maybe that would be enough to convince him.

"Luna?" Aska mumbled, rubbing his eyes. "Why are you still up?"

"Wasn't tired." I shrugged defensively, watching as he spun around in bed and laid his head in my lap.

"Don't lie to me," he groaned.

"I'm not." I lied again.

He nuzzled his head into my knee gently. "Your voice is squeaky. Meaning you're either lying or you have something to say."

"Trust me, I'm fine." I twirled a strand of his hair around my finger.

"I trust you," he yawned.

I smiled secretly. It had been too long since I had seen him decently normal, without a fatal injury, I almost didn't want to ruin it.

"Aska?" he groaned in response to his name. "Jay asked me to leave with you guys. He said I could be useful as a medic." I felt the muscles in his temples move as he opened his eyes and shifted away from me onto his elbows.

"What did you say?" he asked quietly. Behind his eyes I could see remnants of the fire that had sparked the last time we had this conversation.

"I said I would discuss it with you."

"You already know my answer, Luna" he stared me dead in the eyes, searching them for some sort of disagreement.

"Aska, I promise to do exactly what you say-"

"Somehow I doubt that" he muttered, rubbing his temples like a disappointed and tired father.

"But first- please just think it through. The machigai are dying. I'm not your only family, you have others you should be protecting."

"I will protect them. And you."

"But just-"

"NO! You're not leaving, that's final!" he raised his voice. The ferocity in his eyes almost scared me.

"Don't yell. Please."

Before I could react, all the cracks in the window boards were lit. Bright red and blue lights shined in my eyes as sirens rang out around the walls, getting louder and louder so I couldn't think. Aska had already jumped to his knees, which I strongly doubted was good for his leg. Jay banged down the stairs, half-dressed in a sleepy panic. I slid two pistols from the void and steadied them both directed toward the door just in case. Aska nailed his eyes shut and the vein on his forehead bulged, he was searching for victims of sin.

"Don't!" I dropped one of the guns and grabbed his shoulder. "Not until we know what they want!"

"They aren't gonna keep us alive long enough to ask!" He protested.

"Onyx's right, they might not be here for us! If you kill them now, it will only give them confirmation!" Jay screamed. Aska glared at us but obeyed for now. He picked up the gun that I dropped and turned the safety off as I did the same.

"BlueJay! Bird's Eye!" he yelled behind us. Jay gave a little nod and disappeared in his bird form through a back window. Then it was just two. We sat there for a moment, not daring to speak or even to breathe. The sirens were fading, the peak was over, but we could never be sure. An injured chirp echoed throughout the kitchen followed by a fit of coughing. I risked a glance at the scene as Bluejay stumbled a few times and fell to his knees. Aska vaulted over the back of the couch, grabbing the bucket on his way. I slid off the side of the bed carefully and backed toward them without taking my eyes off the windows and doors. Never once faltering the hold on my gun, I stood over Aska as he helped Jay drink water. A hand gripped my arm from behind making me turn from instinct, prepared to shoot whoever dared to touch me.

Jay simply shook his head and croaked, "Not us."

For a moment I studied my friends and the door with only light highlights of pink and soft blue. I turned the safety back on my gun but didn't dare put it back in the void.

Aska and I helped Jay to the couch and eventually back to his room. Aska went back to bed but my nerves had been frayed. For a while, I watched him sleep, carefully breathing, peacefully. I must have fallen asleep sometime during the night because the next morning they were both gone.

Chapter 7: Cinnamon Will Kill Ya

The 3rd disappearance didn't bother me. Maybe because of the previous night's excitement, I thought they would be safer. Perhaps it was because I knew they had people to help, or maybe I had finally accepted that Aska had a different life. With only me, I ended up activating my curse a lot less; I even found more time to go to the library, but still, there seemed to be more and more wanted posters appearing in the streets. Of course, they only showed a dark shadow, but it didn't stop my anxiety from haunting the few normal dreams I had.

I didn't want Aska to return any more. The Machigai Enforcement Squad seemed to be everywhere at once these days. The news often covered the massive rise of applications for Toyls Academy. There were many controversial opinions; some people were against the idea of such young people being trained to kill, while others claimed the machigai were simply diseased, making the students at Toyls doctors, not psychopathic murderers. Either way, the philosophy was demented.

The days I wasn't at the library or gathering supplies, I spent at cafes just watching the numbers rise, knowing that one of those kids would most likely kill me. They showed tours of the grounds and their new toys; everything looked so ordinary that it made me nauseous.

I began using my money conservatively, only purchasing necessities. I took note of police sitting in alleys outside of convenience stores, waiting for me to strike in my usual areas. Summer was an excellent time to be alone; the public showers at the swimming pool were free, making me look more like a teenager and less like a sewer rat.

After about two months, the money ran out. Usually, this would be a simple fix, but there were cops at almost every alley, all with modified cars designed to encapsulate machigai. After nearly two days of starvation, which would have been a breeze a few months ago, I settled on a tiny gas station about two miles from the city. It was small, with likely very little money, and it would take much longer than I typically spent on these trips, but I was desperate.

I went to sleep that night on a still empty stomach that longed for the food it was promised for the next day. Sadly, fate was not in my favor; that night, the nightmares flooded my sleep.

After almost a month without any sign of my curse, I could feel the heat radiate from the monster's hide, burning my skin as it neared. He was my least favorite of the creatures that haunted me; his eight eyes dripping green acid-like tears onto my face and shoulders. Each drop burned like a thousand suns, sinking into my skin layer by layer. I wanted to cry and scream, but as always, I could not. It resembled a spider combined with a woolly mammoth, its abyss of black fur seared as it brushed my face, but I was stuck. My eyes watered as the welts formed, and I woke up.

It took me too long to wrap my wounds up in the morning. The blisters burned and occasionally burst as the clean cloth covered them in white. I threw a hoodie on and tossed my empty bag over my shoulder, wincing as it made contact. To make things worse, my stomach was growling, and my head was being held hostage by rushing thoughts and a significant headache. The steps on the stairs creaked with every aching movement I made; the living room was painfully quiet, which had never quite bugged me till now. Everything about the day seemed cursed, more so than usual.

I took the bus to the stop just before the gas station. I had to walk a little farther, but it would be worth it once the news coverage got out. The store was deserted, with only a middle-aged man at the counter. The food aisle looked so delicious I began stuffing everything into my backpack, from ramen to oatmeal to candy and water. I was so hungry I even tore open a Snickers right there, the creamy chocolate melting in my mouth like ice. It was sweet and salty; finally, eating something felt so good. Then, someone cleared their throat. I was caught. The man from behind the counter was standing behind me. I swallowed the chocolate when he pursed his lips and pushed the candy bar at him apologetically as he pointed to the security camera above the isle. I must've looked foolish because he began to smile and then laugh, and then he was practically doubling over on himself. I couldn't help but grin a bit.

"Go ahead, we've had no one all day. Plus, you look like you are starving." Was this a joke? Did he already call the cops and was stalling for them to get here? What could I do? But what he did next was unexpected. He walked to the hot food table, picked up various sandwiches and pretzels, and shoved them in a checkout bag with Cheez-Its and other goodies. I should have run. Everything would've been better if I did. He handed me the bag and made a "stay here" gesture with his hands. Returning, he offered a weird piece of rolled-up bread with a glaze.

"Here, try this. My daughter made them. It's a cinnamon roll." I took a small bite out of the sticky dessert. It was warm and humid, leaving a slight tingle in my throat. I loved it.

"Why are you being so nice?" I asked through bites, sitting down next to the now-destroyed shelf. The man slid down next to me, his nametag read "Micheal."

"Just cause." He shrugged. "A part of me misses what this city used to be, before the machigai persecution started. I have two kids and—" he paused. "It hurts to see so many young people with bright futures living hungry on the streets. I figured if I can help just one then, ---" he trailed off.

I gave a slight cough, trying to clear the once enjoyable tingle that had turned bothersome. "So, you don't hate the machigai?"

"I'm not sure it's that simple. It's like being asked if you hate all of humanity. Sure, some can do awful things, but that doesn't mean everyone is like that." Again, I tried to clear my throat, but the air that I pushed up just hit a wall, so I tried swallowing. Then my teeth bit down on my tongue very hard, but I could hardly feel anything. Not to mention, I could sense the edges of my tongue touching almost every corner of my mouth, which wasn't normal. Something was wrong. The more I tried to breathe, the harder it became.

"Are you alright?" Micheal asked, his brow furrowing with concern. He slid a hand behind my back, helping me sit up straight as I clutched at my throat. The truth was no. Obviously no. The panic of not breathing was setting in tremendously, and with the panic came the shadows. I started crying as suffocation blurred my vision. I wanted to tell Micheal to run, but he stayed by my side as I watched the shadows lunge out at everything around me. The last thing I heard was Micheal's piercing screams before everything went dark.

Two nightmares in twelve hours was never a good combination—welts on welts. When I woke, everything was gone. The store had been through a tornado. Shelves were knocked on their side, the only shelf that remained standing was the one I had been sitting against with Micheal. A tiny smear of blood and my rapid heartbeat were all that was left of the previous scene.

"I'm so sorry," I whispered to the store as I stumbled away with a few bags of food, making sure to clean out the registers.

***

The streets were dark by the time I got back to town. No one had called in the destruction of the gas station yet; it might even be days till they noticed it was abandoned. Pain and overwhelming guilt found my senses, leaving me weakened and afraid, but more than anything, I just wanted the day to be over.

When I finally reached the dark, abandoned neighborhood I called home, something was off. There was a faint light shining from inside the creaky house. My knife was lodged deep in my backpack, so I had to take the whole thing off to retrieve it.

The screen door in the back was barely open, a habit Aska and I got into when we were younger, making quick getaways and sneaky entrances. I studied the blade as I emerged from what I assumed used to be a laundry room into the kitchen. One tall figure was hunched over the couch that, for once, was actually in couch form. I couldn't see much, but they had a flashlight which illuminated the living room just enough to highlight their silhouettes.

"Have you just given up on knocking?" I asked aloud with a glare. Jay turned around, and I could see distress written across his face. Something was wrong, definitely wrong.

"What happened? What's going on?" I took a few steps towards him, scanning him for injuries.

"Help, I-I don't know what to do." His eyes glistened with tears and fear.

"Jay. . . Where's Aska?" He pointed to the couch. The body was buried in blood and grime. There were a few smears of dirt where it appeared Jay had tried to clean around some of his wounds, but even with his feeble attempts the corpse was still a disaster. His face was drained of color, and every inch of his body was covered in scrapes and soot from an unknown source. I had never seen a body lie so still, at least not one that was still alive.

"Oh god. . . Is he-" I couldn't finish the sentence; I thought they would be fine on their own; he had trained people to protect him.

"I don't know," Jay whimpered quietly. "Please, help. I don't know. . ." He crouched down against the back of the couch with his head in his hands. I could see him trembling as he anxiously pulled at the sides of his hair.

"Okay. . . Okay. . . Okay. . ." I grabbed him by the shoulders. "I need water bottles, lots of them." He gave an uncertain nod and ran to the cabinet where we kept the water; it was still nearly barren, but he grabbed what he could.

Meanwhile, I stole some paper towels from the counter and returned to the couch to clean the edges. He was breathing, but only slightly and there was no guarantee how long he would stay that way. I poured Jay's water on the towel as it soaked the floor beneath me, seeping into the fabric of my jeans. I tried to avoid the actual wound for the time being, since I didn't know much about its depth and didn't think it wise to go too deep.

A lot of my time at the library, I had spent reading not just fiction but information about how to treat different types of wounds, different knife styles, and damage caused by them. *Propper planning prevents poor performance.* I heard my uncle say in my head. I wasn't sure if that was true, because even now, with all my planning, I was performing very poorly.

I hadn't treated a fresh wound since- I couldn't remember. The two previous had been sitting for probably days; this one couldn't have been more than a few hours. The blood pooled in between my fingers as I gently tried to apply pressure; soon, both of my hands were stained red.

Eventually, Aska's limp body was coated in light beams from the window. I heard every single one of Jay's steps as he paced behind the couch, but as my ears and mind wandered, my hands stayed concentrated on their job. Once the bleeding had slowed, my task became to find the source.

After hours of cleaning and recleaning, I found a gaping hole in his side, almost directly below the ribcage. All I could do was hope that whatever it was didn't pierce the spleen and cause too much internal bleeding. Jay kept bringing me water to rinse the blood until the cabinet was empty, and I was left having to open the void to use what was in there. Soon, I was drained between my lack of sleep and overuse of my curse. But I couldn't stop. Underneath the caked blood were dark bruises covering most of his torso; there was nothing I could do about those right now. Most of the problem was gone, but the actual cut was still bleeding, maybe slower than before, but if I had to guess, he had probably lost over a liter of blood. Cleaning any more was far too risky. I needed to stop the bleeding.

"Hold this on the wound for a second, please." I handed one of the towels to Jay as I directed myself towards the kitchen. We only had a few clean cloths, but I grabbed the closest one and returned to the couch. Jay was trying to be gentle, but with the amount of pressure he was applying to the wound, I was afraid he might cause more damage. I gently shooed him towards the other side of the couch, where he sat on the coffee table and began fidgeting. Part of my mind wanted to comfort him; the other told me Aska was more dire right now, so I returned to work. I shifted onto my knees, so I was hovering about a foot above his actual body, and started applying gentle pressure to the wound using the palm of my hand. Luckily, my recent involuntary fasting made it easier for me not to involve too much pressure.

"Onyx? Do you want to switch for a bit? You've been at this for hours." Jay sat down next to me on the floor.

I found it sad that he was almost the same height as me, sitting down as I was on my knees.

"No." I shook my head softly, keeping my concentrated gaze locked on Aska. "Thanks though."

"Okay-" He struggled for a moment to stifle a yawn, and I turned to look at him for a moment. Be careful not to release the pressure.

"You know you're always welcome to the bedroom upstairs if you like that."

He shook his head low. "Don't think I could." He leaned forward and rested his head on his hands to stare at Aska.

"Do you know what happened?" I asked.

"Not really. No," his voice cut out. "He left to borrow food from the local grocery store like we always do. Didn't come back. Blaise got anxious and sent me out, but when I got there, the store was rubble. Found him buried in it, panicked, and brought him here."

"So, Blaise doesn't even know he's here."

"Don't worry. I texted him while I was waiting." He took a profound sigh of disbelief. "They destroyed an entire building just because there was a chance he was there. I've hated them for so long, but this. . . There could've been innocent people in there. There probably was."

"Sometimes, I don't think they hate us that much," I confessed, staring at the floor, and thinking about my time at the convenience store yesterday. Then I looked back to Aska, his young, mangled body. I glanced up at Jay, just seventeen years old, the same age as me, and I thought about how neither of us would likely live to adulthood.

"But they do. They really do."

Chapter 8: Escape

We spent the rest of the day in silence. Eventually, the bleeding slowed enough to wrap it in gauze properly. After that, all we could do was wait. Jay eventually fell asleep with his head on the couch; the opportunity was perfect to retreat to my bedroom to steal some blankets. The weather was strangely bitter for August, leaving the house cold and me yearning for a warm shower. My room was mostly empty except for the little corner I used as a bed. I kept blankets organized on the corner of the floor where I slept, stacking them on one another, and pulling them out when it came time to sleep. I grabbed three and sat them on a small coffee table we found abandoned in an alley (not a bad find, really). Turning back to the tiny closet that stored my few possessions, I grabbed the almost empty gauze roll.

I threw my hoodie on the ground and began to unwrap the previous layer of bandage. It was soaked in liquid puss from the exploding blisters, but they seemed to have scabbed over for the moment.

For a brief second, I caught my reflection in the mirror; my skin clung to the layers of ribs just below my bra, cheeks hollow, and lips chapped. My brown hair was a ratted mess and so greasy it might've been black, and the blue highlights had faded tremendously, but I didn't care. My eyes were stuck on the stuff underneath all the blisters, the white scars from Rosemonde's rage. The knives that caused them were hopefully far gone by now; the whole house was probably sold or demolished, and Rosemonde? She would never be found.

I quickly tore my gaze from the mirror and wrapped my blisters in more gauze. Grateful for something to cover me. I snatched a beige cardigan from my closet and paired it with a black tank before tiptoeing down the stairs with the blankets.

Jay was still out like a baby, yet snoring like a pig. I gently shifted him from the couch to the floor and slid one of the blankets under his head and a second over him. Aska got the third; I placed it over him as carefully as possible. I didn't like it; things were too quiet. The past few months had been nothing but calm, but now that they were back, I didn't know how to think. It seemed to me like we were in the eye of the hurricane, and things were still ready to get worse. I started fidgeting violently; pain exploded in my elbow as I knocked my funny bone on the table behind me. Walking to the kitchen, I began to pace. I was drained yet restless. It seemed like there were too many things to do, but I couldn't decide which to do first, so I was stuck.

Breathe, just breathe. OK, OK, first we need water. We had used what was left in the cabinet to clean Aska's wound. I also desperately needed a shower and food. Water, shower, food. My backpack was still on the kitchen floor. I emptied the food onto the counter and counted the money stolen from the register. Only about $500, typically what store owners kept for change. He must've thought he would have customers; too bad, really, his poor daughter and wife. Those thoughts had to leave my mind; I couldn't save him anymore; $500 was enough for now.

I ran upstairs to grab my shampoo, conditioner and some old body wash before jotting down a note for Jay and leaving it on the table.

***

The pool was empty. It was maybe 10°C and freezing outside; a perfect day to be inconspicuous. Living in a house without heating gave me some perks, such as adjusting better to the cold than others. The pool was free, and the on-duty lifeguards were nowhere to be seen, so I just slipped into the locker rooms and selected the largest shower.

All of this before realizing I was a moron.

I had just applied new bandages less than an hour ago, and now they were wasted. Tossing the still spotless cloth into the trash was mentally wounding, but the warm heat of the shower took it all away. My wounds burned with the contact, but I honestly couldn't give a damn.

At least thirty minutes were wasted in the shower before I finally had the will to leave. Oh, how I wish I could've lived there, but nonetheless, there was more work to do. While drying off, I made a mental checklist of what we needed.

Somehow, I ended up spending over $100 on groceries alone, something that I didn't usually succumb to. It was easy to say we would be set for a while on sugary cereals and blueberry pop tarts, you know, the essentials (and also peanut butter, bread, and granola; seriously, I'm not that irresponsible). The sun was setting again, and my hair was almost completely dried. For once, I felt at peace, normal even, just walking home from the pool and store. It was. . . enjoyable, laughable even, and not the sarcastic laugh I usually bore. I wasn't sure I had ever experienced a real earnest laugh. That was the thought that haunted my mind the rest of the walk home and was still lingering as I opened the front door. I looked inside. Two packages of bottled water fell to the floor with a bang, along with some of the cereal that couldn't fit in the backpack.

"Aska?"

Jay was kneeling next to him, but Aska was bolt upright. As I shuffled closer, I noticed odd things about his composure. His eyes were wide open, and the more I looked, the more I saw how dilated they were, with less than a millimeter of iris.

"Aska?" He didn't acknowledge me or even flinch, so I went to the next source of information.

"Jay? What happened?"

"Not a clue; poor boy was like this when I woke up. Can't get him to move, or anything really, but I did manage to give him some food. Did you get some water?" Jay's tone was casual but his shoulders bore a certain stiffness that alarmed me.

I nodded toward the two packs behind me and knelt next to Aska as he retrieved the bags.

"My Captain Crunch!" Jay muttered behind me excitedly. "WHAT THE HELL!"

"What?" I half turned toward him, surprised by his sudden exclamation.

"Why'd you get *All Berries*?! The squares are the best part!" He put a hand on his hips and pouted like a four-year-old.

I slowly blinked my eyes. "Is that really a priority right now?"

"I have low blood sugar!" He held the cereal boxes in his hand and threateningly waved one toward me.

"You're seventeen! Not fifty! If you don't like the cereal, choose another. There's like four billion different kinds."

"What about fruity pebbles?" I rubbed my temples, all the energy that I had gained from my shower washing away from me.

"I don't understand how someone can be simultaneously five and fifty."

"It's a true gift." I rolled my eyes and he shrugged, seemingly pleased with the fact he had made me smile.

"Hurry up with the water."

"Already done." He appeared next to my side with five bottles.

After he had managed a few sips of water, I pushed Aska back down to the couch to prevent tension in the wound.

There was no visible response to me waving my hand in his face, snapping, or anything else I tried. There was no soul behind those eyes, not even a glimmer. Snatching one of the bottles from the table behind me, I felt its ice-cold condensation leak onto my palm. Removing the lid I remember thinking, *one last hope,* before pouring it down his back.

His shrieks were probably heard throughout the entire neighborhood.

Jay bounced backward and stumbled over something behind him, falling to his backside as I clamped my hand down over Aska's mouth. His body spasmed back and forth to the point that I couldn't control him.

"JAY! Hold him down!" With one hand over his still screaming mouth and the other placed over his chest to help Jay avoid too much of a thrashing, I turned my head toward Jay and gave him a piercing glare.

Jay ran to him and threw himself onto the spasming body. "Aska! Stop! NOW!" Shit. This wasn't good; I should've let the wound heal a bit more before trying to wake him. At this rate, he could split it open even more. Jay was practically lying on his body, using all his strength just to keep it as still as possible.

"Gently!" I yelled, afraid of him snapping one of Aska's boney limbs.

"You're kinda contradicting yourself there!" He shouted back at me. I couldn't feel the vibrations of his screams anymore; this was my opportunity. I bolted up the stairs.

"Where are you going!!" Jay yelled at me. At the end of the hallway was the tiny, singular bathroom in the house. Of course, nothing in it worked due to the lack of electricity or running water, but it was where we kept our wide variety of drugs. Mostly weak ones from convenience stores, but some others from purses or other personal belongings. Those were typically stronger prescribed painkillers of all types and varieties. Aska needed one that would work fast, or else there was no point. It took me maybe thirty seconds to find it in the medicine cabinet: Oxycodone, a precious gem I had stumbled upon about a year ago.

Sprinting down the stairs, I no longer cared about the noise it might make. Aska's thrashing looked like it had subsided at least a bit, but from his expression, it wasn't because the pain was gone. His energy had dipped, but his hands were clinging to the bandages, scraping them even more.

"Stop!" I pried his hands off of them before they tore. "You'll do more harm than good," I whispered in an attempt to keep my voice sweet. He let out a little whimper of pain as I wrapped his hands around mine and set them gently on his abdomen.

"Jay?" I said in my panicked soft tone. Without taking my eyes off Aska, I handed him the Oxycodone. "Crush one of these up using the bottle, please."

"Ya- ya OK." He grabbed the bottle and spilled all the pills out onto the table.

"Relax. Everything's OK, look at me. Look at me and breathe." I whispered to Aska as I heard the thuds of Jay turning the pills to powder behind me.

Finally, Jay tapped my shoulder. I shifted to grab the note from earlier that was still sitting on the table and brushed a little bit of powder into it. After rolling it up and helping Aska snort the dusk (sending him into a fit of coughing). I sat at his side, holding his hands tight until his grip lessened and his eyes went dull.

Once I was sure the meds had kicked in, I retreated to the grocery sacks still on the floor. Over $100 was spent on cereal and little Debbie cakes (lord, have mercy). I put the cakes in one cabinet, the cereals in another, bread and peanut butter on the counter, and then the water in its typical cabinet. My stomach growled as the door to the final cabinet shut, leaving me staring longingly at the Strawberry Cake Rolls, snatching them in my grasp before heading back to the couch.

"Lil' Debbie? Really?" Jay said with raised eyebrows.

"Coming from the guy who likes Fruity Pebbles." I tossed the box to Jay and unwrapped my own cake.

"Hey! Fruity Pebbles deserve your respect and admiration."

"Whatever." I watched as Jay took one from the box as well and we ate in silence.

"Not as good as pizza, but still, not too bad. Should we try to get him to eat." Jay gestured to Aska but the boy was already sleeping peacefully. There was a dusting of Oxy dust on his nose which made it look like he just ate some powdered donuts. I wiped it away and shook my head at Jay.

"Let's just let him rest for now."

After we consumed almost an entire box of desserts, Jay finally agreed to get some sleep upstairs, leaving me alone. I knew Jay needed his sleep, but a part of me wished he'd stayed; without someone to talk to, my thoughts had no filter. It was rare that I entertained the thought of death. Only seventeen years old, yet for a machigai, my lifespan was already more than halfway over. I stared down at Aska and his already corpse-like features and wondered just how much time he had left; I couldn't imagine it being any longer than two years.

I turned my back to the couch and tried to push the dark thoughts away. Two years might be a stretch at this rate; two days had yet to be confirmed. Not even two hours. I thought of something my uncle told me when I was only a child. *Our worries give us nothing but grief. If you truly care for someone mon chou, use what time you have left with them. Use it wisely.* But what could I do with the time I had now?

"Since you've been gone," I whispered without thinking, talking to him like we were just friends having coffee after a long separation. "I've spent a lot of my time at the library. It's peaceful, quiet, not quite your style, I guess." I shook away the idea and stood. Before I left, I bent down to look at him, bony and frail, but still him, still Aska. I brushed back his untamed hair; the skin beneath was ice cold, and I whispered with tears in my eyes. "You can't die. You know that, right?" My hand shook as it lay on his forehead, his eyes remaining still. With that, I crept up the stairs and into bed.

***

I must've been screaming, not from the monsters for once but from a regular nightmare. He opened the door at night and woke me. I couldn't see well or stop apologizing for being too loud. When he started to leave, it confused me. We had an unspoken agreement we would always be there, but when I asked him to stay, he hesitated. Weird. Aska, how much have they changed you? Eventually, he stayed, but not how he used to; he fell asleep on the other side of the room on the cold, hard floor. Nonetheless, the presence was enough to keep the night peaceful.

When I woke up, it was surprisingly nice. I could hardly feel the welts, and the air had warmed into typical August weather. Downstairs, Jay was talking to a barely conscious Aska. He turned to me and gave me a bright smile as he heard my footsteps reach the ground floor.

"Morning. Sleep well?"

"Better than usual," I took a sip of water from the kitchen. "How bout' you?" He shrugged as I sat down, then pointed at the bandages, now stained pink.

"He bled through during the night."

"Shit." I quickly put down my water.

"What do you want to do?"

"Not much we can do, other than rewrap and hope the oxycodone is still in effect."

"Why not just give him another?"

"That stuff is strong; and I don't know how much could end in an overdose." I tore the blanket off and folded it into a pillow, stuffing it behind Aska's head for support. "Third cabinet from the left is medical supplies." Jay stood and walked to the kitchen, counting the cabinets on his fingers before opening the right one.

"Okay, what do you need?"

"All of it." He obeyed like an obedient little puppy, bringing me back all the supplies I needed. He even filled the bucket with water without me ever asking. Maybe this situation wasn't hopeless after all.

"You might need to hold him still for this." I scooted the table closer to the couch, so the advantage point was better. Hopefully, this could be finished fast and with as minor damage as possible, but that was doubtful.

I could see the panic light up Aska's face as I gingerly touched the edge of the bandages. The concept of adrenaline was a mystery to me; it was unfathomable how the brain could store energy and only tap into that energy when your nervous system sensed danger. Every muscle in his face screwed tighter than a dog wearing a puppy's collar. For a while, he was only flinching when my fingers got a little too close to the wound, but everything went downhill after the first layer was unwrapped. The light flinching turned into sudden jerks of his limbs. Even with Jay holding him down, a stray elbow hit the side of my jaw, the impact making my eyes water, but we did what needed to be done. A few kicks, a couple of punches, and about a dozen scratches later, Aska had brand new bandages and had managed to calm down. The only thing I was grateful for? Since there was no opportunity to activate his curse, the cut contained no black fluid, lowering the chance of infection. It also proved to be more accessible without having to stop every five minutes for him to vomit.

By noon, he was passed out again, breathing heavily. Jay retrieved a bottle of water for me to hold against the growing bruise on my face. We were silent until he finally turned in. Staring at Aska and thinking how much fear there was last night, that he would die and how it was still a possibility, something about my mindset changed. So that night, instead of heading to my room, I peeked inside Jay's.

I sat on the corner of the bed as he finished his daily check-in with Burn. He took a deep breath and leaned against the backboard before saying anything to me.

"Do you need something?"

"A favor," I said. He said a quick goodbye into the phone and walked to me as I started spelling out my vision for him to understand. He agreed with me after a moment, and we plotted. Plotted my escape.

Chapter 9: The Machigai

The bliss of August was fading by the time we could put the plan in motion. For once, I was yearning for Aska to leave. I did everything I could to improve his stature, and after a few more days, he was aware of his surroundings again. After two weeks, he was sneaking around, trying to strengthen himself behind my back. It was around that time Jay left. The plan was that once he saw Aska return to wherever they went, he would return for me. I had spent so long in one place that the idea of leaving was almost absurd, but we both understood there was no use in bringing Aska back to heal when they would only jump into gunfire again the second he left. At least if I was there, he had nowhere left to run. No more lies left to tell.

Jay told me to pack as much as possible since we probably wouldn't return. For once, I was compelled to go shopping. No matter how much Jay wanted me there, I had no confirmation the others did; first impressions were everything when you knew nothing. There was no money for fancy stores, but I found that the thrift shops and Goodwill had more than people gave them credit for. My budget ended at $50; we couldn't afford anymore, especially because Aska was still at the house. Keep it simple: a few pairs of jeans, leggings, and maybe some nice shirts. Sadly, the options were limited since I wasn't comfortable with exposing enough skin to reveal my scars; forcing me to stay within long sleeves for now. Sacrificing an extra $20 on a purple and black suitcase at Target, I began to pray that Aska would be asleep by the time I got back. Just in case, I snuck through the back door, searching for the sound of his obnoxious snoring. When none was to be heard, I stuffed the bags behind an old wooden shelf in the old laundry room before emerging into the open.

There was no evidence he could hear me, so I quietly snuck up the stairs, wincing in fear at every creak. I returned a few hours later to make it seem inconspicuous that it was afternoon and I hadn't woken yet.

"Must've overslept. What time do you think it is?" I faked a yawn in the kitchen. When he didn't answer, I risked a glance over the couch. Gone. The whole act had been pointless, but that also meant that packing was tremendously important now because I was leaving tonight.

It was shocking how many of my possessions fit in the suitcase, so many that I even threw in a container of Aska's hair bleach and dye. Then, I had hours to burn.

***

My eyelids had become lead by the time I heard a small bluebird chirp outside my window. Sliding it open, the bird stumbled, collapsing on the floor in a fit of feathers and coughing as it transformed into a fully grown boy. I rushed to his side as he spat a wad of blue on the hardwood floors.

"Sorry," he gasped.

"It's fine. Do you need a minute?" He sat up and propped himself against the wall. As he panted in and out, he shook his head.

"I'll be fine. Do you have your stuff ready?" I clutched the handle of the suitcase and nodded. "Good. Are we leaving through the door or window?"

"Back door. Are you sure you'll be okay?"

"I'll be fine," he repeated and stumbled towards the door. After almost falling down the stairs, Jay finally agreed to sit and drink some water while I peeled an orange and shoved it in a Ziplock for later.

He guided me through the back alleys, skirting around the good part of the city, the sun peeking over the horizon once we finally approached a tall golden hotel. I had never stepped foot in this part of town; there was too much security for my liking, but it was beautiful. Every building stretched taller than any I had ever seen. When I was young, adults would rant about the beauty of the city, and after ten years of living inside, I could finally see the image they were trying to find the words to. Jay took my hand and guided me around the back of the most spectacular hotel, where we entered through a small worker door into a cramped hallway and down three flights of stairs until we reached an area closed off with construction tape and marked- "Working on Renovations. No entry." I hesitated momentarily but Jay slid right through the tape into the darkened area before I finally began trailing after him. We walked silently in the dark for a few minutes before I heard Jay halt in front of me, following the click of a key in a locked door. As Jay shoved me through the doors, I was forced to squint while waiting for my eyes to adjust. He shut it quietly behind us as I took in the scene.

Tables scattered themselves across the maroon and dark oak colored room, three of the walls were covered in stunning old-fashioned paintings that hung on the walls equal distance from one another, every one perfectly angled. A long counter with tall stools sat on the side of the room where we emerged from, the fourth wall behind it covered with shelves that held a wide variety of glasses and alcohol bottles. The room, obviously designed to be a bar, was vacant for the time being.

"What now?" I asked as Jay locked the doors.

"Take a seat and wait for the others. Then we will see if this was a mistake or not."

"Don't back out at the last second." I warned, taking a seat at the bar and staring at the wall of different liquors.

"I'm not." He walked around to the back of the bar and began mixing himself a drink. "I'm just saying, the next few hours will be. . . interesting." He poured a light pink fluid into a margarita glass and tapped a lemon slice off the edge.

"What's that?"

"Cosmopolitan, my personal favorite. Wanna try?" He poured what was left in the shaker into a tiny plastic shot glass and pushed it in my direction. The tinted fluid held a sweet fragrance, like cranberries combined with the tartness of lemons. As I took a small sip, the taste hit me like a brick; heavy hints of all different kinds of bitter fruits tickled my tongue as the orange flavor took center stage—the perfect balance of bitter and beautiful.

I was contemplating the cons of asking Jay to make me one of my own when the door on the opposite side of where we entered opened, and two people emerged deep in conversation. A tall male with dirty blond hair so tainted with flecks of brown it looked like he had been rolling around in the sand for hours, the boy sported a black t-shirt, ripped denim, and elbow-high leather gloves. He paced in behind a relatively young girl with meadow blond hair and a flowy blue shirt that kept catching on an oddly placed stick at her side. The boy's eyes landed on Jay in the bar and then trailed to me.

"Jay? What did you do?" he asked, raising an accusing eyebrow in Jay's direction.

"Exactly what you've been asking me to." He hurdled himself over the bar, landing surprisingly gracefully. "Burn, Lina, I would like to formally introduce you to Onyx." The sheer speed at which the boy in front of me changed everything about himself was surprising. One second, he looked like a brooding teenager, blink once, and suddenly, you were standing before a diplomat. He stood straight and made direct eye contact with a smile that seemed out of place and somewhat unnerving. Slowly, he made his way across the room, towing the young girl behind him as she stumbled in our direction. He held his hand out to me and shook it softly. Charming as he was, my eyes were focused on the girl whom Burn introduced as his 'baby sister.' Her eyes were an unnatural and unfocused shade of gray behind a thin frame of glasses, and now that I was closer, I could see that the stick at her side was a white cane.

The boy flooded me with questions about my past, Aska, Jay, healing, and how I survived. As nice as he seemed, I kept my walls up, only giving him the vaguest of answers for each question. I couldn't give away too much about Aska or my past; each piece of information was a weapon that could be used against us. Soon, more people poured into the bar; some kept their distance, some were curious, and some were children. A woman, maybe forty, trailed a girl with stunning olive skin and shoulder-length black hair wearing a white apron. The girl smiled at me as she shooed Burn aside.

"It's good to finally meet you, Onyx! I'm Lily; this is my mother, Vivianne." She offered me breakfast and told me stories about Aska and Jay. They were all lovely, but their openness to new people felt off-putting. Lily, in particular, was unnerving. Her smile seemed to lighten everyone else up, but then the door opened for a final time, and everyone went quiet.

A ringing voice erupted into the bar. "Everyone! Hallway! NOW!!"

Everyone, even Burn, followed the booming orders out into the hallway, everyone except Jay and I.

"Ask-" Jay pleaded.

"I'll deal with you later." He glared; his jaw set in a hard line.

"Deal with me now. I did this, not her." Jay took a step towards Aska, who looked like he might swing if prodded any more.

"I'll deal with you later," he repeated more sternly, through gritted teeth, glaring Jay down until he finally conceded and joined the others in the hallway. I refused his gaze for a moment, even though he was studying me up and down.

"Go home, Onyx," he said at last, crossing his arms. For six months, he had never stood straight up, always slouching or leaning on someone. I had forgotten how tall he could be, but sitting on the barstool, my eyes were just above his chest. He stood so close it was a strain to stare up, but I sat with crossed legs and a grin spread from ear to ear.

"No." I said blankly. He snapped back at my forever smart-ass demeanor.

"I'm not asking! You have no choice! This isn't a debate! You leave, or I force you to!" I rarely ever saw Aska filled with rage. This was not the wounded boy who slept on my couch and covered me with blankets when I was an ill child.

"Then force me! Cause I'm not leaving on my own free will." I leaned back in my seat to stare him down; this was a favorite game of ours when we were young. It all came down to willpower, and neither was budging. The fire behind his eyes was growing; a part of me liked it. In our few interactions over the last eight months, he rarely had the energy to speak, much less fight with this much rage. It was good to see him alive, but he had no argument to back up his sheer power.

"You can't stay," his voice softened only slightly, but his eyes were still tearing into my soul.

"Why?" Pushing harder, I felt every unspoken word between us; not all were kind. I pressed on, sliding my knees underneath my torso on the stool to reach him in height. "Why can't I stay? Do you think that when I'm not present, the whispers of you jumping into gunfire don't make it to me?" My voice quivered softly, rising by the moment, fueling myself with the anger I had been suppressing so heavily the last half a year. "You're confusing bravery and stupidity, and it will kill you. Don't have any doubt about that." My ears burned with rage as I leaned closer, his anger fueling my own. "Who will you help when you're dead, Aska?! Who?"

Chapter 10: Toyls Academy

Without a breath between seconds, I was on the floor, feeling a new bruise form on the side of my face. Aska stood towering before me, the anger dwindling from his eyes. A million things rushed through my mind in the moment that passed: confusion, anger, shock, more anger than anything else. We stayed still for a second, only a second, our heavy breathing the only sound to fill the room. Finally breaking our mutual gaze, he glanced down at his hand, making the connection as to what he just did and stumbling backward.

"Lun-" My body acted before my brain, jumping up and brushing myself off the floor before pushing past Aska toward the exit. Looking back, it was not the most mature thing to do in this situation. I burst through the doors angrily and stomped through the crowd with their ears pressed against it.

"Onyx!" Jay grabbed my arm. "Where are you going?" There was no response; there wasn't anywhere to go, just away. I shook my head as he held my shoulders firmly.

"Then calm down and come with me." Jay shoved me down the hallway to a room labeled -2.

"Negative?"

"Ya, this whole floor was meant to be a club and rooms for important guests, but no one wanted to pay extra to stay underground. So, it was closed off and used for storage. Mrs. Madalini was nice enough to let the machigai use the few rooms down here; that leaves us with three bedrooms and two rooms Lily uses for the infirmary." He opened the door to show a decently sized hotel room crammed full with two sets of bunk beds and four broken-down dressers.

"Not exactly paradise." A voice announced from inside the room, making me jump backward into Jay.

"Relax, it's just Blake." Jay shooed me into the room, closing the door behind him. On the bottom bunk of the bed on the left sat a young man with short, greasy, dark brown hair with a white cast up to his left thigh.

"Onyx meet Radio, also known as Blake." Jay pointed towards the boy absently.

"Lovely to meet you, Onyx," Blake said as he shifted around in bed to shake my hand.

"For the time being, you will stay here; you'll bunk with Blake, Lily when she's working in the infirmary, and me. Blaise, Alina, Tresa, and Aska stay in room negative one, and the younger kids stay in room negative three."

"Younger kids?" I took a seat on the lower bunk across from Blake; the only bunk in the room that appeared abandoned.

"There's just a few; the youngest is five, the oldest is ten, plus two seven-year-olds." Children? They were doing all of these illegal activities while living with children? How long did these kids have left to live? They were already written off as dead to the rest of the world. The reality set in: none of the people here would live another 20 years. None would grow old. Most wouldn't even make it another year.

"Who's the oldest overall?" I asked, leaning my hands back on the bed.

"You mean of the machigai? Blaise is 20."

"Aska turned 21 in June." I said quietly, as Jay sat down beside me as a soft knock caused me to jerk away.

"Someone's jumpy today," Jay giggled before his eyes fell to my shaking arms. "Everything okay?" I gave him a sturdy nod as Burn entered with my bags.

"You left these. After you're settled in, come and see me. There are some things I would like to discuss." I nodded, and he left.

"This will be your dresser" Jay stood, gesturing towards the small table with drawers closest to the bunks on the right. He slid the bottom drawer open, revealing its empty interior and tossing me one of my bags that Burn had left. I glanced around the room once more, taking in it's contents further.

"How did you guys come to have access to this place?" I asked, as Jay resumed his position sitting on my bottom bunk, allowing me to begin unpacking my belongings messily into the drawers.

"The hotel? It was all Lily really." He shrugged. "Her mother and father own the hotel. See here?" He traced the edges of the bed frame, revealing a symbol of a letter M found within a circle engraved in every wooden corner of the frame. "The Madalini logo, they own hotels all over the continent, this was the first. Her father built it as a marriage proposal to her mother after they first met."

"That still doesn't explain how *you* ended up here." I asked pointedly, flicking Jay in his forehead.

"Ouch. Sheesh. Okay, I was getting there." He sighed and leaned back into my pillow. "I suppose it began when Lily found Tresa on the street, however many thousands of years ago. Took pity on her and begged her mother to let her stay in the penthouse with them. Her mother conceded eventually and the little street-rat moved in. Next thing Mrs. Madalini knew the two of them brought home yours-truly." He gestured to himself with a goofy smile.

"That's the real street-rat" Blake muttered from his bunk.

"Hush, you weren't there. I was positively delightful." I could almost feel Blake's eyeroll from across the room. "Anyways, after that came Burn and Lina and with the penthouse so crowded, Mrs. Madalini encourged—"

"Demanded" Blake corrected.

"Politely encouraged us to move into the basement. After that, it was Burn who turned his attentions towards helping save others. Fighting for all machigai, instead of just ourselves. He created this whole thing. We had become quite the force, before the incident a few months ago…" The room fell silent as I tried hard to prevent my gaze from traveling astray to Blake's leg. Words evaded me, as I struggled desperately to fill the silence. Unsuccessful in my endeavors, I finished unpacking my things without a sound from anyone in the room.

***

Burn was walking around the empty infirmary dramatically. After standing and waiting for him to notice me, I awkwardly cleared my throat, snapping his attention my way.

"You wanted to talk to me?" He gave an uncertain nod. "About what?" I egged on.

"Where we can place you in order for Aska not to rip all of our heads off?"

"I assume you had something in mind?" I leaned back against one of the creaky beds.

"Um, ya. . . Jay's already explained the recent. . . tragedy?" Nodding was the only way to respond; Burn was obviously on edge about something, but he took a deep breath and continued.

"We had already planned the next move before that, but it was thrown off by the. . . losses."

"What was the next move?"

"Infiltrate and rescue. You're familiar with Toyls Academy?" Again, I could only nod. "Our plan was—well, I suppose that doesn't matter now. Anyway, we need someone around your age."

"Why do you need to infiltrate the academy?"

"That's a simple question. Toyls Academy released last year that they had added a Machigai Studies class into their second semester's schedule. Enforcement squads have been less keen on killing us on the spot-"

"So, you think they are studying live machigai?"

"That's the jist of it, ya. There's been a few reports claiming such a thing, but for the most part they've been dismissed by the general public." He nervously itched around the edges of his gloves. "You don't have to. If you want to fight on the front lines, I understand that too, and there's always a possibility that you won't even make it past qualifications. If that happens, we'll try something else; brute force has worked for us so far."

"No, it hasn't." A voice behind me interrupted, I stared at the ground and desperately tried to remain composed. "Onyx is right about one thing. Running head-first into gunfire doesn't work, believe me. We need to play practical, not dangerous."

"Nice of you to finally join us, Aska. I trust you've calmed yourself?" Burn said.

Aska gave a sturdy nod without acknowledging me.

"Good." Burn looked between the two of us. "Well, I'll let you two. . . discuss." He walked out of the room and then, it was just me and Aska. I slid back on the bed as he hung his head quietly.

Silence. Fidgeting. No eye-contact.

"I'm sorry," he said at last. "About everything. Your life isn't mine to control." Did he mean it? Probably not. Who was this boy? What reason did I have to trust him?

"Look, I'm not just apologizing, so you'll go home, but please at least consider it. You have no idea what you're getting yourself into." He held out his hand toward me.

I slid back off the bed, rolled my eyes, and headed for the door. This wasn't gonna turn into a mature discussion; that much was already clear. He stood in front of the door to block my path.

"Move." My voice was hard as a stone, but he didn't budge.

"Please, if you refuse to believe me, come see for yourself. Please," he said, taking my hand and dragging me down the halls, through the bar, and into a single door. I struggled against him for a while before curiosity and defeat got the better of me.

The bright August sun burned my retinas to a crisp. I hadn't realized just how dark the machigai's headquarters were kept. There was a large path of stone stairs leading up and out of our little den. Aska guided me gently into a large fenced-off area with beautiful trees taller than our house downtown and more vibrant flowers than I could name. A secret garden of sorts, maybe that was the purpose, but Aska continued to guide me down the stone pathway deeper into the garden. We turned a sharp corner, and my eyes tried to make sense of what they were seeing. The garden opened into a square grass area with small stones set in neat rows. A Japanese stone garden? Why would Aska want to show me this?

I knelt in front of the closest stone.

Engraved onto its surface were the words - *Kristiana "Petra" Wade.*

Chapter 11: Garden of Graves

My whole world seemed to fade out as the truth of the garden sunk in. Stumbling backward on the ground like a scared crab, I turned to the next stone. *Dieuwier "Dew Drop" Banks.* Next one. *Alexis "Trick-Shot" Sashi-Frie.* Next one. *Jae "Rubberman" Donne.* Name after name, I counted maybe ten memorials. I recognized the alias of some, like Trick-Shot. Her posters used to hang up on every street in town. Rumor said her gun was alive. It never missed. It knew your name, what you'd done, and how afraid you were to die. A legend, now dead and buried among her comrades.

"Some were before my time, but most . . ." Aska muttered quietly. I had forgotten he was there. "Please tell me you understand now. I won't bury you next. I can't."

"You won't have to. Neither of us is gonna die, not yet. I promise." I glanced back at him over my shoulder, still not willing to provide any comfort past that one statement I had held onto for all this time.

"Then at least consider what Burn told you about Toyls. Please."

"Considered it pondered." I turned and walked out of the garden of graves, not wanting to spend a second more thinking about how we were all going to end up there, even if we didn't fight. We walked back in dead silence.

That night was the first; Lily made us poutine for lunch, and more of their ranks began introducing themselves after she excused herself to deliver Blake his food. One of those whom I didn't meet earlier was Tresa, apparently the second eldest among them. She stood taller than me, with what appeared to be unevenly chopped black hair wrapped up in a plastic shower cap, the aura she let off was intense, as if she had already been thoroughly pissed off for the day, but she didn't act hostile towards me at all. In fact, she never said much at all to me, or really anyone but Lily, throughout the night, but the others seemed to look up to her plenty. A leader just like Burn, I suspected, but less diplomatic.

Aska continued to sulk in the corner with Jay and Burn as Lily entered with a train of children in hand. After dishing each child's plate full of delicious fries and cheese, she took my hand and dragged me to one of the round tables to sit with them while they ate. Four children, three girls and one boy. As Lily introduced them, all four remained quiet. Clark was the youngest and sole boy, energetic and just as happy as a five-year-old should be. Jamie, the eldest, was quieter, never leaving her younger sister Ilse's side for the whole meal. Among them, Lulu stood out as the liveliest— a petite Filipino girl who shared Ilse's age and smile.

The boys joined us after a bit; forcing Burn and Aska to push another table together to join ours while Jay entertained the children.

"You could help, you know?" Aska griped through gritted teeth, pressing against the table. Jay swooped Lulu up in his arms as Ilse giggled on top of his shoulders.

"I am helping," he laughed, picking up Clark by his underarms and swinging him around as Lulu played bongos on his head, still giggling like crazy. Aska rolled his eyes as Tresa joined to aid the table struggle.

It was a strange sensation. Thinking back, I couldn't remember ever actually eating in a group, even if not all of us were eating. Sitting around a table with a proper meal was a luxury that I had never experienced. Jay played with the kids, who seemed to brighten up in the presence of his terrible uncle jokes. Burn clung to Alina, who, despite her gentle smile, was obviously weary of her brother. Lily choked on her food from laughter a few times while conversing deeply with Tresa.

"Why would you want to hide this from me?" I whispered to Aska next to me with a grin.

"It's not all sunshine and rainbows." He poked at his still-full bowl of poutine with a tiny smile. "But I suppose it can be pretty nice."

***

I sat on the bunk below Jay, listening to him and Blake snore louder than pigs at slaughter. Lily had stayed up in the penthouse with her mother for the night; the back of my mind wished she was here; something about her put my racing thoughts at ease. Everyone here had a strange way of making me feel safe without ever having to say anything directly to me, but they were all asleep, and it was painfully dark in the room. Nightmares flooded behind my eyes, mocking me for when I gave in and went to sleep. Even if these people seemed nice now, weakness or trust was never an option, and I wasn't quite ready to reveal that part of myself to them, not yet.

The urge to sleep was strong, leaving me no choice but to stand to stay awake. The door creaked shut behind me, and I stumbled down the hallway back into the dining area. Behind the bar sat an alluring coffee pot, still half full and waiting for me. Stealing a glass from above, I poured myself some and took a sip. My lips puckered at the taste, bitter and strong. Coffee wasn't one of my favorite things in the world, but if it could keep me from going to sleep, then it could be my vice for the night.

I trembled as an icy breeze bit my shoulder; someone had left the door to the garden wide open. Wrapping my jacket tight around me, I shuffled to the door with my coffee in hand. The garden was lit with small lanterns, dotting the black sky with tiny rays of light. The birds and bugs sat silent and still; even the wind refused to whisper. I took a step forward and began to follow the path Aska had led me down earlier. As the memorials came on site, so did a figure on the bench.

"Mind if I sit?" I asked.

Burn gestured to the open space freely. "Couldn't sleep?" I continued. His eyes were locked softly on the stones in front of us.

"Something like that." He shrugged and broke his gaze towards me with that overly political smile people wore when they were trying to win you over. My shifted away from his face, and I found myself glancing down at his hands. They were bare for the first time since we'd met; he had ditched the elbow-high leather gloves and exposed himself to the icy cold of Quebec nights. His skin was crinkled and red, at least of the small portions that remained; most of Burn's forearm was missing at least three layers of skin and tissue, leaving the flesh underneath without any raw and exposed.

"Are you-?" I began, but he just waved a hand to silence me. I hated how quickly I obeyed his commands.

"I'm fine. They've been like that for years." He shifted away from the graves and connected his eyes with mine. In the lantern light, he almost looked like a ghost; pale and ethereal, the moonlight reflecting through the lighter parts of his hair. "Have you put any thought towards my offer?"

"A little." His gaze was so expecting and pleading. I felt sorry for him. I pulled a leg up in front of me on the bench to rest my head on. "Aska seems to be hesitant."

"Well, his choice isn't the one I'm looking for." He leaned backward, and for a moment, I saw his hands almost make contact with the stone, but he caught himself and pulled away.

"How often do you come back here?"

"Every night. I think it's important to honor those who died for the cause. Most don't have anyone else to mourn them."

"How many did you know?" I asked. His eyes had found their way back to watching the graves in front of us, but mine rested on his features, trying to analyze the sincerity of his words.

"All of them. The graveyard was Alina's idea. We've been lucky, but others haven't." He closed his eyes, almost as if in a trance, and took one deep breath.

"Tomorrow, Jay's scouting; I've asked him to take you along."

"Scouting?" I asked.

"Observing the area, maybe stealing some cash. Nothing too serious." The thought of Jay jumping from building to building with binoculars was oddly amusing. The idea of a tiny bluebird wearing tiny binoculars was even more so. I wondered if Bluejay had his own walky-talky.

"Scouting. Sounds like fun." I nodded in agreement.

Burn gave me a gentle smile.

"I wouldn't go that far, but it might at least help you decide. Scouting and the occasional raid are pretty much all we do here. It doesn't get us far, but a spy most certainly would." He raised his eyebrows at me, nonchalantly trying to nudge my decision in the way that favored him.

"Ah, and I suppose raiding and scouting are both deadly boring?" I hung my head back and glanced over.

"Not particularly boring, but most definitely deadly." He stood and brushed off his pants, carefully slipping his gloves back on. "He leaves at five tomorrow, so you should get some sleep."

"I should be fine." I grabbed my cup of coffee and stood. "I'm caffeinated."

"Speaking of. Why do you have coffee in a wine glass?" My face heated as he let out a small chuckle. I followed him back through the garden, occasionally chatting about something or cracking deadpan jokes, but everything seemed forced. Faked. A true leader indeed.

"Good night, Onyx." He said as he quietly opened the door to my room for me.

"Night Burn."

With that, he gave a weak smile and closed the door.

Jay's snoring had somehow gotten louder since I had left, but I sat down on my bunk and stared at the ceiling as my eyelids drooped shut. It couldn't be any later than two, but I also hadn't slept for over twenty-four hours, and my body was shot. Today, tomorrow, or soon, things might finally start to improve.

Chapter 12: Scouting

"Rise and shine, sunshine," Jay poked at me from the side of my bed. "Come on. If you're gonna go scouting, you have to be alert. Get out of bed."

"What time is it?" I muttered into the comfortable pillow.

"4:30 in the morning." He responded, shaking me some more.

"Are you insane?" I groaned and rolled over, turning my back to him and curling myself into a safe and cozy ball.

"That's what people keep telling me." Jay grabbed my shoulder and rolled me back towards him, shaking off the warmth of the comforter in the process. "Oh good, you're still dressed from yesterday."

My eyes crinkled open slowly; the lights burned my retina and forced my eyes to adjust. Blake was still fast asleep in his bunk, lucky bastard. Jay sat down at my feet to tie the laces on his black sneakers. His long-sleeved black T-shirt clung to his broad, bony figure underneath a leather jacket. He wore a black beanie that covered his short hair; the style looked strange on his hunger-panged figure. He practically dragged me out the door into the club. Everything sat still as he poured two to-go cups full of coffee and warmed them in the microwave.

"Sugar or cream?" He dropped two sugars into his and looked back at me for an answer, but my eyelids were heavy, and my mind was slow. "Sugar it is," there was a gentle plonk as he dropped more sugar.

Mmmm, sleep. Heavy eyelids weighed down my mind as I drifted off while still sitting upright.

"Ghaa." A freezing shock shot into my spine as two ice cubes fell out of my shirt when I jumped up. "I'm awake, goddammit!"

"Good. Next time, I'll pour the coffee down your back. Let's go." Instead of exiting through the hallway we entered through, he turned to the garden. A ladder I hadn't noticed the day before trailed up the back of the building all the way up to the roof. For a 13-story building, that was a long climb.

"See you at the top." The next moment I looked back, the boy was gone and a tiny bluejay was flying directly up in the sky with both of our coffees in his claws. I took one look at the ginormous ladder and let out some words that would've driven my mother straight to crazy town, before starting the ascent.

By the time I reached the top, my limbs were shivering. The bitter cold had frozen the metal ladder to the point that I stopped to pull my sleeves down over my hands, only a few rings up. Once the top of the roof was within my reach, Jay peaked his head over the edge and hauled me up the rest of the way. The cold floor touched my cheek in an instant as my forearms and calves strained to return to their normal alignment.

"Tresa reacted the same her first time. It gets easier." He handed me my now cold coffee, helping me prop myself up against the tiny ledge.

A small sip of coffee soothed my dry throat; the sugar had made it at least somewhat more pleasant. There was a large bell on the roof that I hadn't noticed before, possibly because it was dark out every time I looked up. The bell was similar to that of a church but slightly smaller; not for the first time, I questioned what exactly this hotel was. Four angelic white arches branched from each corner of the rooftop, forming together to host the bronze bell.

"So . . . now that we're up here. What's the plan?" Jay unzipped a bag he most certainly did not have on him earlier and drug out a folded sheet of paper.

"From here, it's simple." He leaned forward to show me the paper; it was a tourist map of the city, one that you could find on almost every block downtown. "We travel by the rooftops; every time we see an MES officer or police officer patrolling, we mark down their path and the time on the chart. This way, when Aska or Blaise go to. . . work, we know where the law enforcement will be and how long it will take for them to get there.

"What if they change from day to day?"

"We keep hold of all the maps from previous weeks or even months; we know their schedule pretty well by now; this is really only precautionary."

"How come if you're this prepared, people keep getting hurt?"

"By *people*, you mean idiots, and by idiots you mean Aska." He rolled his eyes with a sarcastic grin. "The first two times were raiding MES buildings for prisoners. We can prepare for those, but there's very little chance they will go as planned. As for the third time, we're not quite sure what happened. . . the most supported theory is that the MES planted explosives in all of our typical . . . workplaces. All the employees had to do was hit a button when they saw him walk in and take shelter. It was sickening; they killed several of their employees, not to mention a dozen more innocent Quebecois people in the blast. They blamed the whole ordeal on us." The tones of bitterness and hatred in his voice were so potent it sent a chill down my spine, reminding me of our first encounter. Jay's usual demeanor was his humorous, slightly childish self, but he could become frightening very quickly when it came to the machigai vs the rest of the world.

A plane screeched overhead, and we could finally see the sun peaking out over the horizon.

"We better get going." Jay slung the bag to his side and offered a hand up. The edges of the buildings weren't too far apart, only about 1.5 meters. The one closest to us was about the same distance lower than ours. Jay handed me the bag and took a running leap over the edge, landing with the grace of a dove, his feet planted firmly on the floor of the building. He turned toward me and motioned for me to join him with a slight smile, basking in the glory of me being somewhat impressed by him. Heights had never bothered me, but we were over 36 meters from the ground, and my heart clearly wanted to get as far from this edge as possible. I found my feet edging backwards toward the safety of the middle of the roof.

"Toss the bag!" Jay held his arms. I mustered up my strength and threw the bag as hard as I could, watching it fly towards him. He grabbed it by the strap and slung it back over his shoulder. "Good! Now you!" My eyes looked down at the drop, and I wanted to scream and cry, but there was no way I was going to let him upstage me. I took a long, deep breath and attempted to clear my mind. Slowly, I took a step back, then another. I hesitated.

The drop would be long and hard. I would have no hope of surviving if I did not make it.

I ran.

At the last moment, just before I jumped, my eyes looked down, air caught in my chest, and in a second, there was nothing below me. I moved upward and forward and then downward. My heart seemed as if it would explode.

Thump!

My feet made contact first, then my knees, with a sickening crack. Pain rattled through my lower body, following the impact of the ground.

Jay caught my arms just before my head hit the cement roofing.

"That was good; try to stay on your feet next time. Are you okay?" I nodded, and he let go of me. I put up my hands just in time to protect my face from slamming into the floor.

"Hey!" I yelled, glaring at Jay as he chuckled.

Brushing the dirt off my leggings, I shook my head as I looked back at the gap I had just cleared. In truth, my knees felt like I had just reflex tested them with a sledgehammer, but we had to keep going.

Jay finally stopped laughing. "Does that mean I have permission to mock you for that god-awful landing?"

"Depends. How sophisticated was the joke?"

He scratched his chin, pretending to be deep in thought. "I haven't had too much time to think it through, though there is a high probability it would entail the statement: 'I've seen cement trucks crash with more style.'"

"As flattering an offer as that is. . . permission fully denied." He gave a light-hearted chuckle before striding over to the edge, peeking over, and then snapping back.

"Two police officers sitting in their car." He jotted something down on the map, then continued.

We jumped from building to building, always looking over the edge afterward. It got easier to do each time that I jumped over the gaps. Most times, there wasn't any law enforcement; occasionally, we'd see some police officers relaxing in their car, feet on the dash with maybe a book or coffee. There were seldom any MES officers, though; I suppose they were too important for simple patrols. Our only issue was whenever we came to a building too far away. Jay would have to transform and fly to the other side so I could throw him the bag, then he would tie a rope to the other building, and I would tie the other side to my waist and drop over to scale the side of the building. It got more manageable for me to climb. In fact, I almost enjoyed it; the rope's end resembled a thicker bungee cord absorbing most of the fall so my spine didn't snap like a twig. The wind was perfect and cool, and the sun was finally high in the sky, but it couldn't have been easy for Jay to transform that much over and over again, even if it was only for a short amount of time. Soon, he was beat. As I climbed up the side of a building, I looked up to see him falter mid-air, watching over me.

"Go to the top and rest; I'll be up in a second!" I shouted up at him. The itsy bird looked down at me and nodded. He made it a few feet up great, but then he started to drift back downward, flapping his wings relentlessly but making it nowhere. Panic surged through my veins as the bluejay flipped onto his back, plummeting to my level. I almost missed the catch as he fell into my palm. Latching onto the rope with one hand and the bluebird in the other, the winds seemed to help me scale the building to prevent us both from falling to our death. At the top, Jay fell from my hands as a bird and collapsed onto all fours as a human being, beginning his sacred ritual of choking on the wad of feathers stuck inside his lungs. I searched the bag for anything that might help and only found a few water bottles and a box of townhouse crackers.

Placing the water bottle next to him, I snuck over to the edge and peered off the side, with no police nor MES in sight. That was good; at least we could rest here for a minute. Jay was still coughing where I left him, his face gradually turning purple. For a moment, it looked as if he would die of suffocation, but then the feathers came out, and oxygen returned to his lungs.

My arms steadied him from behind to prevent him from falling into the disgusting gunk as he weakened. He was shaking, and his chest was rising and falling too fast to be healthy. After he calmed down a bit, I dragged him over to the tiny structure that contained the stairs to go inside the building and propped him up against it. Tears streamed down his cheeks even though his eyes were tightly shut, and he allowed me to help him drink a bit of water.

"What were you thinking?" I sat back on my heels with my knees underneath me.

"What?" He squinted his eyes open at me with a dead rasp to his voice.

"You knew you couldn't keep going but didn't say anything. You can't do that. What if I didn't catch you?"

"Sorry." He looked down at his hands; they almost looked tinted blue in the lighting. "I'll say something next time."

"Good. Now rest; I'll wake you up in ten minutes."

"I'm fine. Just give me a second." He tried sitting, but I pushed him back down gently against the wall.

"No, you're not. Sleep. I promise I'll wake you up." He was already drifting off.

"Ten minutes." He sat his wristwatch in my lap and closed his eyes.

"Ten minutes." I agreed. Once he had drifted off, I moved back over to the bag; our coffee was still on the inside, and I was shocked the lid to the bottles hadn't popped off with how much throwing we'd done. The coffee was cold and, honestly, disgusting. There were still plenty of water bottles and crackers, but I wasn't sure how much Jay would need later. Glancing over the building, I saw that the fear from earlier was still there, but it was overcome by the beauty below. People were hustling through the streets, headed to work or back from their night shifts. It couldn't be any later than 10:30, which meant we had already been at this for over 5 hours. Somehow, I felt more awake than I was earlier; the air had a nice breeze that wasn't too annoying. Honestly, it was enjoyable up here despite how Burn had made it out to be. This was the most exhilarating thing I had done in . . . ever.

A crash from behind me almost made me lose my footing over the edge of the building. Jay was already up and causing a ruckus.

"I told you to wake me up!" He glared accusingly.

"You said after 10 minutes. It's only been five." I kneeled down and showed him the watch. "Plus, we can't leave until you're rested enough to fly. We're stuck here unless you sleep."

"I've rested enough." He was still weak; I could see it behind his eyes. Maybe his curse wasn't as prominent or powerful as Aska's, but it was definitely taking its toll on his body.

"You promised you'd speak up when you need rest." With a flick of my hand, the shadow from the wall latched onto him, forcing him to stay put as he strained to return to work.

"If you won't sleep, then eat." I pulled out a pack of Nutri Grain Protein bars and handed him one. He accepted the offer, and we sat and ate a quick brunch on the rooftop.

"Onyx?" he asked, wiping his mouth.

"Hm?"

"Where were you before you met Aska?" He looked up at me through his weighed down cyan eyes.

His question felt a bit sudden, but I answered truthfully. "I grew up in a small town outside the city. Nothing too special. You?"

"Went to a private school in New Jersey for a few years when I was younger."

"Sounds fun." His eyes drifted off, staring at the horizon. "Do you miss your friends?"

"Didn't have too many of those. There weren't a lot of people there like me." He gave a slight chuckle and turned to me with a wink. "That place was whiter than a botanical garden book club." I laughed and he continued.

"Some people were nice, gave me cool nicknames when I was younger." I scooped up my legs and crossed them underneath me for storytime.

"What was your nickname? Blue Jay?" I asked teasingly.

He gave a slight chuckle. "No, nothing like that. I remember being so excited to tell my dad about it. He didn't enjoy it as much, or at all, drove me up to the Dean's office and spent over an hour yelling. After that, the kids didn't like me as much, or at all."

"I'm sorry."

"Doesn't matter now." He took another bite of his bar and tossed the rest to a group of pigeons gathering in front of us. "Truth be told, I don't care too much; the people we were before we were machigai don't exist. We can never go back to those lives, so when I tell that story, it feels like I'm reading from a book. Reciting history." In a way, he was correct; while our memories hint that we had lived before we were on the run, it was more or less simply satire. Something we couldn't change or control because none of it affected us. Our future was predetermined the second we slipped into the devil's grasp, but one thing still didn't add up.

"Jay?"

"Hm?" He finally looked me in the eyes, still tired and dull, but there was a spark, just a small one, but enough to start a wildfire.

"If you grew up in New Jersey, how did you end up in Quebec?" His hand ran up and down his neck, massaging his throat.

"One moment, I didn't feel good, so I went to the nurse; the next she was screaming at the top of her lungs and whacking me with a broomstick out the window. My instincts led me up north; from there, it's kinda blank; I lived on the streets for a few years before Lily and Tresa found me and took me in."

"Oh. . ." I leaned back against the wall, and he turned to face me.

"Don't be like that; I like it here. Plus, I'm better off. The US has serious laws against machigai; you think Quebec's bad? Just giving birth to a machigai child is punishable by death down there; you're considered a vessel of Satan." he gave a slight shudder. "You don't even want to know what happens if you are born machigai. Things are better up here, not by much, but just mildly more humane. Like a fly swatter compared to poison." I gave a weak attempt at a smile. How could he be the same age as me, have been through so much more, and still be able to crack stupid jokes?

He stood and offered me a hand up. "Come on, I am raring to go now. We have a few more buildings to look over before turning back."

"One more question." I requested, staring at his mischievous grin as he loomed over me. "Did you tell that whole story just to distract me from your shadow restraints?"

The spark from his eyes drew itself to the surface, widening his grin. "Possibly."

"Kay, just make sure you don't fall from the sky." I said, taking his hand and hauling myself up.

"Promise."

Chapter 13: Jumping Is Just Falling With Style

We made it back for dinner. I was absolutely starving by the time we hit the final building. Even with the occasional break, Jay was too tired to fly by the time we reached the ladder. Thirteen stories of climbing rails made my limbs ache just thinking about the descent. Jay turned positively green when he looked over the edge; there was no way for him to get down if he couldn't fly. In the end, we settled on tying the rope to the top of the building, and me grappling down with BlueJay in the hood of my jacket.

"You look like shit." Blake sat up in bed as we entered.

"Piss off," Jay muttered, wincing with every small step. He sat on the bottom bunk, leaning his head on the pillar.

"I'll bring back dinner." I looked at Jay, who gave me a slight grin and nodded. "Has Lily brought yours, Blake?"

"Don't worry about me; she'll be here soon. Take care of the birdboy."

"Do you realize how easy it would be for me to strangle you in your sleep?" Jay glared daggers across the room.

"You know you love me." He winked back.

"I loathe you; there's a difference."

"Ooooh, fancy words from Stanford?" Blake prodded.

"If he kills you, you know I'll cover for him, right?" I interjected.

"Don't stress about it; after a whole day of scouting, I'd be surprised if he made it halfway across the room without assistance. I'll be fine."

"Mkay," I slipped out the door and laughed as I pranced down the hallway into the dining room.

"You're back. How was your first day of scouting?" Aska nudged my shoulder as Lily handed me two plastic plates with strange-looking sandwiches on them.

"Not too bad, for me at least; Jay's miserable."

He turned to the table where they were all gathering. "Tell him I'll come visit later, kay?"

"Kay." I responded and started to make my leave when Lily stopped me, her warm fingers pulling me to a halt by the crook of my arm.

"Wait! I'll come with you. I need to check up on Blake anyway." A gave a flustered nod that went unnoticed by her as she ran around the bar to gather two plastic plates of her own and joined me near the edge of the room. "What did you mean check up on Blake?" I asked, us trailing down the hallway side by side.

"His leg was injured in the last MES raid." She stopped walking and turned to face me. "Thank you, by the way."

I slowly moved my eyes from left to right before focusing on her. "What for?"

"The information about the machigai blood, we could've lost so many more. I was too-” she faltered, her constant smile falling not quite into a straight line across her rosy lips. “I was too distracted and naive to even notice the dried blood on the bullets." Her moment of weakness disappeared, looking back up at me with those bright eyes. “You genuinely helped us a lot, thank you.” My face burned from the compliment.

"It-it really wasn't a problem."

"Well, thanks anyway." She nudged me only slightly before creaking open the door and poking her head in.

"'Bout time. I'm starving." Blake grinned as Lily flung the door open.

"Sorry, I got distracted," she said, kneeling at his bedside as I sat on the floor next to mine and Jay's bunk, placing Jay's plate on the tiny dresser.

"Thanks," he muttered sleepily, picking at the sandwich. For a moment, the four of us just sat there awkwardly.

"So . . .?" Lily pulled her knees up to her chest and rested her head on them. "How's the weather?"

The first giggle came from Blake, then Jay, and then finally, I cracked a smile and joined in. The mood was killed when Blake's laughter turned into a mild wheezing, and he leaned back with a smile still planted on his face. Lily calmly turned and placed her hand on his chest. Slowly, I watched it begin to rise and fall with ease.

"Is everything okay?" I asked, shifting onto my knees to get a better view of what she was doing.

"He's fine. Just some side effects of MMB."

"What's that?" She glanced over her shoulder at me before carefully pulling back Blake's covers, uncovering the white cast coating his leg from shin to the knee.

"The result of mixing too many different forms of machigai DNA."

"Apparently, the bastards started smothering their weapons in our blood once they realized we had a Nadadum among us," Jay muttered.

"Nadadum?" I asked with a cocked eyebrow.

"A healer," Lily clarified. "It's one of the five machigai classes."

"Since when do machigai have classes? I thought we were all just machigai."

"We are; Jay just made them up to divide us when we train." Lily jabbed an accusatory thumb at Jay who held his hand up to his heart, miming taking offense.

"After all this time you still don't trust my intellect. Unlike you hooligans, I am actually capable of reading, and they are in fact real categories."

"Sure, birdboy." Blake rolled his eyes.

"Nadadum's like Lil are healers." Jay turned to me beginning to explain."Mentium's curses circulate around a specific element, such as you or Blaise. Tatio's have some sort of physical mutation, like myself."

"What would Aska's be labeled as?" I asked, taking a bite of my sandwich.

"It's not an exact fit, but we consider him an Iliad; a machigai with mental abilities, since he kills without touching his opponents. We also consider machigai who live as regular people, as Sopitam's."

"It means dormant," Lily clarified. "They all have their individual definitions, and the system is pretty flawed. For example, if someone were to have a curse involving speed or something horridly cliche like that-"

"They would be alone," Blake finished, finally lifting his head. He took a long look at us before promptly throwing his head back down onto the pillow.

***

After finishing her food, Lily decided to turn in and climbed up to her top bunk, falling silent soon after. The rest of us, not wishing to wake her, followed suit. In less than an hour, my eyelids were heavy, and I drifted away into sleep.

For once, I dreamt of nothing but the beautiful black sky and jumping rooftops with Jay. Admittedly, sleep was much more enjoyable in its simplicity, without a care in the world. Before it felt like I had rested even five minutes, Jay shook me awake to return to the rooftops.

"Sorry it's so early; we're raiding today, so you'll get more rest later," he said, jumping to the other rooftop with his bag.

"What exactly happens during these raids?" I followed close behind.

"Kinda depends. Most of them are just simple search and rescue procedures."

"What are you rescuing?" I asked, following him closely to the edge of the rooftop. The streets below were just starting to come to life as shop owners yawned and unlocked their doors with coffee in hand.

"Machigai typically, sometimes supplies or blueprints. Whatever Burn gets decent information about."

"So, it's stealing."

"I mean technically, but from military or MES bases, not from the innocent. Burn describes it as a 'rebel cause against humanity.'" He stopped at the third roof and took a bottle of water from the bag. "All I know. If we can save some, even a few, of those kids from getting sent to Toyls or a place even worse. . . then it has to be worth the risk."

"That's either extremely noble or extremely arrogant." I halted as we reached the first significant gap and watched Jay dig through the bag and throw the rope onto the concrete roof.

"That's how we roll around here," he mocked a princess transition and spun around before shrinking down to his tiny songbird form. Picking the rope up in his beak, he stared me down to make sure I secured the other end around my waist just right before he took to the air. On the other building, a now fully grown Jay tightened the rope to an old rod, with little slack between the opposing roof and myself to prevent too much whiplash.

After a quick nod from the other side, I gently walked over the edge with my hands gripping the rope above to steady myself. Adrenaline rushing through my veins, I bent my knees just slightly to cushion the impact of the rigid wall as I made contact. One foot in front of the other, I moved my arms upwards as I felt Jay assisting my ascent from above until my eyes peaked over the rooftop, and he offered me a hand up.

"You're weirdly good at that," Jay commented as I untied the rope, feeling blood flow to the new indents on my abdomen. "We're not going too far today; I still have to get back in time, so we'll only go a few more buildings and turn back, then peek around the east side a bit as well."

"Sounds like a plan."

We did just that, four or maybe five more roofs to the west, then turned back and did them again. For the most part, the roofs to the east began getting shorter after a few, making it much more challenging to get to the far ones without injury. On the second to last building, I loudly yelped as the rope slid and smacked my ribs from a decent ten-foot drop between the buildings, doubling due to the slack in the rope.

"Easy-" Jay grabbed me by the arms as I shouted some very non-Christian words once I reached the top. I quickly undid the stinging rope and turned away to inspect the damage under my shirt.

"Oh god," Jay muttered as I revealed a deep purple line underneath my rib cage. He sat me down and pushed me back against the ledge. "Lean back," he demanded as he rifled through the backpack once more, stealing a bottle of water. I watched as the water flowed from the bottle, soaking a wad of Kleenex and pooling onto the rooftop.

"What in---?" Every muscle extending from my abdomen tensed as the Kleenex burned over the rope's outline.

"Stop! Stop!" I latched onto his arm as he attempted to scrub the burn away. "Will you actually listen for once; you turtle brained fool!" I shouted at him, slapping his face and ripping the tissues out of hand and throwing them over the ledge.

"Turtle-" He had an incredulous look on his face.

"Give me the bottle," I demanded. Turning on my side and flicking the lid off, cool, soothing water trickled over the start of the burn to the finish.

"That's not how Lily cleans wounds," Jay peered over.

"Probably not. No knife, gun, or regular burn anyways." The last of the liquid flowed over my gut as I pulled my shirt down, soaking it. "Rope burns are different; they don't actually break through the skin. Most of the time, cleaning isn't necessary if there's clothing between the rope and yourself."

"So, you wasted water?"

"No, your idiocy did. Tissues should never be near anything that can become infected other than your sinuses. Care to enlighten me on why?" I pushed off my knees, wincing through the sting.

"Not a clue." Stealing his hand from his side, I turned it palm up, revealing a bunch of particles from the Kleenex.

"These should never be inside a wound because you would never want them under your skin." Flicking one of the pieces towards him, I glanced over the edge, scanning for any MES officers, police officers, or onlookers who might've been suspicious of the noise. From what I could see there were none below, none to be seen, at least.

"Seems pretty clear today," Jay commented. "Do you need to rest here?"

"I'm fine; let's just get this done with for the day." In truth, the burn wasn't entirely painful compared to past injuries, but the thought of continuing jumping was just enough to sound miserable.

Jay casually walked around the building, scanning the edges.

"Aha!" he grabbed me by the shoulders and steered me in the opposite direction, bending over the side of the roof. "Fire escape"

"Good eyes," I mocked. "One problem. It's at least two stories down. Unless you expect to jump and break my legs, I'd much prefer to continue as we have been."

"Not jump. Dangle." He held the rope up, sending a shiver through my abdominals.

"Basically, you want me to hang myself and hope all ends well?"

"Not exactly- You'll grapple down the sides, like you have been, but in reverse. I can toss down the rope, and we can walk back to the hotel. Personally, it sounds worth a shot."

So, we did. The rope felt like it was tearing the skin around its previous traces into a million different pieces, but Jay wasn't half bad at ensuring nothing went wrong. He let the rope out little by little, always pulling it tight against the edge to allow me to use my legs for balance. The rope fell behind me after I landed steadily on the fire escape and watched a familiar blue bird fly down and land on the railing.

"Not transforming back?" Making my way down the steep metal stairs, he sat on my shoulder lazily and squawked.

"Lazy bastard," I muttered.

Walking back wasn't that bad; it must've looked odd to onlookers, but Jay's reason for staying in bird form was clear. The amount of wanted posters of him up on the billboards had tripled since we first met; in fact, most of the group was advertised with a warning: **MACHIGAI PUBLIC WARNING! DO NOT APPROACH!** With the number; +1 418-692-4848, for any reports of information. The message stayed the same for every poster, naming the machigai and showing a rather inaccurate drawing of them or sometimes a blurred security camera photo. One of the posters showed a rather well-done drawing of Jay, except with blue feathers coming from off his shoulders and draping down like a Rio Carnaval cape. Next to it was a similar poster, but rather a large dark blob instead of a drawing; under the description, everything was blank.

Jay squawked again on my shoulder, biting my ear in an effort to get me to move.

"Ya, ya, I know." I hurried back to the hotel, staring briefly at its now very visible sign labeled Hotel de Vivianna, before rushing around back to the worker entrance Jay had taken me to before. The moment we descended the corridor and locked the door behind us, Bluejay stumbled off my shoulder, landing on his back, flailing and squawking. As he morphed back into a human, the squawking turned into hard wheezing and coughing. I summoned the void and Aska's bucket, rolling Jay over to his side with the bucket in front of him. Awkwardly, I rubbed his back while he choked out bright blue feathers. For just a moment afterward, there was no noise, just heavy breathing, before he propped himself up and glared at me.

"Sorry, I didn't mean to get distracted." He attempted to respond but just gagged and swallowed. Pushing against the wall, he struggled to his feet, leaning hard on me as we made our way down into the bar area and back to our room.

"Go find Lily," he rasped, careful not to wake up Blake, who was still asleep.

"Why?"

"She can help your burn. Trust me, I need to sleep before tonight anyway." His eyes were already closing.

Chapter 14: Raids and Riots

"Wow, how did you manage this?" Lily ran her hand along the tender skin.

I winced at her touch. "Blame Jay!" I bit out through the pain. I found a point on the opposite side of the room to lock my eyes on instead of both watching and feeling her tease the sore and swollen skin. "Can you fix it?"

"Jay's been doing this for almost a year. I doubt it was 100% him." she said with a lighthearted smile, tracing her fingers across the purple as I watched it slowly fade away. Everything was tingly, like the feeling you have in your leg when it falls asleep. The feeling replaced the stinging and then, faded away, taking my energy with it. With heavy eyelids, I briefly thanked Lily, marveling at the extent of her curse, and stumbled back to our room, using the wall for support.

Jay was already fast asleep, snoring away on my bed, so I shimmied up to the top bunk. Every muscle in my body felt rejuvenated, newly massaged by Lily's ability. Despite my new comfort and it being barely noon, I drifted off. Brief dreams of an artificial childhood, doing homework for school at the dinner table with loving parents, filled my night. The imagery in my dreams was constantly shifting into new, happy things. The sugar plum of the night was walking through the streets with Jay and Aska, the three of us in school uniforms shopping and buying all the junk food we could handle until the sunset. The normalcy of the dream felt like bliss.

Stirring on the bunk below woke me from my sweet delirium.

Peaking over the side of my bunk, I watched Jay violently struggle to stuff his arm into a black jacket sleeve.

I blinked slowly at him, feeling as if I was still half asleep. "Getting ready to leave?" My head dangled over the edge to look down at him.

Jay turned around with a start and raised an eyebrow at what I can only assume was my terrible bed hair. "In a bit. Did you find Lily?"

I slid over the side and sat on the bunk below, lifting my shirt just slightly to show the absence of the purple line. "All patched up."

"Sweet. In that case, you should tag along with us tonight. It's only an intel raid, so we'll be home early," he said, his eyes still on my bed hair which I was trying desperately to flatten.

"Maybe." I shrugged.

"All set?" Burn peaked his head in our room.

"Locked and loaded, captain," Jay slung a bag over his shoulder, finishing the motion with a mock military salute.

"Great. Meet me at the bar in five or less. Understood? That means you too, Onyx." He turned around without a response. Almost instantaneously, Jay began to bow as I snuffed a laugh.

"If you're doing another salute behind my back, then I WILL put you on probation," Burn shouted over his shoulder, barely slamming the door behind him before we busted out laughing.

Jay leaned over on the bedposts and wiped his eyes, stilling the last of the laughter. "Oh god- we should probably get going before he actually comes up with a decent threat."

"Like what? No more alcohol privileges?" I back-walked to the door, mocking Jay's bow as he held it open.

"Now, that WOULD be a tragedy." He giggled as we sauntered into the bar, where Tresa, Aska, and Burn were already waiting.

"Finally," Aska gave a half-hearted sigh. "Were you putting on your makeup, BlueJay darling?"

"As a matter of fact, I was," he motioned to his face with false arrogance. "Does this shadow make the color of my eyes pop?" he said with his face 1 inch away from Aska's frowning countenance. We both slid into the two stools at the end of the bar. "It's not my fault Burn always chooses to call on me last; I was set up!"

"Funny," Aska smirked, standing up from his seat. "Never has to come get us. Can we get going now? We're already gonna have to cram to stay on schedule."

"I wouldn't stress." Burn followed and nodded to me. "You're on probation from raids. Remember?"

"You're kidding. That was months ago, and you're severely short-handed without Blake."

"That's why she's going," Burn nodded to me. Aska's smile evaporated, eyes darting between Burn and me.

"No. Not happening."

"She'll stay safe," he said softly, locking eyes with Aska. "I promise."

"We had an arrangement."

"And I intend to keep it. Relax, it's time to see what the newbie can do." He leaned back on the counter casually, sipping from a can of Dr. Pepper.

"If I go," I interjected. "Then I should show you what I do first, right?"

"Go right ahead." Burn turned his back to Aska and joined the others as everyone circled around. I watched their expressions as my eyes went darker, and their forms turned a variety of reds and oranges.

"Wow, you look. . . Different." Tresa gapped at the dark steam-like substance shifting around my form.

"I've spent years guaranteeing that my face never gets put on one of those wanted posters, and it will stay that way."

"Can you even see like that?" Jay waved his hand through the steam, watching it dissipate and repeat.

"Kinda; it's like wearing glasses, but for all my senses, which can also be a pain in the butt."

"Limitations?" Burn continued to lean against the bar counter behind everyone, observing.

"Nothing, really. It's much more powerful than me, people can't find my actual form through the shadows to shoot; the shadows stay up as long as I need, and there's no repercussions till I take it down."

"And what happens then?"

"Fainting, seizures, vomiting, the whole Shazam. All the reasons she won't go." Aska muttered.

"This true?" Burn pushed off against the bar, staring me down.

"Exaggerated, sure, but yes. It goes away with time, no worse than Jay's."

"No worse than- Jesus Christ!" Aska yelled.

"ENOUGH." Burn cut Aska off mid-rant with a sharp glare, then turning back to me. "Your punishment, your choice. Make it quick. Make it smart."

"I'm going." I said with fierce determination.

"Like hell you are!" Aska began to stand, but Burn pushed him back down on his stool.

"Then it's settled." Jay and Tresa followed Burn's steps to the maintenance exit. "Let's go. We're already behind schedule."

Aska grabbed my arm as I began to follow. "Please." He was the only one who could ever manage to find my actual figure through the shadows.

"What happened to not wanting to control my life? Or was that just a frail attempt at getting me to go home?" I snapped bitterly.

He released me. "No. I- you're impossible." He shook his head dejectedly.

"I'll be back. Don't worry." He gave a hesitant nod, and I disappeared through the door, leaving him behind.

***

Apparently, they owned a van. God, it was awkward, riding in a hollow, lightless car across town to a back alley in complete silence. Not to mention, Jay kept waving his hand through the shadows, watching it disappear and reappear like a 3-year-old. The back alley we stopped in was dark, feeding the shadows surrounding me as the sun set in the sky.

"What exactly is the plan here? Because I think I missed the briefing," I asked, stretching my legs out after the long ride.

Burn made an attempt at grabbing me, but his hand only passed through empty air. A moment of confusion passed over his face before he shook his head and motioned towards a sizeable barbed-chain link fence outside what seemed to be a two-story concrete building. With several meters between the fence and the building, it looked oddly menacing in the darkness. Maybe twenty red and orange blobs moved through the areas in consistent motions, and farther away, another 20-40 figures were out back, leaving too many heat trails for my eyes to accurately trace what they were doing.

"That's a lot of people. Military base, I assume?" I asked Burn.

"MES base. You can see them through the walls?" He raised an eyebrow and I could see him analyzing my abilities and use.

"Kinda. I can trace heat signatures, though only the ones standing in the shadows, but since it's night, the entire

120

earth is technically coated in one. I can also see a toaster on the 2nd floor."

"Good to know," Burn muttered, fiddling with the edges of his gloves. "When we enter, make sure to keep us updated on the number of officers you see nearing; easier to avoid conflict then."

"Got it. Do you mind telling me why we're breaking into a government facility?"

"Inside that facility are documents, filled with locations of hundreds of other facilities and sometimes even blueprints. Within those other buildings are machigai."

"You risk your lives for the notion that you might possibly find enough info to risk your lives again?"

"That's the spirit, Onyx," Jay laughed as I stared at Burn.

"What choice do we have?" he asked. "The machigai in those facilities did nothing wrong. Most of them are younger than Alina, tortured day in and day out. I would want to be saved."

"How long do they last after you find them?" Both Jay and Burn stood still, silent; it was Tresa who spoke quietly.

"Some, like the kids back at the hotel, last a decent amount of time; others make it a few weeks tops. And the rest- the rest never want to live."

"We have to help the ones we can," Burn whispered. I nodded.

"What do you want me to do, captain?"

"Do you have any offensive abilities?"

"Guns and knives."

"Guns and knives. Ok. Flank us on the way in. BlueJay, standard distraction Northeast corner." Out of nowhere, Tresa ripped out a chunk of her hair from underneath her shower cap, handing it into Jay's claws as he took to the sky and dove towards the buildings. I felt a bit stunned at the absurdity of it all but kept my internal comments quiet. Pistol now in hand, we slid around the back, my eyes darting around, trying to trace the red and orange blobs that seemed to be getting closer every second. Suddenly, a small explosion rang through our ears, barely anything, but it seemed to have come from the area where Jay had gone.

"Is he-?" I whispered.

"An idiot. Yes, keep moving." We slid around to the door, locked shut. Removing his gloves and placing his hand over the handle, Burn melted through the entire door, watching carefully as it liquefied and dripped down. Tresa clamped her hand over his mouth to prevent a yelp while the leather gloves slipped back over the peeling dead skin. After a moment to breathe, Burn gained his composure, pushing the door open with his shoulder. Figures swarmed the inside of the building, much too close for comfort. My heart pounded against my chest every corner we turned, thinking I might've missed one.

"Do you know where we're going?" My arm caught Burn by the shoulder; he nodded and motioned for me not to speak anymore. A few more turns and we were deep into the labyrinth; it was then that we stopped. Burn gestured to the door on our left; after I gave him the all-clear, he threw it open, revealing a room filled wall to wall with filing cabinets.

"Grab as much as you can; we'll sort it later." Papers and packets flew into the void and Tresa's backpack faster than humanly possible. Burn stood at the door, keeping watch over us. Soon, the opening of the void began to shrink. If it weren't for the shadow armor around me, I'd likely be dead from the magnitude of how much energy was used to store the files. The moment Tresa's backpack couldn't hold any more wadded-up papers, we darted. My ears pounded against my head as we sprinted down the hallways, no longer obsessed with stealth.

Shouting from guards, down some distant tunnel, alerted us moments before a deafening alarm began ripping through our skulls. Hands pressed tightly against my ears; my speed slowed farther behind Tresa and Burn. Sometimes, it was easy to forget Shadow Guard was only invincible from my curse's effects, not my actual body's. My lungs struggled to inhale the air around me, always coming up empty when I breathed in. Burn reached for my hand, actually hitting his target for the first time, and dragged me along behind him.

"Don't give up now! We're almost there!" Turning a final corner, a rush of nightlight flooded over me, rejuvenating my lost energy and pushing me further. Sadly, as we turned the corner, I made the mistake of glancing behind us. The heat signatures were everywhere, a group of at least five in the hallway we had come from, heading our way. Tugging Burn's hand, he turned and watched the soldiers round the corner.

"Shit," he muttered under his breath. Without hesitation, he ripped a canteen off his belt and poured it out a few meters in front of us. Suddenly, I was being yanked backward as heat exploded directly in front of the guards. Shrieks and clambering echoed through the hallway as the men and women on the other side tried to extinguish the embers.

"Shouldn't it be red?" I gapped at the brilliant wall of deep purple flames.

"Typically isn't." Tresa grabbed my hand and spun me around. "Time to go before BlueJay passes out mid-flight. Burn will cover us." She pointed upwards, revealing the tiniest heat signature circling above us in the sky. I gave a brief sigh of relief knowing my avian friend wasn't dumb enough to get himself killed. Keeping my eyes locked on the sky, I ran, allowing the creature in the sky to guide the way.

Chapter 15: Imagine Dying, Couldn't Be Me

The little bird trailed us the whole way back to the alley. Most of its feathers were slightly dismantled and even burnt on the tips, but it landed gracefully into the car. Tossing the bucket back at him, Tresa and I jumped in the front seats, with her driving while Burn joined Jay in the back as he started his usual ritual of coughing up feathers. This time, they were smoking.

The ride back was just as awkward and uneventful as the ride there. Lily greeted us in the bar when we arrived, making me wonder how much coffee this girl was running on, as it was still the middle of the night.

She was painfully unfazed by my wall of shadows, not even flinching as we entered.

"Where's Aska?" Burn asked, half-carrying Jay.

"He got tired of waiting, I guess." She shrugged and jumped off the counter to grab Jay's other arm. "Do you want me to go get him?"

"Take Jay to rest in the infirmary. I'll get Aska." Leaving all of Jay's weight on Lily, who whimpered as she tried to hold him up, Burn walked away, turning to Tresa and me as he made his exit. "You two go to the infirmary with Lily; I'll meet you there in a second." Tresa nodded, returning to Lily and Jay, and assessed them momentarily. She motioned for Lily to move away and went to pick up Jay. Without much effort, Jay was tossed up bridal style, and Lily giggled a bit as we watched Tresa transport him with ease. Jay let out a few annoyed groans and squirmed, but he was pinned in place by Tresa's huge biceps and shoulders. Trailing behind the two, we turned into the infirmary and watched Tresa dump Jay on one of the gurneys.

"I hate you," he muttered, already falling asleep.

"Why does he hate you?" Burn asked, walking in with a drowsy Aska behind him.

"Cuz' he's a pipsqueak," Lily laughed.

"Fair enough." He shrugged without question. "Onyx, get on the bed."

"Huh?"

"If you're gonna seize when that. . . thing. . . goes away, I'd rather you be strapped down." I sat on the bedside and watched Burn and Aska retrieve thick leather straps from the cabinets. My skin ached, remembering the rope burn from this morning.

"Is that really necessary? Maybe we can get something softer...padded even?" I asked, lying back for them to lock my arms down.

"Maybe not necessary, but precautions can't hurt. This is the best we have." After a few tries to find my arm in the shadows, he strapped my left arm down securely compared to Aska's right arm, which was still pretty loose. Then they added two more on each leg, one at thigh level, the other on my shins, and a final one across my stomach. They were finally satisfied, completely eliminating my ability to move anything below my neck.

"Ready?" Burn sat on the side of the bed. In complete truth, no molecule in my body wanted to drop the shadows. I felt protected inside them, warm and safe. Hesitantly, I nodded, the only true movement my body still possessed.

"On your call." My mind counted down for me. 3. . . 2. . . 1.

All my senses hesitated, unsure of letting down the thin wall of protection.

Then came burning.

Every section of my skin was itching, like a million mosquitoes had just hatched and were biting me from the inside out.

Grains of black came to my vision as panic set in; slowly, they grew bigger until they consumed everything in the room.

I was still conscious, still aware of the pain, and that people were yelling; I just couldn't make any of it out. Then everything went static. A faint buzz filled the void as the monsters came into sight…

"Run… Run. RUN YOU IDIOT!" I thought loudly to myself.

Every time.

There was no movement in my legs, or any part of me for that matter, but every nerve and muscle in my body screamed for me to flee. I was limp, hanging in his bony grasp. Hundreds of deep purple voids stared me down from all over his tall thin pitch-black body, all except a few spots of white, like tiny pores, breaks in the skin. His deep purple, hollowed-out, eye sockets followed me, limbs growing and contorting to make sure no matter where my gaze fell, I could never escape its scrutiny. Deep from within those empty sockets of eyes, rang out screams, familiar final gasps for life. They were always so hauntingly memorable, each of their owners' last expressions permanently carved into the stone walls of my mind. Baths of tears dripped off my chin down my numb figure, the pools around my eyes mixing with acidic drool from Vindicto, burning into my skin and flooding my retinas until the only smell in the air was my rotten flesh as I soaked in the agonizing irony that the only functional part of my body was my tear ducts. I didn't have to see to feel the now acidic tears trailing down my face, removing several layers of skin and muscle on their way down. Nor was a mirror necessary for me to picture the blistering red patches of peeling skin as they flaked off their previous home in clumps, ripping off as much as they could take on the way down. Nor did I struggle to picture the forming burns and blisters, not even Vindicto's cruel, apathetic lump of an expression as his grip loosened, unsatisfied with not completing his kill.

"That's right. Run, you stupid bitch." I thought, face down in the greyish-red soil, waiting for the rest of the shock to fade and the pain to set in. The only trace of any of the monsters was the feeling of blisters heating up and popping and the slight, nearly silent sizzle of human flesh coming from my arms and back. Somewhere far in the distance, the screams were still audible, just waiting for me to return weak and older so he could finish his job.

I didn't know I was shrieking until cold air splintered through my lungs, freezing every crevice inside for a brief moment.

And then the air caught.

If you can picture oxygen as a washcloth, this was the equivalent of it getting caught on an exposed piece of metal in the bottom of your throat. My lungs spasmed, gasping for air through the coughing. Splatters of blood appeared on the palms of my hands as the fit finally relented. I rolled onto my stomach, gasping in pain as one of my newest blisters popped underneath me—stinging puss piercing raw skin. The hard mattress underneath me pressured my chest, making it impossible to breathe easily. Spots dotted my vision with every movement, making it almost impossible to see the small orange pill bottle that sat on the nightstand among a scattered mess of other objects.

"End it." In the back of my head, thoughts rang. "Kill the pain, whatever it takes." My hand reached out in front of me, quivering as my fingers fumbled the bottle through an almost blank vision. There was a small thud as it clanged to the floor, a slip of paper gliding down a few feet away. Pathetic. Only a few more years left, and I wish only to throw them all away—I was a sad excuse for a machigai.

My hands fell as my eyes squeezed shut, releasing the moisture stinging inside them—a slight pounding near an unpin-pointable spot in my skull. I let my body go numb once more as my head tilted off the side of the bed in the direction of my arm; my mind slowly slipping away from reality, into some faraway realm.

Immediately, my nerves were set on fire; with a single touch, my eyes shot wide open. A gut-wrenching shriek escaped my throat without even a moment of hesitation.

"I'm sorry! I'm sorry! I'm sorry!" Someone yelled out immediately, letting go of my shoulder directly on one of my freshest wounds. My own screams muffled, letting the pain burn throughout my body, using the small point on my shoulder as a medium. Aska picked up the pill bottle from the floor and placed it on a nightstand one bed over without a word.

"Luna?" He kneeled in front of me. "You realize you can't stay like this, right? You will one-hundred percent fall off the bed, and believe me, that will be much worse than just letting me help you now."

"Gahf" was the specific noise I remember making at that comment. Still, I was happy that he was the one beside me.

"Just shriek if I hit a sore. Kay?" He ran his hand under my shoulder, carefully avoiding the spot he already hit. A small half-yelp escaped as he brushed the edges of one and stopped.

"Good there?" He asked with a few fingers placed just below my collarbone. Apparently, no response also qualified as a yes because Aska didn't hesitate to carefully flip me over back onto the bed, popping at least five sores on my back all at once. An eruption of burning circles blacked out my vision as my mouth gaped open, and no sound made its way through. The nice new clothes I had just purchased not a month ago stuck into the wounds, rubbing against the raw muscle and bone and ripping off the little skin left near it. Sudden regret of not taking the pills flooded my system as my neurotransmitters pulsed with my speeding heartbeat.

"Luna? Luna?" Aska's voice rang quietly, the ringing in my ears covering up most of his words. "You still there? Wake up."

Wake up? I'm not asleep, am I? Are my eyes even closed? Where am I? Whose yelling? Why does everything hurt?... What happened?

My eyes gently fluttered open, still blurred and grainy. The first thing I could fully recognize was a glimmer of blue in an otherwise bland room. Aska's slim face looked oddly more sullen than usual. There were no tears, but they weren't necessary to read his emotions. I must've looked really awful for him to be this worried.

"Lil, she's conscience-ish," He called, squeezing my hand once before stepping away. Lily stepped into my vision, her soft features a calming sight for my cloudy head.

"Onyx. Blink twice if you can hear me." I complied with her request. "Wonderful! We need to treat your sores before they get infected, a simple two-step process—nothing to fret about. I'll cover them with a thin layer of Vaseline and then wrap you up. Does that sound okay?" Every part of me wanted to scream no, that it was too much. No one had ever wrapped my scars for me; no one had ever seen them. Not even Aska. But Lily didn't wait for a response this time. She gently pulled away my covers, leaving me shivering in the exposed air. Aska grabbed my right arm cautiously. With Lily on my right, they gently sat me up, my eyes almost rolling back with the sudden headache that followed. The back of Lily's soft hand brushed over a blister, making me wince slightly as she gingerly rolled my shirt up.

"Hold this," she instructed Aska before dipping her rubber-gloved hands in a small metal container. The ointment felt freezing against the feverish skin; unlike Aska, Lily didn't apologize or console me after every wince; she simply paused and continued. Admittedly, ignoring the temperature, it did feel significantly better after she completed an area. Like adding chapstick to very dry lips, it still hurts, but somehow less. I had no idea how shallow my breathing had been since waking, but suddenly, it felt like someone had removed a lead weight from inside my lungs, and the air flooded in with ease. My hand gripped the collar of Lily's shirt as she loosely wrapped gauze from my ribcage to my hips. Soon, I was tightly bundled, and the two of them laid me back, gasping for the new quality air.

"Get some rest; I'll be in with lunch in an hour or so." Lily smiled and waved goodbye after she finished putting her supplies away. Aska gave my hand another gentle squeeze and followed her out. A newfound exhaustion flooded through my body. My limbs went numb, and my eyelids drooped.

Chapter 16: Untrainable

Lily broke her promise. She wasn't back in an hour with lunch; Burn was. I was barely conscious when he casually knocked on the doorframe. He strode in with a tray and casually put a desk/armrest thing in front of me to set the tray on. Tomato soup and crackers. I grabbed a pack of crackers and started chipping away at them before noticing Burn was staring me down. I suppose there might've been a reason he brought lunch, not Lily.

"I've come to a conclusion." He sat up straight with his hands on his lap, like someone posing for picture day, if you excused his stone-cold expression.

"About?" I raised my eyebrow.

"You. Every time you use that… 'thing,' it sends you into an episode, correct?"

"Well, yes, but-"

"In that case, as valuable as it is on the field, it's not worth it."

"I have other abilities that can be useful." I don't know why I was fighting so hard to be in the center of the action; these people were strangers, and the cause honestly didn't matter much to me. To be honest, it just felt good arguing.

"Even so, as impressive as I'm sure they are. They're nothing compared to what you could do for us. Off the field."

"You're still set on me going to Toyls?"

"In short? Yes. I asked you to consider it, and I think now is the perfect time for an answer." I fiddled with the spoon lying in the tomato soup. The entire purpose of my coming here was to watch over Aska. Despite things being strained with him since arriving, somewhere deep down that was still what I wanted. "It's what he wants you to do, you know? You'll be safe there while also providing us with valuable information."

"What makes you think I care what he wants?" I shot back. Burn just shrugged.

"Just a hunch. So?"

"Review with me here. What exactly are the options?"

"Well, we can't let you go to raids with us if just going injures you. So, I suppose your options are number one: stay here and help Lily take care of things around the base and help BlueJay with scouting, number two: go to Toyls as a spy and help us from the inside, possibly freeing thousands of helpless machigai children or number three: leave."

For a moment, everything paused as my brain mauled over the choices. "Are you absolutely sure that Toyls is the right choice?"

Burn sat for a bit, playing with his wording like always, finding a way to state the truth while still influencing others to get what he wanted. "It would be the most beneficial for everyone, yes."

I cocked my eyebrow like a gun as we stared each other down, waiting for one or the other to concede. My will broke first, mainly just in the hopes he would leave me alone to finish eating.

"What do I need to do?" A grin broke through his shaded features.

"Train, but we can begin that once you've healed up. For now, eat and rest; also, if you can, the faster we can get those files, the better. I'll return tomorrow." He stood and walked to the door with a sense of accomplished swagger, turning back briefly. "Thank you… Onyx. You won't regret this."

"I better not." He smiled and left, shutting the door behind him. I took a sip of my soup. It was lukewarm and kind of clumped at the bottom, but I finished it and munched on some crackers; only barely attempting not to make a gigantic crumb mess. Sometime shortly after Burn left, I drifted asleep. No dreams, thankfully. When I awoke the following day, my muscles were still sore, and occasionally, there was a familiar explosion of pain as another blister exploded, but it was a significant improvement from the day prior. I threw my legs over the side of the bed, flexing my joints in and out, searching for pain or discomfort. A slight throbbing just below my kneecap indicated that there was likely either a blister there or it was the result of the leather straps they had used earlier. Maybe both. That was an awful thought. Stumbling off the bed, I leaned on the post, watching the spots appear in my vision and then fade away. Once my balance was caught, I kind of waddled/walked through the door. The wall was my support, blundering through the hall into the bar.

"What are you doing?!" Lily's voice rang as her hands securely gripped my waist. With her guidance, I somehow made it to the bar and awkwardly wriggled into one of the tall stools as she frantically checked my heart rate and pupils.

"I'm okay, I'm okay."

"Really? 'Cause you kinda look like shit," Jay said from beside me, taking a long sip of his light pink drink.

"Same to you, but that's not outta the ordinary, is it? Make me one of those, will you." My hand lightly gestured to his drink.

"One of those?" he asked mockingly.

"Columbus or whatever." A ghost of a smile spread across his tired expression. The clock read 6:30 am, but it felt hours earlier.

"Cosmo or Cosmopolitan if you wanna sound like a prick." He looked over to Lily for confirmation as she fretted over my wrinkled bandages. Her hand glided back and forth over them, unsuccessfully trying to iron them flat as I winced. Gentle eyes looked up to meet Jay's. She shrugged before looking back down.

"Can't be any worse than what she's already doing."

Jay rolled his eyes and hopped over the counter to mix the drink.

"How was your hangover?" I asked. Watching him gently fill a glass with cranberry juice.

"Same old, same old. Better than yours, apparently, although it seems we have similar remedies." He raised the shaker in his hands, hinting towards it.

"Seems that way.'"

"I could never do it," Lily said quietly, sliding onto the bar countertop; the girl didn't seem to have much love for chairs.

"Hm?" Jay handed me the poorly made drink.

"The whiplash of the curse."

"You get your own form of whiplash," Jay said, crawling back over the bar.

"A headache and sleepiness is nothing compared to the rest of you." She took a sip of her coffee.

"So what? You also don't have as powerful of a curse, meaning you have to stay here all day. Even trade, I think," My mind tried to gauge how many drinks he'd had. Not even Jay was foolish enough to consider that a fair trade. From that moment, we just kind of sat there. Jay finished his drink and stumbled away back to the room. Lily kind of just started fiddling with the apron strings around her waist.

"Lily, do you know-"

Burn barged in. "Oh, there you are."

"Know what?" Lily asked.

Burn ignored her question, instead inspecting me, running his eyes along my frame and studying my condition.

"You're well enough to walk?" He raised an eyebrow.

"Yes?"

Burn latched onto my wrist and started dragging me away; I barely had enough time to finish my drink before we were at the garden door. The outside was bright, too bright. What time was it? 2-3 pm, maybe. A tiny breeze whistled past, nipping at the side of my cheek. "May I ask what we're doing?"

"Today is August 17th."

"Yes. And??" My eyes rolled; this kid was way too serious.

"Entrance exams are in two weeks precisely."

"Entrance exams?"

"You didn't think they would just let you in, did you? Don't answer that." He paced in the shape of a soft square; this boy was either ADHD, a trained diplomat, or just really, really stressed. "There are three main categories, all physical; they'll worry about your intelligence later. You don't pass the first semester with at least 3.87 for your GPA; you're expelled without a second thought, no redos." He stared me down to drill that into me; no *pressure* I thought. Burn continued after a moment. "But we'll worry about that later. First, we have to get you through the door, then we'll keep you there-"

"What are the three categories?" Burn stopped and looked at me for a moment as if questioning how he had just been cut off. "Sorry, you were rambling."

"I-uh, yes, entrance exams. . . Sharp shooting, physical testing, and team strategy."

"Team strategy? How would that test you individually?"

"The whole team doesn't always pass; they watch you to see how you handle other people and new ideas. A dumb dog can't admit when they're wrong and might get other officers killed on the field."

"Genius wanted to start with sharp shooting until you're more healed." Tresa appeared in the doorway, lounging against the frame with her arms crossed. A small bundle of dark hair was free from her black shower cap.

"Tresa, your hair," Burn reminded her as she tucked it back in.

"Here," she handed me a silver Beretta 70. "Show us what you can do." I flipped the gun over in my hand, weighing it in comparison to my father's.

"Loaded, I assume?" I looked back up at her.

"I hope so; the ammunition is still locked inside."

"What am I shooting?" Burn removed the glove from his left hand, tossing it on the bench behind him. Small puffs of smoke rose up in nearly perfect circles, filling the area with the smell of burning flesh. How was he not screaming in pain?

"Get it as close to the circle as you can, and try not to shoot either of us." My fingers ran over the gun, feeling every crevice until they flipped the safety off. Starting with both hands, I fired a single shot at the highest smoke bubble, trimming the edge. My left arm dropped down to my side as I took a step back, lining my body up with the direction of the gun. Three consecutive shots through the next three bubbles. They all hit but needed to be centered better. Depending on how the scoring system was set up, just hitting the target might not be enough to pass.

"Not bad shrimp tail; ever handle anything heavier than a pistol?" Tresa rested her elbow on my shoulder; the girl was a decent amount taller than me, just barely shorter than Jay.

"A few times, not a fan of carrying large machinery." The void opened beside me, popping out the largest gun I owned, a sniper. I picked this one up a few years back in a pawn shop next to a grocery store we had raided. With a little click, it loaded and locked up the shot. I brought the gun up, guiding it to the bullet's destination.

DING.

The bell on the roof rang as the gun lowered. My shoulder popped back into place, forcing me to expect a bruise the next morning. Two more shots were fired before my collarbone had taken enough of a beating. The distance and power from a sniper were better than my pistols, but my aim was sloppy, and I didn't need my weapon causing more damage than my opponent.

"That'll work." Burn shook off his hand, a few flakes of ash tumbling to the ground before he reapplied his glove. "I'd place my bets that they'll hand you something similar to that, along with a pistol and a rifle.

"What else?" I asked, tossing the gun over my shoulder into the void.

"Well, there will be a generalized physical fitness test, long-distance running, sprints, and weights. The bar is very low to qualify in those categories because they will absolutely grill you on them later on. The final category is strategy or team strategy, depending on the year. Likely some sort of child's game, like tag, turned gruesome with fake guns. You might be placed in a team or a partnership, or they might put you on your own. It's a bit different each year; last time was capture the flag with tasers and stun guns.

"Real stun guns? For a high school tryout??"

Tresa scoffed. "They would give you real, real guns to shoot at each other if they saw fit. Laws don't apply to law enforcement. Every year, dozens of kids get injured during these trials, and the MES don't care, as long as they get their pick of the crop."

"But," Burn sat down on the bench. "You have an advantage. You're machigai. Brief me on what all your abilities entail."

"Well, I can store stuff in the void, but the more I store, the more it's likely to get lost and never return. If I'm standing in a shadow, I can control it, like it's a part of my body and-"

"Give us an example," Tresa demanded, her eyes lit up like a wolf stalking its prey.

I awkwardly shuffled back to the side of the building, close to where she was standing in the doorframe. The familiar chill of the shadows bulleted through me, an ice bath in my veins. My pistol popped out of the ground beneath me. It's hard to explain because I couldn't *actually* see it, but I could feel the shadow's point of view; I could feel the trigger of the gun as it lifted up, surrounded by the steamy puffs of dark storm clouds. BANG. A single shot, followed by the aggressive thud of my knees against concrete. Nausea overcame me, wiping out my vision in a startling reminder that I was still recovering from the raid yesterday. I could feel Tresa and Burn's eyes locked on me as I swallowed some bits of my earlier crackers. Wobbling, I stood once more, trying to ignore the spots that danced in my sight and the jackhammer behind my eyes.

"I-uhhh, I can also- cloak, l-like- uhhhh." Burn waved his hand in a "zip it" motion.

"That's enough. Tresa return her to the infirmary and get Lily from the penthouse. Discretely this time if you would."

Tresa rolled her eyes at his final comment before approaching me steadily. Before I could utter a word, her arms swept below my legs, throwing me up in a bridal style carry. For a brief moment, I attempted to resist before realizing it was pointless.

"That's really not necessary-" I uttered, just barely avoiding my head getting smashed by the doorway. Her shower cap favored her left side, angling just enough so that chunks of uneven black hair fell out, almost scraping her shoulders. Eyes so dark the pupil blended into the iris, forming a singular circle that made it impossible to only look at them for a standard time frame; you were either warded off from direct contact or sucked so far in you would never escape. The rest of her features were just as sharp, with dark chestnut skin, pursed lips, and a thin nose bridge.

When I looked closely, I could almost make out freckles blanketing her nose and cheeks; then again, they may very well have been spots in my own vision.

Entering the infirmary, she once again nearly crushed my skull on the doorframe, just barely giving me time to shift my neck out of the way. She placed me on the edge of the bed, and though she hid it well, I watched her chest rise and fall with quick, shallow breaths. She must've anticipated more of an effortless trip than what was provided.

"Lily will be in shortly," Tresa half grunted under her breath before turning to leave.

"Thank you," I shouted back after a moment, yet I doubt she heard, nor cared for my gratitude.

The unspoken and spoken promises of the day mauled through my mind like Miley Cyrus on a wrecking ball. I had told Burn that I would be attending Toyls; my fate was soon to be placed in the very hands of the people whose life goal was to bring me and my family to extinction. *Family*. What a strange and undefined term. I suppose no matter how irritating and irrational he may be, Aska will never not be my brother, blood or otherwise, but what about the rest of the machigai? Whether justification called for it or not, somewhere inside, Jay was someone I cared for. Burn and Tresa on the other hand seemed less concerned with connections and bonds, and instead, their minds were set on justice and strategy. *"Not necessarily a bad thing,"* My mind echoed; breaking ties with the world was a rather appealing option for someone who had no given place within it, but then again, where would I be without connections? My life had always been put on the back burner for Aska's;

it was a choice that I put it there, but that didn't erase the amount of times my stomach ached from starvation to ensure that his never had to, the amount of times I was forced to endanger myself to retrieve him from a mission gone wrong or tolerate his poor housekeeping skills. It's easy to lose myself in the sacrifices made, but despite that, in the back of my mind, I know that without him, I would've been dead years ago. That debt forever sits in the pit of my stomach as one that will never be repaid. One that cannot be repaid.

Part II:

Toyls Academy

Chapter 17: C. Everette

The weeks that passed were long and, to be completely honest, draining. As diplomatic as Burn seemed when we initially met, that mask had dropped completely the moment he convinced me to attend Toyls. The boy was quick to anger, especially as our time began to dwindle, and I continued to fall short of his physical expectations.

"9.02 seconds," he said, glaring at me after the 3rd 50-yard dash of the day. "You had 8.8 last week; you aren't trying hard enough."

I simply nodded through my breaths.

During the first few weeks, a comment like that would have likely earned an irritated retort, leading to a lengthy yelling match that I always seemed to lose. Eventually, Jay taught me it was easier to bite my tongue than waste time arguing with a brick wall. A shadow passed over the ground beneath me; looking up towards the building, Tresa climbed the wall like a nimble spider. Although from here, my eyes could not spot the rope, I knew it was there holding her up. I longed for Sundays, when Burn allowed me to join Jay in scouting while he and Tresa met with informants. The rest of the week was packed with what felt like 24/7 conditioning; Mondays, I sparred against Tresa while Burn watched, correcting my every move and explaining why she continued to beat me in all fields; sword fighting, wrestling, chess, even gun fighting with paintballs. On Tuesdays, he would train my curse, which was not nearly as intense as the physical activities. Burn may be short-tempered and mild-mannered, but he was not an idiot. A dead machigai was a useless machigai. If that wasn't the case, he'd already have an army.

Instead of murder, he guided me to simply work on accuracy, and even pushed me to open two voids at once, transporting items between them; although it was a challenging ability to hold for very long. We spent Wednesdays constantly testing my physical abilities; sprinting, weightlifting, how far I could jump, and how high I could jump. Without the aid of my curse, there would be no chance for me even to be considered for the academy, but Burn showed me how to lift more using the shadow of the bar to lift with me, doubling my natural ability. I could also jump higher with the shadows pushing me up in the first few seconds, but there wasn't much my shadow could do to increase my speed, making Burn grow evermore paranoid that it would be a major red flag to have such a broad weakness.

"Do it again." His voice was just barely lower than a shout, mimicking a drill sergeant. A brief moment passed when I thought for certain he was about to start referring to me as "maggot." My heart spasmed inside my chest, begging for a break that was not to come. It must've been nearing peak noon, and my senses were engulfed by the scent of the lasagna Lily was preparing in the kitchen, making my stomach grumble. *Just give him what he wants, and he'll eventually relent.* I passed underneath the shadow of one of the garden's trees, the tips of my fingers buzzing with a new energy. If only I had spared Tresa in the shade when my capabilities were at their peak, that might at least put us on an even playing field. The silver line of spray paint glinted against the sun. Fifty meters, almost stretching the complete width of the garden. I lowered myself into a set position, feet shoulder width apart, one hand down and one hand in the air.

"3. . . 2. . ." A gunshot rang through my ears, but before my mind could think, I was shooting through the air. The crisp wind slapped my face, whistling through my hair.

"8.937. Not awful," he said begrudgingly, clicking the timer off. "That doesn't mean it's even remotely near decent." I focus my line of sight beyond him, intentionally gazing longingly toward the hotel and the delicious cuisine inside. Just as I'd hoped, Burn followed my eyes, likely recognizing his own appetite steadily growing. The timer clanked, hitting something at the bottom of the bag. "I expect you back here by 14:00 sharp; every minute you're late will be an extra kilometer dash. Understood?"

"Yes, sir." My eyes locked onto Burn's, holding his gaze with a straight face until finally, he gave a sturdy nod, excusing me for lunch. A grin broke through my mask of seriousness, returning Burn's nod before hastily turning to the ladder that scaled the building.

"Don't even think about it." Burn latched onto my shoulder from behind. Warmth radiated from underneath his leather gloves. He didn't mean it to be threatening; I had learned that by now. His skin, especially his hands and forearms, were permanently searing, a never-halting reminder of his dastardly and ever-approaching fate. "They'll be nearly done by now, and even if they weren't, it's counterproductive for you to join. It'll both stall their progress and drain you further than necessary." For a moment, something flickered through his eyes that hadn't been there before; either irritation or the dead look of a diplomat, but it was gone momentarily. "Go get something for lunch; I think Lily made lasagna. I'll be in soon." His hand slid from my shoulder to the bone just below, giving a slight nudge in the direction of the door. My eyes fell to the ground in disappointment.

He was right, of course, but Sunday seemed so far away.

***

Sunday was not far away. In fact, it passed too quickly; the weeks flying by in one giant translucent blur. Before there was time to comprehend, I was standing outside the looming gate of Toyls Academy. My hand nervously tugged at the helm of my jacket while the other gripped the inside of Mrs. Madalini's elbow.

"Relax, my child, you will do wonders," she said in her broken accent, placing a steady hand atop my own. Her silky black hair glinted in its tightly pulled bun, with only a few pieces falling down to curtain her round face. At one point in her life, I suspected she once looked very similar to how her daughter did now. For a moment, she gripped my hand tighter, keeping her eyes forward and her voice low. "This plan is absurd and reckless, but as long as my flower insists, I shall aid your people's brigade."

"We are forever grateful, Ma'am." My attempt at a sweet smile was feeble, but she seemed to accept it.

Your people's. The words stung worse than they should. Mrs. Madalini had welcomed me with open arms, but the look in her eyes was still cold towards anyone who wasn't blood. She was not an ally, more or less a resource. She stopped short of a fork in the gravel path; people veered to the right, heading towards a grand building that I assumed was the meeting hall we were instructed to congregate in before exams. Mrs. Madalini didn't turn. Instead, she looked up at me with a tight jaw.

"Repay your so-called gratitude by not getting caught; mistakes will cost us all dearly, darling." She dug into her purse, revealing a folder filled with different files. Shoving the folder into my hands, she spoke calmly, "These are everything you will need: Lily's birth certificate, her transcript, everything is there. Don't even think about doing anything foolish." She dropped my arm coldly and walked back through the gate. She was undoubtedly correct about one thing: this plan was insane. For it to work, I would need to pose as Lily, whom I looked nothing like. Her skin was pretty light for an Italian, and my training had given me an unwanted tan but that was very much where the similarities ended. She was just noticeably shorter than me, with lighter, healthy chocolate brown hair in contrast to my oily dark brown. Jay had to cut a decent few inches off of my own to even pass for the length hers was in her school photos last year; leaving the ends choppy and uneven, nothing like how she wore hers. The list of differences could go on and on, but Burn was confident that it could pass without trouble. Then again, he wasn't at risk of getting caught.

Clutching the files closely to my chest, I entered the meeting hall. Tall ceilings shrouded the bustling crowd below; a center stage made of brick fell directly under one of the largest glass domes ever seen. Four sections of brilliant, sleek black seats with white accents surrounded the stage; from a quick estimate, the sections probably had around fifteen rows a piece, each row about twenty or so centimeters higher than the row prior. If I had to guess, I'd say each section held a little more than a hundred seats, making four hundred in total. A small scoff nearly escaped my throat; Toyls was notorious for its small graduation sizes, but this was just sad.

Looking up, there was a balcony above, overlooking the main stage. This room was nothing more than a boast of power, meant to draw people in for the minuscule hope that one day they'd afford a place with these same silver and white pillars with animal toppers.

Wait. I turned back to the pillar and looked up. It reached up just below and in front of the balcony, so close that if you reached your hand through the railing, you could almost touch the mane of a giant bronze lion topper, one of four shoved on the single pillar. Looking around the room, there were eight pillars in total, two guarding each set of stairs to access the higher rows of seats and two guarding the entrance. Each had four lions facing separate directions, the only distinguishing difference being engravings on a thick belt the lions perched upon. Straining my neck to get a better look, I studied the horse carved into the two pillars I was closest to, then turned my attention to the other six pillars. An elephant posed gracefully inside the belt of pillars guarding the right stairwell, a lion in its place on the left, and glaring at me from across the room, a cow or buffalo of some type. No, not a buffalo. Suddenly, my stomach was in my throat; memories of my time in the library flooded my vision. No, that wasn't a buffalo. It was an ox. These were cheap knockoffs, well definitely not *cheap,* but a mockery of the Ashokan Pillar at Sarnath nonetheless. I'm not sure what caught me off guard so much. People made recreations of important monuments all the time; my uncle used to tell me fables of his time spent in some place called *Vegas* when he visited the States. Apparently, they had their own Eiffel Tower, Pyramids, and even the infamous Caesar's Palace, but those were tributes. These just seemed. . . disrespectful, not to mention horribly inaccurate.

"ATTENTION!" A voice boomed from center stage; a small, plump woman in a matching brown pants suit stood speaking against a microphone, a jumble of papers in her clutch. For a brief moment, I thought it might be the in famed Headmaster. Madam Toyls didn't appear much on the news as more than a voice for security reasons, but something about this woman didn't match the aura of confidence and supremacy that radiated from the image of Toyls founder.

"PLEASE BE SEATED; WE WILL BE---MO-- ---TARILY. Jesus Christ almighty, can't a girl get a decent mic around here?" There was a wave of giggles followed by the lady's face draining of color when she realized we could all hear the second part. I found my seat in the back row of the western section, closest to the exit. My hands shook as I tried to hide them inside the fuzzy interior pockets of my jacket. I was certain people could see right through me and they were just plotting how beneficial it was to keep me around.

"Nervous?" The boy seated next to me asked, looking at my hands. "It'sokaymetoo," He spoke with a fast and high-pitched tone, jumbling several words together despite desperately trying to act cool. He took a deep breath, waiting for my response; when I didn't give one, he continued. "Sorry. I hear no one even knows what the exams are about. God, I hope they're not strength based."

"I'm sure they're not," I lied, turning straight ahead to watch the lady fumble with more papers.

"Ya..." His voice was nothing more than a disappointed whimper, sending a pang of guilt through my stomach.

"Attention again!" The lady spoke through a new microphone. There were about two dozen upperclassmen handing out pamphlets to each of us. "Before we can begin with exams, you must complete a physical examination and register."

I looked around the packed room; there had to be at least three hundred of us, and I couldn't imagine this taking less than forever. "I'd like to say welcome to all of you, and I hope to see the majority of you succeed today. I'd like to remind you that not being selected this year is perfectly okay. You can always work harder and retry again next year; do not be discouraged. With that happy note, physicals and registration will be held in Gymnasium #3." I took a couple of pamphlets from the girl walking past, handing one to the boy next to me, his face lighting up at the empty gesture.

"I wish you all prosperity and luck!" The lady spoke before exiting through a small spiral staircase located on the upper left corner of the stage. People began flooding out the doors. God, this was a bad design, only having one exit for a room designed to fit a little over four hundred people. Once we were outside, the gym was relatively easy to find, seeing as it was just down the path a bit.

"I'm Calvin, by the way. Calvin Everette." The boy from the auditorium said, struggling to keep up with my intentionally fast pace.

"Lu-Lily," I conceded finally. It was apparent I was stuck with him for now, but at first glance, there was no way this short, awkward boy would be enrolled by next week. Thin, close-cropped strawberry blond hair and shocking blue eyes provided a strange combo with his childlike face and even more childlike frame. He didn't look older than thirteen. What was he doing here?

"Well, Lulily-" he began, getting cut off almost immediately; my stumble earlier was practically costly.

"Just Lily," I said, trying to hide the disdain in the lie.

"Okay, Lily, what made you want to join the MES?" Panic welled up inside, this was not a question Burn and I had gone over to prepare for.

"I-umm, same as everyone else, I guess; the machigai are dangerous and need to be contained." How convincing was that? Mrs. Madalini was right; this plan was doomed to fail because of me.

"I wouldn't say everyone, but it's a solid reason, yes." He stared at the ground.

"What about you kid? What's your reason for being here?"

"Me? Oh well, I- I'm. Really. . . I just want to understand them." Ahh yes, my favorite form of learning about a creature - brutally torturing and slaughtering them until they go extinct. The urge to roll my eyes and leave was unbearable, but we were only a few paces away from the gym, and Burn would absolutely annihilate me if I left before exams ever started.

"What's there to understand?" I muttered, trying not to let my emotions shine through too obviously. Either this kid was really oblivious to tones, or he simply didn't care.

"You don't seriously believe everything the news says, do you? The average life expectancy for a machigai is 25 years old. They're children; what compels them to kill and destroy everything they encounter?"

Kill and destroy. I've done my fair share of both, but it was always necessary. The rules were to kill to see another day or stay pure and die of starvation on the streets.

"There's no correct answer to that. As far as we know, they still have nervous systems and comprehension levels, meaning each machigai will have different reasons behind their actions." I quickly added at the end: "It's our job to make sure their actions have consequences." *Severe consequences.* "Either way, I'd better go get the forms and stuff taken care of." I took off towards the female side of the gym, desperate to escape the awkward conversation.

Chapter 18: Exams vs. Escape

Physicals weren't nearly as bad as I believed they were going to be. I simply handed the files Mrs. Madalini had given me to the lady sitting at registration, she opened them and gave me an unreadable look.

"You dyed your hair," she said pointedly, staring at my faded blue highlights. They really deserved a touchup. The last time I redyed them was before Jay took me to the machigai, over a month ago. Oh, Lord, it *had* already been over a month. Everything still felt like such a fever dream; like I would wake up any moment in our old house. I gave the lady a feeble nod and tried for a sugary smile. This seemed to please her. "It looks good," she said, returning my smile.

I breathed a sigh of relief. "Thank you, ma'am," An attempt at fluttering my eyelashes was made, but there's an 80% chance that, from the look on her face, she thought I was close to having a seizure. I quickly scuttled out of there to avoid her comparing me to the I.D. picture any longer. I made my way to the first station for the physicals and then to the next. One by one, I was weighed, my eyesight was tested, my height was taken, and the physician used a tiny hammer to apparently "see if my reflexes were working properly," although, by her facial expression, it wasn't far-fetched to say she just wanted to hit me with a hammer. She even did it a few extra times despite my leg twitching after the first hit. I was sure I'd have a bruise on my knee later in the day.

At the end of the examination, she handed me a small file that contained a few pamphlets explaining the history of Toyls, as well as a barcoded card on a lanyard that I was instructed to always keep around my neck. She then assigned me the letter A and pointed me to a gathering group of people in the far corner. In the wise words of John Mulaney, "Yeah, oh, we were a swell bunch of kids in Group A," or something of that magnitude. Most of his act was some big blur that escaped my memory, but the joke seemed quite fitting in a terrifyingly ironic way. All of us in group A sort of shuffled around nervously, a bunch of scared children in a place they didn't know.

"Lily!" I had to stifle a groan before plastering a fake smile and spinning around to watch Calvin waving me down, approaching from his side of the gym.

"Group A?" Even my own ears heard the irritation bleeding into the question, but Calvin didn't even flinch.

"Yessir, you too?" I nodded hesitantly, almost thinking it was worthwhile to lie and flee to another Group. "That's awesome! Now we can look out for each other- I wonder what tests they'll have us pass." A part of my brain tingled, wondering how exactly Burn knew what we were going to be doing and how many resources the machigai actually had.

"Not a clue," I lied bluntly, once more tugging on the hem of my black jacket.

The shadows under my shoes buzzed with every step as the rest of Group A, my new puppy, and I followed a tall, dark-skinned woman dressed in retired MES garments. I held my breath with every turn of her head to look back at us.

"Nervous?" the puppy whispered as we entered a metal building that appeared to be a shooting range.

"A bit," I shrugged; anxiety was an easier answer than the truth. "How's your shooting?"

"Eh, average. Not my worst category. I might possibly be screwed if we have to do hand-to-hand combat. I'm best at strategy, or sometimes strength-agility maybe? Not fully sure, just NOT AT ALL good at hand-to-hand combat- you know? Anyways, I'm working on it, but it's hard to practice hand-to-hand by yourself- you know?"

"Mhm," I zoned out as he continued speaking, focusing on the instructor and the little gold tassels draping the figureless black suit she wore and the small maple leaf flag patchworked onto her chest. *T. Hammele,* her tag read. It didn't ring a bell, which wasn't surprising since any MES officer I'd been close enough to read their tag was likely a corpse.

"Lily?" Calvin aggressively poked at my shoulder.

"Ow! What!" I whisper yelled at him, rubbing my soon-to-be second bruise.

"Oops, sorry!" Calvin shrunk back, making him look even more pitiful. *This kid's gonna get eaten alive.* I took a deep breath and leveled my voice.

"Apology accepted; I'm sorry for snapping. What were you saying?" A huge smile cracked through his face as he looked up at me with those big blue puppy eyes.

"I was askin-"

"THAT'S ENOUGH!" The crowd of 100 or so in Group A fell to an explosive silence as Hammele spun around, only slightly, on us first few applicants. A sarcastic urge to say something dumb over the silence was bit back by the intimidating aura of the MES officer in front of me, her pencil-straight spine exaggerating her already towering height. "LISTEN UP," she spoke with power and volume, yet levelly; she didn't quite shout; she simply made her regular tone louder. Odd. "I WILL BE YOUR DIRECTOR AND PERFORMANCE MANAGER FOR THE DAY; YOUR FUTURE -OR LACK THEREOF- HERE AT TOYLS IS RELIANT ON ME. MY NAME IS THEADORA HAMMELE, BUT YOU WILL ONLY ADDRESS ME BY LIEUTENANT, LIEUTENANT HAMMELE, OR PROFESSOR HAMMELE, ANYTHING ELSE, AND YOU WILL BE REMOVED FROM THE PREMISES IMM-EE-DI-ATE-LY!! AFFIRMATIVE?"

"AFFIRMATIVE LIEUTENANT!" the crowd shouted in return.

A ghostly smile peaked through Hammele's stony expression; she enjoyed the respect, and I couldn't blame her. As loaded as the title Lieutenant sounds, the MES divides their officers into two sections. The lower officers: the privates, corporals, and sergeants; were nothing more than secretaries, file workers, and assistants, maybe occasionally disposable pawns against smaller machigai. As far as the higher-level officers: the lieutenants, captains, majors, colonels, and generals; the lieutenants were the lowest ranked you could get. Maybe they could order around a private or two, but mainly, they spent their time training detectives, working as lab assistants, or doing pitiful favors for Toyls', such as showing around a bunch of potential students who would one day surpass them. As tall, muscular and physically flawless as Lieutenant Hammele was, chances were I could overpower her on the spot with minimum effort. The thought gave me a sickly buzz of power. The shadows under my heels suddenly felt much more controllable as they welled up with energy. *I could kill everyone here; why should I be afraid of THEM?* They had killed so, SO many of my people, and they made my brother and my family suffer immense pain; why shouldn't I take back just a little bit right now? Unfortunately, that wasn't an option, cutting off a fingernail out of an entire army would do nothing long term. Burn was right; we needed to cut off the head for real vengeance.

"Obviously, your first exam will be all about gun power and accuracy. File into eight lines, into each of the ranges."

We followed her instructions; Calvin and I both fled to the farthest-over section as several students fell in line behind us. The section was bordered by bulletproof glass, tunneling around a single target. I had no idea how shooting at the same target repeatedly could possibly test someone's skill accurately.

"Inside your files, there will be a key card; remove it and scan it over the screen before you." Hammele now sat in an isolated glass box that hung above the center section. She was speaking through a microphone that echoed through the range, like a child screeching in a back alley in the dead of night. That was certainly a visual thought…

In our section there hung a standard 9mm pistol. I fiddled with the trigger on the gun for a moment, weighing it in my palm, it was heavier than mine, with a much stiffer trigger.

"Girl in section #1," Hammele rang. "You are being time-limited."

My first shot fired.

***

Turns out, the one small target could shift between 30 and 100 meters and could measure exactly how close your bullet was to the bullseye. We were given ten shots with each gun, which sounds like it would go by fast, right? No. Not even close. One hundred kids, eight different guns: a 9mm pistol, .50 caliber sniper, 20 gauge shotgun, MP5 smg, a crossbow (most people didn't do well on that one), compound bow (or that one), .45 Colt revolver, and an automatic rifle. It took maybe an hour or so to get through the collective 8,000 shots, which was especially painful, seeing as I wrongfully chose to start my section. I was one of the first to finish and was stuck waiting with Calvin for a decent amount of our time there.

Finally, we were freed from the musty, gun-powered, and BO-filled range that had most definitely caused permanent hearing damage that would haunt us for the rest of our adolescence. FUNSIES FIRST DAY. But no, Madam Treetop led us completely across the campus back down to the entrance, but instead of leaving to peacefully return home, we were drug across the main lawn into possibly one of the largest open-sky arenas I had ever seen. Wait, had I actually ever seen an open-sky arena? Well, there goes that comparison, lovely. You get the idea, it was big, like REALLY BIG. Doming upwards only slightly to reveal one of those balcony-catwalk thingies that no one actually knows the name of, but in operas, it's really expensive to sit in despite not having the greatest view of the stage, ya, that thing. The base was nearly a kilometer stretch of sod terrain; like I said before, REALLY BIG.

"You are standing in the world's largest, most advanced, most realistic, terrain morphing training facility. Everyone take a few steps back into the entrance please." Hammele shooed us off of the sod as she turned to a silver keypad attached to the wall, A1A324. *A1A324, A1A324.* I could not forget that. My hand slipped into my jacket sleeve, summoning a small void, barely the size of a fingertip, which dropped out a sharpie before evaporating into thin air. While Hammele was turned, I jotted the code onto my palm and zipped the sharpie into my jacket pocket.

"What was that?" Calvin whispered.

"I-ummm, the code?" I stuttered and panicked.

"Ohhhh, ya. Smart. Like if the teachers all get killed or something, understandable." My brow furrowed questioningly at him, before simply accepting his statement with a concerned nod. Hammele removed a single garage door opener from behind the keypad. With a single click, the sod fell out from below the arena, and a new floor of sand was covered by a thin sheet of crystal glass. The glass slid back away, leaving a stunning beach of white sand.

"Lieutenant?" Calvin asked meekly. For a moment, I saw his hand raise up to poke her like he did me, but he apparently rethought it.

"Yes, private?"

Calvin flushed. "Well-I, Ummm; I wouldn't say- not a private yet, Lieutenant. Glass!"

"Glass?" I resisted the strong urge to laugh at the confused expression plastered all over the Lieutenant's face, and the identically funny expression of embarrassment that plagued Calvin's. Taking a few deep breaths and regaining my composure, I tuned back into their still awkward conversation.

"YA! Sorry... Lieutenant, but, ummm- why the glass? If it just gets removed, Lieutenant."

Hammele smiled; she very obviously enjoyed the feeling of intimidation she produced. "They tried it without, but the sand just slid off into the mechanics below; the designers added sides and the glass top to it in order to prevent such a thing; the sides stay up, and the glass top leaves. Question answered?"

"Yes, Good- good design." Lieutenant Legs nodded and headed onto the sand to help some privates arrange strange-looking boxes amongst other things. I nudged Calvin in the ribs, followed by a slight eyebrow raise, causing him to flush once more and look away. Stifling another laugh, we watched as Hammele approached us from the sand. A group of over a dozen officers dressed in standardized MES field uniforms, tight-fitted black shirts with loose matching BDU pants, topped off with their signature gun holders along with gold and blue embellishments, trailed closely behind her.

"For your next section of the exam, you will be tested not only on your speed and strength but rather your battle comprehension and strategy. Quick thinking is how you will survive now." Hammele shouted, her voice no longer as power-hungry as it had been through our other exercises. "Behind me stand the province of Quebec's seventeen Machigai Enforcement Squad Majors. You are in the presence of some of the best officers in standing service to our great province." Oh, that's why her confidence was wavering; she was hopelessly outranked and outclassed. It was one thing to be able to manipulate your mind to believe that you were special in the presence of meak children, it was another to convince it of your own power while being circled by people who could crush you like a bug beneath their heel without even an ounce of effort. . "They will not only be your judges for this but... also your enemy." Murmurs went through the crowd behind me; really, *a dramatic plot twist?* A little cliche, a little boring, and a lot expected.

"Thank you, Thea." A slightly shorter but extremely muscular man amongst the Major's patted her shoulder, dissipating the last of the Lieutenant's rigorous display. She awkwardly shuffled up the staircase leading to the balcony. "Major Malcome #3" the tag attached to his chest read. Unlike Hammele I did recognize him, not from real life, but rather the TV at the cafes. He was the major commanding the Capitale-Nationale branch, which was held in Quebec City; in fact, the high-security zone we raided a month or so back would likely been one of their facilities. Malcolm spent most of his energy posing for the press at conferences and drafting wordy statements about the MES's recent "steps towards machigai containment." When Aska first went missing, he was always the one I pictured in my mind delivering the announcement that the gruesome Soul Stealer had finally been put down, citizens cheering in the background as they often did during such marvelous achievements. My fingers wriggled and squirmed, trying desperately to relieve some of the tension in my muscles without drawing too much attention as the major instructed us on what the next exam would entail. From what little I gathered from the discussion, we were playing a lengthier and more complicated game of tag (really impressive, I know). The twelve majors would play against one hundred of us on a square kilometer stretch of land. As someone who had been outrunning the majors my whole life, it seemed rather familiar. That familiarity was outstretched when Major Malcome pressed the second button from the remote, and all the boxes they had placed earlier expanded into small to medium-sized buildings, creating the cutest miniature city you had ever seen.

"Cheap knockoffs," Malcome muttered. "Those of you who are enlisted will get to experience the real simulation during training; sometimes your teachers will have you build them yourselves, but most times, the stage is set by privates."

"That being said," One of the other majors approached. "GO!" For a moment, we stood there, slightly confused on the premise, before those of us in the front were soon pushed forward by those in the back, and everyone took off.

There were most definitely cameras everywhere, which made discrete aid from my curse more difficult, but on the bright side, scouting with Jay and Tresa made me very comfortable with heights and the tops of buildings. Almost immediately, I found the tallest building; disappointment sat in when I entered. The buildings were all hollowed out, no stairs or rooms, which made sense logically due to how compact they were in the containers, but there were a few items placed sporadically. Nothing too useful: random household stuff mainly, some (slightly creepy) stuffed animals, a pillow or two, and clothes hangers. Then I struck gold. One domestic house's exterior was decorated with strands of Christmas lights, and the roof was decently low set, allowing me to use one of the hangers to jump and hook the lights, ripping the beginning of a strand down. I yanked the end to test how secure it was, then took off up the side of the house. Once at the top, I removed the rest of the strand. This house had a horrible advantage, not to mention it was short enough that one of the taller majors would most definitely pull themselves up, and there would be nowhere for me to run. I had removed the lights, but without Jay holding the end, there was no way to actually use them.

A loud buzzer sound startled me to the point of nearly slipping off the peaked roof. Following the noise, my eyes made contact with a mega projector screen, possibly the size of one of the houses, that hung on the western wall of the arena. Names lit the board, and one by one, some were crossed out. Every time a line appeared through a name, shortly thereafter, a number appeared next to it. My first thought was that the numbers were scores, how well the person had done, but after a moment, it dawned on me they were the region numbers of the major who had tagged them out. The screen shifted to a new group of twenty, and then another after that, all listed in alphabetical order.

I pried my eyes from the screen. All there was to know was that I hadn't been tagged out yet, therefore I had to keep moving before a major found me. A house to the left of me had a makeshift satellite dish attached to the top. *Perfect,* I thought before tying the end of the lights into a loop. *Dear whoever the god of yee haw cowboy-isms is, please let this work.* Whoever they were, seemed to take pity on my soul because, on the 5th attempt, the lasso latched sturdily around the dish. From there, it was a simple rope and repeat, just like scouting. Suddenly I was bursting with excitement just to shove it in Burn's face that my "days off" scouting, instead of rigorous training, were actually saving his ass (pardon my French).

It felt good to be high off the ground again. Not all the buildings were close enough to jump to or had anything the lights could use as a proper pillar, but out of the four surrounding sides, there was always the option to turn back, or typically there was another solution. Three majors gaped as I passed them from above, two of which attempted to climb the side of the house I was on at the time, but once they were on the rooftop I had already hopped to the next house, leaving them in my trail. Despite knowing discreteness was key, during the first twenty minutes or so, my ego thrived off the boost that came with every applicant or major's stunned expression upon seeing me. Once their looks became boring, I, in turn, lost my show spirit, ducking behind peaks of houses or hiding in nooks to catch my breath. Some others attempted to copy my strategy, only to either fail to mount the roof or get stuck, not knowing how to switch to the next house.

With only thirty applicants remaining, they crunched the final names to only one screen, so it no longer shifted. Apparently, Calvin was shockingly still alive, probably hunkered down hiding somewhere.

As I caught my breath on one particular house, something glinted in the burning sun below, catching my eye. Before I could tell what it was, someone came screeching around the corner. They dramatically summer-salted down half the alley before popping back up, and half ran- half hobbled away. Tight on their tail was a major, who did not see the need to slow himself down with a summer salt when in high pursuit. Big mistake. If you ever see someone do something seemingly inconvenient during a high-adrenaline scenario, question it, please, because this particular fellow did not. The glinting object was clear duct tape; several long strands, stretching from wall to wall, and then another section a few feet behind that and two more behind that one. By the time the major stumbled through all the layers, he looked like a fragile package all wrapped up, and the kid was long gone.

I unfortunately laughed at this precious scene, attracting the attention of a very unhappy wad of tape. The major's eyes locked on me and he began to scale the base of my house with frightening speed and agility; I quickly turned to the opposite side and tossed my lights, something that, with practice, had become second nature. I tightened the remaining slack and jumped, already running when my feet made contact with the siding. The major had already pulled himself up to the building behind me as I wrapped my lights back up and jumped to the next building just for safety. The major gave me a stern glare before running and jumping off the house he was at. For a brief moment, I thought he might've died, hit the pavement, and went splat from his ego, but two sets of fingers peeped over the edge. I muttered a few inappropriate phrases and took off, lassoing to the farthest possible roof. Every time I checked, he was no more than two roofs behind me. My mind raced for a solution, a subtle trick that he would overlook, allowing me to escape, because when it came down to endurance, it was blatantly clear who would win. It never came to that. Soon enough, he was gone, fallen hopefully, with lots of injuries so he wouldn't prove a problem again.

The scoreboard revealed that another ten kids had been caught, leaving only twenty of us remaining. A glimpse of something in the alley below caught my eye, and then another. I peeped over the roof to see the duct tape kid setting up his newest trap. The hood of his jacket fell down briefly, revealing pale strawberry-blond hair.

"Calvin?" He turned around, and his face lit up as he approached. The hobble from earlier was apparent in his right leg. "What happened?"

"Landed poorly on my ankle while rolling under duct tape. It's nothing. How's roof life going? I've seen you jumping; everyone is quite impressed."

"Not a lot of excitement, to be honest, but it's a safe route for--6 O'CLOCK!" A major turned the corner, maybe five or six blocks back.

"What?" He flinched, looking around.

"BEHIND YOU! 6 O'CLOCK!" In a moment, he was off, although his hobble was slowing him down tremendously, allowing the major to gain ground. I hopped from roof to roof, keeping up with Calvin as he twisted and turned. I called out how far back the major was every once in a while, so he didn't have to check. "Five blocks, four blocks!" Then at three blocks, something hit me. Dashing ahead, I called to Calvin while dropping down the end of the lights.

"Climb!" It took him a second to register before taking the makeshift rope. As he climbed, I lifted, helping him to the top and out of reach from the major in no time. The major didn't even try to jump up; he simply stood there smirking before-

"AGH!" Calvin screamed next to me, a hand gripping my shirt from the back, lifting me just a few inches off the roof.

"Tag."

Chapter 19: The Blind Side

The major who caught us was the same from the roof chase earlier. Undoubtedly, the whole thing was a ruse—a good one, I'll give them that—but a ruse. We allowed them to scan our cards and as we walked back to the entrance, the scoreboard crossed us out. Major Necussor from branch #9 took claim over me, and Major Charon from branch #8 took claim over Calvin. No wonder they worked so well together; their territories bordered each other. Necussor and I walked together in dead silence. He was the officer responsible for the chase on the roof, and it was apparent from the gashes of blood on his hands, that he was not mine or Calvin's biggest fan at this moment in time. Charon on the other hand was a rather chatty fellow, him and Calvin hitting it off immediately, comparing strategies and complimenting each other's techniques. I think at one point in our lengthy walk back I even overheard the Major giving Calvin advise on women.

The majors abandoned us about one hundred meters away from the entrance, without any instructions as to where we were to go next. Calvin's mood quickly deteriorated as we searched for our classmates and the Lieutenant.

"We did fine if that's what you're worried about."

He nodded. "You were really great out there. You wouldn't have gotten caught if you didn't try to help me. I know that, and they do too; it'll be taken into consideration." Panic rose up for a moment; if Burn ever found out what had just happened… He'd call me weak. Foolish. It was instinctual, just like helping Aska or Jay… yet it was enough to be considered a near criminal against my own kind. No, he could never find out.

Out of nowhere, a female with slicked-back red hair came sprinting up behind us. She was a few centimeters shorter than myself. The convincing deer-in-headlights look led both Calvin and me to stare behind her, waiting for the MES officer in pursuit to turn the corner, but no one ever did.

"Tag and tag." She tapped us both, dropping the frightened expression and quickly pulling her badge from her back pocket. *Major Monet #6.* Region #6 would be around Montreal. Montreal stood at the 4th highest machigai crime rate in all of Canada topped only by Calgary, Victoria, and Brampton. Which in turn meant the highest machigai population and highest death rate in Quebec. Depending on where you look, the Montreal MES squad was either hated or worshiped, no in between.

"Sorry, Ma'am-"

"Major," she cut Calvin off softly, but with an edge, a subtle command that hung in the air.

"I'm so sorry- I didn't mean- I."

"Major, I believe what my comrade is trying to say is that we've already been tagged out." I gestured to the board and then offered my hand to shake. "Lilian Madalini and this is Calvin Everette"

"Pleasure." She took my hand; her skin was calloused and rough. I'm not sure what I expected from her line of work, but then again, MES officers rarely lived long enough around me for me to shake their hand.

"I don't suppose the others will need my help to tag out ten untrained teenagers; I'll walk you two back to the balcony to meet your lieutenant."

"Thank you, Major," Calvin said softly, trying to shrink up from his cocoon.

"No need to withdrawal over a single mistake, young man. You'll learn that soon enough once you begin training; now hurry up; your day isn't over yet."

***

"When I met her, she seemed so nice." The garden was stunning at this hour, just before sunset. My uncle used to call this part of the evening shimmer time because of the way the sky gave everything beneath it, a shimmering metallic glow, but then again, he also drank a lot. My arm looped through Burn's as we walked through the trails, listening to the fall birds chirp. Once I returned to the hotel after exams, he immediately drugged me outside to inform him privately of all that had happened.

"She tends to put on a sweeter facade around her daughter," he laughed for the first time since the night I arrived. Everything felt lighter now without the vigorous training and screaming, without the stress of exams weighing over our every moment. Now, what was done was done, and we simply had to wait till next week for results.

After the very intense and mature game of children's tag, we concluded with generalized testing. After a day of abstinence, my curse had been itching for some use, bumping my lifting up nearly sixty lbs from my natural strength and fifteen lbs from my average weight session with Burn. "See what happens when you actually give it a break?" I had joked earlier. Even with the massive boost from my curse, my maxes for almost every lift were still only slightly above average, especially by Toyls standards, but it should be enough to push through to the top 25% of applicants.

"The only machigai other than Lily she's even remotely warmed up to is Tresa." Burn continued, pushing my thoughts back to Mrs. Madalini.

"Well, who wouldn't adore Tresa? She's a sparkling conversationalist." He gave a half laugh.

"She's loyal and powerful, with morals, but yes, verbal communication is less than her specialty." He did that dramatic stare-into-the-distance thing that you always see in movies when people talk. Burn was something of a sort; most of the time, I couldn't distinguish what was an act and what was personality. At moments, he seemed no less than make-believe, but then again, don't we all feel that way at times? "She's my number two, you know, second in command?"

"Your number two." I looked him dead in the eyes. "I guess you could say she's the shit."

After a long pause where he just stared deadpan at my face, he turned and said, "Jay ruined you," and continued walking.

"Maybe," I shrugged, "It's kinda odd, though, isn't it?"

"What is?"

"You know those stupid cliche machigai gang-style movies, where we are made out to be like mob bosses?"

"You think the cops scare me? I am machigai!" he banged on his chest, mocking an awful Russian accent

"Why are we always made out to be Russian? Russia only has ⅔ the machigai population we do! It's insulting!"

"Out of all the awful things in those movies, that's what you choose to be upset about?"

I shrugged and carried on. "Those movies, they always end with the head machigai dying, and everything is left to his young, innocent next of kin; what's with that?"

"No clue, blame The State's trash Hollywood for perpetuating those stereotypes."

"Believe me, I blame more than just them. Would you ever-?"

"Not a chance," he answered without skipping a beat, his arm tensing beneath my fingertips.

"You didn't even know what I was gonna say!"

"You were gonna ask if I'd ever leave this mess to Lina, and the answer is dead no, it's too dangerous for a little girl."

"You're right, I suppose. How is Lina anyway? I haven't seen much of her the last few weeks," he untensed, as if glad to have strayed from the topic of his sister's future.

"Probably hiding out either in the penthouse or the first-floor lobby. She conned her way into a job helping Mrs. Madalini in the hotel," he smiled. "Assists room service, customer complaints, reservations, anything that she doesn't need sight for. Great tips; the guests love her."

"Who wouldn't?" I laughed. "I'll have to go visit her sometime."

"She'd like that. No one except Lily can really go up there. There are too many people, and most of our faces are too well known these days," he shrugged, turning us back towards the door and picking up the pace ever so slightly.

"Burn?"

"Hm"

"Are you trying to use me to spy on your little sister?"

"Yes, now run along, little shadow." He slightly nudged me inside and pointed me towards the stairs leading to the main hotel. "Thanks for catching me up on exams, now shoo." He slammed the doors shut behind me.

"You would think spying on an extremely secure defense school for eight hours would be enough," I muttered, slumbering up the long staircase. "Nooo, now I have to spy on my own ally because someone's a helicopter brother."

The moment Lily's eyes fell on me in the front lobby, I was done for. She charged and swooped me up in a hug, leaving my feet a few centimeters off the ground. Her skin was comfortingly warm against mine, leaving traces of a fruity-like fragrance- strawberries, possibly.

"Girls!" Mrs. Madalini snapped in her pristine tone from behind the counter.

"Sorry, Mom!" Lily took my hand and began dragging me down the left corridor. "Let's go up to the penthouse, and you can tell me everything about the exams." She clicked a polished silver button that stood out against the sweet cream-colored walls. The upper hotel was so shiny and well-kept compared to the basement; everything seemed to glitter with gold or silver, leaving my eyes burning while still longing to see more. For a moment, everything slipped away, just me and Lily in some amazing, wondrous place. She scanned a special card on a touchscreen pad, and then, just as the elevator doors began to close, my hand latched out forcibly, stopping them.

"Alina!" I said, probably a bit too loudly. "I was gonna talk to Alina." For a moment, something passed over Lily's face, making her already doe-ish features even more sad.

"Lina- Lina, of course!" she said, regaining her pep. "She's on break upstairs anyhow, so I guess that'll work out splendidly. I released the doors; a part of me twinged to reach for the hand I had so ungratefully dropped a moment ago but ultimately decided against it. Lily hummed awkward elevator music as the numbers slowly went up one by one: L 3, L 4, L 5. Did I offend her by asking about Alina? L 10, L11, and we came to a smooth halt on the floor labeled Penthouse 28.

"28?" I asked Lily as the doors slid open.

"It's my mother's lucky number; Papa designed the whole hotel in her honor when they married; everything is supposed to be a subtle homage to her. Romantic, right?"

"LIIIINA!" she shouted as we entered. The penthouse was huge; there was no other way to explain it, except maybe "grand" or "impressive." okay, maybe the phrase "No other way to explain it" doesn't really fit that well; if anything, there was too much to describe, an open entrance hall with creamy walls and oak wood accents, ceilings higher than you would think possible for a single floor, and across the room there was a marvelous polished oak floating staircase leading up to a loft larger than most people's apartments.

"I'm currently robbing your room. Can you come back later?" Alina shouted from up in the loft.

"No can do! You have a guest!"

"Guest?" Her head popped out of one of the lofted rooms. "Who?" she asked, staring nearly directly at us.

"Onyx," I shouted up to her.

"Ugh," she groaned. "Brother dearest sent you, didn't he?" She half laughed, gracefully gliding down the stairwell. Lily bounced across the room to a little living area, a couch, and a 150 cm television on the wall. She sat down On the fluffy wool rug, and I took the couch. Alina reached us and felt along the back of the couch before maneuvering around and walking into Lily.

"Ow," Lily laughed, rubbing her shoulder. "Watch it."

"Haha, you're so funny." Alina sat down next to me. "Sooo Onyx, do tell me, what's new in the basement?"

"You haven't heard?" Lily asked without turning around. "Onyx took Radio's place at Toyls; she was actually just going to tell me about her time at the entrance exams before we made our way up here."

"Ohhhhh, that sounds interesting. Lot more fun than running around the hotel. How'd it go?"

"Decently, I think, not a lot to tell, really. We did the standardized strength testing and gun range and played tag. Less than eventful."

"Do you think you got in?"

"Good question… I guess we'll find out." I shrugged and leaned back. Lina laughed.

"That all sounds amazing, I wish I would've gone,"

"What do you mean?"

"Soul Stealer never told you?" She softened her voice. "Figures, Blaise never tells me anything either."

"Blake was the original," Lily started. "Seemed perfect; before the incident, he was in pretty good shape, mobile, fast. Burn trained him just as hard as he did you. Not to mention, his curse is radio; he can speak through other people's minds, as well as knock out electricity, so it fits that he should be the one to be a spy."

"But then Blaise made the mistake of taking him on a raid, *the raid*," Alina said quietly. "He was out of commission; that's when Bluejay started going off on rants to my brother about you and how you would fit the role. Stealer was less than thrilled at the idea of getting you involved and turned to me. Started training me, and eventually-"

"Was he the one that-"

"Did this?" she gestured to her gray, unfocused eyes, raising an eyebrow. "God, no, that was mainly Blaise."

"What?!"

"Different story for a different time, darling," she patted my knee. "Basically, Soul Stealer started privately training me, with the idea that with the right persuasion together, we would convince my brother to send me. It was a win-win: you would be safe, and I would get out of that stuffy basement. In short, Blaise found out and metaphorically ripped Aska to pieces, nearly locking me in our room for the rest of my life. Aska was put on probation, along with several other punishments, and has stayed that way." She took a remorseful breath in. "Poor guy, if anything, he sold Blaise on bringing you here. My brother pretends to be all logic, but in reality this whole scheme might as well just be a middle finger right in Aska's face."

"Don't pity him too much; his idiocy was the one who sold me to come here, to begin with. If it wasn't for that, I probably would've stayed home, and you would've gotten your freedom."

She laughed. "You make a compelling point."

Chapter 20: Lil' Schoolgirl

We spent the next several days in excruciating anxiety, waiting for something, anything. That was the issue; Toyls never even told us how we would know who got in and who... well, didn't. According to Lily and Alina, the news typically would broadcast a list of the new students, but we had no way of knowing when that would be, so together, every day, the twelve of us would gather around the bar, silently staring at the 6 pm news. Even Blake, who was slowly gaining more mobility, got wheeled out to watch.

Finally, one day, we got something. I twiddled my thumbs, arms wrapped around Ilse, who sat between my legs on the countertop. Lily braided Lulu's hair next to us, and to my right, Clark sat atop Jay's shoulders on the barstool, giggling as he bounced up and down. Suddenly, the news reporter's false smile grew as large as the Grinch's heart on Christmas day.

"I'm sure you all are waiting for the same thing out there; here it is," She spoke proudly. "436 applicants, one of the largest turnouts in years, and only 80 accepted to the most prestigious training academy in the country. These are the next M.E.S. hopefuls." The screen went dark, as one by one, names slid into the 80 slots alphabetically; the reporter recited each individual as they joined the others on screen.

"M. M. M." I could hear Burn muttering.

"Chaise Lindsey. . ." the news lady continued. I gripped Ilse's hand, trying not to squeeze her frail bones too hard. "Fruydence Luide. . ." No one dared move or even breathe. "Irene Lysine. . ." Behind the counter, the shadows of alcohol bottles seemed to melt towards me. "Duke Macow. . ." *Come on, please.* "Lilian Madalini." the room erupted immediately; Lulu fell off the counter as Lily jumped up. Aska picked her up off the ground and swung her around before placing the young girl back upright and sitting down, panting, but with the biggest smile. Lily embraced me and Ilse, the tingly static feeling radiating through my whole body warmly. She fell back onto the counter, giggling with beads of sweat pooling on her temple. Clark screamed, suddenly landing hard on the stool as the familiar BlueJay took to the air, circling the room and cawing excitedly.

"Enough!!" Burn shouted, silencing the room. BlueJay landed on my head quietly as Burn lifted his glass of sparkling cider. "A toast! To Onyx!"

Jay fell back off my head onto the counter, shifting back into his regular self and laying flat. "IT TAKES AN INCREDIBLY SPECIAL IDIOT TO PULL OFF WHAT YOU HAVE DONE!! " His complexion was only slightly greener than normal. "To our lil' schoolgirl!"

"Here! Here!" Everyone else shouted; even Burn had a stupid grin as he ripped off his slowly melting leather gloves. Tresa tossed him a new pair from behind the bar, then resumed watching over the already half-asleep Lily. Looking around the room, you would think we had just returned from a raid, not that we were celebrating. Aska had retreated to the corner of the room, cautiously scanning over his hands, which had turned a purplish-black at the fingers. His curse was searching for a sinned soul. It would die down soon enough, but for now he was hyper-aware of how dangerous he was. In the meantime, Tresa handed Jay a precautious bucket as he struggled to resume an upright position. Lina beamed at me briefly and mouthed what looked like a congratulations before she returned to facing Burn, who seemed to be demanding she allow him to guide her back to the lobby entrance. I only caught bits and pieces, but there was something said along the lines of "Dear lord, Blaise!! If I could roll my eyes, I would." Before Lina promptly made her leave, her cane still hanging on the loop of her belt, up until she neared the door. It was quite impressive how well she had the basement layout mapped in her head, although from what I could tell, she had spent quite a bit of time here. Without Lily's supervision or Jay's entertainment, Clark, Lulu, and Ilse circled Blake like vultures, climbing on his wheelchair and attempting wheelies. For the most part, he excelled at covering up pained grimaces every time one of the little monkeys stepped on him.

"You did good, kid." Burn moved to the stool Jay had abandoned. "Hand me the whiskey."

"Thanks." He reached over the counter to dump his cider into the sink. "Which kind?" I asked, sliding off behind the bar.

"Crown, please." I poured him his drink and screwed the cap back on.

"What's with the cider anyhow?" I slid back onto the counter, leaning back and allowing Jay to rest his head on my lap.

"What do you mean? I enjoy the carbonation; it's like swallowing acid." He gave a smile that I couldn't quite translate between sarcastic or badly faked genuineness.

"Bullshit," Jay half coughed. "Burny here doesn't drink around his sissy, mainly because he's a hypocrite."

Burn basically shot his drink, rolling his eyes. "She's underage," he muttered.

"Aw hell, I was 10 when Tresa challenged me to my first shot contest."

"That was a good day," Lily giggled.

"See! Lil's on my side!"

"Don't," Tresa warned from Lily's side.

"I'm just saying!" Jay slurred. "It wouldn't hurt anybody if-"

"Enough, it's late." Burn downed his second glass and stood. "Onyx, you did great. Seriously." He patted my knee. Even with the gloves acting as a barrier, his hands were still hot to the touch.

"Come on, pal!" Jay grabbed his hand. "Don't leave, we're celebrating!"

"Goodnight." Burn took his hand back and promptly exited.

"Party pooper," Jay mumbled, rolling onto his back.

"He's probably right." Lily sat up and swung her legs over the counter.

"You can't seriously-!"

"About it being late, chill. I need to take the kids to bed." She slid off the counter and whistled.

"I'll take care of the kids." Tresa walked around the bar; she was probably the only one who didn't simply jump over the counter to get around. "You just take care of yourself and Radio."

"You sure, Tres?"

"Ya, I got it. You just get some sleep."

"Will do! Thank you." She turned to the kids, who had worn themselves out already. "Listen to Tresa, I have to go." She wheeled Blake out, Tresa and the children following in their wake, leaving only Jay, Aska, and myself.

"Hey, Soul Stealer! You still here?" Jay shouted, his eyes closed.

"Ya," Aska sat down at one of the corner tables.

"Still got killer paws?"

"Ya," he muttered, staring down at his still purplish toned hands, with a slightly sad expression.

"That's unfortunate."

"Here." I jumped off the counter, leading Jay to bang his head.

"MY PILLOW!" He propped himself up and glared. I tossed Aska a pair of Burn's gloves.

"Those should suppress it until you go to sleep."

"Thanks," he paused, before looking up at me with that brotherly smile I had learned to crave. "I'm proud of you, Lun."

"Save that for once I actually manage to get any useful info, but thank you." Jay lolled back on his arm with his eyes closed. I glanced back at him and then at Aska. "I suppose it would be smart to drag his ass to bed, preferably before he blacks out. You gonna be okay here?"

"I'm not a child; I'll be just fine. Go get some sleep." I jumped to the other side of the bar and pulled Jay off.

"Goodnight, Onyx," Aska said, his voice tinged with sadness and remorse.

"Night, Soul Stealer," I replied gently.

***

It didn't take long after that until a letter arrived upstairs, giving explicit instructions for orientation in a week. Every day it neared, I felt a mixture of anxiety and excitement well up inside my chest. It was one thing to get into Toyls, but now… if I ever got caught. No, I wouldn't get caught. Burn cut off training for that last week, allowing me to scout with Jay more and, in my free time, visit Lily and 'Lina in the penthouse, where Lily would brief me on some of her family, medical, and educational history.

Soon enough, I was once more at Mrs. Madalini's side, a folder stuffed full of different forms attached to the handle of Lily's suitcase, like her identity, on loan to myself. The handle shuddered, just barely, trembling in my grip, as we approached the gate. With a subtle nod, she released my hand and allowed me to continue forth to the meeting hall.

Unlike last time, the hall was nearly barren down below the balcony. An usher stood at the north entrance and took my papers and suitcase as I entered, directing me to the right section, between the lion and horse figures. 60- possibly 70 people sat in the same area, the largest group in the hall. To our left, between the lion and ox, there were maybe 30 kids chatting amongst themselves. The other two sections only had about 20 or less present. I suppose the upperclassmen really had no use in actually attending orientation, or… there was a rumor on the news that Toyls had been sending them out and paying them as privates early in place of their afternoon training classes. Logically, it made sense; there were at most 5 MES specialized academies in Quebec , while most weren't as harsh as Toyls, producing nearly ten times their average class size, even that was only about 400 per class, but that was still only about 2000 officers per year spread across all of the province of Quebec. Strict regulations are great and all for getting the best quality officers, but they were largely less effective on the quantity of said officers, they need more men. Ironically, despite most of the high-ranking officers coming from Toyls, the majority of the lower ranks were made up of drafted city police or military. Combining the rest of Quebec, there were at max 7000 officers per year. A minuscule number, really, but in comparison to the 1/10000 birthrate of the Machigai, not to mention our quartered lifespans… well, somehow, even the MES's pathetic numbers outweighed us. Where was I? Ah yes… numbers… they're tiny, we're tinier… moving on.

"Lily!" A familiar voice echoed through the open hall a bit too loud, my face flushing as several people near us went silent. "You made it!" Calvin slid into the seat next to me. "Well, I knew you made it- my dad and I watched it on the news- but I thought you might have well… like… I don't know, missed it or something like that- and then the letter might have got lost in the mail- or- or-"

"You're forgetting to breathe," I said deadpan, a smile tugging at my lips. When we had watched the announcement, everyone was so focused on whether we did it, that the annoying albino chihuahua had completely slipped my mind.

"Ya. . .ya. It's just-" His breathing slowed to just barely faster than a normal person's. "It's just good to have a friend."

A foul taste occurred in the back of my throat. "Friend… ya- it is." I knew it was a lie, still, together we watched as a few late arrivals flooded the four entrances. Soon enough, the lights slowly faded, leaving us with only the rising sun's rays for sight. The golden beams illuminated the sides of the oxen pillars, the silver absorbing them to make itself glitter even more, while the white reflected it around to the other statues. The whole thing was so subtle; if one were to simply glance over the room, they'd never be able to pinpoint the thing that made it all so… connected.

"Ah-hem," the same old woman from entrance exams cleared her throat in the mic, gathering the student body's main focus. "Welcome, students," she said into the mic, much more collected than our first brush with her. "As many of you are aware, my name is Madam Bassette, although the majority of you may know me as Captain Bassie."

"GO BASS!!" a few of the older kids yelled out, pumping their fists before being promptly shushed by their ushers.

"Yes. Thank you, thank you," she added, with just a touch more primness in her tone. "Toyls was not available for training back in my prime, yet even if it had been, it would not be the trademark that it is today. The legacy. The MES top school. The legend. All of this was created by our lovely headmaster, who shall speak with you now. Headmaster Lealli Toyls."

Chapter 21: One Day I'll Understand (Doubtfully)

The woman was angelic. Sincerely, there were no other words. A modest yet elegant, evergreen dress clung to her wide hips, highlighting every curve and muscle. The long arms of the dress exposed a gap between the tight halter neck and the flared finger-length sleeves. Waist-length, auburn waves cascaded down her back, the streaks of natural silver occasionally catching the light as she walked up to the podium, adding just the perfect contrast to her deep caramel complexion and round face. Oval nails, tips painted sage green, lightly wrapped around the microphone, one by one.

"Soldier's heart-" her voice was strong, cutting through the air while also dancing on the electricity. Strong and powerful, while also swimming through the breeze, like sword arcs slicing through beings as they fall, like rocks tumbling off a cliff. "Lamb's head." The majority of the upperclassmen echoed her final words. "And yet, beware the king's screams."

"The king's words, the poet's words-words," Calvin muttered next to me.

"What?" I nudged his shoulder.

"Nothing… it's- when Toyls first was founded motto was "Soldiers heart, lambs head, but beware the poet's words, for he shall be our savior or our doom." He looked up at me. "No news station ever reported on the sudden change in the motto ten years ago, which seemed odd. You think with how much the news covers Toyls, they'd report something like that." Someone shushed him from the row ahead and he flushed, turning back to the stage, but his words stayed with me.

The headmaster didn't speak for more than a minute or two, the same old speech as any other orientation: "Welcome in," "We feel so blessed to have you," et cetera. She then turned us back to Madam Bassette, or, as the upperclassmen insisted on calling her, "Bass," who sent the 2nd, 3rd, and 4th years on their way before calling upon us, the 1st years.

"Well then! Let's not sit around like creepy dolls. We have a campus to explore!" From the meeting house, we traveled north to the gym, back to the gun range, and then we moved to actual classrooms. A science center with blue-tinted windows and little green frog-stained class portraits, something straight out of children's fantasy. That plus the armory was it for the East Campus, but even from the Science Center, you could see the 5-story dorm building's shadow looming over us, just over 100 meters away. If anything... it was underwhelming. The bottom floor was made up of brick, the rest a beige terracotta, all with windows equally spaced all around its 2D capital T shape. We were promptly told that we would return to the dorms after the tour. Bess dragged us out to the Main Lawn, which overtook the majority of the West Campus. From there, she pointed out the Math and English buildings to the Northwest, and the obvious Training facility that scaled the entire landscape to the Southwest. I tried to create a visual map of the place in my head, but she moved on to the next building almost too quickly for me to remember the last. By the time we were done with the tour, my feet were sore, and my head was spinning.

Finally, we were allowed into the dorms. The lobby floor of the 5-story building was made up of a large dining hall, with an impressive buffet-style bar divided into 5 sections: The first section contained plates, silverware, and drinks. The next had a variety of fruits, berries, melons, and every other fruit you could imagine. Then, there was a huge salad bowl, carrots, mushrooms, onions, cherry tomatoes, and all other kinds of nutritious veggies. The last two sections, as you could probably guess, were filled with meats, fish, shrimp, and finally, pasta, bread, and quinoa. The whole thing was so elaborate and terrifying, not a single soda or pizza, waffle or fried foods, no sweets or chips. Jay probably would've blacked out after he saw the lack of grease all over the food. As someone who had done the majority of mine and Aska's shopping for the last 5 years, I didn't even want to think about how much funding went into the fresh fruit alone. I remember seeing the price for mushrooms going into three digits – insanity.

Other than the dining hall, the lobby floor also contained a nurse's office and infirmary suited to handling 40 patients at a time. Considering that the school had around 200 students at a time who focused entirely on physical activities and often used guns, this seemed a bit less than impressive.

"Your dorms will be on the 4th and 5th floors." Bassie-goddammit, they have it in my head- *Madam Bassette* yelled over our crowd. "For security reasons, no student is permitted to use the elevator. Once it arrives, I shall give you your room keys, which will grant you access to your floor and room number only." She handed a key card from her pocket to a boy with buzzed beige hair and short, stocky muscles, who stood in front of the crowd. Before releasing her grip on the card, she asked the boy for his name.

"Jake Derrien, Ma'am." He held his grip on the card and attempted to size her up.

"Jake… what a strong name. Well, Jake, could you watch this card for me? It grants access to all floors. Use it for the 4th and the 4th only. Understood?"

"Yes, Ma'am." She released the card, sending Jake back a step or two into another student.

"Good." She clapped her hands, "because as good a boy as I suspect you are, the school directors don't take my opinion into consideration for such severe matters. Such as if something were to happen to a high-security key card." The threat in her tone was far from subtle, and for a woman who at first glance looked like someone's crazy Aunt Ruth, she could glare daggers that made you feel as though an ice spike had lodged its way into your chest and you were just waiting on whether it would kill you, or simply melt, leaving you chilled to the literal bone.

"Yes, Ma'am" Jake's voice had only lost the shine of its edge, but he stood tall (metaphorically… physically, well, to the least he was lacking in that department.)

***

"Four flights of stairs," one of the girls gasped for the 3rd time since ascending. "We have to walk these every day??" I tried focusing on her hair as it waved and bounced back in forth, not her nagging voice that was driving daggers into my skull. Her hair was beautiful; in all fairness, I couldn't even tell what the natural color was, but it constantly changed from cheery red roots into teddy bear brown, followed by golden blond tips. Watching it mix and swirl occupied me for the first huge flight of stairs just to get to the 3rd year dorms on the 2nd floor. It's silky and soft volume reminded me of a fox's coat.

"What are you staring at?" She snapped. For a moment, I nearly jumped into Calvin, but she wasn't even looking at me, but rather at a skyscraper red-headed boy with lean muscles and flakes of an incoming mustache.

"Not much, apparently," he shrugged. "Just kinda wondering how someone so stuck up made it into Toyls'- they obviously have us walk these to show that we are still students under their thumb. It'll stay that way until we earn their respect, therefore shut the fuck up."

"I don't think that's it," Calvin interjected from next to me. He stood pressing against the golden railing; I'm not sure why he crowded himself so close to the wall, seeing as the majestic stairwell was wide enough to fit 6 people shoulder to shoulder. "It's-it's a metaphor. 1st years on the highest floor because we're farthest away from the exit, or rather our goal. With each year, you get closer to leaving. It's brilliant, actually."

"Or they want to torture us… I'm just saying." The whiny girl shrugged.

"I agree with Danny," Jake still walked at the front of the group, running Madam Bassette's key card between his fingers. "No one puts that much thought into a dorm building; probably just flipped a pair of dice."

"Rolled," I stated dryly.

"What'd you say, sweetheart?" He turned to face me, so he was walking backward up the stairs with shocking coordination and poise.

"You roll dice, you flip a coin."

"And I suppose you grew up in a casino from your superb knowledge, Omb*rr*e."

"Ombre?" Calvin raised his eyebrow. "Her name's Lily; that's not even remotely close."

"Her hair is Ombre, and generally, I could care less about her name either way. Same for you, Q-tip." Calvin flushed, breaking his eyes away and leaning back onto the railing.

"Okay, by that, completely horrible logic; shouldn't her name be Ombre?" I pointed to the girl with the red roots.

"Not even remotely, she's Danny Rose. Always has been, always will be."

"Danny Rose?" The red-headed tower from earlier snarked.

"Daneila Rosalind to you dick-breath." Danny snarled at him, her eyes glaring daggers.

"Down, girl," Jake muttered. "We're here, anyways." He turned to the door and slid the card twice through the metal scanner below the doorknob before the little signal turned green, and the door slid open flawlessly.

"Fred Bumguarder, in case you were wonderin', sweetheart." The carrot top attempted to kiss Danny's hand, but she pulled it away and marched through the door behind Jake.

"I'd rather lick the toilet seat," she muttered as she passed.

The stairs came up at the end of a 6-door long hallway that led into a large, square main room. Madam Bassette sat directly across from us in a bay window couch area surrounded fully by blue-tinted glass. To her right was a booth-style L couch sat in the back left corner, with a glass coffee table in the joint of the booth. A matching set sat in the corner across the room, framing the doorway that separated them. On the opposite side of the room, two sets of kitchenettes sat on each side of the opposing doorway.

"This," She stood gesturing to the large room, "With a great deal of luck; will be your life for the next 4 years. I, along with the rest of the faculty, hope that by then you will truly be able to understand the honor and grand responsibility that has been placed on your shoulders." For a moment, her blinks slowed, and she really did look like a MES Captain, strained by years on the force. "With that being said, find the door with your name on it. You will find you key inside on the dresser; it will grant you access to this floor and this floor only. For those of you who do not find your room, meet me back here and I shall show you to the fifth floor. DISMISSED."

Chapter 22: So. Much. Work.

We all flocked into the hallways like sheep on the run, breaking off in different directions. The eastern hallway was labeled for men, so Calvin parted off to search that way while I turned to the opposing side.

After a crowded and, quite frankly, irritating wild goose chase for mine, or rather Lily's-name pinned on a door, I gave up in the western hall. The northern hall which we had entered from, didn't have a big metal door to unlock. Instead, it was an open spaced entrance that tunneled down, revealing the large bronze elevator doors that loomed over the end of the hall, accompanied by the meek students' stairwell oak door. Two doors down from the elevator, on the western side of the hall, I finally discovered the sparkling chalk sign that read "Lily I. Madalini" in silver lettering. I slid the door open, allowing it to disappear into the wall as I slipped into the room, making sure I locked the door behind me. The room was simplistic enough; in the back right corner, a twin-sized bed sat up about nearly a meter off the ground, with drawers underneath. At its foot, an over two-meter-tall wardrobe towered over me, my keycard lying on top just as Madam Bassette had said. Finally, a surprisingly nice L shaped corner desk sat in the corner by the door, paired with a non-shockingly entertaining spinny chair (objectively my favorite part of the room).

Flinging myself down in the chair, I turned round and round, keeping my eyes fixed on my suitcase ballet style, challenging it to unpack itself. When the suitcase so rudely declined, I figured logically I should probably move myself in, then redecided to procrastinate by doing further exploration.

An open doorway sat next to the headboard of the bed, only a porcelain sink visible through it. Shuffling my feet against the nice hardwood floors, I pushed myself and the chair over to the door frame for a better look; the wheels rolled against the floor, making a really satisfying noise. This thing was getting too addictive too quickly.

I peered into the doorway gently, preventing the wheel from taking the tiny fall from the hardwood floors to the white stone tile. The bathroom was insanely nice, if not slightly petite, only about two and a half meters squared; pressed against each side of the wall was a full glass shower with marble tiling and a full porcelain toilet stool, while the sink still stood facing the door.

Since there was no electricity nor running water in our house, Aska and I had very few options when it came to using the restroom; my go-to was typically just using the public restroom at the library during operating times. Aska, his face actually being decently known, had far fewer options. Compared to that, this was beyond imagination.

Finally, having explored the full room, I turned back to my suitcase. Unpacking didn't take too long, seeing as I had only a singular suitcase packed. An eight-class schedule lay on the desk, taunting me as I unpacked. It read:

Period 1: 6:15-7:20   English/French Language Arts

Period 2: 7:25-8:30   Physics

Period 3: 9:35-10:40   Trigonometry

Period 4: 10:45-11:50	Machigai History per Region
Lunch 11:55-12:40	
Period 5: 12:45-13:50	Chemistry
Period 6: 13:55-15:00	Foreign Affairs
Period 7: 15:00-16:05	Poisons and Ointments
Period 8: 16:05-17:10	Sharp Shooting and Combat

After School Activities: Weightroom, gymnastics, agility training, grappling, psychology, and undercover work.

I sat the schedule back down, wandering over to the wardrobe. Attempting a casual façade, I slid the hangers over and out of my peripheral. The glistening of a small camera caught my eye from the corner of the wardrobe. Grabbing a midnight blue and purple hoodie, I returned to the bed. Praying that keeping my fitted jacket on underneath a hoodie wouldn't seem odd, I slid the cover over my head, mocking a struggle in order to catch a clear view of the entire room's ceiling. Within reason, there was likely another camera within the fire alarm; I also caught a glimpse of something odd attached to the top of the door frame. *Creepy,* I thought to myself, but it was understandable. A high-profile school can't risk any scandalous behavior. *They're doing, oh so great at that.* I thought before flinging myself down on the strangely comfortable bed.

***

The next morning, we were briefed on how everything would go. The schedule was pretty self-explanatory; apparently, we were supposed to design our own after-school schedule as long as we had more than 30 credits by the end of the semester. We were shown how to get to each class, and after that, the week seemed to turtle walk across the street as I avoided getting crushed. Turns out, formal first-grade learning followed by self-teaching in the library when given time, is not the greatest source of education. English/ French and history were okay. I had always enjoyed reading, from non-fiction to French drama; when you don't have easy access to a TV, books are an incredible source of entertainment. Math and Science were far different; neither had ever intrigued me, and while I had found a few common core books in the library, they never held my attention for more than a few weeks at a time. In all, I had less than a freshman understanding of math, leading most of the words to come off as gibberish.

The fast pacing of each class certainly did not improve matters. It seemed that they spit facts like acid; drowning us in pages of notes that were more direct quotes than true understanding.

The layout was much different than I expected; for each class, we were assigned 4-9 assignments on the first of the week, all due before the next Monday, and then we were taught how to complete them gradually over the week. Ten-centimeter-thick binders were assigned in each class, explaining in detail everything we would complete before the end of the quarter. Our days ended with intense training, finally making it back to our dorms by 18:00. The dining hall was open at all times between then and 20:00, and if you desired to eat in the dorms, you were allowed one Styrofoam box. The rest of the night was spent intensively fretting over any homework you didn't complete while at lunch or dinner.

By the time Friday rolled around, every muscle and organ in my body ached worse than any repercussion from my curse. We were allowed to stumble home for the weekends to recover in the presence of our families, or in my case, receive criticism and curse training from Burn. I limped down the long streets of the city, staring up at the rooftops to guide my way. It was far too late in the day for Jay to be out scouting, but the futile hope relieved some pressure from my chest. Finally, I fell into the shadow of the looming figure of the hotel, as I slipped through the back alleys to the basement entrance.

"Onyx!" Lily shouted from behind the bar as I walked in, hurdling the counter to race towards me. The kids all sat up on the bar stools, chowing down on hamburgers and apple sauce.

"Where is everyone?" I asked, pulling her to arm's length in order to rememorize the soft features and welcoming smile that I had missed desperately in the last week.

"Lina's upstairs working. The others ate early and headed out to scout a location Burn is wanting to raid tomorrow night. A new machigai 'hospital.'" She made hand quotes in the air directed to the word hospital, we all knew the machigai that entered those were never meant to be cured or to ever leave.

"Aska is off probation?" I slid onto one of the bar stools as Lily climbed onto the one next to me.

“He was borderline insane having nothing to distract him this last week; Burn thought it would be the best solution. Don’t worry, I don’t see a reason why he would need to activate his curse, just as long as Burn is with him anyways.” She giggled a bit. “I’ve gone with them once or twice, back when Blake was… before, you know? Scouting and planning those things can be quite fun, kinda like a video game. All strategy and overly deep intellectual thought. Very cool, if you’re into that kind of thing, you know?” She nudged me with her arm. “But, hey, since they won’t be back until late, that means we have the whole evening together.”

“What did you have in mind?” I jumped up on the counter, resting my arms on her shoulders, exposed by her flowing pastel pink top. She leaned back between my thighs, the top of her head resting just below my ribs. She lingered for a second there before turning back towards me; her pupils doubled in size.

“MY LORD! You don’t have any wanted posters, do you?!”

“No, none with my face, that is.”

She beamed in response, bouncing up and grabbing my hands to yank me off the counter.

“Kids, go brush your teeth and get ready for bed; if you need anything, Blake is in his room.”

“Where will you be?” Jamie asked, jumping down before helping her sister off her stool.

“The mall, picking up lots and lots of presents for good girls who do as they’re told.”

"I wanna go, I wanna go!" Lulu laughed, falling off her spinning stool, Lily scooped her up onto her hip bone.

"You know you cannot, mi amour. It's safest for you here."

"She knows," Jamie said, taking Lulu's hand as her feet hit the floor. "We all do."

Chapter 23: Girl Talk

After spending a rigorous hour tucking the younger kids into bed, Lily dragged me up the taped-off stairs into the main lobby. Dozens of families from the Friday evening rush scurried about, trying to find luggage and get checked into their rooms before dinner. 'Hotel de Vivianna' was carved into the marble backsplash behind the front desk, tinted with golden accents so the letters reflected across the room.

"Hotel de Vivianna," I whispered under my breath with a grin.

"My father named it for my mother when they married." Lily stopped and joined me, staring the sign down; she gave a light chuckle. "Most people travel for their honeymoons; my parents opened their first hotel."

"They opened their second in Ontario shortly after I was born; currently, my dad is working on expansions in Europe." Her face fell, the ghost of her smile being wiped away at the mention of her father. "Anything to avoid his machigai daughter." She took my hand and dragged me to the elevator, away from the lobby, scanning a card from her pocket against the pad which granted her access to the penthouse suite. The urge to pry into the meaning of her words was washed away by the very un-Lily-like expression on her face, so I turned my questions elsewhere.

"I thought your mom's name was Vivianne, so why is the hotel's name Vivianna?" Lily turned to me and mustered a sweet smile.

"My father met her while he was studying abroad in Italy; he used to joke that "Vivianne" sounded too Canadian for a purebred Italian like her, that she should change her name to *Vivianna*." She added a thick Italian accent over the name, smiling from cheek to cheek. I turned to watch the floors go up one by one, currently level 8/13.

"So, your mother lived in Italy?"

"Born and raised," she giggled that sweet sound. "They struggled for years to get her a Visa before they married; my father was determined to have no rumors that it was an immigration marriage. No rumors that he was marrying her for anything other than undeniable affection."

"That's… sweet?"

"He can be *sweeter than sugar*." She exaggerated her vowels to shape her voice into a Southern American accent. "When he wants to be, of course." The doors to the penthouse slid open, revealing the grand room.

Lily turned towards the stairs leading up to the large luxury loft/second-story above. "Make yourself at home; I'm just gonna change real quick." She waved at the top of the stairs over her shoulders. "Be back in a jiff." I took a seat on the half-circle sofa facing the TV, unsure of what to do.

"Onyx is that you?" a voice rang from the direction of the kitchen.

"Lina?" She emerged from the shadows, heading in my direction and taking a seat next to me on the couch. "I thought you were working?"

"Yvette, the night shift caller, came in a half hour early after a fight with her boyfriend, so now I'm here, killing time and making food."

"What are you making?" She leaned back on the couch.

"Oh, just a frozen microwave meal… it was pretty crap, if I'm being honest. What are you doing up here?"

"Lily wants to go shopping."

"I HEARD MY NAME, ARE YOU TWO GOSSIPING WITHOUT ME?" Lily shouted from above the loft.

"OF COURSE WE ARE, HURRY UP AND WE MIGHT ACTUALLY LET YOU JOIN!" Lina shouted back. I heard a few laughs upstairs before Lily trotted down the stairwell in a new blue plaid dress with black tights and a black long-sleeve shirt underneath, her wavy chocolate hair was now pulled up into an effortlessly attractive messy bun.

"Will you be accompanying us grocery shopping, Lina?"

"I can, ya. Are you guys leaving now?"

"That's the plan." Lily swung her legs over the couch, resting on the back of it. "We'll have to walk, of course, since Tresa and the others took the van."

"Oh… I may stay back then," I stated, my muscles still aching from my short time at Toyls.

"No! Don't say that! Why?" Lily shook my shoulders, giving me her best puppy dog eyes. I laughed and leaned into her knee.

"Training at Toyls is definitely nothing to be messed with, even compared to your brother's death circuits," Lina smiled gently.

"Oh, that's nothing a little Lily love can't fix; where's the hurt."

"As endearing as that may be, I doubt you'll have much fun shopping if you're worn out from your curse."

"Coffee was invented for a reason; it wasn't this one, but it was a reason." Lily's hands hovered over my legs, then my arms, and finally my back. Spreading that sweet, sleepy, warm sensation across my body. In the end, I yawned and leaned into her, free from the pain that plagued me a few seconds prior.

"Come on now," Lily slid off the couch, stretching while obviously straining to keep her previous energy levels. "There's a lovely coffee shop around the corner we can stop in on our way." She bounced her way to the elevator. "Follow in a suit, my dear lassies; dinner is on me."

We did as she said, Lina grabbing her white cane, which was mounted on the wall.

"Not to be ignorant, but aren't you supposed to have that with you at all times?" Lina shrugged, her brows furrowing slightly.

"When you spend every day for eight years on the same fourteen floors, it becomes more of a nuisance than anything. Although I do have to be pretty particular in where I set it down, forgetting is a bitch."

The doors to the elevator clicked shut, and we began our descent. "I once walked into her on her hands and knees, scurrying around like a little mouse in the penthouse trying to figure out where she put it," Lily laughed, mimicking the movements with her hands.

"Blaise would flip a lid if I ever lost it." Lina shook her head.

We exited through the lobby, which had calmed down tremendously. We took a left outside and then crossed the street to find the little coffee shop Lily had described. *'Flour Petals Bakery & Coffee'*, the pink and black sign out front read, accompanying pictures of flour and roses. Inside, the smell of lavender scones and sweet coffee wafted through the air. I scanned over the menu for myself, baffled by various options.

"What's your favorite?" I asked the barista. She tucked a strand of her short rainbow hair behind her ears, turning to the menu.

"It kind of depends; what do you like?"

"Anything that doesn't have cinnamon," I responded with a laugh, bitterly remembering the incident at the gas station only a few months ago. She flashed a smile back at me.

"How about a peppermint mocha latte? It's our owner's specialty." Memories of the soft peppermint candies my uncle used to bring home from work danced on my tongue.

"Perfect." I said, returning her smile.

"Alrighty then, I have one lavender latte with oat milk & whip cream, one sunshine smoothie, and one peppermint mocha latte. Anything else for you ladies today?"

"Yes, we'll take three of the chicken ciabatta wraps with a bag of chips each." The barista rang in our order, allowing Lily to pay before we took a seat next to the window, watching people pass. Lily set Lina's cane against the wall, but a few people still took a second glance when they saw it, trying to find its owner. I wonder if Lina could feel the unnecessary stares from on-goers. She had ditched the sunglasses she sometimes wore, leaving her gray eyes unfocused and exposed, staring off at an unseeable destination. The barista brought us our drinks, Lily thanking her as she promised our food would be out soon.

"You said Blaise and the others took the van; what have they run off to accomplish today?" Lina asked, sipping from the thick pink straw in her drink. Neither Lily nor I were granted straws for our coffees, just small holes in the lid that steam and tasty fragrances seeped out of. The peppermint flavor was strong against the thick creamy chocolate base, almost reminding me of a more bitter peppermint cocoa.

"Scouting for a hospital raid tomorrow, we'll have to be quick; they should be back by eight."

"An hour and a half, we can work with that," Lina nodded back.

“Do we have to be back before them?” I leaned back, staring out the window.

“She does.” Lily nodded towards Lina.

“Oo, which reminds me. Don’t let it slip to my brother that I went out with you guys.”

“I would never. Lying to Burn is my specialty.” I gave her a wink before remembering she couldn’t see it. I wasn’t sure how you could forget something like that, her eyes were locked in my direction, red in the corners, hollow everywhere else. Small scares inches around the bottom and top of her eyelids; how I hadn’t noticed them before was baffling, but then again, Lina held herself so normally that if you weren’t paying attention, it was difficult to notice anything was odd with her.

“Is Tresa driving or Blaise?” She turned to Lily.

“Jay, for once. I watched him beg for the privilege.” Lily laughed.

“Which means Tresa will be driving back, which means we have an extra quarter-hour at the store.” Lina took a large bite from her wrap, smearing a bit of orange sauce on her cheek. She looked so young outside the hotel; anywhere else it was easy to forget she was only thirteen.

“Lina, you said earlier you’ve been at the hotel for eight years, right?”

“Almost, why what’s up?”

“That would have made you five when you moved in?”

"Just barely six actually. Blaise met Jay back when he was still street fighting for money. Jay convinced Lily here, who convinced her mother to remove us from our… let's say, quaint tent on the riverside. We were the first machigai to move into the basement."

"Mom said five kids in the penthouse was too much," Lily said with a laugh, popping a chip in her mouth. "I still stand by the fact she was just sick of Tresa accidentally blowing stuff up."

She turned to me and mock whispered, "Before we found her a hairnet."

"Blaise was the one who turned Lily's makeshift orphanage into an actual organization; up until a few months ago, he made sure the five rooms in the basement were full at all times with people he deemed useful. That and, of course, us original five." She took a breath, allowing her a moment to take another bite of her sandwich. After she swallowed, she continued. "A little more than a few years ago, somehow, he and Tresa managed to strike up a deal with this tiny little Machigai town that's taken over Greenville. Every time we have any excess people, Tresa takes them West, along with any supplies we can spare; they send back weapons and ammo."

"And fresh berries," Lily winked.

"If you guys ship off excess people, what's with the four kids at the hotel?"

"Ilse and Jamie haven't been with us long, but Blaise saw a lot of potential in Jamie's curse. She can turn solid things into liquid; you can see how that could be useful, especially for hospital raids like the one they are planning for tomorrow. He wasn't as thrilled when she refused to separate from Ilse."

"Especially after Jamie lied about Ilse's curse." Lily took another fist full of chips.

"She lied about her sister's curse?"

"About a year ago, when they first arrived, Jamie told Blaise that Ilse could talk to people in their minds but that she wouldn't let her because it gave her severely incapacitating migraines. Despite this, my brother being the stubborn asshole he pretends he isn't, talked Blake into secretly attempting to train Ilse while Jamie was training with Tresa. It took two months of wasted time before Ilse let the lie slip and told Blake that she was actually human."

"I'm sure Burn was thrilled," I laughed, picturing his face at the news.

"His hair caught fire." Lily giggled. "I have photos; I'll show you back at the hotel. He was bald with third-degree burns on his scalp for months."

"If I could bring back my sight for one day, it would have been then," Lina smiled. "Anyways, yes, he wasn't too happy, especially since we already were housing Clark and Lulu permanently."

"What's the story with those two?" I finished the last bite of my sandwich and then took another sip of my coffee, which was slowly getting colder.

"Jay found Clark tied to a lab table during an info raid two years ago; he was only three years old at the time.

After that, the kid refuses to leave Jay behind; he's the only one he trusts. As for Lulu… Lily care to comment?"

"Jay got an apprentice; I wanted one, too." She leaned back in her chair. "Plus, she can make the prettiest flowers with that curse of hers, and they really bring the hotel and the bar together."

"How did you convince Burn of that?"

"In technical terms, I'm the only one he can't boss around." She winked, before setting her chair back down on all fours. "We should probably get going before it gets too late." She handed Lina her cane back and tidied up the table, stacking all the plates neatly and leading us out of the shop and about ten blocks north to the closest grocery store.

Chapter 24: Hostile Hospitals & Hypocrites

We greatly underestimated the amount of time shopping would take, or maybe we simply got too distracted goofing off in the toy section or trying on graphic tees with stupid text in the clothing section before we ever even got the food Lily would need for the next week. Either way, it was 8:30 by the time we arrived back in the hotel. Lina opted to return to the penthouse and sleep before she, and likely us received the undeniable lecture from Burn. Lily and I braved our way to the bar, bags of loot hanging heavily off of every space available on our skin. When we opened the door Aska, Burn, Jay, and Tresa were circled around the corner table, files spread over every inch of its surface.

"Shit, run, run," she whispered, turning to shoo me back out the way we came.

"Hold it." Burn turned to us. "Onyx, good to have you back." He nodded to me first. "Lily, what have you done with my sister?"

"What do you mean?" Lily asked, portraying her innocence shockingly well.

"I used the phone to call up to the penthouse to check in on her. No response, which is odd, seeing as her shift ended at six."

"Don't be so serious, Burny Poo." She ruffled his hair a bit, pushing past him and behind the bar, setting the bags on the counter. "Your sister is a grown woman, I don't keep tabs on her."

"She's thirteen." He snipped. I thought for a moment, I saw a blaze of red flash behind his eyes.

"Almost fourteen, and that's past middle age for a machigai therefore she's basically forty and probably just asleep. I'll go up and check on her as soon as Luna and I get these groceries put away. And don't worry, I'll make sure she calls you back so you can hear just how fine she is."

"Mhm, I'll believe it when I see it."

"What a pessimistic worldview; poor Lina would never be able to believe anything."

"Watch it," Burn glared, a bit of steam pouring off his gloves. Lily's smile fell off her face at this, turning back to the groceries and removing them from their bags. I snuck behind the bar, setting my bags down as well.

"Onyx, come join us. Lily can handle that; I want your input on some of this." I turned to Lily, who squeezed my hand and gestured for me to go with him. I nodded back.

"Rough day?" I asked Burn as we walked to the others. He rubbed between his temples, a tic I had noticed he used often.

"Oh, it's been a day, for sure. Not to mention, I'll still have to get your report from Toyls later tonight." He cracked his neck in a circle, yawning.

"We can take care of that Sunday or tomorrow when you're back." I shoulder nudged him playfully. "Promise I won't forget anything."

He smiled back at me, sparking hope that I had succeeded in brightening his mood. "I don't know; a distraction might be just what I need tonight." We approached the table with the others. Tresa sat with her hands laced together, staring at the files on the table, which were now revealed to be sketches and blueprints of the inside of the hotel. Aska sat with his back to me, turning to face me at my arrival. Dark, baggy circles hung under his eyes.

"Luna," he gave me the Soul Stealer branded nod and smiled.

"Aska." I nodded back, then gave him the Onyx branded disappointed leer. "You haven't been sleeping."

He mustered a smile, tracing his boney fingers under his eyes. "You know how nights can be; it comes and goes," he shrugged with a smile, turning back to the blueprints.

"What all has Lily filled you in on, Onyx?" Burn asked, taking a seat to Aska's right.

"Just the basics."

"Then I'll cut to the chase, I would like you to join us tomorrow. If you're feeling up to it, of course."

"Burn-" Aska protested.

"Aska, if you wish to return to your sabbatical, please continue." I saw Aska twitch a bit, but he stayed silent. "Wonderful. Now Onyx, do you remember that move we've been working on in training? Transporting humans through shadows, from the side of one thing to another?"

"You want me to do that with a bunch of kids at the hospital? While in shadow guard?"

"No shadow guard. You have school Monday, and the relapse time for that is far too long. Tresa is going to blow up both the generators…" He pointed to a small square on the paper behind the hospital. "Jay will use her hair to bomb the backup generator." He pointed to another small square across the map. "There will be no cameras and as long as Aska here can ensure there are no witnesses; you should be in the clear to use your regular form."

"Even so, isn't transporting all those kids dangerous?"

"Less dangerous than them staying in that place. Not to mention, this way, we can have three teams instead of two. More teams, more kids saved in less time." He sat up on one knee in the chair, tracing his way over the papers. "The goal is to be in and out in thirty minutes from the moment Tresa blows the generator at precisely 7:00. Aska and Jay have no way of getting into the cells, so they will act as guards and scouts for Tresa and you. Jay will go with Tresa so he can fly her mini bombs to cells ahead and get away without getting hurt. You and Aska have worked with each other for years, so your partnership here should be no problem." I squeezed Aska's shoulder lightly, feeling his apprehension at Burn's words. "I will go my own way, and we will meet back up here," he pointed to a marked position on the east fence. "It is incredibly important you arrive at this fence at exactly 7:30, no earlier, no later. I will melt a small hole in the fence here and get everyone across. Jay will then drizzle a healthy dose of gasoline across this section of fencing that I will ignite as we leave to ensure no one follows us back to the van. Tresa will transport the kids to our associates in Greenville the next morning, before the cops have the opportunity to find a trail.

"How many kids do you plan on saving?" I asked.

"Ideally? All of them." Burn said with a grin straight from the face of Swiper from Dora. "Realistically? As many as we can." He stood, stretching his arms behind his head. "Onyx, I think I'll take your advice and call it an early night. The rest of you should do the same; meet back here at 5:45 am; we will gear up and load the van to leave by 6:30 am." Jay and Aska collectively groaned, both muttering about the early start as Burn took his leave and walked out of the bar.

"In that case, nightcap, anyone?" Jay stood and headed to the bar, Lily had slipped out sometime during our conversation, likely headed up to sleep in the penthouse tonight.

"Not for me; I think I'll turn in for the night as well." I twisted my spine, stretching it.

"I'll join you." Aska stood to follow me.

"Guess that leaves you and me, Tresa. What are we drinking?" Jay called, already behind the bar.

"Crown Blackberry tonight," Tresa called back, leaning against the wall.

"Goodnight, you guys," I waved to them both, taking Aska's outstretched arm and turning us towards the door.

"Goodnight," Jay and Tresa echoed.

Aska rested his head on my shoulder as we walked down the corridor.

"How is Toyls treating you?" He asked quietly.

"Oh, it's so luxuriously exhausting."

"That is such a drastic change from the restful homeless chic of the house." He chuckled slightly.

I returned his laugh. "Homeless chic, I couldn't have described it better myself."

"That's because I'm simply better," he yawned, stopping in front of my door; turning to me with a more serious look. "I've missed you this last week."

"Says the man who spent the last year disappearing on me for months at a time." I crossed my arms and glared at him.

He smiled sleepily and shrugged. "I've been disappearing for a lot longer than just the last year. You were better off without me."

The casualness of his tone irritated me so much that I wanted to kick him in the shin. I had to use every shred of my willpower not to do so. I huffed back, turning to the door, but he grabbed my wrist and pulled me into a hug.

His arms around me were firm but soft. "I missed you every time I left," he said.

I sat there, a million questions and insults echoing through my head, but I stayed silent. Instead, I enjoyed the feeling of leaning against his chest, feeling his body get heavier with exhaustion every passing second before finally pulling away.

"Goodnight, Aska."

"Goodnight, Lun."

***

Jay's alarm went off at exactly 5:30. While I was already rolling over to shove my face back in the pillow, he was jumping off the top bunk and landing hard on the ground next to me.

"Quiet it down; I don't have to be up," Blake muttered from across the room.

"Agreed," I responded, groaning.

"False information, you are coming with me," Jay said tugging on my arm, dragging me from my comfy bed and onto the cold hard floor. I stood groggily and followed him into the hallway to knock on the other door. Tresa emerged with Aska in tow.

"Good morning, sleepy heads," Jay clapped Aska on the back.

"It's too early for you to be in such a good mood," he groaned back, taking my arm and laying his head on my shoulder. The doors to the bar swung open and Burn approached with a tray of coffees in his hand.

"Drink up and suit up into your equipment." He commanded, passing the tray to Jay. We each took our coffees before separating into different parts of the basement to prepare.

Only a half hour later, we were loading up into the van. Burn wore an entirely black outfit with long sleeves and a new tactical vest that held his small containers of gasoline, as well as a slot for his gloves and some standard burn cream, gauze, and painkillers. Aska wore a similar get-up; except he had binoculars and water attached to his vest. Bags of hair dangled off Tresa's chest in the same spot where mine was plain. Jay wore his regular clothes; I suppose he would be in bird form the majority of the time, so his clothes were less than important.

Tresa and Burn took their front seats in the van, loading Jay, Aska, and I into the back. Aska leaned over, resuming his place on my shoulder, softly snoring after a few minutes. It only took a short quarter hour to arrive at our destination just outside town. Tresa parked in a grove of trees surrounding a creek just off the road, inside a valley to ensure we were out of sight of the watchtowers.

The hospital loomed across the skyline, peering just above the collections of trees that circled it. A tall fence with barbed wire toppings traced its perimeter, only a few meters away from the gray outline of the hospital's stone walls. Bars covered its small windows, except for those in the middle, and two watch towers stood guarding the front entrance. A slight glance passed between me and Aska as we followed Tresa and Burn to the edge of the tree line.

"Remember, you'll have only 1 minute to drop the bag and get out once you're out of Tresa's range," Burn told Jay, setting two of Tresa's hair bags on the ground.

"Oh, believe me, I remember after last time." Jay shuddered, transforming into his small little Bluejay. The bird picked one bag up in his claws and another in his beak before flying off towards the towers. We waited, watching for his return. Soon an explosion crumbled the tip of the left tower, shortly followed by a twin blast on the other. Emerging from the ruckus came flying our familiar bluebird.

With steaming feathers on his rear, he flew down, latching onto another two bags from Tresa and then resuming flight towards the building. He disappeared into the smoke cinematically; Tresa kept her eyes locked on him the whole time; her brows furrowed together.

"What is she doing?" I whispered to Burn.

"Holding the explosion, we've been working on it in her training more recently. If she concentrates enough, she can buy Jay up to a minute before the hair ignites. Naturally, they would just explode once they got more than a hundred meters away from the source or whenever she chooses to ignite them." He explained quietly.

We watched as Jay reemerged from the smoke, finally allowing Tresa to release her tension; another explosion echoing from the distance. Jay collapsed to the ground in his human form, panting heavily.

"Generators. . . out," he gasped, raising a thumbs up.

"Perfect, thank you" Burn helped him to his feet. "Onyx, your turn"

"My turn?"

"Her turn?" Aska echoed with an eyebrow raise.

"I know it's a lot to ask, but I was hoping you would be able to blend the five of us into the shadows- like we practiced- just until we are inside the building."

"I can do that- I think." I stuttered, trying to connect to the shadows around me; teasing my abilities to check their power. "Everyone grab on and stay connected." I reached out and allowed Tresa and Aska to take my hands, Jay, and

Burn joining on each of their other sides. Together, we slipped around the side of the 'hospital.' When we arrived at the fence line, I watched as Burn, still concealed in shadows, traced his finger along a invisible path in the metal wire. Every spot he touched steamed and turned a brilliant red orange, snapping apart. After a moment, the final chain broke, and Burn removed the now separate section of fence, revealing a "bad side of town" sketchy version of an Alice in Wonderland tunnel to the other side. I felt Tresa tense ahead of me as one of the still-searing half-links ripped through the upper shoulder of her shirt. Reflex tears welled in her eyes, but she remained silent, knowing any sound may be our downfall. Once on the lawn, Burn led our crew to the back entrance of the building, melting the lock away and revealing the hospital's powerless and vacant interior. On the upper levels, we could hear the congregation of guards, their shuffling of boots, and panicked conversation.

"Check… rooms… machigai." I heard through the ceiling.

"Power…just… nothing…no… worried… I'll… generator," his comrade responded. The clanking of metal souls traveled across the roof, leading us to the stairwell.

Hidden by shadows, we watched as the second man made his way down the stairs. He was a tall man with steroid-like muscles and platinum blond hair grown out just past regulation length. Everything about him made me want to carve the smug smile off his face with a knife, but I never got the chance. At the bottom of the stairs, he suddenly halted; his body seizing and writhing, smoke wafting from his blond hair turning it a crispy black at the tips. He looked as though he had been electrocuted, but there was no sign of the source nearby. That was until I felt a gentle shaking in Aska's hand. Burn caught the man as he fell to the ground, breaking his link to us and emerging from the shadows. He lowered Blondie slowly, careful not to cause alarm upstairs, before turning back to us.

I released the shadows, sparing my energy, but kept ahold of Aska's still trembling hand. Burn gestured to Jay and Tresa and then upwards. He held out his hand, holding up the first two fingers and then three. *Second and third floors.* He then repeated the motion towards me in Aska, but instead with four and five fingers.

We nodded and bolted up the stairs, watching Tresa and Jay split off to the third floor. Scaling the next two levels, I glanced down at the watch attached to my wrist. 07:06. Twenty-four minutes to do what needed to be done. Aska matched my pace to the 5th floor, helping me slide the door open, revealing what seemed like an endless tunnel of padded rooms with one-way glass and heavy-duty doors with food slots guarding them. The door banged shut behind us, alerting three guards in the first stretch of hallway and turning their attention toward us. But it wasn't long after they vacated their rooms and began their pursuit that all three stopped in their tracks. One man, not unlike the guard downstairs, fell to the ground smoking from his tips from electrocution. Another shrieked from the top of his lungs as he raised his arms in front of his face; small trails of blood leaking out of each bruised puncture wound before he collapsed next to his coworker. The third stared us straight in the eyes and smiled as he sat peacefully on the ground, his face turning deeper and deeper shades of purple as he spat out gallons of water on the floor.

I turned to Aska, whose face was nearly as purple.

He took a deep breath and nodded ahead. "The kids, let's go." I nodded back, taking off to check the first few cells. Nothing. Then finally, about halfway down the first hall, a young girl sat leaning with her back towards the observation glass, her black hair pressing against it like a paint blob. I spawned a void beneath her, releasing her at my feet. Her deep complexion was clammy, and her eyes unfocused, but she slowly looked up at me and then to the cell to her left.

"Are you Jesus?" she whispered.

Chapter 25: Windows…. Yay…

"In a sense… yes," I told the girl, hauling her up to her feet. She nodded, allowing Aska to take her hand. I pushed forward, trusting him to watch her and match her pace. A few cells ahead, another girl, just over my own age, paced around her cell, itching at the needle scars and bruises that lined her inner arm. Unlike the first, this girl seemed to be at least somewhat aware of her surroundings. I watched the void open underneath her, releasing her in front of me and summoning a new ringing in my ears. She glared over to me unphased.

I tried for a sweet smile, reaching out my hand for her to shake. "I'm Luna."

"You're no one, just another fake." She stated simply, continuing her glaring. "I'd like to return to real life now," she said, finally looking away. I choked on my words, unsure of what to do next.

"She's not a hallucination," Aska interrupted. "We aren't hallucinations; we are real, and it's time to go. Join us or stay here; it's your choice." He continued on down the hall. Hesitantly I followed, looking back at the girl who seemed to be in a self-debate. Aska stopped a few cells ahead, gesturing inside at a boy bouncing a ball against the wall. I mimicked the motion I did the last two times, dropping him next to us. He looked around confused, ball still in hand. Suddenly, then the ball disappeared.

"I knew it; I knew someone had to come." He threw his arms around me, eyes lighting up. When he pulled away and caught me staring at his empty hand, he attempted a dreary smile that only accented the dark bags that hung under his deep brown eyes. He held his hand out, and the ball appeared again; I held my own hand out, and he sat it in my palm. The ball shifted first from its red rubber form to a mini wooden rocking horse and then to a cell phone before disappearing again.

"It's not real; it's all a mirage." He smiled, shaking my hand. "That's what they call me, or they used to… Mirage. My real name is Lucas."

"Nice to meet you, Lucas." I responded as Aska checked his watch.

"15 minutes left, Lun. We need to pick up the pace. Release and run."

"Got it." I nodded, beginning to take off down the hallway, but I was stopped when Lucas grabbed my wrist.

"My brother, we need to find him. I know he's somewhere on this floor; I can feel him," Lucas said with wide pleading eyes.

"Lead the way," Aska gestured down the hall, forcing Lucus to the front of the pack with Aska still trailing close behind. I took the hand of the first girl, who was still dazed. Behind us, the second girl had also joined but seemed to be keeping her distance. We found two more kids, a boy and a girl, both between five and ten years old, before making it to Lucas's brother's cell. The boy was shaking and curled up in the corner when we found him, remaining in that same fetal position even after being released. It wasn't until Lucas lifted his chin that we saw the first signs of life.

The boy screamed, eyes wide and frightened, darting from each of us to the next.

"No-no, no, no," he muttered, scooting away from our group. Lucas gingerly followed him, grabbing him by his shoulders and pulling him into a hug.

"Shhh, shhh, it's okay, come back to me."

"No-No! They're coming for us, Lucas; they all are! You have to listen to me!" The boy sobbed into his brother's shoulder. Now that they were this close, it was plain to see they weren't simply brothers but twins. The same tight curls ran rampant on the same long, tired faces, topping the same twiggy bodies. The acne across their jawline was identical, even the clothes they wore were the same, their clearly worn jeans clinging loosely on their frail dark skin.

"I am listening, Issac, but no one is coming to hurt us. You are safe. We are safe." He cupped his brother's cheek in his hand. Isaac let a few more tears fall before nodding and accepting Lucas's hand up. He kept his eyes only on his brother as we walked, occasionally snapping his head in an unknown direction or screaming out at invisible figures.

"It's the mirages." Lucas whispered to me as we opened the staircase on the other side of the hall after collecting only one other child on our journey on the 5th floor. Issac's hand was still attached to Lucas's, but his eyes and thoughts seemed to be anywhere else but here. "He makes them too, but they're stronger. They'll rip him apart, take his mind away from reality, create people and creatures that aren't real." I glanced over to Issac, who was muttering to himself while staring at the railing of the stairwell. Lucas must have noticed my gaze because he added, "He's crazy but not even remotely dangerous, not to anyone but himself. I promise."

"We are all crazy in our own ways." I shifted my gaze to watch Aska ahead.

"Tis the life of a machigai." Lucas laughed.

"We should try to make it through the 4th floor too, just run through. No talking, just release and leave." Aska said, turning to the door on our right. He slid it open, and unlike the last one, no guards appeared, leaving us empty in the hall.

We took off down the corridor, making shockingly good time. As we walked past each cell, I simply glanced inside, and if there was someone, I slipped them through the shadows to the outside of the cell. With every kid released, my eyelids drooped, and my head pounded, but we forced our way forward, leaving every kid sitting on the ground in front of their cell. Two more joined our group; the others just sat in front of their cells, sometimes crying, sometimes dead; silent and still.

We emerged into the t-shaped intersection that marked the center of our journey. Aska pushed on, but something else caught my attention. A door hung open at the end of the hall, one unlike any of the others. An office door. I turned back and saw that Aska and the others were a few cells down, behind me Katrina, the second girl we had found and so far, the eldest, stood holding onto Lucas's brother Issac's hand.

"Stay close," I told them both, approaching the door. I grabbed one of my father's guns that was attached to the holster at my hip, kicking the door open to reveal an empty room. Glass walls covered the far side, revealing the green grass and fence line below. A large wooden desk sat to our right and the left wall of the room was plastered with filing cabinets. Issac began shrieking from the added light of the rising sun reflecting through the windows.

"Christ almighty kid. Shut the fuck up," Katrina muttered, covering her ears and stepping up to the window to stare at the lawn. She shuddered a bit, her grimace softening. "It's been a while since I've seen a sunrise."

"Brighter than you remember?' I asked with a laugh, making my way to the desk.

"A bit, actually, yes." I decided to let her have her moment, trying desperately to ignore Issac; still in the door frame, who had begun muttering in between his short, cut-off screams. I examined the mahogany desk, papers scattered over its top, photos of the owner's family in pretty little silver frames. I picked up one and examined it. He stood with his wife and a small child. His wife's eyes bore into me, their frighteningly familiar dirty blue gaze holding mine wherever I went. She was strong, with long legs and muscular arms that were cut off by the fitted black tank she wore. My heart dropped, the buzzing in my ears growing as I traced those arms up to her collarbone. A collar bone marked by an upside-down moon tattoo, the same tattoo that I would stare into as its owner's claws raked my face. The same tattoo I would look at instead of my mother's eyes when she would force me into a half-apologetic hug for actions she never regretted.

"MISTAKE!" The woman jumped out of the frame, shouting at me. I dropped the frame with a scream, shattering it on the ground.

"Luna?" I heard Aska shout from down the hall, but I stood petrified, staring at the frame. Katrina came over and shook me.

"Snap out of it!" I looked her in her eyes, steadying my breathing. Everything was still for just a moment.

And then Issac made impact.

The small boy ran into us both at full speed, with a long barbaric screech, slamming us both through the glass window. The next thing I knew, my hand was latched to Katrina's, staring up at her needle-marked forearm. Her other hand was clinging to the ledge, the only thing preventing us both from falling the four floors onto the cement below. Issac loomed over us, snapping his head back and forth, tears streaming down his face.

"No-Never-Help-Time," he muttered, lowering himself down and shaking back and forth on the ground. Katrina grunted hard, lifting me to the ledge next to her. I winced as sharp shards of shattered glass forced their way into my palms, shredding the muscle underneath my skin.

"Issac, help-" Katrina's voice died out. I looked over to see her eyes turned entirely black, as if two miniature 8-balls had taken their place.

"Help- help is good- relief is good- death," Issac muttered before looking my way. His skin was clammy, but his expression was more scared and scattered than regretful. Then he disappeared, instead in his place was Rosemonde Ray Leonce-Tremblay, wearing the same outfit she was last seen in 10 years ago. Her eyes were still red and unfocused, her skin cloudy, peering through the rips in her baggy red t-shirt that hung just low enough to reveal the crescent upside-down moon that swam just below her shoulder.

"Join me… my beautiful-darling-Anastasia de Lun." *Anastasia.* My middle name. A name I blocked out years ago. The name my mother began calling me after my father left. "Join me." She whispered, stepping forward towards me, kneeling down to my level, and pulling a knife from her back pocket. The same knife I had left on the closet floor that night. She traced it over the knuckles of my hands, a stinging pain and a trail of blood following its path, forcing me to release a blood curdling scream. All of my energy flooded into holding on, even as tears poured down my face. "Join me in death, my girl." She raised the knife above her head, and I closed my eyes, waiting for the blow.

"Luna!" Aska latched onto my wrist; my mother now gone.

"Aska," I whispered back as he and Lucas hauled me up. I looked to my left, hoping to see Katrina. Instead, I found her sprawled across the pavement four stories down. I followed Lucas's gaze to the corner where his brother lay, a gunshot wound leaking blood from behind his still head.

"Lun, you're bleeding." Aska grabbed my wrist, revealing the gory state of my palms. My watch flashed up at me: less than two minutes to get to the fence; we were almost out of time.

"Prioritize the kids" I said, barely a whisper. He opened his mouth to speak, then cautiously dragged me into his arms, holding me there tightly while I held myself together by a thread. Finally, he gently kissed the top of my head before pulling away and nodding.

"Everyone, follow me quickly or be left behind! Let's go!" He shouted, turning back out through the door with one final glance. Everyone turned and followed, apart from Lucas, who instead retrieved his brother's limp body from its resting place in the corner, lifting him in his arms with tears streaming down his face. Without meeting my eyes or saying a word, he stepped out the door with his head held high. I began to follow, but something stopped me before I could make it to the door. My eyes darted back to the desk in the corner, to the shattered frame that peered at me from behind its wooden legs. I brushed the glass away from the photo, looking at it more closely. A man, his wife, and three children, none of whom I knew.

Chapter 26: These People Are Something Else

Upon returning to the hotel, Lily healed my hands before we joined the others in washing up the kids. In total, almost thirty machigai were saved, doubling their last record. Even just getting up and moving around, the basement was cramped beyond imagination, forcing Burn to make the executive decision to have Tresa drive the kids to Greenville as soon as they were able. Then, she would stay the night in their ranks and drive back the next morning.

Despite the events of the day, that night was incredible. Even through my objections, unable to remove the images of Katrina and Issac from my mind, Jay dragged me to the bar. After a few of his espresso martinis, I was in a sleepy, giggly mess, pushing everything else to the back of my mind.

As a whole, I couldn't be too upset; twenty-eight kids were safe because of us. Sometime in the night, someone had turned up the stereo, and we joined together to move all of the tables out of the way and have a mini dance party. As Jay was lugging one of the tables across the room, I noticed him struggling and gave him a "do you need help" look. He sneered back sarcastically, but I approached to help anyways. After almost getting the table piled onto the heap in the corner of the room, he flexed at me, and I decided this was the perfect time to let go, trapping him in the corner with fear in his eyes.

Aska turned on the speakers and started hard rock. Lily shrugged and started doing a weird interpretive dance to the loud music, causing the others to all start laughing before Burn finally turned it back to traditional pop and turned down the volume. For around an hour, the room transformed into a space that could put any college frat party to shame. Aska and I danced together; he even attempted to twirl me around, but his arm got caught in a stray fist bump from Jay, who was totally in his own zone. At one point he even climbed on the bar and screamed, "Check out my dance moves!" Before promptly tripping and falling face-first on the floor. That would be great bullying material later. Finally, after a few hours, the music became so loud that Mrs. Madalini came down, forcing us to turn in sometime in the early morning.

That was the final moment before my half-truth, half-life began.

Calvin began tutoring me in math, every day after school, while I would help push him during training and weightlifting. For the most part, everyone else at Toyls faded into the background, with a few jabs about my hair here and there. Jake's nickname of "Ombre" unfortunately stuck with the majority of the class, which I was grateful for in a sense. The new name definitely helped redefine this new persona. I wasn't quite Lily, but I couldn't be Onyx; instead, I was Ombre. The teasing Calvin endured was worse by far, so I couldn't complain much either way.

Nearly everyone on our floor vexed me on some occasion; their self-absorbed attitudes, their poor hygiene, their mocking tones; it all drove me insane. One girl, in particular, had developed a uniquely terrifying habit of sharpening her blades in the bay window of the main room.

Jake, in his own existence, had several irritating qualities: waking up at 5 am for early training, increasing his muscle mass by the day, and, in turn, his booming footsteps, waking me up from my well-earned rest.

Days turned to weeks and then months. Settling in took time, my grades were probably close to the bare minimum, and my sanity mirrored them. Training got exponentially stranger throughout the semester. On one evening, we found ourselves back in the midst of the large domed facility. New buildings popped up around us, the setting much more elaborate than last time, with different buildings and small land features such as bushes, all placed on sod rather than sand.

Combat class constantly proved itself to be simultaneously my favorite and least favorite of all the courses. Favorite in the sense that it was one of the few times a day I could pummel the arrogant miscreants who were dead set on murdering me. Least favorite in the sense that unless I managed to out-strategize them, a novelty that proved to be less-occurring in an environment where my curse (to everyone else's knowledge) was non-existent, it was more often that I was on the receiving end of the pummeling. Hopefully, that would change today; I had the advantage after all; building jumping was an acquired skill, one that I doubt these middle-class suburban children had much experience with.

"Twenty teams of two," Mr. Gariag, our combat teacher, shouted. He was an older fellow with a shaven head and wisps of salt and pepper stubble. He was about eye level with me, but his years in the MES were well worn into his exterior, with stocky muscles and a pale burn scar traveling from behind his ear and disappearing into his shirt. "James, Danny, you two together. Olivia, Calvin. Harry, Jessica…" he continued on down the list, eventually pairing Jake and myself together.

"Ombre!" Jake high-fived me, carrying on with his falsely friendly demeanor. "We gonna win this?"

"I suppose," I shrugged.

"Confidence, hun, confidence." He rolled his eyes as we stood awkwardly, waiting for our turn.

The concept of the game was very similar to the one we had played the day of entrance exams, except the arena was divided into four equal sections for less mobility, and instead of one hundred students against a handful of MES officers, it was two teams vs. one another. From what the others said, the challenge was simply laser-tag with more space, which was a common occurrence with most combat challenges at Toyls.

Our active uniforms possessed a singular leg garter on each thigh that held our "weapons" for class, in other words, a dagger with a rounded rubber point and a tracer pistol with no bullets but rather a beam of purplish light that connected with our targets. The pistol could convert between three settings: sniper, rapid-fire, and close range. The touch screen pad on the side of the gun allowed the user to switch between the settings, while also enabling and changing the distance on the scope. Each uniform also possessed "kill zones" that were set off by contact with either the rubber of the dagger or the beam of the gun. The five zones were attached to separate locations on our uniforms; one on our silver helmets, another rubbed against my neck from the high collar of the spandex top, two more were placed along each student's spine, and a final one rested above each of our hearts. They were light, almost like stickers, sewn into the uniforms, but it did raise the question of how the staff washed these get-ups every day after class without short-circuiting the technology.

Finally, Mr. Gariag called to Jake and me as a buzzer went off for the last team. We were assigned to section two. Looking down from the catwalk, we could see the buildings below. I watched as Jake carefully examined the terrain with his trade-marked arrogance. My mind similarly began to develop strategy after strategy, silently knowing they would be pushed aside to fit my partner's so very clearly superior plan. Together, we exited down the catwalk to the section entrance; Calvin followed in the trail of the blond girl with knife-sharpening tendencies. *Perfect.* I internally rolled my eyes; I'll have to pummel the sole lifeline to my passing grades, and a girl whom I was 45% sure had removed the rubber from her dagger.

"The queen and the vegetable? This will be fun." I couldn't tell how much sarcasm laced Jake's statement as he marched ahead.

"Vegetable?" I asked curiously.

"Her name is Olive; that's a vegetable, is it not?" He looked back at me as I struggled to keep up with his pace.

"I guess?"

He rolled his eyes and looked back ahead. "Oh, forget it; the joke's ruined anyways."

We set our places for each team on opposite sides of the small sectioned-off area, our suits syncing to our assigned box. We would be disqualified immediately if one team member stepped even a foot out of the zone. The cliche-toned countdown commenced, and in perfect timing with the alarm, Jake sprinted off.

"What's the plan?" I shouted, without response, from nearly five meters back already. Jake jumped up, latching his hands onto the roof gutter, bending it slightly as he pulled himself up. Sadly, I do have to admit the move was quite impressive, the gutter being a bit over two meters, whereas Jake was nowhere near CEBL height. Shockingly, he kneeled on the roof, reaching down for my hand. I hesitantly allowed him to hoist me up, throwing my knee over the side of the building like a toddler crawling out of a pool. Once again, Jake took off to the other side of the roof.

"Olive isn't much one for heights, and judging by his previous performances, I believe Calvin will likely follow her lead. That means our advantage is on the roof's high ground, but they'll figure this out just as fast and likely be stalking us to try to gain first eyes. Olive may prefer close-range combat, but Calvin isn't awful at sharpshooting; they'll try to snipe us."

"Sniping from ground point? It'd be throwing rocks at bees."

"With a scope, but yes, that's why they'll get the highest possible location within the safety of a building; they won't go on roofs."

"Which is?"

He pointed to the tallest building, possibly three or four stories; it was styled like a small office building, nearly completely surrounded by windows.

"Wow, nice eye, but you sure?" I asked.

"Positive."

"So, what's the plan?" I followed as he started jumping to the closer roofs.

"That building has three stories; I noticed when we were waiting before that there another building with two stories directly behind it; we get there and make it to the top to sneak in. I'd expect they'd be close to entering the building by now; we need to hurry." I followed as he leaped from roof to roof in a path so decisive and graceful I could practically feel Jay's eyebrows being set ablaze in rage. Within moments, we arrived at the two-story building, Jake just barely out of breath while I doubled over, panting as he scanned all the floors of the building.

"They're behind schedule, only on the first floor; that'll work perfectly. Shit-" Jake's shoe turned, knocking a few pebbles off the roof. Olivia's eyes darted up first, sending shivers down my spine and locking my gaze in place. Jake had already disappeared from my side, latching onto the window seal on the glass building. Down below, I saw Olivia raise her gun, lining up the shot while Calvin slid open the window (not technically necessary, seeing as it was a laser, but probably the safer bet as Mr. Gariag would've docked their grade for a move like that). "Jump!" Jake yelled, reaching out his hand from the seal as Olivia pulled the trigger. The shot must've missed, but she loaded up her second as Calvin began lining up his first try. A leap of faith and I latched onto Jake, who flung me up next to him on the seal.

"What now?" I clung to the wall and his shoulder, "They'll just climb the stairs and make easy targets-" His hand slipped behind my back, and his sadistically sly smile was the last thing I saw before plummeting through the air.

Chapter 27: Can I Get A Week Off From Dying?

Suddenly I was falling, tumbling through the skies. It felt like an eternity before I hit the concrete with a sickening *crack*, an oddly warm sensation briefly cradling my back on the concrete, my vision -one odd grainy blur- filling with black static. The static also swarmed my ears as I tried to concentrate on the broken pieces of voice I heard.

"Li–" Calvin, he was getting closer. Jake's trap was working at my expense.

"Ca—-It—-TRAP!!" The knife girl screamed. The rest of my vision faded, leaving only my hearing, lasting just long enough to hear the winning buzzer.

***

There was no longer any warmth, only surprisingly mild pain. My vision finally filled in from a shockingly dreamless sleep. I was lying face down on a clean white pillow. The room, long and white, was sprinkled with simple twin beds identical to mine, accompanied by wheeled silver carts with digital alarm clocks on them. A piercing shriek escaped from my lungs, the painful result of attempting to sit up to read the time. The memory of Jake's last facial expression echoed through my mind.

"Oh, you're awake!" A painfully cheerful lady wearing scrubs approached, calmly holding a large bowl filled with broth, mushrooms, and odd cream-colored cubes- tofu if I had to guess. The lady was slightly on the plump side, with faded black bangs and shoulder length hair. She sat the bowl on a wheel table, sliding it as close to the bed as possible, and plopping a comedically long straw inside.

"Drink," she commanded sweetly, placing the straw in my mouth. The soup was shockingly good, weirdly flavorful for broth. "I'm Miss Mary; I'll be your nurse." She introduced herself in such a way, I half expected her to tell me this evening's specials. "You're quite the lucky girl, took a pretty bad tumble there, we were all expecting some form of breakage, but nope! Bruised and cut yourself up quite a bit, though." She fumbled with what felt like the familiar sensation of gauze on my back. Brief panic welled through me, suddenly realizing my front half was covered only by the bed and a backless hospital gown while my back was entirely exposed other than spandex shorts. I had no explanation for the blister scars that covered my torso and arms. Cool air covered the now exposed fresh wounds coating my back, adding a new relief to the burning pain. Mary added fresh cream to the wounds, leaving them tingly but with next to no pain.

"Emver cream." She leaned down and winked at me sweetly. "Toyls' very own chemists invented it a few years back; it treats cuts, scrapes, burns, practically everything." She laughed. "I would hardly know how to do my job without it." She flashed the container at me and screwed the lid back on before setting it on the table.

"They want you released in the morning, so you'd better rest; I'll be back in a few hours to reapply your wrap. Sleep well." She waved goodbye and disappeared from my sight.

***

Sleep wasn't difficult to obtain; the cream left me feeling nearly as drained as Lily would. When I woke, my bandages had already been freshened up, and the clock read 10:00. My classmates would be in trig right now; that was an odd thought. I never knew strictly where someone would be and when; something was off about it.

I sat up in bed, flinching with the remaining pain from my back. My head hung slightly; energy depleted. I looked around the room once more; there were clean white cabinets on the other side of the room, but no cameras or windows. One of my bags sat on the lower shelf of the cart next to me. I latched onto its straps and gently tossed it up onto the bedside; a fresh pair of black leggings and a grey t-shirt sat inside. The t-shirt was short-sleeved, something I would've likely only layered with long sleeves due to the remaining blister scars on my arms, but I couldn't be picky at this moment. Stuck onto the neatly folded clothes sat a small yellow sticky note reading "Get well soon, -Cal" with a small smiley face in the bottom left corner.

A brief feeling of warmth played with my senses before being promptly swept away by the claustrophobic panic and guilt that always plagued the thoughts of the new and growing false friendship I had somehow accumulated. I crumpled the note and threw it back in the bag, trying to shake the feeling and focus on clothing myself instead.

A gasp of pain escaped my lungs from the pressure of fully sitting up. I realized a moment too late that I was still wearing spandex shorts and simply decided to ignore them, sliding the leggings over with mild discomfort; the t-shirt would be long enough to cover the outline anyways. I slipped out of the hospital-style gown and into the t-shirt. Other than the spandex slightly bunching under the leggings, the outfit was oddly comforting, reminding me of something I would wear back at home with Aska, the only place my skin could ever breathe without risking exposure.

The clock now read 10:20 am, 40 minutes before it was no longer considered "morning." Miss Mary didn't exactly seem like someone to avoid punctuality. My eyes danced over the white cabinets as ideas spun through my head.

Standing was next to unbearable; the bandages wrinkled and expanded across my back, digging into the raw flesh as I hobbled over to the cabinets. Their contents were pretty standard: lots of over-the-counter meds, bandages, gauze, etc. One cabinet was entirely filled with small containers of the specialized cream Miss Mary had fawned over so dearly. They were only about 16 oz a piece, a short-lived supply but possibly enough for slight relief. I swiped two containers from the cabinet and gently closed it, silently praying that they weren't responsible enough to keep an accurate chart of the med bay's contents.

Miss Mary showed up at precisely 11:00 on the dot, carrying a small plastic bag.

"Oops! I tried buying you a bit extra sleep time; I didn't mean to keep you waiting. You're all set, I see." I nodded along, allowing her to fill the conversational space alone. "Well, right this way, pretty miss." She grabbed my bag for me and slung it over her shoulder, making sure to keep the pace slow as I gradually followed, occasionally wincing with my steps. It was Thursday, I believed, meaning there was only one day of classes to suffer through before being able to make a much-deserved trip back to the hotel to actually relax. I hadn't been back in nearly three weeks and had hardly spoken to Burn or Jay alike over the phone either. Both were risks, and I was no longer in crippling pain from soreness at the end of each week, forcing me to return home to be healed by Lily. Not to mention I hadn't gathered any severely important information other than training schedules, fighting styles, and weaknesses in securities. But nearly dying, and acquiring the specialized cream seemed a good enough reason to visit.

I followed Miss Mary past the staircase to a double set of elevators us students had only ever dreamed of accessing, she scanned her key card on the door and stood in the doorway, allowing me time to make my way in at a turtle-like pace.

"We really aren't supposed to do this, but I've never quite been one for following everrry rule." She giggled, encapsulating the energy of those woman that would walk into stores and ask about samples while constantly saying how they were being "so bad" by breaking their middle-aged suburban mom diets.

Once I was fully in the elevator and secured to the side, Miss Mary handed me both my bag and the small plastic one she'd been holding.

"There will be a meeting in Madam Toyls' office during your lunch break tomorrow for the injury report. I'll be by your room to escort you and Mr. Derrien there at 11:50."

Being escorted anywhere in the presence of Jake currently was an unpleasant thought to say the least. With luck, he would be expelled, eliminating any chance of other students suffering a worse fate than me, while also allowing me more rest in the mornings without his loud footsteps in the halls waking me up before dawn. I pushed the thoughts away and focused on Miss Mary, who pointed to the plastic bag and lowered her bright and happy tone down to a more serious whisper. "There's three containers of cream in there; apply it generously to the wounds." She paused and stared, a bit of pity in her eyes. "It works on blisters, too." My skin tingled in remembrance of my scars, open for the world to see. "I don't know what or who's..." she hesitated, letting the word sink in. "Responsible, but you should know, Toyls' medical staff is fully equipped with therapy and counseling professionals; all you need to do is ask." She smiled sweetly and tilted her head, the same look people used to give me when I was young and begged on the streets. People are always so willing to help only enough to help satiate their own guilt before continuing to turn a blind eye.

I nodded, attempting a look worthy of her sympathy, like a lost and injured puppy. It was a familiar act, a familiar mask, like a daily makeup routine.

Miss Mary clicked a button in elevator, the second to last one from the top. On its surface the number four was printed in gold lettering, the 1st year dorms. She scanned her key against the pad on the inside, granting all clearance, and stepped away, allowing the elevator doors to slide closed.

My eyes darted across the elevator, searching for something to read or focus on to avoid thinking about the implications of Miss Mary's statements or tomorrow's looming confrontation; they landed on the other elevator buttons. The fifth floor held 1st years dorms, just as the fourth floor did. The 1st years were the only class to have two floors, due to most students not passing that year alone; the third and second floors were 2nd and 3rd years. Most 4th years were rarely on campus and didn't live in dorms, the entire year was mostly a work-study, with an occasional class or request for help with the lower classmen. For the few that did choose to remain on campus, they could easily fit in with the 3rd years. The second to last button was labeled with a captial letter 'L', marking the lobby. Then it got confusing. Underneath the lobby was -1, teacher and staff offices, then -2 and -3. We had not been informed of these levels at orientation. Opportunity and fear alike tugged at my mind, slamming my hand impulsively against the -3 button, but it was no use; without a card, I had no access to any other floor than my own. I watched helplessly as the doors slid open onto my own floor.

Chapter 28: I Hate This Place

I wasn't back in my room long enough to even catch some shut eye, before Calvin came barging in. I suppose he still had a key card from packing my clothes.

"You're back!" He jumped on the bed, forcing me to wince as it shook my back. "I'm sorry, I'm sorry," he said, grabbing my shoulder gently, propping some pillows up behind me, and helping me sit up with less pain.

"You're okay," I muttered quietly, trying to mask the mild irritation in my voice.

"Is there anything I can do?" He was sitting on his knees, staring me down with those big puppy eyes. How was this kid going to survive life as an MES officer? He'll be torn to pieces in the field.

"My homework," I chuckled slightly, trying to lighten the tone.

"Okay." He immediately got up and sat down in my desk chair.

"Calvin, sweetie… sarcasm." I rubbed my temples exhaustedly, a habit I traced back to watching Burn do it too often during training. "But I do actually need to finish this week's homework, so could you bring me the English binder and a pencil?" He nodded and sat the binder down on the bed to my side, resuming his place as well.

"How are you back so soon, anyhow? You fell two stories; we were all assuming you'd be gone till at least Monday, with a few broken bones at a minimum- and you look better than expected- not that you look good–I, no that- you don't look bad, it's just-"

"Calvin?" I opened my binder; I only had one assignment left from English this week, as I tended to have more motivation to finish it than in my other classes.

"Hm?" He looked at me with those sad embarassed puppy dog eyes.

"Shut up," I stated dryly, coaxing a smile from his lips.

"Yes, ma'am."

We sat in comfortable silence for the rest of Cal's lunch break; he ran down to the first floor to grab a to-go lunch we split while working on our respective projects before he returned to class. Miss Mary had left a note on my desk stating I was excused from classes for today and tomorrow. Excused absences were a rare thing at Toyls, typically only awarded when the school itself was involved in the reason you were absent, such as work studies or being called to the field. Excused absences really only meant you would be sent a briefing of the lessons for those days, unlike unexcused absences, when you were responsible for catching yourself up. The briefings were actually very helpful, allowing me to make significant progress through my homework before drifting to sleep.

***

I woke up with Calvin gently closing the door, reentering the room with two Styrofoam boxes in hand. A blanket had spawned over me sometime during my rest and all of my homework had been moved away and neatly stacked on the desk as well.

"Sorry, I didn't mean to wake you…" He blushed. "Just dropping off dinner." He smiled, handing me a box and some plastic silverware.

"You managed to con your way into two boxes?" I raised my eyebrow as he sat on the foot of the bed, opening his own box.

"One of the nurses was passing by when I was trying to explain why I needed two; she vouched for me and convinced the cafeteria man to give me a pass for a bit. Nice lady." Calvin was much more mellowed out than in his high-energy state earlier; training usually did that to him, understandably.

We once again ate together and worked on our assignments. I vaguely remembered him falling asleep at the foot of the bed, but by morning I was unsure when in the night he had left.

It was past 10 am when I woke. *I have to stop sleeping so late before Monday.* I thought to myself silently, cursing the abrupt change in schedule while also sliding out of bed. I had completely neglected my bandages the day prior. After I showered, I added another layer of the special cream, which meant their condition as of today was a wrinkled and scrunched mess that dug into my abdomen in deep red indentions. Carefully, I reapplied them with spare gauze and struggled to throw on a slightly nicer outfit for Madam Toyls. Jeans and a fitted long-sleeved black shirt; I was not informed of any dress code, so this was a proper middle ground. My dyed tips had faded tremendously quicker after I was granted easier access to a hot shower; the blue was hardly even visible anymore. I made a silent mental note to touch them up as soon as I had the chance.

Miss Mary knocked on the dorm door at 11:48, two minutes early. She came in and checked to make sure the bandages were properly changed before meeting Jake, already in the hall; I glared daggers at his still-toying smile. The kid held no remorse for his actions, not that I expected any, but it certainly didn't help matters. *Lord, let his absence from Machigai History per Region not be excused.* That was a particularly fast-paced class, not necessarily difficult, but certainly a lot of information to process, and incredibly torturous to catch up on without notes.

We were not granted the pleasure of the elevator today, and while the pain had been reduced, the stairs were still treacherous, and with only 10 minutes to get to Mrs. Toyls office on the main level, Miss Mary was less kind with her pace. Within half of the time frame, I sat next to Jake in matching red lounge chairs centered in a hexagonal room. The room was not overly large, seeing as there wasn't much space to spare on the lobby floor. The desk in front of them, on the other hand, was less than humble. With hundreds of tiny engravings, it reminded me of sleeve tattoos, millions of arts morphing together to create one piece in grand mahogany. A glass door to our right revealed another slightly larger room with a bed and other living arrangements. I suppose running entire training facilities really was a full-time job.

I shifted uncomfortably in the chair, the bandages on my back grinding against loose pieces of skin, gradually ripping at them. Jake was unreadable, sitting straight up in his chair, staring down the desk's engravings and the arrangement of marigolds and poppies on the corner. Somewhere in the back of the room, Miss Mary had yet to leave, occasionally moving just enough to be heard. Sitting in silence had already begun fraying at my nerves, the shadows bending only slightly towards them, creating static in the air.

"Breathe," I muttered to myself quietly as the door gently creaked open behind us. Jake stood without hesitation; I followed, awkwardly hitting my knee on the chair. Madam Toyl smiled and gestured for us to sit. She wore a white pantsuit with a red rose attached above her right breast. Her heels clicked as she trotted to her chair, breaking the staticy silence of the room. The meeting was brief; she sat silently as we reviewed the training tape. I hadn't actually seen the events that followed my fall, Calvin had sprinted out of the building, shouting my name, Olivia chasing after him, aware of the trap, but clearly not enough to save either of them. Neither stood a chance against Jake's quick draw; the buzzers had sounded multiple times, indicating a new record. The tape clicked off, and Madam Toyls turned her stoney grey eyes on Jake.

"You sacrificed your own teammate, not even quite for the win, but for the quickest win?" she asked simply.

"Yes, Ma'am," Jake responded, still not faltering in his confidence.

"Miss Mary has provided me a report of Ms. Madalini's injuries, along with several images of the severe bruising and cuts caused by the concrete. They should've been even worse; Ms. Madalini was very lucky." She pushed a file across the table to Jake; I caught a few glimpses of the extent of the damage on my back, everything a deep blackish purple in the photos, and enough stained blood to cover my scars. It suddenly dawned on me just how much skin on my back I was missing and that when it grew back, for a short period of time, it would be untainted. *What if a nightmare comes before it's healed?* I internally shuddered at the thought; blisters on the already painful open flesh sounded like an inhumane level of pain.

"Doesn't look pleasant, does it?' I nodded to Madam Toyls statement before realizing she was still talking to Jake.

"No, Ma'am."

"Do you feel regret, Mr. Derrien?" Her voice was sharp.

This meeting was turning into something that felt more like an interrogation quickly. I felt a pang of sympathy for Jake; this was his dream school, and he was about to be kicked out before the first semester. Toyls was not above such; since the beginning of the school year, three kids in our class had already been expelled, with another five dropping out at the severity of the curriculum. *Weak.* I thought to myself, yes, the work was difficult, but in reality, it just took extra time and effort; it was far from impossible.

"No, Ma'am," he responded confidently, staring her down, mirroring the authority in her voice while maintaining his level of respect.

She raised an eyebrow. "Why not?"

"On the field, our lives do not matter; only civilians do. Every second a machigai is active within city limits is another life at risk. I chose the course of action that was likely to get the enemy detained with the least amount of time, and it worked—a school record on that course, if I recall correctly." His words were laced with arrogance.

"I see your train of thought, but sacrificing another officer like that would never have the same effect on a machigai as it did on Mr. Everette."

"Every scenario is different; I analyzed the information I had access to and used it to adapt a plan specific to this scenario."

Madam Toyls paused for a moment; I briefly thought I felt a wave of anxiety come off Jake at her glare. We sat, waiting for her to speak. One second, then another passed. I soon lost count as we avoided the gaze of the Head of School. This woman radiated power like no machigai I had ever met. Confidence and sophistication, beauty and ruthlessness, wrapped all in one package. She sat up slowly in her chair, placing her head on her hands and focusing her eyes on Jake.

"Pride can poison one's soul from within, it blinds people to reality." She spoke dryly to him before cracking a slight smile laced with warning. "But it can also allow us to see just enough, to act without question, and make the right decision without wanting or needing others' approval. Balance it just right, and I'm sure you'll rise through our ranks very quickly." She sat up straight once more, done with her playing tone. "I will advise you not to underestimate the wrath of your superiors; you have much less control over your own fate than they do. You are dismissed, Mr. Derrien.”

“Thank you, Ma’am,” he said, standing and bowing his head to her before exiting the room. Her wavy, auburn locks bounced in their ponytail as she turned her head to me.

“I reviewed the tape of your entrance exam, Ms. Madalini. I see your friendship with Mr. Everette has only grown stronger, and both of you maintain trust in people who seem to be getting you in trouble recently. Kindness will get you killed in this career. I wish that wasn’t true, but some things cannot be changed by wishes alone. I’ve sent significant compensation to your mother for your injuries and hope that you continue your time here at Toyls.” She pulled paperwork from her desk and began to work on it, not looking back, even as she dismissed me and Miss Mary.

Chapter 29: Dyeing in Misery

I didn't waste any time after returning to my dorm before packing. This week's events had created a deep seeded longing to return to the hotel, to escape the specific breed of psycho that Toyls specialized in. Within the hour, I was walking the streets home. Quebec had turned icy overnight, the October weather bringing in the first snows and cold spells. The chill felt nice over the heat of my skin, but a large distance loomed between Toyls and the hotel. It also did not help that my injuries stung and tensed at the feeling of Jack Frosts icy grip, forcing me to stumble and shiver my way through the streets, until I was practically dragging myself into the building. When I did, though, Lily, the real Lily, was hysterical, throwing herself at me, sobbing into my shoulder. Pain shot from the tip of my tailbone throughout my neck, bringing tears to my own eyes, but I clutched at her nonetheless, grateful for the affection of a real friend, even if it was rather sudden and confusing. Behind her, I locked eyes with Burn and Tresa; the rest of the congregation was out of sight. Both gawked at me; Burn held a glass of whiskey; hinting Lina was nowhere to be found.

"Where is everyone?" I wondered aloud.

"My-my mother-" Lily choked out, clutching onto me tighter to the point I gasped in pain.

"Mrs. Madalini? Is she alright?" I groaned out, a sharp discomfort throbbing through me.

"Tresa, get Lily to release the poor girl." Burn stated, still seeming off. Tresa stood as directed, gently prying Lily away until she collapsed into her own arms, still sputtering as Tresa comforted her. Burn stood, gently removing my bag from my grip and taking it in his own.

"You're injured," he stated plainly, examining me up and down.

"Burn, what's happened to Mrs. Madalini?" I stared into him; he shook his head softly.

"Mrs. Madalini is perfectly fine. You are the issue."

"Aren't I always?" I cocked a grin, which he did not return. Fear cramped my chest. "What did I do?" A million situations ran through my mind. Had someone followed me here? Had I been discovered at Toyls? Was Aska dead?

"Wednesday evening, Mrs. Madalini received a letter from Toyls- a check for $5,000 and a card that read *'Our deepest apologies and condolences for the accident involving your student during her time on our campus.'*. Deaths occurring at Toyls are not unheard of, although they are well covered up by the media. I suppose you can infer the rest." he half laughed, then cleared his throat, sharpening his semi-drunken gaze. "Infirmary now, Tresa, try to get Lily reined down, please." Tresa and I nodded in sync. As she sat Lily down at one of the tables, I followed Burn to the infirmary.

"Show me," he stated simply, not meeting my eye. I attempted to place a calming hand on his shoulder, but instead, I was greeted by shock and brief pain as his t-shirt caught flame. I yelped and jumped back on the bed. Burn also appeared startled by his own combustion, gasping with

257

pain, an act unusual for his typical composure even while ablaze. He calmed himself and patted out the flames.

"That shirt's ruined," I muttered, staring at the new, smoking hole.

"I'll wear a jacket," he half whispered. He fondled his new wound, failing to hide his discomfort. I reached for my bag that had fallen from his shoulder to the floor. I withheld a groan caused by my creasing bandages, hyper aware that any cause of concern may lead to more than a shirt aflame. My hands found one of the specialized creams from within the bag, pulling it out and unscrewing the cap. I gestured for Burn to sit on the nearest bed. Surprisingly enough, he obeyed, allowing me to climb onto the other side, propping myself up on my knees directly behind his back.

"Lean forward," I commanded. With a confused look, he once again obliged. Gingerly, I slipped my hands under the bottom of his deep red t-shirt, my fingers skimming his still searing sides as I pulled the shirt above his head and folded it next to me on the bed. His torso was a cacophony of deep red and white skin writhing into itself in contorted patterns over his deep and defined muscles. I thought of the time I had accidentally touched the stovetop as a kid, and the pain that had accompanied my burnt hand for days afterwords. Then I thought of how often Burn activated his curse, almost daily, if not at least weekly. My chest grew tight as I felt the warmth radiate from his skin, so much so it felt like sitting next to a fire. The cream on the other hand, was nicely chilled from my extensive walk through the cold and damp outside. Burn shuddered at its touch, a noise escaping his throat, but I could not pinpoint whether it was from pleasure or pain, maybe a touch of both. I watched as his hands clenched and unclenched repeatedly, his legs tapping restlessly on the ground, and his eyes looking everywhere except forward as water gathered at his lashes, steaming gently and evaporating into the air before it could ever be released. I finished applying a thin coat of the cream to his shoulder and shifted to his side, taking his hands in mine and applying another layer to the scars that generously coated their surface. Finally, I screwed the container lid back on, careful to savor our short-lived supply.

"Better?" I asked, raising an eyebrow.

"What is that stuff?" he asked, still avoiding eye contact.

"Toyls' specialized cream, a gift from one of my nurses."

His eyes finally landed on me, and his brows knitted themselves together tightly. I gently placed my hand on his pant leg in a strained attempt to be comforting. I saw his hand twitch towards mine briefly, before pulling away. Finally, he took a shaky breath. "What happened?" he asked, barely a whisper.

I explained from the start, making sure to include specific details, such as the mysterious buttons in the elevator. "I'm sorry- for not calling; I- didn't think they would send anything, I didn't think-"

He shook his head at me. "It's not your fault; it's those people, not you," he paused. "I-we," he corrected. "At the beginning, I used to think we were invincible as a team until- well, we learned quickly how fragile we actually are. I think occasionally the others still allow themselves to believe in that invincibility, which only makes things like this worse when they come. Bluejay hasn't laughed or chirped; Lily hasn't smiled, Lina-" he choked, "My sister h- hates, hates me. I hate me," he whispered and continued. "I expected equal fury from Soul Stealer."

"Expected?"

"He's done nothing, not to me, not to anyone. He hasn't eaten, hasn't spoken, just laid in bed; his-" he sputtered, once again not meeting my eye. "His curse hasn't deactivated since, to my knowledge, yesterday morning. He hasn't slept; he's just… there."

I nodded. This wasn't uncommon for Aska. He had a history of shutting himself down, stopping eating, and lying alone for days; it was terrifying, with or without a curse.

"I take it he's in your room?" I asked, already standing. Burn nodded, no longer looking back at me. "There's more cream in the bag; please put it away in here. I think it will be useful," he nodded once again, searing more tears away.

***

Burn did not lie. When I entered the room, Aska was nothing more than a corpse. The little weight he had gained in my first month here had fallen away. His fingertips ombred themselves in soft purple, not his full ability but enough to eat away at him, deplete his appetite, and his life.

I sat gently on the foot of his bottom bunk. I had swiped a pair of Burn's gloves from the infirmary and slipped them on, a precaution. Aska did not need his hands to kill, nor did he even need to touch someone, but this added just a small barrier between life and death. The room was static, physically so, with his grief.

"Aska," I said, placing my hand on his leg. The purple faded from his fingers, flooding out like a river without a dam. He opened his eyes slowly, looking up and widening them.

"You're not here." He stared me down, not blinking.

"You're an idiot," I managed a weak smile. His brow broke, then his lips; the rest followed, shaking. I grabbed his hand and yanked him to a sitting position, frightened by the lack of effort it took to push him around and even more frightened by the feel of his ribs against my hands, but it was once again another thing I simply chose to ignore, there was nothing to easily remedy that now. Instead, I clutched at his outgrown hair, burying myself in his grip, attempting to spread my warmth to his shivering body.

Suddenly, I winced deeply as my hip hit the floor hard, compressing my already abused spine. Aska sat straight up, shaking and staring at his hands, which were pure purple to the wrists.

"I'm sorry-I'm sorry- so, Lun-, please, go. I can't-" He gasped through waves of tears.

"Hey," I moved to my knees to look at him, steadying myself. "I'm not leaving. Breathe, it'll fade, it always fades." More tears flooded his face.

"Lun- I"

"Shut up." I snapped without raising my voice, moving closer despite him shifting away. I placed my hand on his knee, stroking its boney surface with my thumb absently.

"Focus," I commanded. He took a breath in; I did as well, forcing him to maintain eye contact, ignoring the sharp and growing pain in my chest. With the fading of the static came the fading of the purple and, in turn, the fading of the pain. I moved to his bedside and wiped a tear from his face.

"You can't keep doing this," I muttered to him, sitting by his side. He did not move, still staring at his hands quietly. Instead, I moved to him. Not afraid of his curse, I rested my head on his shoulder. It was uncomfortable with his bone digging deep into my temple, but I stayed.

"I don't know how to stop," he whimpered, leaning back into me. I took his hand in mine despite his protest.

"We'll find a way." I twirled a lock of his hair; it had grown out to past his ears, his tips no longer blue but dusty, bleached blond, and unbrushed. "Your hair's awful," I stated honestly, laughing through the welling tears. He smiled and turned for me to hug him. I did, and then pulled back cupping his cheek in my hand, our faces so close our noses nearly touched. "We'll find a way," I whispered again, squeezing his hand tight before releasing it. "I'll be back shortly." With a quick kiss on the forehead, he released me without a fight.

I returned as quickly as I could, hair dye, scissors, numerous brushes, a few towels, and a plate of crackers and cheese from the kitchen. I knew how depleted his curse left his appetite, how nauseated he must be, but I appreciated the effort he made at the crackers while I brushed his hair out, cutting it back to regular length before I wrapped a towel around his neck, and applied dye to the ends of pieces at random. The dye rested in his hair while I rebleached the ends of my own, adding almost four inches to the previous one or two remaining from Jay chopping off my hair to match Lily's before I started at Toyls. Aska leaned back, still lost in the distance, and pushed the plate away, less than half finished, as I wrapped up the process.

"You okay?" I nudged him.

He shook his head, flushed, with squinted eyes. "The bleach," he attempted with a frail smile. I lidded the bleach, aware that it was futile; we were already surrounded by its pungent fumes

"Do you need water?" I asked, taking his hand again. He shook his head. "Is there anything I can do?" He shook his head again. I shifted his shoulders off the wall, allowing his head to fall on my lap, not caring about the dye staining my jeans a new vibrant purple. I rubbed circles over his arms with my thumbs.

"You don't hate me?" he muttered; eyes still closed.

"No," I returned.

"Why?" he begged.

"You saved me." It was true, he had years ago, but now; he was my family by choice, and I couldn't hate him, not now, likely not ever. He started to argue but bit back his words screwing his eyes shut tighter. My heart winced; he didn't need my pity, but this had been our lives for some time. He had been in consistent pain for so long, in every form, and it broke me that I couldn't help. He breathed in sharply.

"I'm sorry," he muttered.

"You have nothing to be sorry for," I stated blankly.

"I failed; I tried to protect you and hurt you instead. I'm older; I should be the one saving you, and yet-" He lurched a bit and held his tongue, quickly I summoned the bucket from the void, catching it in my left hand, but he shook his head, still quiet. I sat it silently to my side and wrapped my hands tighter around him.

"Save the apologies; we'll have plenty of time for them later. Rest now."

***

Aska was quiet the rest of the time the dye set. Over the years, I had gained a decent grasp over when it was time to wash it away. Today I pushed it slightly past the right time, afraid that stirring Aska may result in vomit on my shoes. Eventually, I shifted him to break free and wash off my own bleach in the bathroom sink before returning to retrieve Aska to rinse his dye. I hated how his eyes began to glaze over every time he stood up, how much he had to lean on me, and how easy it was for me to support him even with my still injured back. He was never the largest or strongest kid, but this was another level.

"You can't keep doing this," I muttered again, helping him back into his bunk. "Promise me." He just looked up at me in response and shook his head; the short walk to the bathroom had obviously taken its toll on his energy. I rubbed my temples in response, knowing that even if he had promised, it wouldn't have been that simple, but I was disappointed, nonetheless. I stood, knowing I still had to see Jay and Lina. I probably should also check in on Lily and Burn, but Aska grabbed my wrist, his hand gently shaking.

"Stay. Please, just for a bit," he whispered. "Remind me that you're real."

I sat next to him obediently, letting him sit up so he could realign himself, resting on my chest with my arm around him. I had to admit, his new hair was fun to play with, twirling its damp strands through my fingers as he shut his eyes.

"Aska?" I whispered, setting my chin over his head and closing my eyes as well.

"Ya, Lun?" he responded drearily.

"What if I can't do it?"

"Can't do what?"

"Toyls, the machigai, any of it."

He looked up at me softly, pushing himself up and away just a bit so I could continue. I trusted him; he wouldn't risk outing me to the other machigai, and he couldn't lie to me, even if he tried.

"The people there, they aren't all awful, or at least they don't seem that way all the time; they're human, not monsters. They want to know me, but I can't tell them anything. We're watched all the time, and if I slip up—" I hesitated, unsure of how to articulate my fears. "I don't know if I can kill them. They aren't random faces in the crowd anymore, occasionally they actually seem like my friends."

He stared me down and nodded, no judgment in his expression; I was more grateful than he could know for that.

"Humans and machigai-" he struggled with the phrasing, pausing for a moment. "We all laugh, we all love, we all cry, we all have humanity, but it's easier to believe that the other side doesn't, because we can't stop fighting. Machigai need to fight humans because we aren't welcome in their society, but we have nowhere else to go. Humans fight machigai because they're afraid and want to protect themselves and the people they care about. It's hard to see the truth and keep fighting while knowing it's not as simple as killing monsters." I nodded along, unaware of where this sudden sentiment was coming from. He continued, "I do understand where Blaise is coming from with the importance of Toyls, his reasons for sending you, but our lives- machigai lives, are short, don't waste them wallowing in a decision you'll regret."

"We could run?" I suggested, "Find another city, another house. We'd make it. Alberta would be nice this time of year." Even as I said it, I knew the answer: Even if he wanted to, Aska couldn't make it cross-country in his condition. I could always get him better, bulk him up again, and then we could run, but he wouldn't.

"My reasons for being here haven't changed, Luna." He laid his heavy head back down, resting his eyes once more. "The others won't be mad if you back out of Toyls; I wouldn't let them anyways," I stifled a sarcastic laugh; the thought of Aska preventing anyone from doing anything at the moment was bittersweet amusement. He smiled, too, knowing my thoughts all too well. My mind couldn't force itself to stay planted in the nice moment, instead its thoughts drifted back to its previous train. If I left Toyls, the machigai would be set back at a minimum of a year, and Blake or Lina would be at major risk with weaker aliases than my own. No, they would never turn against one of their own, but I would never be able to look at any of them again without guilt. Plus, if Aska couldn't leave, then the decision was already made.

Chapter 30: Fight for your right… not to party

I slipped away after Aska fell asleep, grateful for his rest, knowing the next week would be miserable from the consistent state of his curse. With my homework completed, the weekend at the hotel was paradise. I finished dying my hair on my own, the same stunning lilac as Aska's. I admired the finished product, purple was by far my favorite color, and it had been far too long since my hair had been this vibrant.

Lily, once she had calmed down, healed a decent amount of my injuries. She couldn't heal them all; firstly, it would look very suspicious to the community at Toyls. Secondly, she simply couldn't heal them all; the "luck" of not shattering my spine on the concrete was my curse, forming a shadow and absorbing the impact. Where the shadow had touched was immune to Lily's abilities.

The weekend blew by, and when the time came, I was half tempted to tell Burn I would rather not return to Toyls, or if I did, I'd rather not return home; so tired of playing each side. Instead, I checked on Aska a final time, hugged Lily and made my leave.

Classes at Toyls continued to creep by, day by day, at a snail's pace so steady I could practically feel the weight of time bearing down on my shoulders. Nights got shorter, and mornings got earlier, mainly because of Jake's workouts burrowing their way deeper into my rest hours. My wakeup call crossed into nearly 4 am by the time November's cold chill rippled through the crisp air, snow falling gently onto the training grounds for hours to days at a time.

On one particular morning, Jake's footsteps were so heavy and loud that I couldn't even fain ignorance of them. Eyes heavy, I rolled over and groaned loudly into my pillow before rolling off the bed, less fury and more irritation motivating my movement. I slid the door open gently, shutting it softly because, unlike some people, I respected my classmate's well-deserved rest.

The scene before me was unexpected, to say the least. Jake leaned heavily against the railings, skin clammy and eyes dull. I had never seen him stand less than his full height and it brought me an uneasy feeling. He smiled slightly before his hand slipped on the rail, slamming his head onto it on the quick journey to the floor (sincerely, thank you, Mr. Railing, <3). I groaned deeply, wishing nothing more than to leave him in his heap but knowing that it was impossible. His room keycard hung around his neck in a lanyard. I slid his door open easily and dragged Jake's limp body parallel to his bed, yanking his body up first by his torso, followed by his legs. I retrieved a glass of water from the main room and moved the trashcan to Jake's bedside before returning to my own bed to attempt further sleep before sunrise.

Jake did not show up to classes for the entire first half of the day. It was the talk of the semester, Toyls' golden boy, for the first occasion, not being the first in his seat at each lecture. Murmurs flew, some of concern, some of indifference, some of relief, having a day's break from his egotistic monologs. I, however, began the day indifferent;

but cracks of weakness in my hatred appeared as the hours went by without Jake's return. By the time lunch rolled around, knots had appeared throughout my stomach, followed by anger at my own concern.

The door to his room slid open at the touch of the key card; there was no Jake inside; he appeared to be entirely absentee from where I had deposited him earlier on the bed. My ears caught a strange noise; I turned toward the bathroom. The door hung wide open. Running water. Shit, shit, shit, shit.

"Hey, Jackass?" I knocked on the door, merely a gesture. No response. "Jake?" Nothing. Turning the corner, the shower door was open, water pouring out from the bottom, Jake's limp body covering the drain. I shuddered with discomfort, reaching over and shutting the shower off. I grabbed one of the towels from the wall and tossed it over him. Kneeling down, I tried to analyze the best way to go forward with this, doubtful that pouring cold water on him would do anything. I was not looking forward to dragging this man for the second time in the last 12 hours.

"Get up," I nudged him; his skin was burning, which made sense, seeing as the shower had been steaming hot for who knows how long. The watermarks looked like the world's worst sunburn, but that had to be an issue for later. Jake's eyes opened very slightly, rolling back into his head while their lids fluttered a bit.

"If you pass out, I absolutely will leave you here. Don't test me," I muttered, shaking him a bit more till he looked semi-conscious. "Can you stand?"

He looked at me, but his head fell to the side, and there was no response again. "Too bad, you're gonna." I managed to get him in an upright sitting position against the wall before finally retrieving the robe marked JD, slipping him half into it before hauling him up. Despite being vertically challenged, Jake wasn't small. Even with him partially holding himself up, his weight hung down on my shoulders like a 100kg barbell. I kept my arms firmly around his waist, with his wrapped around my shoulders. He was making an attempt to assist, but his feet dragged against the ground, making movement very difficult and slow. Eventually, I dumped him off onto the bed, propping him up with a few pillows.

"What on earth is wrong with you?" I muttered, glaring and violently gesturing in the direction of the bathroom.

He gave me a sly smile, pulling up the blanket. His waxy skin was tainted with water dripping down from his buzzed hair. "I was cold, and a hot shower sounded nice."

I rolled my eyes, but he grabbed my hand with a terrifyingly weak grip, his smile fading away. He seemed almost drunk with delirium "Why are you being so nice to me?"

I paused. In all honesty, I was unsure myself as to why I was helping him. Not only was he a blood enemy, but he had very few redeemable traits. "You're pitiful," I said finally.

"Still, you hate me, and yet you're currently going out of your way to help me."

"As I recall, you pushed me off a building; a little animosity is called for."

"As I recall, we have a plaque downstairs with our names on it from that adventure."

"I'm not sure it was worth it." I muttered, remembering the soreness in my spine. For a moment his eyes softened, and I thought I saw humanity peak through.

"I'm sorry," he said. I rolled my eyes and stood, but he caught my wrist on the way to the door. "I owe you one Ombre."

"This means nothing," I stated flatly before turning away. "Sleep," I said on my way out the door. I had already wasted away over half of my lunch period, leaving barely 20 minutes to return to the cafeteria and hurriedly eat. Calvin was already waiting for me at our usual table.

"Where did you go?" he asked, eyebrow raised at the homework he had laid out before him. The cafeteria was suited for the entire student body to eat at once, but most ate in their rooms or out on the lawn, so most days, it was next to empty, with light music playing in the background. Faintly, I could hear Guns and Roses' Paradise City echoing along the tall ceilings. Calvin hummed along softly, subconsciously.

"Had some stuff to take care of." I sat down and rubbed my temples, helping myself to the grilled chicken breast I had selected for lunch, with some baby carrots and ranch on the side.

"He's not a good person, Lil," he muttered, shaking his head. I shrugged and focused on my chicken; Calvin didn't press the topic any further and instead explained his math homework as he did it, more to fill the silence than to help me.

We returned to class shortly after, but there was a major shift in Calvin's composure compared to normal. He and Jake didn't have the best of relationships, nor did Jake's chosen companions favor Calvin or his comparably odd mannerisms, but his lack of compassion was terrifyingly out of character.

The division of people at Toyls was certainly unnerving; the machigai were a united cause, all on the same page on at least one topic, but things were different here. It seemed that the cause that united Toyls' students was either not as strong or that the students were simply too self-indulgent to see past their own differences. Whichever one, the thought of Jake's disaster of a personality, along with Calvin's sudden withdrawal, were both causes of great irritation throughout the remainder of November.

***

As finals began to approach, classes somehow increased in difficulty, as did our workloads and training. The time between my returns home grew, with little information of any secret affairs within Toyls. On a few occasions, I did hear bits of discussions between the upperclassmen and some more favorable classmates about the Machigai Studies course that would commence next semester. With increasing stress and decreasing sleep, Toyls became more divided than ever. Fred and Calvin seemed to clash during training more than ever, Jake and the rest of their merry gang of pinheads following in his trail. Calvin continued to help me with my homework, but our conversations were significantly chilled in comparison to before. I would watch as he disappeared away from me, slipping into the crowd every time Jake came my way to engage in conversation between training activities and classes. Every time I began to dwell on the change, it didn't take much to remind me that it was for the best.

As the other boys began to get more aggressive during training, it was occasionally difficult to restrain the urge to jump between the raging bags of fleshy testosterone, well that and whatever you may consider Calvin.

"Calvin." I knocked on his door on one particular day, sliding it open with the spare key card he had gifted me, overcome by vexation caused by a later unremarkable equation written on my homework. "I can't seem to understand this problem." He sat at his desk, facing the corner, unphased by my abrupt entrance.

"Leave it on the dresser; I'll do it when I'm finished with the others," he said without ever turning to face me. Something was off in his voice, it was cold and almost too hard. Even with our recent distancing, his voice never sounded like that.

"Do it? No, I only meant—Cal..., is everything alright?" I asked, steadily advancing towards his still unturned chair.

"Fine-everything's fine" he choked softly; I placed a hand on the back of his chair.

"Turn around, Cal," I spoke, hardly a whisper, anxiety, and fear building up in my chest. "Turn around."

The chair spun slowly, Calvin not meeting my eye, but I met his, his bruised and bloody eye. A gash the width and nearly the length of my pinkie finger stained his forehead, just above the right eyebrow; two other bruises were forming on his shoulder and neck, accompanying a fourth on his left jaw. His bottom lip quivered against his swollen upper as he worked his way to finally meet my gaze. Rage burned underneath my skin, seemingly willing my body to fight someone, but I couldn't tear my eyes away from the boy in front of me. My hand gently but sternly lifted his chin, guiding it at my will to further examine the damage on each side before finally turning back toward me and forcing his eyes to meet mine.

"Who did this to you?" I asked, knowing the answer but wanting to hear it bleed from his lips.

"Lily, no. No one did this, please." He removed my hand and held it, begging.

"Who did this?" I repeated, a stoney chill to my voice.

"Lily, I'm fine, hey- it's fine."

"It's not fine, Calvin."

"It will be. I can fight my own battles." He held my gaze, digging into me with those painfully blue eyes, looking a bit possessed with his good eye overly wide while his damaged one was only half open.

"You can, but you won't."

"Probably not," He admitted with a shrug. His voice was still shaky but gaining back its composure, "but that's my decision to make, not yours. Promise me you won't do anything."

"Cal-"

"Promise me," he said, cutting my defense off.

"I promise," I relented.

"Good." He stole the math homework from my hands and studied it meticulously. "We can probably knock this out in an hour or so." So we did. I struggled to smother out, or at least disguise, my still boiling anger. My constantly distracted eyes, which refused to leave Calvins gnawed and beaten features, were not ideal for completing complicated equations, so by the time we had finished, Calvin had nearly drifted asleep after essentially spoon-feeding me every question. I tossed a blanket over him on the bed and shut the door behind me, gently leaning into it and taking a deep breath. My logic had seemed to regain control, and perhaps Calvin was right. He didn't want or need my protection, and I should respect that and let him handle his own life. I took a step towards my room, listening to the gentle slide of a door behind me. Turning around to face the newcomer, my eyes narrowed, followed by a sudden explosion in my chest. Before my vision could even clear, my forearm made contact with the figure's throat, pushing him back into his own room and against the wall. Jake gasped and clutched at my arm.

"Om-bre." His face was slowly turning discolored, and his eyes bulged, making him look more like a monster than a man. I quickly removed my arm, placing my hands on his shoulders and using the falling force to knee him against his groin. Hard. He crumpled to the ground, moaning in a heap. I kneeled down at his side, pulling his hair to force him to face me. "You ever touch him again, I'll end you."

"I'm sorry," he muttered quietly, looking semi-ashamed or possibly embarrassed. I let his head drop down again and slammed his door in my wake.

Chapter 31: An Olive Branch

The day after, I was Calvin's bodyguard, refusing to leave his side at any cost. It was apparent that he was growing tired of my presence as the day went on. I can't necessarily blame him, even I was getting bored with the charade by the time lunch rolled around. After all, what is the need for a guard when there's no one to guard from? Jake, Adise, Fred, and Noham had all failed to show up to our evening courses, and by the time training rolled around, they were still nowhere to be seen.

Whispers fluttered through the weight room about where they may be. Some people thought they had heard Adise talk about how they were dropping out as a protest against the lack of vegan protein in the cafeteria. Others thought they had all gotten food poisoning or were hungover, but none of the rumors seemed to hold any merit. By the time our sweaty and smelly class made our way up the large flight of stairs and into the common room, everyone pooled together, circling the couch on the far wall bay window. Chatter and laughter erupted so gradually and loudly that you could barely make out any one conversation. I took Calvin's hand and dragged him through the crowd to peer over the first few gatherers of people.

In a giant struggling heap on the couch laid all of our missing students, exposed in all ways except their tightie whities. Their hands were rope tied behind their backs so tightly, I couldn't imagine how any of them hadn't dislocated their shoulders yet. Their ankle ties matched their wrists, and they were very clearly not sober, but the most distinct features of their apparent abduction were the smears of rainbow colors across their chests. Eventually, someone from the crowd, Danielle, I think, took pity on them, grabbing a knife from the kitchen and cutting their bonds. A few others joined in helping the boys up and beginning the search for their clothes as Calvin tugged me away into the east-wing hallway. He whispered harshly in my ear.

"I thought I said to leave it be." He growled with a look of betrayal. I giggled, finally letting the insanity of the scene sink in. "I didn't do it!"

"Then why are you laughing?"

I clutched onto his arm, turning and pointing towards the chaos ensuing in the common room. I watched him finally loosen up and let out a small giggle before laughing along with me.

"Because whoever did this is a madman and a genius, and I would kiss them if I could," I said, hugging Calvin by the side.

"They deserve it," he muttered, staring at Danny helping Noham to his feet and down the center hall towards his dorm, moving around a figure in the doorway. Olivia made brief eye contact across the room, and we froze in our laughter, standing straighter as she stared our way, stuck in time. She let out a small smile and wave that sent shivers down my spine before she pulled one of her knives from her cargo pockets, began twirling it in her fingers, and turned her back to us, crossing to the west-wing hallway to head to her dorm.

Calvin and I locked eyes, and he raised his eyebrow. "That's terrifying."

"Oh ya." I agreed, staring back to the spot where it felt like Olivia had vanished like a phantom, despite the fact we watched her walk away.

"Should we talk to her?"

"You can; I'm staying five feet back at all times." He rolled his eyes and tugged me through the crowd, approaching Olivia's dorm in the west-wing. He halted in front of the door, hesitating before knocking.

He leaned over to me and whispered, "I don't care if you're five feet back; I will still be using you as a human shield." The door slid open, and Olivia raised her eyebrows.

"May we come in?" Calvin kept his head up; I suppose he had worked with her a few times in training; maybe the hard edge was just an act. She stepped aside, nonverbally inviting us in with a stony expression.

Her room was spotless, well-swept, and mostly minimalistic. She sat down hard on her forest green bed comforter that matched the decorative vines falling down her walls behind the bed. Her entire room was a beautiful, clean forest with a cascade of deep greens, blues, and grays. I briefly shuddered at how much she and her family must've spent on this design. I had once tried to make Aska and I's house more homely; it cost us the same as three weeks of food and still only looked half finished by its completion.

"Why'd you do it?" Calvin interrupted my analytics of the room. Olivia just shrugged.

"They called you a queen," she sighed, leaning back on her mattress, "amongst other things. You weren't going to fight back against their bullshit; I wasn't going to let them get away with it. Even trade."

"Not even trade!" Cal sat down next to her. "They'll report to administration; you'll be expelled." She dryly laughed and rolled her eyes.

"Even if they did, the administration wouldn't do anything without a name, and have you seen that group of guys? The chance of them giving any form of credit to a woman is absurd. I have two baby brothers; if I leave guys like that to get away with stuff like this," she gestured to Calvin's face. "Then things don't stop, and by the time they're older, they'll either be the assholes or well- you."

"Ouch," Calvin muttered.

I stifled a laugh, making him look up and smile.

I smiled back, then turned to Olivia. "That was quite the handiwork," "How'd you get them unconscious?"

"Midazolam, the less you know, the better." Her lips twitched just slightly before falling back down; a grin was something she didn't display often, but it spread a tingling across my chest to know I helped cause it.

Chapter 32: Something to Believe In

Finals killed me. As the weeks approached, Calvin, Olivia (who had encouraged us to call her Olive), and I stayed locked up in Cal's dorm, studying ferociously day in and day out. December rolled around, snow blanketing the streets, making it ever more difficult for me to complete the trek back to the hotel. Because of this, my visits became further and further spaced.

While I was there, Burn somehow managed to exhaust me more than even Toyls could manage. He was convinced the void was travelable over long distances, which, in theory, made sense but, in practice, was proving to be more draining than effective. The idea was to send my body through, just as I would an object, and have it appear through another opening; the issue was that I could not open the void while inside of it. The first attempt was utterly terrifying, no oxygen existed in my creation between worlds, nor did anything else. I simply fell, weightless, and lost from every living thing. Burn would tie me to an anchor, typically a rope attached to a nearby tree, forcing me to crawl out with his help at every failure.

If you've ever considered rope climbing while experiencing suffocation, 1. You're a freak. 2. Don't.

Eventually, I could manipulate and transport my body within the space, just as I could any other object I stored in there, summoning it at will. This new skill could allow me to hide within the shadows, an ability that would've improved my life on the streets immensely. After we accomplished that, Burn was set on me being able to summon portals in areas I could not see, such as through walls. It was possible, yes, but I had to picture every last detail of the place I was going and keep it more focused in my mind than I thought my brain was capable of. By our last visit, I was able to summon the portals, but they were far too unstable to travel through, leaving more than half of our test objects stuck in the world between.

With finals in view, it had been nearly a month with no return home. Burn made no attempt to hide his irritation with the lack of information Toyls had brought, agitated at the fact his seemingly fool-proof plan wasn't even fireproof apparently (don't ask). If I passed finals, that would mean another semester of tuition that the machigai would be forced to pay for, and I could feel everyone's support wavering; even Lily was quiet on the subject.

A part of me hoped to fail finals, to live simply one life instead of balancing so many secrets. The other was embarrassed to admit my own weakness in allowing myself to grow attached to a select few at Toyls. Those were the two thoughts that warped my mind as I sat in that ever-so-silent test room, staring at the blurs of words that slid past each testing sheet. Minutes passed by in hours as each breath of my fellow participants acted as a cheese grater against my brain, every scrape of a pencil or every turn of the page pushing me closer and closer to insanity. Six hours we were held up in that test room, some of us stumbling as we exited, others celebrating as if they had just landed on the moon. One of the most shocking occurrences of the evening was the amount of people from opposing classes or higher grades waiting for their significant others with large banners asking them to the winter formal over the weekend. Olive and I laughed at one girl who ran past us jumping into her boyfriend's arms, as Calvin's face flushed. We returned to the dorms as he shuffled his feet awkwardly.

"Could you guys maybe just stay here? Just for a moment- I can- I'll be right back!" he said, abandoning us in the hall before briefly struggling with his key and darting into his room.

"What's that about?" I asked, turning to Olive, who was twirling one of her knives while leaning against the wall.

"Who knows with him." She shrugged.

We waited there for a brief moment, hearing a bit of commotion echoing from the door. Finally, it slid open, Calvin clumsily stumbling through it with a large paper board covered in paint splatters. *OLIVE, IT'd BE PRETTY Sweet If YOU WENT To WINTEr FORMAL w/ Me.* It read in giant, sloppily painted letters with a small package of candies attached to it. He panted just slightly and glanced up from the board. I wondered why he felt the need to reread it knowing he was the one who painted it. Nonetheless he smiled up at Olive with those big puppy dog eyes of his. Now, it was my turn to lean against the wall and watch with my arms crossed. I stared back and forth between my two friend's exchanges, waiting for either to falter.

"No," Olive shook her head before walking off calmly, still twirling her knife. I glanced at Cal, whose eyes had followed her until she was out of view.

"You did kinda jump her with that." I shrugged. "Put the board away and go apologize." He nodded, letting a few tears fall as I led him into his dorm. I intentionally took longer than I should've to shove the board into his wardrobe, giving him extra time to pull himself together. Knocking on Olive's door, I stood out of the way, allowing Calvin to be the main sight in the door frame. She slid it open and stared him down with an icy expression.

"Yes?"

"I'm sorry, I sh- shouldn't have sprung that on you. I swear I didn't mean to make it so sudden, I guess- I don't know, I'm sorry." She allowed him to stumble through his words before gesturing her head for us to come inside. She pulled the chair out from her desk, sitting faced towards the backrest, resting her chin on it and gently shaking her head.

"Say something," Cal said as he sat down on the floor in front of her, staring up.

"I'm thinking!" she snapped, forcing his gaze downwards. "I'm sorry." She pulled his chin back upwards and then looked at me, struggling to find words. "I shouldn't have snapped, and I shouldn't have overreacted at your… proposition."

"You didn't-"

"I won't be going to winter formal or any dance with you-"

"I understand, I-"

No, no, no- shush." It was weird seeing Olive's eyebrows scrunch, given her usual poker face. It looked almost unnatural.

Cal sunk back down, finally keeping quiet.

"I will not be going to the winter formal, or any other dance for that matter, with you or with any guy." A few tears bundled at the rips of her eyes, never quite falling; I suppose she was too proud for them to. She clutched Calvin's hands in her own, never once breaking eye contact.

"I don't want to go with a *guy,*" she repeated slower this time.

Calvin began nodding his head slowly at first and then faster, showing that he understood. Tears streamed down his face as she began nodding along with him, half a joke as they bobbed their heads and laughed. A smile spread across my expression; Calvin turned around and reached out to me, pulling me towards them. Olive stood and hugged us both, finally allowing the corner of her eyes to leak a single time before hardening her exterior again.

I think we were probably the only people who had ever seen her cry…at least at Toyls.

"You guys do good on finals?" She tried to disguise the gasp for breath in her words, but instead, it came out as a half laugh.

I laughed and flung myself back on the bed, asking myself that same question as I stared at the ceiling.

"I think I did okay," Cal laid down next to me, Olive following in trail.

"I definitely failed the science portion," Olive stated.

"Don't say that; we all killed ourselves studying. I'm sure we made it," Cal said, looking a bit worried.

"I'm sure you made it, Cal. Personally, I guessed on at least half of the math section. I plan on working as a waitress for the next decade." I laughed.

"Until you get yourself a sugar daddy to pay the bills," Cal replied.

"Or… sugar momma," Olive corrected Cal with a wink.

"Exactly, exactly," I said, giggling.

"I do have a question." Cal sat up and looked at us both. "So, we all are staying till the dance on Saturday, right? Just not going together?"

"I'm planning on it at least, one day of fun to make up for a semester of exhaustion," Olive said as she stared at the ceiling.

"Not me," I shook my head. "I promised my brother I would head home tomorrow; I haven't gotten to see him for a while."

"Oh, come on," Cal shook my shoulder, forcing a grin, "you'll have almost a whole month to spend with your family, they'll be fine. By the time it's over, I know I'll be begging to get away from my dad and sister for another semester."

"What about the rest of your family? Don't you want to spend time with them?"

He shook his head at my question.

"Just me and them; my mom was killed by a machigai when I was eleven and we weren't ever close with our extended family."

"I'm sorry," Olive stated immediately; I simply sat there, unsure of how to proceed, a familiar thought tugging in my brain. Images began intruding my mind: the sounds, the screams.

"Which machigai?" I shifted my eyes, trying to disguise the emotion in my voice.

"Onyx."

My breath caught at my name, trying to place Calvin's features with any of the dozens of women that haunted my dreams. One woman, one terrified boy, one fateful day.

"That's awful." Olive once again formed words where I could not. After all, how could I express remorse for this poor boy's mother? I was the one who took her from him. "I can't imagine getting that kind of news."

"I never had to; I watched her die. We had always stopped at this little gas station on our way into town for donuts. Onyx arrived while we were there; she was so young-"

"She?" Olive asked. "I thought Onyx was a guy."

"That's what the police always say, but I saw her. She was our age-younger even- and looked like she had been through a hurricane, with this crazy dark gaze. She kinda just stumbled in and began tearing the store up, eating stuff straight off the shelves, shoving the rest into her bag, or just throwing it around. When the worker confronted her, she lost it, collapsed, and suddenly-" he paused, regathering himself "Suddenly, black was streaking through the place, in tendrils, sucking in anyone in its path. Before I knew it, my mom was gone, and so was everyone else. She looked up at me and told me to run, so I did."

"That's awful." Olive placed a hand on Calvin's back, gently stroking it in a paternal manner.

"I suppose." he took another deep breath. "Sometimes, I still dream of her expression. She was in pain. Young and confused. Lost and afraid. Both feared and forgotten by all of society. That's why I enrolled in Toyls; something must change. Obviously, it isn't true for all, but so many of these creatures are just sick; instead of hunting them- we could work to cure them or even provide them jobs in homeland security."

"You want to help the people who killed your mother?" Olive shook her head, returning to her cool composure.

"Well, no. I-I just-"

"I think it's admirable," I interjected. Trying to make sure they could not see my shaking hands.

"That is if you can reason with killers," Olive muttered under her breath, but both Calvin and I ignored her.

"Does that mean you'll stay till the dance?" Cal asked me again.

“I suppose.”

Chapter 33: And Something To Take It All Away

"They are requiring a few days of casual testing, along with a school function on Saturday. The teachers and other faculty members should be absent from the building to monitor the function, which may provide an opportunity to explore some of the lower-level offices and campus grounds for information." I messaged Burn after returning to my dorm for the night.

"K," he responded almost immediately.

Guilt clawed at my chest. I lay in bed, clutching my pillow to my stomach and leaning into it. I thought of my promise to stay and the promise I made to Aska to return. I thought of my loyalties to my people, the ones who took me in and protected me. Worst of all, I thought of Calvin's mother, trying to grasp every last detail of her expression before she died. Picturing how her funeral must've looked to young Calvin, without even a body to bury. Those thoughts consumed many of my dreams for the next few days until I woke up on Saturday. Knocks rang at my door, and two sets of hands banged up against the metal frame. Quickly, I covered up, hiding my scars beneath a cardigan and wiping the tear stains from the night before away.

I opened the door to see my two friends. "What time is it?" I asked, leaning against the door frame.

"Half past noon?" Olive responded dryly.

"And you woke me up this early, why?"

"Earl- Never mind. We were going to go shopping for the dance tonight." Cal grabbed my arm, steering me to the stairwell.

"I don't have money."

"We do, you'll be fine." Before I knew it, I was deep into the upstairs of a mall on the northern side of town, just outside of Toyls. Aska and I were partial to the lower security portions of the city, less likely to be caught and more likely to find a house to squat in if ours ever got commandeered. The more I thought about it, the likelier we were to be somewhat close to the hotel. I stared at the rooftops, hoping to catch a glimpse of Jay finishing up his morning scouting. Something inside me ached to be so close to home and not able to return there, wishing nothing more than to just make a run for it.

Olive picked out a lavender skater dress with a lace back for me. There was no denying its beauty, but with only a halter top neckline and a skirt that fell just above my knees, my scars were open to the public view.

"It's cute," I said, exiting the dressing room and handing the dress to Olive. "But I think it needs a jacket- maybe some tights too."

"We can do that," Olive said.

By the end, Calvin, Olive, and I each left with our own full outfits, and only a few short hours later, I was standing in my room staring at myself in the mirror. That sounds conceded, I know, but it was hard to help. I had gained 8 kg since starting at Toyls, and it filled out my new outfit perfectly, allowing the lavender to cling to the edges of my skin and roll over my hips. Paired with the black leather jacket that loosely hung over my shoulders and the tinted tights sculpting my thighs that had all but doubled in size and definition, I wasn't shocked Calvin didn't recognize me. I was a stranger to even my own eyes. Over the last three months, my hair had lightened to a softer brown, no longer darkened by layers of grease, and my skin had gradually darkened from so many evenings in the sun. Olive had done a thin streak of eyeliner across my eyelid, along with some mascara and a splash of blush across my cheekbones. It wasn't anything extravagant, I wasn't anything extravagant, but compared to the heaping mess of a girl I was nearly a year ago when Aska first disappeared, I was a new person entirely.

Finally, I turned away from the mirror and to the window. Lights lit up every inch of the lawn below as kids danced and laughed, basking in their normalcy. The effects could nearly fool you into thinking this was a mid-summer late-night picnic instead of an early winter affair. A thin, invisible sheet covered the campus from the outside, creating a controlled environment that the administration rarely deemed suitable for snow to peer in. Instead, our grass was barren, and buried beneath it lay hundreds of high-tech heaters and AC units that almost always remained at a perfect 20 C.

The building was too high for me to truly know, but I could almost make out Calvin and Olive congregating next to the punch bowl with a few of the upperclassmen. That was my cue, as good as any, to make my entrance. Excitement overtook me and I leapt down the first four flights of stairs, taking them two at a time. Suddenly, I slammed into a figure, nearly knocking us both down the remainder of the stairwell. Two strong, soft hands grabbed me by my shoulders as their owner smiled that oh-so-charming smile at me.

"Careful, my love, no need to rush; the party will still be there if you walk." Madam Toyls took my arm in hers. "Here, we may walk together." I did as she instructed, carefully traipsing down to the lawn by her side. Her presence was always slightly off-putting to me. If anyone on this campus were too see through my disguise it would be her, with those stoney, calculated eyes that hid behind her beauty and odd respectfulness. She reminded me of the goddess of wisdom, calm and self-assured enough to strategize each of her moves; anticipating her opponents next actions before they even know themselves. Sometimes I wondered why did didn't work for the MES, if she was a general, I doubt I would've stayed alive this long. She blinked down at me with those hard eyes that hid behind a gentle smile; forcing me to flush and look away to escape the feeling of being completely unworthy of that gaze.

"I truly am sorry about your unfortunate state at our last meeting, my dear. I hope you don't hold my ruling against me." she said, gently stroking my hand in the nook of her arm.

"I don't." I responded shortly, while still trying to convey the amount of respect the headmistress expected.

"Good, good, I'm glad. You have much potential, you and Mr. Everette both." She tilted her head towards me with a wink.

"Calvin?" I asked, still facing forward. Her tone was so light and playful that I couldn't tell if she was drunk or perhaps about to end my life.

"Yes, yes. I do try not to pick favorites with my students, but his training videos are remarkable. That child's mind is a work of art indeed. I hope you two remain such close friends and you continue guiding him down the path he's on. He'll do great things for this institution."

"May I speak freely, Madam?"

"You may."

"What has you in such a grand mood this evening?"

"Life, darling, life. I'm still riding the metaphorical high of some excellent news I received only a few days ago. This weekend, I will return to my country home to properly celebrate justice."

"Justice?"

"Several years ago," She started, almost casually but with a tone of caution. "After I had opened Toyls, I made the mistake of taking pity on a machigai child. He was invited into my home, slept in my beds, and ate my food, but he appreciated none of it. In those days, the long-term goal of Toyls was to be able to cure machigai, to help them exist instead of simply sponging out their species. I thought I could do that for this young lad." She paused, pain peering through her confidence. "He murdered three of my children as well as my husband. My eldest son and I were out of the country; we came back to nothing." My heart caught in my chest, listening to her story, praying I didn't know the monster responsible for damaging this diamond-like woman.

"Aneska, Ameer, and Aska." The world slowed to a halt around me, holding my focus on her words. Trying desperately not to break my composure and beg for answers, millions of stories forming in my mind, each more unlikely than the last. "My babies, lost to an unforgivable fate. A few days ago, my men apprehended the machigai responsible for their deaths. One of the deadliest machigai in Quebec City has been removed from the streets at last." She was lost in her own glory, no longer speaking to me but basking in her revels aloud. We arrived on the main floor after what felt like an eternity, she turned heading in the direction of her office, turning back and bowing her head.

"Thank you for your company, Ms. Madalini. It was nice to talk to someone, I do hope you enjoy the party."

She waved a hand over her shoulder as she left towards her office, likely the most casual gesture I'd seen her act out. "Soul Stealer awaits me!"

Part III:

Betrayal

Chapter 34: FML

I broke. Sprinting across campus and through the gates. Somewhere along the way, I heard Calvin shouting my name, but the pounding in my ears was louder. My brain was overloaded receiving so much data in so little time. I had no explanations for hardly anything, but the three things I knew were clear. Aska had an unshared connection to the Toyls family, he was in major trouble, and no one had told me anything. I ducked behind an alley and threw up over a sewer grate, the panic pouring out of me and leaving behind nothing but burning rage. I pulled out a knife that I kept strapped to my thigh. Wiping my mouth dry, I glared across the alley to the shadowy brick wall, dead sprinting into it full-out Harry Potter style.

Then it all went black.

My knees hit the floor first as I swallowed a second round of vomit, black spots swirling in my vision.

"Onyx!" A voice shouted, Lily perhaps. She grabbed my shoulders as I gained my bearings, mainly trying to ensure all my limbs were still attached. My eyes landed on Burn at the bar, looking fearful, like a kid with his hand stuck in a candy jar. My left leg took the first step, launching me up from the floor and against Burn. The knife I had summoned from the void pressed to his neck. Droplets of blood formed around the edges of my blade, each of his hands clinging to my wrists. His palms were warm but not hot. He could melt my skin off and force me back if he wanted, but instead, he just pleaded with large, tired eyes.

"Onyx-" I dropped my blade but held my position, my point already made.

"Where is he? How long has he been gone? And why did you hide it from me?" Without my adrenaline, my vision was gray and my balance unstable, but I couldn't show weakness. As of right now, these weren't my friends. Out of the corner of my eye, Jay was still gawking at me. He looked worn, with eye bags rivaling Burn's and a ruffled mop of short, loose curls atop his head, replacing his shorter cut. I hadn't noticed those the last time I was here, but then again that was a month ago now. Another wave of guilt slammed into me, fueling my rage at the scenario.

"We wanted you focused," Burn said, brushing off his shirt. "I'm sorry. As for your questions: We are trying to figure out where, and he's been missing five days."

"Five days." I bit, the knife still in my hands itching to raise again.

"We are gonna get him back, Onyx." Burn swore to me, placing both hands on my shoulder. I shook him off.

"Ya, we are, and I think I have an idea as to where he is."

***

The next twenty-four hours were the longest of my life. From the way Madam Toyls talked to me, I had to assume Soul Stealer was on her personal estate, waiting for when she got home. At the same time, that meant we had a very limited time frame before he was dead.

Jay, Lily, and I spent the night searching through thousands of records to find an old blueprint of Toyls Manor, including its personal, high-security jail in the basement. The manor was five stories, two below ground and three above, and even in its currently uninhabited state, it was likely swarming with guards. I stared up at it through the blanket of night; hidden by the grove of trees that engulfed us. The manor glowed in the night, golden beams leaking through every window. I was close… so close I could feel it pressurizing in my chest.

I turned to Blake next to me. His mobility was severely limited still, and you could sense his exhaustion and pain as he leaned on his crutches. Lily only ever stood a pace back in case he needed extra support. In any other scenario, I would never have asked him to come with us, but I was unwilling to make even a single mistake. He nodded back towards me, being well briefed on his purpose. Together we all watched as the lights flickered out of the house, no power, no internet, no cameras. Radio was maybe the most versatile machigai I had met. He could absorb electricity and use it as his own power to communicate with us through his own thoughts. Unfortunately, we had no method of responding. I understood why they had wanted him at Toyls; he never would have had to wait or leave to inform the others of any updates. It would have been perfect.

"No generator?" I asked after a moment when the lights never reappeared.

"Already taken care of." He grinned back, obviously enjoying his time out of the hotel.

"Good." I placed a hand on his shoulder, turning to face Lily. "Take him back to the hotel and move the van. Quickly, we shouldn't be more than an hour or two… Thank you both for this."

Lily nodded, but Blake protested. "You guys need me in case they have a spare generator, not to mention most of those guns are mainly electric these days."

"No, we aren't putting more people at risk than necessary. You did your part." I responded, turning away from them.

"But-"

"You'll stay in the van," Burn interrupted. "In case we need to leave early. Rest and save your energy, we'll call Lily if we need you"

I nodded, still unsure of leaving them so close to the fight but unwilling to disagree with Burn's authority. My worst-case scenario was that a guard strayed off and found the van. Lily had a chance of defending herself or at least running, but there was no end to that thought that resulted in Blake still alive. Hopefully in the end, it would all be simply speculation.

Lily steered him away, occasionally holding a hand out every time his crutch caught on a rock or a divot in the terrain.

"Instructions clear?" Burn asked, turning to the remainder of the crew: Myself, Jay, and Tresa. We nodded, breaking away in separate directions. Burn headed around the left to the gardens, and I took to the right while Jay and Tresa held the center, waiting for Burn's signal. I stared at the back entrance, calming my nerves. In only a few short hours, I would have my answers. I would have Soul Stealer.

Smoke billowed from the gardens; I could just barely make out the tip of a growing flame over the manor's great walls. I melted into the shadows of the bushes surrounding me, feeling my physical shape shift away into nothing more than my soul. From there, I emerged onto the grounds, watching as guards appeared from inside and called to the remaining dozen in the yard. They fled to handle the fire. Burn would try to keep them there without conflict as long as possible, but once they got the hint that the fire wasn't natural, they would begin searching for the culprits. To protect Soul Stealer, the guard's focus had to be elsewhere. I could stick to the shadows and never be found and if necessary, I could fight, but he couldn't.

We took too much time to plan. I thought to myself, paranoid about all the events that may have occurred due to our lack of haste. If my theory was correct, Madam Toyls would be home by morning. The cameras were down, but we still needed to exercise severe caution when crossing the grounds. I kept my eyes peeled in every direction, wary of anyone who may catch wind of my movements. Once the guards were out of sight, I continued forward. I hadn't slept nearly at all in the last two days. Instead, I spent my nights studying the blueprints of this cage; at this point, I likely knew more about the layout than many of the guards. Making my way through the house was easy and quick. With no light, shadows painted my skin, allowing my abilities to strengthen in this extensive playground.

On an ordinary day, I would be frozen by the brilliant architecture that lay inside the house; the deep mahogany floors, modern art, and rooms separated by large doors with detailed carvings etched into their surface. The whole palace was the epitome of Quebec's French Upperclass, an undeniable show of wealth and power, but as I slipped down the staircase to the first basement, I was transported into a different world. Golden statues, shrines, and something that couldn't be found on the previous floor: colors. Carpets of all sorts covered the floor accompanying the large variety of pillows and couches that scattered themselves around the large open-concept area. Madam Toyls had never struck me as a very cultural woman, but her basement could not contradict that more. Warm-colored beads hung from the tall ceiling, shaping it out in intricate designs; red-toned curtains framed each doorway, and dark woods covered the whole place. The interior was essentially a large wedding venue, deep down I wondered if she rented it out for such a purpose.

Shaking the change of scenery off my mind, my eyes found the right hall leading into an office of sorts. From what I could see, this may have been the only room on the level with a door and lock. With the power out, all the electric fingerprint sensors were useless, leaving only the spare physical lock. Keyholes were essentially swimming pools for shadows, deep, dark, and useless when you can manipulate them. Okay, maybe that last point was only relevant to keyholes and not swimming pools but give me a break I'm under a tad bit of stress. The shadows stiffened and morphed to the shape of the key, lifting the pins until they clicked into place.

The door to the office dramatically swung open, and my formless form drifted inside. Dust covered much of the furniture, including a large dark-oak executive desk and matching cushioned chair. A man's photo sat on the edge of the desk, absent of the dirt that coated the rest of the room. He had light skin and soft, curly brown hair topped with an American Naval Officer's hat. His high cheekbones and thin frame mimicked Soul Stealers to a tee, but this man had lived easy. He had lean muscles and a sparkling smile; I could almost picture him winking at every girl he saw on the boulevard, a well-lived glint in every feature. It was as if I was staring down a version of Soul Stealer he never got the chance to be, the version he was supposed to be.

Other pictures hung on the wall too, including a large family portrait behind the desk. The man from the first photo stood in a black and silver button-up next to a golden-encrusted chair. His hand rested lovingly on the chair's inhabitant; a young Madam Toyls in one of her signature form-fitted black dresses with a gold-laced black shawl. In her arms was a tiny baby, maybe only a few months old, and standing to her side was a young boy. A tired expression crossed his face, his gray eyes staring into my soul like an X-ray. I knew those eyes. I knew that face, although years younger and far less worn. Soul Stealer had not killed the young Aska Toyls after all, only his image. My eyes darted to the other figures in the photo. The navy man's spare hand gripped the shoulder of a taller boy with a mop of dark hair so messy and similar to how Aska's used to be that it made me wince. His jaw and cheeks were also Aska's, but his skin tone was a few shades lighter, more of a warm caramel in comparison to Aska's deep chestnut, and he had his father's dark eyes with the same glinting smile. Ignoring the baby's featureless lump, the only other child was a girl, the same height as Aska, but from what I knew she was a little over a year younger. Aneska. He had accidentally called me that name once or twice when we were younger; I never asked why. Suddenly, our "don't ask, don't tell" rule over the years seemed so childish; we were together for so long and knew virtually nothing of our lives prior to becoming a machigai.

I looked up at the clock, scared of how much time I must have wasted on these photos. It was half past midnight, only half an hour later than when we arrived, but still far too much. I grabbed the edge of the portrait and swung it open, revealing a steep and long staircase with little to no light. I narrowed my eyes and slid into it, more motivated than ever.

Chapter 35: This World is Sick

The stairs led into a wide tunnel that seemed to go on forever, but shadows didn't have friction, so I moved at the speed of my will and nothing less. The world slid by in a blur, there was no feeling, no wind, nothing holding me back, just freedom in its simplest form. Soon, I had to slow down as small cells began appearing on each side of the walls. First, only a scattered few, then more, transforming into a never-ending jail.

The cells were odd; occasionally, one would be personalized and labeled with a golden tile hanging above. A few used thick, murky glass instead of bars, trapping their future inhabitants within a glass jar. "BlueJay," one of these specialized containers, was labeled. A lump formed in my throat, picturing Jay's bird form flying up against the solid glass, desperate to escape and make it back home.

There was still no electricity, and I couldn't sense any upstairs either, so I allowed my body to solidify against the ground, regaining my balance step by step. I checked each cell, aware of how much time was slipping out of my hands.

"Who's there?" A squeaky voice echoed a few cells ahead. I peeked inside, straining my eyes to see the small figure in the corner.

"Hello?" The cell was barely customized, but I was still cautious as I moved the shadows apart. A small boy with tears streaming down his face was locked inside a titanium cast, chained to the wall. He couldn't have been any older than four or five, terrified and weak. My throat caught at the sight.

"I'm here to help," I said without thinking. Burn likely wouldn't be thrilled at stowaways, but he would just have to buck up and deal with it. After only a few minutes back as a physical person, I melted into the shadows, cueing death-piercing shrieks from the little boy. I reformed back in front of him, hoping that my being there would quiet him and not alert any remaining guards. It did not work. His screams grew, clutching his eyes as more tears poured out. I cupped the side of his face and shushed him softly.

"I'm sorry-I'm sorry, I should've warned you. It'll all be okay; I'm right here." The locks on his armor were all simplistic, essentially non-existent master locks with minimum protection. They clicked off easily, and I tugged them away, opening the large cast and allowing the boy to fall into my arms. He clung to me, to my hair, to my clothes, anything he could grab, sobbing into my shoulders as I picked him up and let him rest on my hip.

"We're gonna get you out of here; we'll fix this," I whispered to him. A void opened, placed as close to the bars as I could manage, another one appeared just on the other side. They were so close the boy hardly even noticed when I stepped across. The more confident I grew with using the void for transportation, the more stable it seemed to be holding, especially for short distances. I knew that using my curse so willy-nilly was going to catch up to me soon, but I just had to hold out until we were back. No more than an hour.

The deeper into the jail we walked, the more personalized and high security the cells became. I counted my friends off as I saw them. Burn. Tresa. Myself. I stared at mine for a moment. It had glass walls on each side, with lights coating every inch behind them. Without electricity, the lights weren't on, but even still, it caused a slight feeling of unease. I tried to come up with a way I could escape if I was inside but came up blank; it was completely debilitating to my curse, and without being able to open my eyes because of the blinding lights or move because of the shackles to the floor, I would be useless. A lamb for slaughter. I clutched a bit tighter to the kid, grateful for his company.

The hall was coming to an end, and there was no sign of Aska, until the final cell. The cell was possibly double the size of the rest, with gold-plated tungsten forming close-knit bars that were only separated by a few inches. Laying curled up in the corner, arms held tightly behind him with chain cuffs, was a still Aska.

"Aska!" I yelled, the rope around my heart finally loosening for the first time in days. I set the kid down, sprinting to the cage, shadowing just long enough to run through the bars and landing hard on my knees by his side.

"Aska! Aska!" My now free heart swelled with fear. A thick strip of metal was wrapped around his head, covering his eyes and ears. At first, he didn't move at all, and I thought maybe the worst had come, but when I grabbed his arm, he jolted awake.

"It's me," I whispered, knowing he couldn't hear it. He muffled a few cries, shifting away from me. His t-shirt was torn in several spots, bruises covering his skin, but other than that, he seemed mostly fine. I slid a hand to the back of his neck, startled by the chill of his skin. If he could tell it was me, he didn't acknowledge it; his resistance was weakening but only just barely. The metal band was locked in the back, almost making me roll my eyes at how predictable this was becoming. The satisfying click tinged my ears, the shadows undoing the second clasp and allowing the contraption to slip away to the floor with an echoing clang. A deep red line ran across Aska's forehead and another across his cheeks. It would have been almost comical in another scenario. He fell into me, soaking my shirt in sweat and tears. He didn't hold me, just laid into my chest numbly.

"You shouldn't be here," he rasped at last, another tear falling.

"This is the only place I should be." I lifted his face to look it over, hating every inch of despair painted on it. Instead of sadness, I was filled with rage. Someone would pay for the way our people had been treated. They say we're inhumane and then lock us in pungent cages for experimentation and torture. We're the evil ones when they force us to scrounge for food; we cannot be hired for honest work, and our families throw us away. Instead of helping us, they hunt and kill us, then label us as the hunters and killers.

I undid the rounded gauntlets restraining Aska's hands and helped him up. He swayed slightly when he stood alone, so I wrapped his arm around me, supporting most of his weight.

"You've improved," he whispered quietly as I opened a void to get us out of the cell. We stepped through, forcing us both to shudder on the other side.

"Some things are worse than fear," I replied. The kid was still waiting patiently on the ground outside the cell. I took his hand in my spare.

"You ready to get out of here?"

"No," he said softly, shocking me a bit.

"No?"

He shook his head up at me.

"A girl. We- we can help her too. This way." He tugged at my arms, and I resisted, looking back at Aska. My watch told me we were slightly past one a.m., behind schedule by a decent amount. The manor was outside of town, far from the police station; nevertheless, swarms of cops would be arriving soon. The kid pleaded with his eyes, living off playing hero.

"It's on the way back?" I asked.

He nodded again.

"Let's go."

Chapter 36: Sick of this World

"Stay here, drink something, and eat." I sat Aska down on the wall, summoning a large bag of trail mix and some bottled water. He squeezed my hand gently and nodded, not resisting for what may have been the first time in our joint lives. The kid had stopped us in front of an apparently empty cell.

"Nala?" he called out, listening to the echo. I watched the hall, expecting guards to come running.

"George?" a young girl called back. I could swear I had checked all these cells the first time through, but I walked through the bars, nevertheless. Near the back, handcuffed to the wall, sat a young girl, Alina's age possibly. Suddenly, it was clear why I hadn't seen her before; her skin and hair were translucent. I undid her cuffs, allowing her to stand and fully stretch her legs. Her strawberry blond bangs fell in thick, greasy strands across her forehead, nearly covering her eyes. A memory from my past life resurfaced; my uncle clicking the TV on in his apartment while he cared for my too-drunk mother. That couldn't have been more than a week after my father had disappeared. Strawberry Shortcake was playing that day, and now, fourteen years later, she stood in front of me, greasy, tired, and disappearing. That may be a bit dramatic, but I could swear Nala had every characteristic of my favorite childhood character, right down to the stunning green eyes and studs of freckles that crossed her sullen and drained features.

"Who are you?" she asked, those green eyes locking in on me and forcing me back to reality. I snapped my head up and locked my mind onto its previous task.

"Onyx. We don't have much time. Let's go" I grabbed onto her, half dragging us both across the bars.

"How did you do that?!" Nala latched onto my arm, shaking. It only now occurred to me I probably should have warned her before dragging her through an alternate dimension.

"I'm like you. We all are," I said, gesturing to Aska and George. In the quick glance, I noticed Aska had drunk all of his water and even ate a bit of trail mix. Air seemed to suddenly flow through my lungs a bit easier than it had a few moments prior. Maybe it was just my mind tricking me, but he looked more like himself than before. I'd known my time with him was limited for a while now, but hopefully, we could milk a few more years out of his drying life before saying our goodbyes.

I offered him a hand and helped him up, allowing him to stand on his own this time. It had only taken me ten minutes to get through the tunnel before, but now, I had two children and one barely conscious adult that I had to keep pace with, which could take up to double the time we already didn't have. Upstairs, Tresa, Burn, and Jay were likely already fighting the guards and local police. Tresa and Jay would be fine, they could hide in the tree line; Jay dropping Tresa's explosions down onto the further back troops. Burn didn't have the same luxury; he would be on the front lines, circling himself with the fire he could afford to spare. Fire does little for bullets, and the thought of his already damaged skin wilting under the searing heat made my insides crawl. Even so, I trusted the three of them could take on the police and the guards easily, but once the MES showed, we were all screwed.

***

We made horrible time down the tunnel. The stress was enough to unhinge me, but George's constant complaining could have sent anyone over the edge. Once the kid was out of his initial shell shock, he never shut up. At a slower speed I now noticed the purpose of having such a long tunnel. Motion-detected guns hung from the ceiling, as well as many other precautions. I had eventually given in and begun carrying George, allowing Aska and Nala to fall only a few steps behind us. After only a few minutes, my arms began to lock up, and I started to pop my shoulders excessively.

"I can take him for a bit if you'd like," Aska offered. Hesitantly, I handed over the kid, who was half asleep (go figure…glad he could rest during a time like this) and watched him settle into Aska's arms. He smiled down at me, and I told myself we only had a bit more time until-

The lights were on.

"Don't move!" I shouted, but it was too late; George stirred in Aska's arms, and the guns turned to them both.

"Down!" I pushed Nala to her knees behind me, watching as Aska turned to shield George with his own body. In less than a second, I had a thin layer of void surrounding us, absorbing every bullet. I held my arms up, shaking, willing it to stay even as the light surrounding us

313

threatened to wash it away. George's screams echoed through our little bubble, deafeningly paired with the shrieks of a thousand bullets. Seconds turned to minutes, Nala's arms clinging around my waist. I had no plan besides fighting till the end.

The lights flickered off, and the guns and I fell in unison. My elbows clanged against the ground, skin ripping apart. Inside, I felt as though I had just forced the void to consume an entire supermarket; so much in such a short amount of time. George's screams no longer dueted with the flock of guns but now sung along to the fast pace of my heartbeat. Nala's hand rested on my shoulder, reminding me I was not in solitude. On a good day that company might have brought me comfort, but now it was a morbid admonition of the people depending on me. Slowly, I sat up, regaining my composure.

"Everyone alright?" I turned to face them. Just behind me, Nala was shaking slightly, but gave a nod. George was still sobbing with his neck pressed deeply into Aska's shoulder, who had his eyes locked somewhere off in the distance just past my right collarbone; the corners of his mouth numbly limp in an expression that wasn't quite a scowl but was far from a smile. He looked almost mournful.

"Aska?" I stepped towards them. "Aska?" He snapped back to me; for a moment, there was an expression of pain and fear, but it quickly washed away into a soft grin. Time stopped and for one simple second we were kids again, just happy to have another person and a roof over our heads.

"What's that look for?"

"You grew up." He gestured around us just slightly. The four of us stood in the center of a perfect circle of bare floor surrounded by bullet shells in every direction.

"Apparently before you," I jested back, before turning back to our path in a futile attempt to hide my smile. The stairwell leading up to the office loomed in the distance, teasing the edges of my vision.

"We don't have much further." Aska took Nala's hand, and we began our way to the stairs.

Halfway up the stairs we could hear the gunfire from above. There was hardly any light, forcing the others to be more precise with their movements. We emerged into the office and even there I could tell everything above was chaos. No one was in the house, but smoke had already filled the walls of the basement while alarms sounded in every direction, to the point we had to cover our ears and mouths.

I motioned to the others to be quiet as we took our first few steps through the office. A deep paranoia seeded itself inside me that a lone straggler guard would be waiting around any corner. Inside I knew it was an irrational fear, all the decent guards would be fending off the machigai attack above, without thinking about the possibility of one below; still it was an image I could not erase from my mind.

"Mr?" George's voice echoed through the room. I swore this kid was going to be the death of me.

"George," I whispered harshly. Turning around it took me a moment to process the scene. Aska was leaning heavily against the wall, eyes glazed over. My heart plummeted.

"Aska? You okay?"

No response.

"Aska," I repeated louder. This time, he snapped back, standing rigid.

"Ya, what's up?" At that very moment, my eyes spotted the red stain spreading through George's pants where they met Aska's side.

"Nala, take George" I commanded so sternly it startled even me. The girl did as instructed, both her and George's eyes passing between Aska and I.

"Sit," I bit at Aska a bit more harshly than intended.

"No," he snapped back. "We need to move and get back to the others"

"You were shot and didn't say anything," I hissed, lifting his shirt to reveal the bullet hole pooling blood around the right side of his lower stomach.

"Because I knew you'd react like this. I've been shot before and it's never as bad as it seems. I'm upright and I'm alive, the quicker we get back the less we are all in danger. Please, I'm okay." He placed his hand over mine on his stomach. I watched as his own blood stained his palms red. He gently removed my hand and placed it to the pulse on his neck. I locked eyes with him as the beat pounded against the tips of my fingers. It was faster than normal yes, but that wasn't the point. He was proving to me that it was still there, he was alive, and he would stay that way.

"I'm okay" he repeated quietly. The way he spoke was more level than when we would pick arguments in the past. He was calm, almost convincing me it would be fine, other than the slight slur in his words.

"Your eyes are cloudy; you're not okay." I said the anger draining out of my voice, leaving only concern.

"I have hardly eaten since being here. Once we are home, I'll be fine." He gave me a smile that made the world stop around us. *It'll be fine. We'll be fine.* I repeated in my mind, trying to place my thoughts back on our friends fighting for their lives outside.

"You're right."

"I am?" he asked, slightly shocked at my lack of persistence.

"Ya, just let me quickly patch-" he grabbed my wrist as I lifted it to open the void.

"Luna, you're drained. You've been over-activating your curse all day. We can use the stuff in the van. Just get me there." I nodded, suddenly taking in all his features. Why was he so calm? *How* was he so calm?

"Let's go then." He took off strong in the lead as if he had walked these halls a million times before.

"Aska Toyls," I said quietly, not having moved a step yet and instead looking back at the portrait behind the desk. He turned at his full name, eyes wide, but did not say a word.

"That's you, right?" I jogged over to him, gesturing back at the image of his family, taking his hand for a bit of extra support.

"It was." He shook his eyes from the portrait and me, turning back to the exit.

"You never told me."

"That was always part of the rules, right?" He shrugged. He said the statement so plainly, without any hardness or cruelty, but it still stung. We had known each other for so long, while at the same time we never knew each other at all.

"Rules made by children, for children? I think they may need a few revisions," I nudged him slightly with an attempted smile. He laughed, then clutched his lower stomach, making my heart skip a beat.

"Giving you my life story means you'd have to dish over your own." I thought of my past; days that didn't even feel like my own anymore. I nodded up at him in agreement to our new terms.

"We get through this, and I swear I'll tell you everything," he said, squeezing my hand.

"We get through this, and I promise I'll listen. We are a team. Just make it back, okay?"

"I can do that," he said sloppily with drained features. He let down his guard, leaning on me just a bit. My damsel in distress would be safe once again. He had to be.

Chapter 37: The End...

The closer we got to the exit; the harder Aska fell. Nothing was slowing his bleeding, and I withheld the urge to beg him to slow his pace, but he was determined to leave this place. Smoke filled the halls, falling down onto us like a thick sheet, strangling us to death. I held Nala's gaze as Aska hobbled up the stairs, watching her eyes flicker to every movement of light through the windows.

"Where will we go?" she asked

"Home." She forced a smile and nodded, clutching onto George just a bit tighter as we followed the stairs to the main floor; gunshots echoing through the corridors.

Weaving through the house, we could spot the gentle light of the brilliant moon reflecting across the smoke plaguing the aflame gardens. Calmly, I walked out, feeling the intense heat of the purple flames. They were beating back and forth in the wind, no less alive than a human heart itself. I reached out and let the flames consume my hand for no less than a second. An involuntary scream shot itself out from the bottom of my lungs at the sudden and searing pain, the licks of fire revolted back from my red, blistered hand almost guiltily. I took a deep breath and tried to suppress the pain, thinking of how Burn experienced it every day; the feeling of skin melting, ripping itself away and exposing the raw flesh and bone below. As bad as it was, the sacrifice would be worth it. He once explained to me how he could feel every item inside his flames and understand it, similar to how I could my shadows. From the way the fire had retreated I could tell he knew we were out, alive, and incredibly late.

I shook off my hand, watching a piece of my skin shrivel up. Nala looked up at me, wide-eyed. I knew I must look like a sociopath, but at least the others were updated; they would be here soon. My ears clung to the gunfire in the distance, desperately wishing to help my fighting friends. I took a few steps towards the west, hoping to catch a glimpse of BlueJay in the sky. Behind me Aska stifled a cough, then another. I turned to look at him; the smoke around us was encapsulating and made even my lungs ache. He clutched at his wound, wincing with every attempt at breathing. I summoned a water bottle from the void, giving him just enough time to shoot me a glare before his coughing fit forced him forward a bit, blue in the face. He removed his bloodied hands from his wound, grasping at his throat with one hand and holding onto my shoulder for balance with the other. Smears of red appeared everywhere he touched. He fell to his knees, and I knelt with him.

"I'm fine— I'm fine," he gasped through watery eyes, taking the bottle. I looked over at the other two, their fearful expressions covered in soot and ash. I had to get them back to the van; the others could wait. As soon as he seemed ready, I pulled Aska back to his feet, wrapping my arm securely around his waist.

"Let's get out of-"

"Onyx!" Burn yelled from within the flaming mansion, parting the smoke and fire from around us in a clear path. Jay and Tresa appeared by his side, the lot of them running to greet us. Relief flooded through me for the first time in the last hour. Aska untensed, resting nearly his whole weight against me. I realized how hard he must've been trying to stay strong this whole time, but we were safe now. We were all together and headed home.

Burn smiled a rare smile as he approached, his gloves were gone and his fingers were blackened, but he was alive. They all were.

"Why is he bleeding?" Tresa asked, gesturing to Aska.

"Because he's an idiot."

"I didn't realize idiocy caused people to spontaneously bleed from their abdomen." Jay shifted Aska's weight from me onto himself. Aska groaned in pain but grinned up at him.

"If so, you may be doomed, my friend," he clapped Jay on the back weakly. Jay smiled and whispered something to Aska.

"We have to move," Burn said, head tilted towards the incoming gunfire.

"Lead the way, Captain." I gestured ahead, falling in formation to his right as he took off through the grounds.

***

The openness between the manor and the woods was our downfall. MES officers swarmed around the sides of the building, catching our tail end as we wove through the gardens. Bullets sizzled past our ears, George's screams echoing our every move to the officers.

Burn tried shouting something to me, but it fell on deaf ears. Instead, he took my hand in his own, running side by side. I could feel flakes of crisp skin crumble under my grip. He was still warm.

I glanced over to Jay, who clung to Aska in his arms like he was nothing more than a feeble child. Fear was broken across his normally bright expression. He wasn't meant to be on the front lines, they were both dead if we had to participate in short-range combat. To their right, Tresa had taken George as her own, running full speed with him leaning into her shoulder, propped up from her hip.

"The tree line!" I yelled, yanking Burn towards the woods. The pitch-black void from the canopy of leaves shielded us from the moonlight, fueling me. I threw Burn's hand, falling to my knees and hardening the night around us. A sheet of shadows traced the lines of the trees as far as I could manage. My arms shook, and a pressure like a sheet of lead rested on my chest, sucking the remaining breath from my lungs.

"RUN!" I shouted to Burn. "Take everyone and go! I'll hold them off as long as I can and find you guys later!" Jay set Aska against a tree. Both of them were soaked in blood. Aska's eyes were closed against the bark, and a part of me wondered if he could even hear us, another part of me wondered something worse.

"We aren't leaving you!" Burn said as the first soldier hit my defense. I felt the impact like a punch to the throat, forcing my eyes to water.

"GO!" I shouted again, voice breaking with panic. For the first time since I met him, Burn looked his age. He was young, lost, confused, and defeated. His hardened exterior was shattered, his hair disheveled, and his skin sweaty and seared. I now recognized a familiar look, the same look he had when I failed an exercise he challenged me to. Once upon a time, I believed that look to be disappointment; now, it was something else entirely. Worry. 20. That's how old Alina had told me Burn was. Just barely an adult and trying to lead a revolution. He was blinded by fear and desperation, always trying to save everyone.

Burn threw an arm out, steadying me forward as another man slammed into my shadows, an army close behind him. He held me close there for a brief second, clinging onto me like a scared child.

"Just keep the shield up, and I'll burn them from this side!" He yelled back at me.

He summoned fire in his hand; I watched in utter uselessness as the flame broke my wall, making contact with one of the men; lighting up the night around us like a bonfire of burning flesh. I felt my renewed strength from the woods evaporate, leaving a ringing in my ears that was just barely noticeable above the resumed rain of bullets. I summoned my father's 9mm, aiming it into the crowd. Jay fell on Aska, shielding him from the fire. I moved in front of them, taking down who I could with my bullets. Burn made them easy targets, lighting them up against the dark sky, but two against an army was never going to end well. Suddenly next to me Burn roared in pain; I turned to see him grasping onto his side.

Piercing pain shot through my right thigh, knocking me off my balance and onto the ground.

Another shot rang, latching into my shoulder.

I looked down as my blood pooled through my shirt, leaking onto the ground.

Aska reached out a limp arm to me and I grabbed on, allowing him to pull me up against the tree with him. I could feel all the bones in his chest shake as he heaved hard breaths. His arm wrapped around my waist, squeezing me in tight like a child needing protection. My head was spinning, and red dots danced in my vision as the officers closed in. The bullets had slowed, Burn and I were down, and the rest were unarmed. They won.

"Luna, I'm not ready," Aska whispered to me, tears streaming down his face. I clung to him tighter.

"I love you," I whispered back. He gave me a quick kiss on my forehead as a response, then pushed me away harshly. Leaves stuck to my wounds as I hit the ground, shrieking in pain.

"Aska!" I yelled, his eyes were pitch black, and the world around him seemed to wilt away as he sat straight up from the tree, tears still streaming. Static filled the air, swarming with unbridled power. Guards fell around us, stopping in their tracks. Some appeared to be shot; others clung to their hearts or were choked out on an invisible poison.

Soon, we were alone, and the woods were silent.

Aska fell to the ground with a thud; stiff. Words came from my mouth, but I couldn't hear any of them. Instead, I clung to his body.

Chapter 38: Le Deuil

The days after that were silent. I lay in the infirmary alone. I slept most of the time, walked a bit, but mainly I spent my time watching Jay dig another grave in the garden. Two days went by. No one said his name, then we all met outside and watched as Tresa and Jay lowered my oldest friend into a hollow pit in the ground. His eyes were closed and he donned the same ragged clothes he had worn at Toyls manor. In most ways, he looked the same in death as he did in life, but there was nothing. Nothing there. When Burn spoke his name, in that so casually even tone he always bore, Aska did not stir. He stayed there and allowed himself to be buried alive. Burn delivered a speech, which I caught Lily mouthing along to.

"He— I—" Jay started through misty eyes. "I don't know how—" Tears fell down his cheek, and he turned away from us all.

"May his death be more peaceful than his life," Tresa said pointedly, kneeling down and gently laying a bouquet of black roses on his chest.

"Thank you for your service, Soul Stealer," Burn whispered, and it all came crashing down. I stared around at the stones surrounding us, and I didn't know what to do; I just knew it needed to stop. Grave after grave. The stoic faces of my allies, so tired of burying their friends. I turned my back to his grave, marching off, holding back another round of tears. I would not break, not until I broke the people that caused this.

"Onyx! Onyx!" I heard Burn calling after me. "Luna!" I halted in the door to the infirmary, spinning on my heels, letting the tears evaporate.

"Excuse me?"

"I– I was just-"

"You don't have the rights to that name; NO ONE has the rights to that name!"

"I'm sorry, I-"

"You what?" I felt rage well up inside me, the impact of the last few days hitting me like the crash of a cold wave. "You're sorry? You could've gotten them out. You could've ran. They would've followed you! You were supposed to protect him, Burn!"

"You're alive because of my decision; I need you alive." He tried taking my hand, but I shoved him away, pushing against his chest. My tears had resumed, burning trails down my cheek.

"He's dead because of it! Gone! Because you traded his life!" I tried to breathe, but it was all too much. Everything was lost; I had failed. "How would you feel if the roles were reversed?" I pushed him into the wall, hearing him wince from the still-healing wound on his side. "How would you feel if it was Lina in that grave instead of Aska?"

"Onyx don't-" He warned weakly.

"She told me how she lost her sight, Burn. How you stole it. How would you feel if I took the rest of her?"

"You wouldn't-"

I summoned my dagger from the void. "How would you feel if you walked into me dragging this very blade across her neck?" I mimicked the motion softly against his throat, holding his head back to the wall by his hair. Tiny droplets of blood followed the steely edge's sharp path. Not enough to harm, just to sting. "How would you feel if I was the one to end her? If you held her as she faded away. Staring at you with those empty… innocent… dead… gray eyes-"

He grabbed my throat and threw me around to the wall, holding me a few inches from the ground. Smoke filled my lungs. The clinking of my dagger hitting the ground echoed through the empty room, but I didn't fight. Burn's eyes were not his, as he stared me down. The skin on my throat sizzled with his heated grip.

"Do it," I rasped, daring him to rejoin me with my lost loved one, but his gaze softened into fear, realizing what he was doing. My knees hit the ground, sending a shock through the hole in my thigh. I clutched at my throat, coughing and ripping at the burnt skin. Burn stood staring at his steaming hands, tears falling.

"Onyx, I'm so sorry- I didn't mean-"

"Now you know," I croaked, leaning back against the wall. He sat down and gingerly embraced me without reciprocation. We sat there like that for a minute, just two people unsure of what to do next.

"I never meant for it to end this way," he whispered.

"Neither did I."

****

The weeks of holiday from Toyls were a blur of disillusion and disinterest. The other machigai stared and made faces at the marks on my neck, but no one ever asked any questions. They didn't have to. Even with the help of the remaining special cream from Toyls, a white scar in the clear shape of a hand had wrapped itself around my throat, but I didn't care. In the grand scheme of things, it was one of a million scars that I had gathered over the years.

Jay attempted to reach me, occasionally entering my room or taking me to the roof, but his false positivity would consistently crack only a few minutes in. I didn't cry. Not past the day in the infirmary with Burn. Some days, I hated Jay for his tears, but every day, my loathing for myself grew past that hatred. I felt his absence with every passing moment. I avoided mirrors for fear of the highlights in my hair. I hated my face because it wasn't mine, it was Luna's. Who was Luna without Aska? I did everything; I did nothing.

Burn hinted several times that he thought it might be smart to resume training, but that wasn't happening. I spent most days on the roof or in the garden. The air was chilled, freezing almost, and the sun set early, revealing constellations that I couldn't even pick out from the inner city. I hopped from roof to roof, occasionally using the shadows to appear on the other side. My nightmares increased by the day, tearing down my body with them, but I continued until one day, I found a house. Our house. Our house, on the bad side of town, with a partially broken roof, mold, no water, and no electricity. Our house; the only remnant of a time in my life when I was truly happy. The roof below me creaked, likely suffering from the same ailments as our own. The concrete below looked so far away; two and a half stories. I stumbled hazily down the slanted roof, the bitter wind blowing against me. Jay always warned against standing too close to the edges, especially on shorter buildings. There were too many pedestrians in the streets below, but today, the streets below were empty, except for a few homeless people. Again, my eyes found the short 1.5-story house sitting on the corner. I remembered the day he brought me there and wondered how long he had lived there alone before I came along. "Our house" wasn't ours; it was his that he chose to share. And now it was no ones.

My heart caught in my chest as the wind whipped against my face, tumbling through the air. The ground sped at me, becoming all more real by the second. *Jake pushing me off the roof.* Closer. *Shopping with Calvin and Olive.* Closer. *Burn training me.* Closer. *Drinking with Lily and Jay.* Closer. *Aska's first disappearance.* Closer. *Playing Clue with Aska on a late night in summer.* Closer. *Ranting about my most recent book to Aska over dinner.* Closer. *Aska teaching me how to ride a bike at midnight in the streets.* Closer. *Aska.* Closer. *Aska.* Closer. *Aska.* STOP!

I never hit the pavement. The shadows caught me, just as they had the day with Jake. I counted the constellations in the sky, watching them blur as tears flooded my eyes. Sobbing, I clung to my knees, shaking on the side of the street until the blistering cold of Quebec's winter night was too much. The familiar brush of the front door against the ragged green carpeting was all but a welcoming hello into the rickety house. Upstairs, I ignored my old room and instead creaked open his door, watching a rat scurry out from under the bed and through the window. The clusters of old clothes and blankets scattered on the bed were a warm comfort, a protective shield against the rest of the world that night.

Chapter 39: I Study Myself

I received an invitation to rejoin class at Toyls a few days into January. Burn offered for me to drop out, but anything was better than the silence and stares that filled the halls of the hotel. A week later, the campus's grand presence loomed before me once again.

Quebec's winter chill provided the perfect excuse to camouflage my newest scar under layers of sweaters and scarves. That plus my constant solitude allowed me to answer as few questions as possible. Calvin found me almost immediately during the second semester orientation. My heart gave a small lurch, unable to look him or any of the others in the eyes again. They were not responsible for the events that unfolded at Toyls Manor, but one day, they would all be at the hands of hundreds of deaths just like it. In a few short years, it was possible that one of them would finally end my life, many of the others dying at my hands. They weren't my friends. I had said that before, but now I more than thought it; I felt it and I meant it.

"Welcome, students," the science teacher, Madam Teresty, began. "To machigai studies." A few students clapped at her theatricals. Machigai studies was the only course that every grade level, even the 4th years who were rarely seen around campus, had to take. But Toyls would not begin the work until the second semester due to its rather… inhumane nature… 1st semester was meant to weed out the weaker-minded 1st years; those who could not keep up with coursework or training or merely lacked dedication. A few times, it was told to me that the academy enforced it in such a way as to prevent infiltration from spies and reporters wanting to know about the Machigai studies (great job, really impressive work, you fucking imbeciles). It seemed that, for the most part, it was effective; only a few articles had been published telling of the "methods" used in the study course. Those articles quickly gained traction, feeding the media with horrifying stories of machigai strapped to tables and dissected, amongst other grueling things. Even for the generalized public, that seemed a bit far, not to mention dangerous to exist in the same room as a machigai (again, fantastic job, people. Round of applause).

"During this semester you will learn and study the simplistic classifications of machigai, machigai history, the current 'high impact' machigai in the city, as well as anything you may need to know on the streets if you are so unfortunate to come upon one of these creatures." *Insert eye-roll.* "Let's begin!"

"There are five simplistic classifications of machigai: Mentiums, Nanadums, Tatios, Iliads, and Sopitams." She wrote them on the board as people around me took notes. Jay had used a few of those terms before, but I had never thought much of them until now.

"Sopitams." She clicked the board with a long stick. "They are by far the least dangerous machigai. They have the gene, but their abilities have never been initially activated, many go their whole lives without realizing they are machigai. We also occasionally refer to them as dormant machigai or crossbreeds. Next, Nanadums."

"This class is Nana-dumb," I heard Fred whisper behind me, igniting a diluted roar of snickers around him.

"Healers." Teresty continued, ignoring the comment. "Their abilities have differed; in the past, some more peaceful ones have even been employed by the government in exchange for immunity. Not dangerous… unless on the enemy's side." Lily.

"Next. Tatios. Mutants, if you will. They can be peaceful but are more often far from it. Some have been seen with tails or wings. Others are abnormally tall or small etc, etc, etc." *BLUEJAY* popped up on the board behind her in large letters, slipping away to the top and revealing two blurry photos and a rough drawing. I almost had to laugh. Wanted photos were notoriously inaccurate, but this… oh lord. Jay was maybe 7ft tall and about 3 shades lighter than he should be. His sparkling smile was washed away with dark, sullen eyes, making him look like a druggie on the street. But the most noticeable mistake was the large blanket of brilliant blue feathers drifting down behind his arms like soft mystical wings. Below the awful drawing was a list of all of Jay's personal information, or rather statistics from the eyes of the other students.

All around me kids pulled out their phones and began taking photos of the screen to copy into their notes later, I did the same and made a mental note to show Aska the photo the first chance I got. It took me a moment after that thought before the familiar rope around my heart tightened. I deleted the photo and threw my phone in my bag a bit harder than I meant to. No one seemed to notice my odd display of aggression, no one except Olive who shot me a questioning look from across the room. She tried to mouth something to me, but I turned back to the front of the room; digging my nails into my palms.

"BlueJay, otherwise known as Jay Faeleen." Madam Teresty gestured to the image. "One of the more notable Tatio terrorists in the city. 17 years of age, male, African American, 2.9 MDR, born in New Jersey, America. No one is certain how he ended up in our humble town, but he is often regarded as one of the most dangerous Tatios in all of Quebec City." *One of the most dangerous Tatios in all of Quebec City.* I mauled that over for a moment, trying to picture Jay as anything but bubbly, sweet, and far to innocent for all he had seen. Briefly, I wanted to believe he was only regarded as dangerous because of the company he kept, but then I recalled our first meeting. I remembered his frightening speed, and the rage in his eyes; the same rage that had made even me quake just a bit. Suddenly, dangerous seemed appropriate under the right context.

"Next. Mentiums; curses revolving around the elements. Fire, water, air, ice, as well as several honorary elements that you will further define next year. For example..." My heart skipped a beat as another name popped up on the screen, this time my own. "Onyx. Age: unknown. Race: unknown. Name: unknown. 4.0 MDR. He manipulates shadows," Teresty stated simply, staring down the class. "Uses them to suffocate people, strangle them, steal, every crime you could think of. When Onyx first surfaced, he was initially referred to as a Tatio. He surrounds himself with a shell of shadows to hide his identity, which experts believe to be his real form. It wasn't until years later when Onyx was connected to a convenience store murder spree from prior to what was thought of as his first appearance in the city, that our officers on the field realized that it was just a disguise." The images behind her were clear photos of my shadow form, taken from store cameras all around the city. A sting of pride struck me. They knew nothing. Even after all these years of cat and mouse, they had nothing on me, and I had everything on them.

"Finally, Iliads."

"Like the story?" Calvin asked.

"Like the story," Teresty confirmed, "They have mental abilities: hyper-intelligence, mind control, forced hallucinations, telekinesis, location, clairvoyance, telepathy, the list goes on and on. For this example, we are forced to stray a bit further from home to Suffield, Alberta, where the machine is known as "Coon" reins. Coon is known for her animal control and as the only machigai that has successfully taken an entire military base and held its control for longer than a month. Because of her, Suffield has been brutally known as the first "machigai town" in Canada." A machigai town? Jay had drunkenly discussed the idea of them before, but honestly, they seemed more like an intoxicated fantasy than fact. Machigai were social creatures, like humans; we longed to find the families that we lacked. This led most machigai to end up working with other machigai to survive, both as a tactic and an unquenchable thirst for normalcy. Machigai towns were meant to uphold that normalcy. They functioned similarly to that of a town - you worked instead of killing for your spot, and all machigai were welcome if they contributed something. The only issue was finding enough alive machigai to actual form a civilization

"Finally-"

"You said Iliads were the last thing," Calvin said, digging his notebook back out and beginning to scribble on the pages.

"They were the last classification, yes, but there is one other thing we will be applying to all of our units in the next few months. Are you all aware of machigai ranking?" A few students mumbled agreements. There was a top ten most wanted list in each province. Unfortunately, I had never made a list. Aska had peaked at 7th but quickly fallen off. Burn has held a spot on the charts for the last year, hovering between 8th and the honorable mentions. It was an impressive feat considering how many more machigai Montreal and the northern cities had in comparison to Quebec City; then again, our MCR (machigai crime rate) was much higher than theirs as well.

"You are all likely thinking of machigai placements on Quebec's wanted list, but those don't necessarily equal a high ranking. Can anyone tell me how the machigai wanted list is determined?"

"Maximum sentences for each recorded crime," Jake answered, leaning back in his chair. "My father works for the agency that publishes the list."

"Very good, Mr. Derrien. I'm aware of your father's position; he would be proud." A look of satisfaction washed across Jake's face as he sat his chair back on the ground and continued notes. "Every crime that a machigai commits is recorded, whether it be murder, theft, assault, or something more. For example, number 10 on Quebec's most wanted list; Metas. She turns things into metal, like King Midas, but less valuable. She is listed for 123 cases of murder, divided into different degrees, 18 robberies, 1 account of removing a band aid in public, etc. The maximum sentence a civilian can serve for each of these crimes is tallied and compared to other known machigai, and that makes the ranking for the wanted list. We will not be focusing on those rankings though, instead we will be using the MDSC, otherwise known as the machigai danger-score chart. Can anyone tell me how machigai danger scores are calculated?"

No response.

"How disappointing." Madam Teresty shook her head before grabbing chalk and heading to the board, her heels clicking behind her like hoofs. "This will be the simplest equation you will learn in this class. Known casualties over known appearances equal MDS; write that down. An MDS will allow you to determine a machigai's true rank, between 1 and 5. 1 being the most dangerous and 5 being the least. Fives have a MDS of less than 2 and are considered not a threat. Four's lay between 2 and 3; caution is necessary, but you are free to approach with little backup. Threes are between 3 and 10; call for backup before approaching. Twos are where it gets complicated; they are between 10 and 17. It is against protocol to approach a two before the full backup squad has arrived. One's…" The bell rang, cutting her off. "Above 17 kills on average per appearance, do not approach." Everyone began packing up to leave. "Study these numbers; we will use them all semester for classifications!"

Chapter 40: Another Mental Breakdown (Who's Shocked, Anymore?)

Machigai studies was oddly informative, and bone chillingly enjoyable. I remembered the guilt I felt last semester; that feeling had faded into a dim, constant black cloud. During machigai studies, that cloud found a way to surge to the surface of my chest until it felt like my ribs were cracking. This feeling followed most things I found enjoyable, shrouding my thoughts in a dim, desaturated coat of gray. I had escaped nothing by returning to Toyls, but at least this time around, I was useful. I voice-recorded every class with Madam Teresty, sending them over to the machigai for the others to review. Teresty supplied us with a schedule of units and exams for the semester. Four weeks would be spent on each machigai classification, leaving the last few weeks of school to review all of them before the finals.

Weeks went by, and I soon discovered nadadums were more interesting than I could have imagined. Teresty began our semester by weaving tales of the nadadums that worked for the government. They were always kept under total lockdown and forced to use their curse frequently until there was nothing left of them or their powers. Still, this was seen as mercy, allowing a cursed creature to work instead of being hunted. Providing them with food, water, and actual rooms. I almost considered persuading Lily to review the forms, but two small facts slipped my mind: 1) "Lily" was already an enrolled student at Toyls. 2) MES officers held close watch over the homes of machigai, under a "find one, find them all" philosophy. The others would be found immediately, and we would all be executed, Lily included.

"I have a special surprise for you all, " Madam Teresty said, entering class in her normal full MES uniform and four-inch heels. A few students had joked in the past about her heels secretly being weapons to kill people who interrupted class, but of course, those were just rumors (I think). "To commemorate the last day of our nadadum unit, we have a guest." She flipped the top of the island that sat at the front of the room like a dissection table, revealing straps and wires. Two men rolled a gurney in, shuffling its inhabitant over to the island. She was a girl, no older than Nala. Her cheeks were sunken in, carving around her young face. I had to resist the urge to trace my finger around her eye sockets that were so far away from her real eyes she looked like a perfect Tim Burton life action character. She didn't resist as they moved her, the only sign of life being in the slight groan she made when they threw her onto the table. My eyes widened, taking a step back. Our machigai studies class wasn't more than 20 people, but still, the room felt suffocating.

"Meet Emilie Veronique; no alias, age 12, MDS 0, ranked a 5, French-Canadian, nadadum…" she rattled off the rest of the girl's data like reading from an over-read script, but the noise faded out over the ringing in my ears. All I could see was the vacant look in Emilie's eyes, so young and already one foot in the grave.

"She's been at Toyls with us four years, longer than any of our other machigai. How many of you have been to the infirmary in the last five months?" Almost everyone in the room raised their hands. "I assume you've all been treated with our famous 'Emver Cream'?" Nods wove their way through the room. "I expect you to show your manners and thank Emilie for her generous DNA donations to help create that cream, as well as almost every anti-nadadum weapon in the MES's arsenal." The room erupted into sarcastic applause, causing the girl to whimper and shake.

"Anyone have any small scrapes or wounds they would like to part with?" A boy from the back of the class volunteered, shedding his jacket to reveal a gnarly wound from our fencing unit in training yesterday. Why they gave unbuttoned and sharp fencing swords to teenagers still baffles me. Teresty led him to the girl, placing him directly to her left so we could all see. She then tightened the straps, holding Emilie down one more time, unbuttoning her loose shirt, and attaching a few wires to her chest. "Hold here," she instructed the boy, handing him Emilie's limp wrist. She flipped a switch, and the girl began screaming at the top of her lungs. Teresty flipped the switch off quickly. "Oops, forgot. Silly me." She grabbed a cloth gag from under the table and stuffed it in Emilie's mouth as tears streamed down the young girl's face. The switch flipped back on, and her screams were muffled. We all watched as the boy's wound faded away, leaving his skin clear of even acne. The color drained from her fingers and up her hand, leaving them a flakey gray. The switch flipped off, but the color did not return as her hands dropped down to the side of the table. The two men moved her back to the gurney and escorted her away.

***

The door to my room shut behind me, providing a safe haven for my emotions. Sinking down against the wall, I clung to my knees like a child, gasping for breath and letting the tears fall. She had a MDS of 0; she had never killed. An innocent kid tortured for nothing except being born. A knock sounded at the door.

"Ombre?" Olive asked. She could forget it; they could all forget it; I wasn't coming out to face these people. "OMBRE!" She banged on the door louder. "I know you're in there! Open the door, or I will!" Begrudgingly, I wiped my eyes and slid the door open.

"Hey, I- Are you okay?" she asked bluntly as if she hadn't been threatening me only a moment ago.

"I'm fine; what did you need?"

"Calvin is worried about you- frankly, so am I. It's been four weeks into the semester, and you haven't so much as smiled at us."

"So now you're all for women smiling?" I raised an eyebrow, not showing so much as a speck of remorse.

"No, I just- did we do something wrong? Did I do something wrong? You didn't come to the dance like you said you would, and then we didn't hear from you at all during the break."

"Not you guys; everything's okay, I swear."

"I don't believe you but be that way, but if you insist then prove it. Come to the mall with us this weekend."

"Can't. I have to go home?" I stated plainly.

"Visiting your brother again?" She raised an eyebrow, and I stared her down, fueling my words with every ounce of bitterness from the last month.

"My brother is dead." Her face fell. I suppose even the toughest people can be shut up with the right turn of phrase. Even so, her sudden change of expression reminded me solemnly of what exactly those words meant.

"Shit, Ombre-I-"

"You didn't know," I shrugged, trying to suppress the regret and new wave of tears. "It's okay."

"How did he- you had mentioned he was sick, but I didn't realize-"

"He was killed on the streets," I said shortly, not wanting to hear any more about what she presumed. My own lies had more comfort. "I got the call right before the formal; I'm sorry."

"No, you're good." My hands started to shake, and my eyes locked on the ground. Olive, uncharacteristically, pulled me into a rough hug, forcing the rest of my control away from me. Her skin was chilled, and honestly, you could tell she didn't have much experience with hugs because she kept readjusting her arms, but she was there, which was all I needed right then. I clung to her jacket like it was my last breath, feeling myself break and mend for what seemed like the millionth time. I heard her knife clatter to the ground as she wrapped both her hands around me tighter, lifting me to her hip and over to the bed. Untangled in her forestry scent, I released all of the frustration from the last month, letting it out in ragged, snot-blocked screams. My lungs were on fire, and everything spun around me, leaving only Olive.

Eventually, my throat went raw, and I couldn't muster the energy to hurt anymore. I leaned against Olive and rested. My newly plateaued emotional state, combined with the events of the day, helped me draw two conclusions. 1) I couldn't stay here much longer. 2) We had to get those kids out.

Chapter 41: Ruthless

"That's awful," Lily said, gingerly ending the voice-recorded playback from her perch atop the bar. I twirled my empty glass, watching Jay mix another round of cosmos.

"You think they are being held on campus?" Burn said, ignoring Jay's offer for another pour of Fireball.

"Madam Teresty hinted at it. I watched the gates, and no vehicles or people went in or out in the hours after. The basement is likely designed for it. Not to mention, realistically, it just makes sense to hold them there."

"Still, we have to be sure," he said as he downed the last of his drink. "Does anyone remember if we have blueprints to Toyl's in the archives?"

"We did," Tresa said.

"That was years ago. They remodeled only a few months after they realized they were missing," Jay poured me another drink.

"They remodeled because of you guys? Must've been expensive." I raised my eyebrow.

"Remodeled is underselling it. They essentially tore the place down and rebuilt it. No cost is too great to preserve their secrets." Burn rolled his eyes at this fact, but I just grinned back at him. He froze in place, his glass just barely touching the tabletop. "What?"

"Madam Toyls must keep those pretty close now, safeguarded."

"Her house?" Lily asked, flinging her legs over the counter and resting them across my lap.

"I don't wanna go back there," Jay muttered softly, I gave him an encouraging smile, knowing the feeling.

"She only goes home every few weeks, sometimes not even for months." I said, shaking my head to Lily's initial response.

"Does she live in faculty housing on campus?" Tresa spoke, tracing her fingertips over the veins on her arms; a habit I had noticed she took to when she was in deep thought.

I shook my head.

"She has a small living area attached to her office."

"How small?" Blake asked. I hadn't even noticed he had rolled in using his wheelchair during the conversation. The wheelchair was becoming a formality. He could move around and walk pretty well these days; it just wasn't the most comfortable. It was better for him to preserve his strength.

"Small enough." I shrugged.

"Just like Burn," Jay said, causing Lily to spit out her cranberry juice all over a seemingly very displeased Burn.

"What's your plan, Onyx?" Burn asked, wiping a bit of red from below his eye.

I explained what I had in mind. Blake was thrilled to help, while Lily was a bit skeptical of him leaving base. Eventually, she agreed to my idea, but we would have a very limited time frame.

"If that's all settled then," Burn stood. "I would like to take a shower to become less… sticky." Lily and Jay giggled a bit behind the bar. "Onyx, walk with me" he commanded.

"Yes, sir." I stood slowly, knowing I had probably pushed casual drinking a bit too far today. We exited through the double doors towards the bunks and infirmary, and I tried to remember the first time I had seen these doors, not even a year ago.

"What did you need?" I asked as we crossed through the doors.

"I was actually going to ask you the same thing," he laughed, an unusual sound coming from Burn. He probably had also passed his casual drinking limit for the day. "We are under your command for this one. We know what you need from Blake, but what do you need from the rest of us." I smiled somberly; this was his way of making up for the events at Toyls Manor. The gesture was kind, but all I could think of was the reason behind it.

"I need you to listen to me on this one. If I say get Blake out of there, even if it means exposing me, you have to trust me. We have no real proof that these blueprints will even be there, but if they are, and those kids are being held in the basement-" I paused, thinking of what would come after that. "Attacking small MES facilities is nothing compared to what would await us if we tried to attack Toyls at full force. Our only focus is to save those kids, not to take revenge on every faculty member and student on campus, as tempting as it may be. If it does come down to it and they begin to approach, I want you to burn that campus to the ground. Everyone inside." I thought about the friends I had made at Toyls. It hurt to think they may lose their lives in the crossfire. But the things I had seen and the things I had lost… they could not be ignored nor forgiven.

"So, what's the plan then?"

"I don't know, but we'll figure it out if, and when, the blueprints prove us right." I followed Burn into his and Tresa's room, trying not to stare at the empty bunk below his. Burn followed my eyes regardless, and his face fell.

"He'd be proud of you, you know? Leading like this." He gestured to the bunk, placing one hand on my shoulder supportively.

"Like what?"

"Ruthlessly." The word slipped off his tongue like the most holy compliment one could give. I couldn't even protest before he began again. "You're sacrificing your best friends, the only chance of normalcy you have, for the greater good. For those kids. And I can tell you're willing to sacrifice even more."

"They weren't my friends-"

"Oh please, Onyx, I'm not naive. You've been home every weekend since the second semester; you used to only come back once a month or so."

"I *realized* they weren't my friends," I said coldly, anxious to get away from the topic. Burn shrugged and slipped his gloves off onto his dresser. His skin had only gotten worse since the night at the manor.

"Have you been using the cream?" I asked, once again picturing the scene where the process of making the cream was demonstrated. My stomach turned.

He laughed dryly.

"I never liked that stuff, but after today? Humans harvesting machigai…" he shook his head. "I'm never using it again."

I couldn't really blame him for that, but we had work to be done.

"If you are going to burn Toyls to the ground, you need to be at full capacity. That means healing your hands and not activating your curse."

He signed, resigning himself from the conversation.

"That poor girl," he shook his head somberly. "What was her name again? I want to commit it to memory; we have to honor her."

"Emilie," I paused, thinking about his words. I remembered her screams. "Do you think she'll live long enough for us to save her?"

"I'm not sure she'll want to," he shrugged, pulling a spare set of clothes from his dresser. "The end of machigai lives are messy and painful. After four years of what she's been through? She wouldn't be the first to give up."

***

We didn't waste time for once (I know, shocking). The Wednesday after I returned, I heard a familiar voice from my dorm room.

"All set up outside; wait for the cue," Blake echoed in my thoughts. Madam Toyls was scheduled for a press conference this evening further uptown, and with the long nights of winter still with us, we were almost completely protected. That was unless Blake and Jay got caught in the van parked just beyond the gates. I walked to my window, slipped it open, and stared down at the campus below. Faster than a kid going back for dessert, one by one, each of the building's lights flicked off.

"Go time," I thought to myself. My heart silently pounded against my chest in a steady rhythm, but I ignored it, closing my eyes and picturing Toyls office. With no light, my curse was at its peak, dropping me through the shadows to the bottom floor. A slight chill ran its way through the office as I moved silently toward the living space. It looked no more luxurious than a hotel room, with a simple king-size bed, kitchenette, TV, wardrobe, and safe. Safe. Bingo. It was maybe a foot shorter than me, plated with steel and gold, a large bank vault-style combination lock plastered across its front half, and a gold wheel right below it. Combination locks were a pain in the ass to crack for my shadows, but that didn't mean there weren't other ways of getting in.

"Find them," I commanded aloud. The shadow lifted, nodding its figureless head at me before disbanding and slipping through the cracks of the safe. A moment later, the void opened, producing file after file of papers. I scrambled through them, using the shadows to sort through the important and unimportant. My watch told me it had been around 10 minutes since Blake had cut the power; I had to find the blueprints quick. Something made contact with my back. Imagine the feeling of an ice cube down your shirt, but a million times more powerful, and you'd have a fraction of the experience. I turned to see a shadow fall back into its natural form, leaving behind a folder of royal blue papers.

"Perfect." I checked the folder to confirm my suspicions, allowing the rest of the papers to be swallowed up by the void before falling in myself. Jay was by my side in an instant as my knees hit the floor in the dorms. Fear briefly overcame me, thinking that I had left a lung behind in the space between when I couldn't catch my breath. I made an attempt at stifling my coughs to avoid unnecessary attention in the dorms, but it was futile. I scratched at my throat, feeling swells build up within my chest, pressing hard against my ribs.

"Onyx!?" Jay caught me as I fell forward, panic surging up. "Breathe, breathe." Just as my vision started to go black, my throat loosened, coughing up globs of puss and blood onto my nice, clean dorm room floor.

"Hey-hey, you okay?" I groaned, laying back on my floor, not enjoying the taste of iron that resided in my mouth. "I think it's time you cut back on void hopping."

"I agree." I handed him the blueprints along with the rest of the files. "Get back to Blake and get out of here."

He nodded, and I watched as BlueJay fluttered through my window into the cold, dark air, clutching those kids' only hope in his claws.

Chapter 42: Salute to the Fallen

The next day, MES officers raided every student's room, searching for the missing files. Lucky for me, for the first time ever, I did not procrastinate cleaning up my room the night before. I used the void to swallow up the majority of my blood mess, wiped the rest up with a shower towel, and promptly tossed that into the void as well.

A full investigation was conducted over the events that had transpired the night before. It was good I had no intentions of staying much longer, because the faculty was convinced there was a rat amongst the residents on campus.

During the first semester, I hadn't used my curse nearly as much as I was currently, and the drastic change was catching up to me. The next week, as investigations commenced, rest did not come easy. The few times I did manage to sleep, my dreams were haunted in all forms. Some nights, Vindicto visited me, his formless figure draining my will. Some nights, it was another creature, a new one, smaller than Vindicto, with purple streaks blazing across its tall, bony body (how a creature with no bones can be boney, I'm still unsure). He didn't touch me, just galivanted around my shadow realm, watching me with those sunken eyes. Even so, it was the nightmares outside the shadow realm that persuaded me away from rest the most.

"Just like our eyes, our hearts have ways of adjusting to the dark- of adjusting to the loneliness of being surrounded by people," my father stated in a steady one-handed grip, aiming for the target on the other side of the yard.

"CEDRIC!" mother exclaimed from inside the house, storming out in her Louis Vuitton black heels, a present from father after their last fight. They clashed horribly against her gray sweats and wine-stained t-shirt, but she was proud of them and would always claim that the day they left her feet would be the day she got a house dropped on her. "What have I told you about having that thing out around Luna?" My father turned to me and rolled his eyes with a little glimmer before quickly shifting his aim from the target onto a rabbit just beyond it. I felt the dream shift away, happily replaced with more recent memories. I was grateful for the absence of Aska in the dreams, afraid of seeing him only to wake up to a world where he no longer breathed.

A few times, I gave up on sleep and simply headed out to the shooting range. With the recent unrest, I was not the only one out there in the early hours, often accompanied by Olive or Jake or even a few upperclassmen I wasn't familiar with. I suppose everyone has their own demons at night. I rarely exchanged words with Jake or Olive, allowing them to take their frustration out on the targets and not me, but I did make an attempt at learning more about the upperclassmen. Specifically, their class schedules. ¶

***

"You sure this will work?" Burn asked, sitting by my side out in the garden.

"I'm never sure, but what do we have to lose?" We stared off at the stones together, just as we had a million times before.

"Those kids, our family, our shelter, our lives-"

"It's a figure of speech, Burn," I said, not needing the reminder of all they were risking for my plan.

"Blaise," he corrected. Since he gave me the lead on this mission, he'd insisted I call him by his real name, just as I did the others.

"Fine," I rolled my eyes, not enjoying the change so far. "What kind of parents name their kid Blaise anyways?"

"They met in Greece, both from Ontario, and both there to study the titan of the sun, Helios." He stared off into the distance, picking at the flakes of skin on his palms. So far, he had followed through on his promise to not activate his curse until the attack on Toyls, and because of it his hands had finally begun to heal; something I doubted they had ever thought possible.

"All those years in the same city, never knowing each other, just to meet in a country across the ocean?" I asked, basking in his parents' story.

"They liked to claim the sun brought them together. It was a major symbol in our house growing up, both Alina and myself were named after it. She just got the more normal side of the deal." He laughed slightly before his laughter was stifled by a sad look. "Anyways, back to the plan. 16:30?"

"16:30," I repeated, confident in my answer. "The 1st years will be the only ones on campus, 2nd years are touring different MES bases around town to prep for their school to career next year, and all 3rd and 4th years are at their designated MES jobs after lunch."

"Nala will turn us invisible to get in, we'll enter the basement through the worker's stairwell in the back of the building, and Jamie will liquefy the cells to let the kids out." Blaise recited simply.

"You're taking Jamie and Nala? They're just kids." I furrowed my brow disapprovingly at him, but he only shrugged.

"If things go south, we need more manpower than what we currently have. Without Jamie, Tresa would have to blast the bars, which could hurt the kids and likely alert the staff. Nala is almost 13, so she can take care of herself. Plus, she's our only guarantee that we won't be caught entering."

He noticed my displeased look and nudged me slightly on the bench. "Tresa has been working with them both, they know how to protect themselves if things go badly." When I didn't seem convinced, he squeezed my hand and added: "I promise I'll keep them safe. It'll be quick in and hopefully a quick out."

"*Hopefully*," I repeated, but I looked up at him and attempted a smile. "You trust me; I trust you." He smiled and stood, offering me a hand up

"I'm going to go in and help Lily with dinner; that way, I can brief everyone on the plan and get some sleep before tomorrow. You coming?" I shook my head, not accepting his hand.

"I'll be in shortly," I said quietly. He gave me another smile and headed in; I waited for him to be completely gone before I slid off the bench and took a few steps towards the graves.

The dirt was still loose as I knelt before his stone, which was covered in a light dusting of snow. Underneath his name, carved into the gray surface, read; December 18th, the last day he opened his eyes. Jay must've added it since the funeral. Tomorrow would mark two months. Somehow, it felt both like yesterday and a million years ago.

Dirt fell through my fingers as I broke apart a clump of snow. Fresh flowers sat in vases on each side of the stone. Roses. He hated roses and marigolds- and poppies, he despised poppies. I never knew why. Foxgloves were his favorite, but he loved the smell of morning glories. I made a mental note to bring some of both when I returned, but that wasn't the reason I was here right now.

"I failed you, but I won't fail them," I vowed.

Chapter 43: Too Late for a Coffee Break?

The alarms began sounding far too early. At around 16:40, the sirens screeched in the middle of our training, causing a few kids to drop their blades and one to accidentally stab their opponent. Blue light shrouded the room.

"Code Blue," I heard Professor Mourir mutter, the only person in the room not clutching his ears.

"What's that?" Jake's friend Noham shouted as our class crowded into the center of the arena, circling the teacher.

"Machigai sighted on campus," Calvin shouted back before realizing who he was answering.

"Stay calm," Professor Mourir instructed the class. He made his way casually to the control panel against the wall of the arena, typed in the code, and then flicked a switch.

"Then what's the plan of attack?" Olive uncovered her ears, approaching the professor. He merely turned to her and half laughed.

"For you? Nothing, little girl. I will join the rest of the staff in the meeting house to await the arrival of the MES and handle the issue appropriately. You will all stay here, under lockdown, understood?" Olive glared back at him intensely but didn't say a word.

The blue lights and sirens faded.– The panel began beeping intensely as he snaked through the door, right before steel bars fell down, trapping us inside.

"Yes, sir," the class echoed, all except Olive.

"No, not understood. Our campus is under attack! We should be fighting!" She yelled.

"Sorry kid, our insurance doesn't cover paying off your families when you die at the hands of a machigai only halfway into your 1st year." He turned and left us all locked in the arena.

"Calvin, get your ass over here," Olive commanded, summoning him to the control panel. "Undo it." She gestured wildly to the panel and the door. Cal turned back to me.

"Professor Mourir said to stay here," Noham objected.

"Why do you want to become an MES officer, hamboy?"

When she turned on him fully, he shrank down, and I remembered only a few months ago, he was being held at her mercy while drugged. I also remembered how much he deserved it.

"My cousin was killed by a machigai." He said, an uncharacteristic glint of emotion in his eye.

"What was their name?"

"Tyreed."

"This is your chance to avenge Tyreed. And Jake-" She turned to him. "Think about every night your dad has been called in to analyze a case instead of being home with your dumb ass. Calvin, think about your mother." She turned to the rest of the crowd, addressing them as a whole, with a kind of unitive energy I didn't know Olive was capable of possessing.

"This is our chance to take back just a little bit of everything they've taken from us. We'd be making the front papers before we ever entered the force; we'd be legends! Who's with me?" Some people sunk back down, but the majority jumped up, ready to fight.

"No, we were told to stay here. We are staying here." I interjected, hoping that the others would follow my lead.

"Don't be a buzzkill, Ombre," Jake said, squeezing my shoulder as he launched himself to the panel.

"Knife," he held his hand out to Olive expectantly, receiving only a glare and an eye raise. I watch Jake take a deep breath and his overconfident and egotistical persona fall away, leaving him raw and more human than before.

"You're right, I'm sorry. May I have your knife please?" She relented and handed him one of the daggers off her waist.

He fiddled with the panels, maneuvering between bolts until the front of the panel popped open; he then flicked with buttons to no reward. "Dammit," he swore under his breath.

"Let me," Calvin said, pushing his way through and typing in a code. The bars rose as the rest of the class stared back at him in awe, myself included. He ignored the rest and met my eye with a mischievous grin. "What? You're not the only one who likes memorizing codes." He winked and punched my arm.

Our classmates began gathering their weapons one by one from the floor, strapping their armor, and checking their ammo.

"Don't do this," I begged, grabbing Olive's wrist and whispering. "I can't lose you guys, too." The statement was far from true, but I believed it enough that she did too. Her confidence broke for a moment, but instead of surrendering, she gave me an encouraging smile.

"Hey, don't worry. Calvin is scrappier than you might think. I'm the best fighter this class has, and you haven't missed hardly ten shots since we enrolled here. We'll all be fine, I promise." I tried to protest more, but she pushed past, running back to her corner of the arena to suit up. All around me, my classmates were preparing to fight. -

***　.

I continued to try to look busy while glancing out the door. It wasn't hard to look inconspicuous; other students were doing the exact same thing I was. We were only meters away from the exit, if we stayed here, there was no chance they could escape without a fight. Hopefully, the machigai could sneak by before they were ever found. There was that word again, 'hopefully.' I felt like Marty Mcfly in Back to the Future 2, just trying not to run into the other version of

359

myself. Toyls vs Machigai. It crossed my mind to wipe a few of my classmates into the void, but I couldn't kill enough of them without others noticing.

The arena buzzed with energy, an energy so loud it didn't require a single word. A fury shook through my class like a wave, morphing their overconfident, rich, pompous attitudes into warriors. Young, strong, afraid warriors who had never been more ready to battle. Everyone here had a reason for wanting to hunt machigai, I realized. Everyone had been hurt or negatively affected by my existence; the only thing we truly had in common. Soon enough, our entire clan was weighed down by more weapons than the New York City Police Force.

The energy building within the people around me exploded when the kid next to me, watching out the door, saw the same thing I did.

"Machigai!" he screamed, snapping the head of everyone in the arena.

Chapter 44: Can You Be Dead and Still Breathing?

I saw Blaise first, and he saw me. But there was so much more to take in during such a minuscule moment paused in time. In his arms, he held a small blond child with acne scars grazing his cheek. The boy sat atop Blaise's hip, his hands clinging around his neck. I looked at the other machigai around him; almost everyone who was able-bodied held at least one child. Another dozen surrounded them, holding onto each other and the "grown-ups" that had come at last. Then the moment unfroze, and a rain of bullets and arrows from every weapon in the artillery flooded towards my friends and the children, the machigai contorting their bodies to shield the young with their own lives while fleeing towards the exit.

Without thinking, I melted together the shadows from the arch of the arena's entrance, locking my classmates inside. I felt the shadows absorb into the arena, strengthening every wall. Within me, every sensation, every brick of the building became one. I could see, feel, and hear every perspective that they contained in a sense of painful overstimulation. Through my blur, I looked across the barrier, locking eyes with Jay, who broke into a sly grin that said: *that's my girl* in every inaudible language. Taking advantage of the confusion that ensued around me, I took my first step through the barrier. The shadows tickled my skin like static electricity, allowing me to make my way through the darkness and toward my people.

"Lily?" I heard Calvin say behind me, but I tunneled my vision to the other side of the wall, to my reality. Jay embraced me upon my greeting them, and I allowed myself to release the weight of my decision to him, taking a heavy breath in before releasing him and glancing back over my shoulder one final time. My old classmates were slowly realizing what had just happened, glaring me down through the tinted shield that divided us. Calvin stared through the shadows, his mouth just slightly agape and his eyes never faltering from my own. Behind him, the crowd shifted and faded into one another. I couldn't force myself to focus on any of them any longer, so I turned to Blaise.

"Let's go."

He gave me a stern nod and directed himself towards the exit. Before I could make a single step away from my brief hallucination of a new life, my knees gave way, and my head hit the ground in a buzzing and quick thud.

"Onyx?" Jay rolled me over. Through the ringing in my ears, though, I could hear another voice, one much further away.

"Traitor!! Traitor!!" Olive shouted, stabbing at the shadows with one of her knives. I felt every impact, tearing at my being. Behind her, every student lined themselves into a clear formation, allowing an access point for the barrel of every gun. The sun beat down on me from high in the sky, threatening to dissipate my cage at the slightest change of angle. It was a weak barrier, one of the weakest I had ever made. 16:30. I had chosen the time of day when I was most useless and then put myself in a position where I was being the most relied on.

I faced Blaise and shifted to my knees. "Go!" I shouted through the starry pain. My body shook, latching onto his free hand. He stared at me, fearing the irony and familiarity of this situation.

"Not without you!" Jay tried helping me to my feet, but my eyes rolled back, and my knees gave way again, allowing Olive just enough opportunity to slip through the shadows. There she was, looking as if she had gone mad, sprinting towards us. Her own shadow turned against her, suddenly making me incredibly grateful for her compulsive belief that her knives were the most reliable weapon, even compared to guns. She tripped, scraping the ground as her shadow clung to her, shackling her ankle to the spot where she lay. A gut-wrenching scream of frustration and anger pierced the air around us as she stabbed at her bonds only a few yards from us. Behind her, the barrier remained frail but functioning despite its minor lapse.

"Go!" I shouted again, my voice cracking. Jay picked me up in his arms, preparing to run, but then turned to the kid he had abandoned next to me, unconscious on the ground. He sat me back down and picked up the kid, glancing between us, torn.

"Go," I said once more, softer toward him, then turned to Blaise. "You promised!" I shrieked, allowing my anger to feed into him. He gave a hesitant nod and pushed Jay toward the campus gates.

"NO! NO! WE CAN'T! I SWORE! I SWORE TO HIM! PLEASE!" I heard Jay's voice fade as my vision spotted out with the little blurry black smudges. My focus pulled away, turning entirely towards Olive's presence, her movement struggling close by. Behind her, I could feel the barrier still up, yet faltering by the moment like a staticy TV. Someone behind the barrier had begun banging on it, just as Olive had, weakening me by the second.

"1. . . 2. . . 3. . . 4. . . 5. . . 6. . . 7. . . 8. . . 9. . . 10. . ." I counted in my head, trying to trace the time that passed. "55. . . 56. . . 57. . . 58. . . 59. . ." first minute. "56. . . 57. . . 58. . . 59. . ." second minute. "57. . . 58. . . 59. . ." third minute. "58. . . 59. . ." I felt the barrier and myself flickering out around the 5th minute, and before I could stop it, the shadows dissipated entirely.

"TRAITOR, WE TRUSTED YOU!!!" Olive shouted, coming down on top of me hard, landing a few solid blows before latching onto my neck and applying pressure as she thrust me up and down into the ground, wringing my neck out. I fully expected to lose consciousness when the barriers fell, but I was still there, just long enough to feel those last moments. *I hope he's proud.* I thought as it all went black. ¶

***

I thought I was dead. You know the phrase: "Don't go into the light"? What happened next was something I can only describe as "being in the light." When I opened my eyes, everything was so bright I was literally blinded. Only beams of brilliant yellow filled my vision, and nothing else. I closed my eyes, and it wasn't much different, the back of my eyelids being a vibrant orange instead of a red-tinted black. Time was irrelevant; I was chained to the wall with loose shackles around my wrist that allowed me enough time to walk from side to side of the small confines. I counted the steps back and forth, grimacing through the pain that ached throughout my whole body. Eight steps to the wall directly across from the one where my chains connected. Seven steps from the back to the front wall, which was checker-printed with square holes just large enough to fit my fist through.

Eventually, boredom overtook me, and I sat against the wall, slipping in and out of sleep for what could have been hours or decades; the only true measure of time was the hunger and thirst that consumed me. Occasionally, I would hear shuffling or murmurs outside the front wall, but they faded or ignored my cries for help until I stopped trying.

"Good evening," A familiar voice called from behind the wall. Suddenly, I was being dragged by my shackles towards their origin until they were both tightly pressed against the wall, leaving me uncomfortable and with little to no range of movement. I heard the front wall grind against hard ground as it slid open fully and heels clicked in.

"I said good evening, Lily." Madam Toyls sank down to my level just a few feet in front of me. "Or shall I say Onyx?" I laughed, a dry and cracked sound against my barren throat.

"That's not my name," I stated. "My name is Lunette Tremblay," I said, hoping to drag the investigation of my identity away from Lily and Mrs. Madalini. If they bothered to check police records, there should be a missing persons case with that name on it.

"I see. I'll make sure to give the media that information. A name to accompany the face of the blame. You've caused quite the uproar, haven't you? A machigai infiltrating my campus."

"My bad," I stated dryly. "What now? You kill me and sleep easy tonight?"

"Kill you?" She forced a laugh, such a sweet and lighthearted sound that now froze my blood. "Now, why would I ever do that? It's already so rare I find one of your kind." She stroked my cheek softly, "much less one of your beauty." I scoffed, understanding the mockery. "Just trust my plans for you, my darling; all will work out as it was meant to be."

"How could I ever trust you?" I attempted to stare her down, following the sound of her voice. "How could anyone?" I lowered my voice and fed all my anger and bitterness into my next words, forcing them out barely louder than a whisper. "After what you did to your own son." She moved away from me, granting me a bit of satisfaction.

"Pardon me. I seem to have forgotten your past acquaintance with the machigai once referred to as Soul Stealer. I take it he finally reached his expiration date, yes?" Anger boiled inside me. I thought of my own mother and wondered if even she could have asked a question like that about me with such disregard.

"Aska-"

"Don't call him that!" she snapped; the first sign of blunt emotion I had ever heard the woman show.

"Aska," I continued. "*Your son* passed away on the 18th of December, honorably."

"I had four children; Aska died alongside his father and younger siblings the day Soul Stealer was born. He lost the right to that name long ago.

"And yet I called him by it for over half a decade." I snarled.

"That was your own choice," she muttered, walking towards the door. "You will be visited by guards once a day; they will provide you with a meal and enough water for you to get by. They will also be in charge of changing your chamber pot, which has been placed in the back left corner of your cell. Once every other week, you will be escorted out of your cell to be bathed. Other than that, unless I further command, you will remain here for the rest of your short and meaningless machigai life. Understood?" ¶

I attempted to spit at her in response, but I was far too dehydrated for it to leave my mouth, forcing it to dribble down instead.

"How pitiful," she said, "I have left your first meal and today's water supply right here for your enjoyment. Have a wonderful life, Lunette." ¶

The door slid shut, and I was left alone. I wondered how the rest of the machigai were doing. I thought of Lily's laughter, Burn's stern commands, Jay's jokes, and the way his eyes sparkled. Most of all, I thought of Aska. A silent and final tear fell down my cheek as I scorned Olive for not finishing me off when she had the chance.

Epilogue:

The girl sat alone in her dungeon, back propped up against the wall. She had given up pacing after the first few months; now it was just time. Time to not think about the amount of time she had been there or the amount of time she would remain. Time to not think about the overpowering stench that wafted through the bright room; coming from the chamber pot, her guards procrastinated changing or properly cleaning each shift until it was unbearable. She kept her eyes closed at all times— protecting them from irreversible damage—and allowed her mind to stray from one life to another. It didn't matter how much longer she lived; there would be no more memories made, no people met, and no days lived outside of this place; she was dead in every way that mattered, her mind waiting for her body to catch up to their fate. Of course, it wasn't far behind; the food served met no nutritional standards, breaking the spirits of all the jail's inhabitants within a week. Six days on average. She kept track; with every new inhabitant came new screams— cries for help—but like everything else, they faded to black.

A few months in, the girl received a visit from an old friend. A gift from his so-called "generous headmaster" in exchange for his academic excellence during his first year at the academy. Apparently, setting a new record for ranking 1st in every subject was the price of admission for a single ticket to the zoo. She learned how the previous head of their class abruptly dropped out shortly after the machigai attack on Toyls, as well as how close she had really come to dying at the hands of an angry classmate that day. Her friend judged her, shamed her for her choices, her betrayal, her crimes. She reciprocated, allowing the venom to spew in her words about his self-righteousness and naivety. After that, they sat in silence until, eventually, he slipped out of her cell and left her to her regretful solitude again. Soon, she stopped counting the days, allowing them to morph together, divided only by food, sleep, and the memories of her past life.

Years or months passed, and her broken body became the new play toy for the upperclassmen. She never saw any of her old peers, an intentional ploy from the administration, she suspected, but she had no desire to either. The satisfaction they would be granted from seeing her writhe in pain on a lab table was happily absent from her life. What she did see was the sadistic glances of every student who witnessed her pain, even smiles from a few. Despite her better judgment and pride, her natural instincts forced her to beg them for help with every available breath in her shriveled lungs, and yet they looked on without a second thought. Was it really not that long ago that she was among them? A part of her wondered if that girl made it out with her other friends. Another part wondered if any of them survived; the authorities had been on their way, were they not? This whole ruse, everything, may have all been for nothing. The lack of closure kept her, unfortunately, alive through the moments when it was nothing but a hassle. Thinking, sleeping, and believing for the remaining life of a criminal, murderer, and machigai.

About the Author

Banff Isabella Perkins (Born June 12th, 2006) is a young journalism student and author of the novel Feared & Forgotten. Perkins was raised in a rural southeastern Kansas town named Eureka, Kansas. Growing up, she had a powerful love for finding life's adventures through the pages of books, which later developed into an equal love for creating her own stories in writing. She began her first manuscript, titled Separated, at the age of twelve. After two years of work, Separated was eventually scrapped and replaced by a new project titled Lost. The author finally began slow work on Feared & Forgotten during the summer of 2020, during the COVID-19 pandemic. After many years of gradual work while in high school, Perkins finally completed her first manuscript on December 29th, 2023, at the age of 17. She later signed with New York Book Publishers in April of the following year, officially becoming a published author in August 2024 at the age of 18.